ARLENE JAMES
A Love So Strong

When Love Comes Home

Love Inspired

Recycling programs
for this product may
not exist in your area.

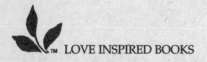 ™ LOVE INSPIRED BOOKS

ISBN-13: 978-0-373-65152-8

A LOVE SO STRONG AND WHEN LOVE COMES HOME

A LOVE SO STRONG
Copyright © 2006 by Deborah Rather

WHEN LOVE COMES HOME
Copyright © 2007 by Deborah Rather

www.LoveInspiredBooks.com

Printed in U.S.A.

CONTENTS

Books by Arlene James

Love Inspired

*The Perfect Wedding
*An Old-Fashioned Love
*A Wife Worth Waiting For
*With Baby in Mind
The Heart's Voice
To Heal a Heart
Deck the Halls
A Family to Share
Butterfly Summer
A Love So Strong
When Love Comes Home
A Mommy in Mind
**His Small-Town Girl

**Her Small-Town Hero
**Their Small-Town Love
†Anna Meets Her Match
†A Match Made in Texas
A Mother's Gift
  "Dreaming of a Family"
†Baby Makes a Match
†An Unlikely Match
The Sheriff's Runaway Bride
†Second Chance Match

*Everyday Miracles
**Eden, OK
†Chatam House

ARLENE JAMES

says, "Camp meetings, mission work and church attendance permeate my Oklahoma childhood memories. It was a golden time, which sustains me yet. However, only as a young widowed mother did I truly begin growing in my personal relationship with the Lord. Through adversity He has blessed me in countless ways, one of which is a second marriage so loving and romantic it still feels like courtship!"

After thirty-three years in Texas, Arlene James now resides in Bella Vista, Arkansas, with her beloved husband. Even after seventy-five novels, her need to write is greater than ever, a fact that frankly amazes her, as she's been at it since the eighth grade. She loves to hear from readers, and can be reached via her website at www.arlenejames.com.

A LOVE SO STRONG

And this I pray,
that your love may abound still more and more
in real knowledge and all discernment.
—*Philippians* 1:9

For Lauren, because granddaughters
are one of God's greatest blessings,
and Granna loves you very, very much.

Chapter One

"Happy birthday! Happy birthday, Marcus!"

Marcus Wheeler lifted his hands and addressed the two dozen or so assembled guests.

"You shouldn't have gone to so much trouble. The church already gave me a nice monetary gift. A man blessed with that and a family such as this can't ask for more." He grinned, then added, "But I'm mighty appreciative, all the same."

"Good grief, man. We have six sisters between us," Vince, husband of Marcus's sister Jolie and scion of the boisterous Cutler clan, stated ruefully. "Did you really think your two sisters and my four would let your birthday slip by without a family celebration?"

Everyone laughed, and the rippling sound warmed Marcus to the very center of his soul. Not so long ago he'd been struggling to hold on to some semblance of his fractured family, and now, thanks to his two younger sisters—especially Jolie, the eldest of them—he had more family than he could keep track of.

"So far as I can tell," drawled Kendal Oakes, husband of

Marcus's youngest sister, Connie, "the Cutlers don't let any excuse to celebrate get past them."

This elicited more laughter and a general chorus of "Amen, brother!"

An only child himself, Kendal confessed to Marcus that he still didn't seem to know what to make of the loving horde who were the Cutlers, but after almost a year as a member of the clan, he was more at ease. Even his daughter, Larissa, who would be three in a couple months and was often overwhelmed by too much stimulation, had relaxed into the midst of what had proven to be a loving, sheltering family.

It was also a growing family, with Jolie and Vince expecting their first child in late June. Marcus knew that Jolie would be as wonderful a mother to her own child as she had been to her nephew, Russell, Connie's thirty-month-old son, in his first year when Connie couldn't take care of him.

"Can't have too much celebration," Connie murmured, smoothing Russell's bright red hair as he leaned against her leg, eagerly awaiting his piece of the birthday cake.

Marcus couldn't have agreed with her more. So much had changed in the past two years.

Connie had gotten out of prison and had since been exonerated of having taken any knowing part in the armed robbery and subsequent murder perpetrated by Russell's biological father. The split that had occurred in the family when Connie had reclaimed Russell from Jolie's care had been mended, thanks to Vince Cutler, who had married Jolie last Valentine's Day, almost a year ago now. Most amazing of all, Connie and Kendal had found each other, and what had begun as a marriage of convenience had joined two broken homes into one strong, Christ-centered family.

Marcus thanked God daily for the masterful way in which He had mended the bonds shattered by death and separation, and the spotty care of the foster child system in which he and his sisters had grown up. Truly, what else could a man of God possibly ask for?

Looking around the room at no fewer than seven happy couples, Marcus had to admit to himself that it was proving to be surprisingly difficult to be the only unmarried adult member of the family. Here he sat, a single minister in want of a wife, and suddenly thirty felt positively ancient. It seemed ungrateful, even selfish, to keep asking God where his mate was, but he couldn't help wondering. Marcus closed his eyes and sent a swift, silent prayer heavenward.

Lord, I thank You for all with which You've blessed me. I thank You for every person in this room. I even thank You for the room itself! You've given Jolie and Vince a lovely home. Connie and Kendal, too, for that matter. And I thank You for my church, Lord. Help me be satisfied with what I already have. That's my birthday prayer. Amen.

Jolie shoved another box onto his lap.

"Ya'll, this is just too much," he insisted, mentally cataloging the stack of dress shirts, ties, bookmarks and religious CDs already littering the floor around his chair.

"Hush up and rip in," Jolie counseled, dropping a kiss on his forehead as she moved back to her husband's side on the sofa that occupied one wall of the living room, to which the party had relocated after indulging the children's demand for cake. "That's the last one anyway."

Relieved to hear it, Marcus eagerly tore away the wrapping paper and pried apart the white pasteboard box beneath to reveal a large photo album tastefully bound in brown leather. A cross and the word "Wheeler" had been embossed on the front in gold.

Somewhat warily, Marcus cracked the cover. The front page contained grainy black-and-white photographs of their great-grandparents Edna and Bledsoe Wheeler.

"I remember these!" Marcus exclaimed happily. "But I thought they were lost."

"Jo had them," Connie apprised him, obviously pleased.

He turned another page and found a color eight-by-ten of his mother, Velma, as a high school senior. The youngest of two daughters born almost twenty years apart, Velma had been the late child of elderly parents and too quickly left alone in the world. After Marcus's father died she'd tried to fill the void with one man after another, eventually abandoning her own children in search of a love she'd never truly understood, only to die in an auto accident.

As difficult as it had been to be separated at ten from his younger sisters, Marcus thanked God that he'd landed with a family who had taught him to love the Lord and saved him from repeating his mother's fate. His sisters hadn't been blessed in that fashion. But now wasn't the time for bad memories. Today was his birthday, a time to celebrate. He and his sisters were back together again. That was all that mattered.

He turned the page and saw a small photo of their father, Carl, who had died of heart failure in his thirties, brought on by extensive alcohol and drug abuse. Marcus barely remembered him. Mostly he remembered the loud arguments that had preceded his departure from the household when Connie had still been a baby.

He'd been a nice-looking man, with Connie's bright, golden blond hair. What a pity that he'd allowed himself to be controlled by his addictions. Still, it was nice to have this reminder of him.

Pictures of Marcus and his sisters as children followed. Most included various members of the foster families with whom they'd resided. Next came a picture of Jolie's wedding. Marcus smiled at that and then at the photo of Connie and Kendal's *second* wedding, which followed. Now that was an interesting story.

Their first ceremony had been a somber affair performed in Kendal's home. They married because Russell needed a father, and Larissa needed a mother. Only some months later did the two realize that God had brought them together for more than the sake of their children and made their sham marriage a real one with a ceremony in church. It had been Marcus's distinct privilege to perform all *three* of his sisters' ceremonies.

He chuckled at photos of his nephew, Russell, and niece, Larissa. The two had taken to each other like bark on a tree. Soon the cross adoption of each child by the other's natural parent would be finalized.

The last picture was a puzzle. It looked like an ink blot at first, and then Marcus realized that it more closely resembled a printed negative of an X-ray. He turned the album sideways, trying to get a better look, prompting Vince to lean forward and announce, "That's your *other* nephew."

Jolie patted her slightly rounded belly with a self-satisfied smile. "We made you a print of the sonogram."

Ovida Cutler, Vince's mother, launched to her feet. All rounded curves and beaming smile, with fading red hair curling about her face, she was the quintessential grandmother.

"It's a boy!" she exclaimed, as if she didn't already have four grandsons.

"And this one will have the Cutler name," one of Vince's sisters pointed out.

"Actually," Jolie said, glowing at Marcus, "we're thinking that Aaron Lawrence Cutler is a fine name for a son, if you don't mind us appropriating your middle name, Marcus."

Marcus glanced at Larry Cutler, Ovida's husband, who was beaming ear to ear, obviously having no compunction about his given name coming in second to Marcus's middle one.

"I'd be honored, sis," he told her in a thick voice.

Fortunately the doorbell rang just then, preventing the whole room from erupting into happy tears.

While Vince hurried out to answer the door, Marcus quickly flipped through the remainder of the pages in the photo album to be certain that they were empty, then yielded to the clamor to pass it around. Within seconds the women were all "oohing" over the sonogram. Marcus himself hadn't seen anything that actually looked like a baby in the print, but that didn't lessen his delight in having it. Aaron Lawrence Cutler. Wow.

He wondered if he would ever have a son whom he might want to name after himself.

Vince returned with a girl in tow. Striking, with long hair the color of black coffee falling past her slender shoulders, she wore a somewhat outlandish costume of lime-green leggings, a long, straight denim skirt, a black turtleneck and muffler, a sky-blue fringed poncho and red leather flats. The shoes matched her gloves, which left only her wrists, ankles and heart-shaped face bare to the February chill.

A lime-green headband held back her sleek, dark hair, revealing an intriguing widow's peak that emphasized her wide, prominent cheekbones and slightly pointed chin. It was an exotic face, with large, round, tip-tilted eyes that gave a feline grace to a small nose and a wide, full, strawberry mouth. What galvanized Marcus, however, were the shiny tracks of tears that marked her pale cheeks.

Without even thinking about it, he was out of his chair a heartbeat after Jolie's mother-in-law, Ovida, and was striding across the room, certain that he was needed.

"Nicole Archer!" Ovida exclaimed, opening her arms. "Honey, what's wrong?"

The newcomer shook her head, eyes flicking self-consciously around the room. If her hair was black coffee, Marcus noted inanely, then those sparkling, soft brown eyes were café au lait. The cream in the coffee would be her skin.

Despite her lithe build, she was not a teenager, he saw upon closer inspection, but not far past it. He liked the fact that she wore no cosmetics, her skin appearing freshly scrubbed and utterly flawless.

A number of private conversations immediately began, their intent patently obvious. Marcus felt a spurt of gratitude for any effort to put this obviously troubled young lady at ease.

"I'm sorry to bother you," she said in a soft, warbling voice as Ovida's round arms encircled her slender shoulders.

"Nonsense. Suzanne's daughter could never be a bother to me." Ovida pulled back slightly and asked, "Now, what's he done?"

Those coffee-with-cream eyes again flickered with uncertainty. Sensing her discomfiture, Marcus stepped up and pointed an arm toward the door beyond the formal dining area as if he had every right to offer this young woman the use of the house.

"It's quiet in the kitchen," he suggested.

Ovida looked up at that, her worried gaze easing somewhat. She patted his cheek with one plump hand.

"I don't want to impose," Nicole protested softly, sniffing and ducking her head.

"No problem," Marcus assured her as Ovida turned the girl toward the door and gently but firmly urged her forward.

A couple of Ovida's daughters rose to follow, but Marcus lifted a proprietary hand. They would, of course, want to help, but ministry had some privileges, and he found himself compelled to exercise them for once. Both instantly subsided, and he nodded in gratitude before swiftly following Ovida and her guest.

He caught up with and passed them in time to push back the swinging door on its silent hinges. As she passed through into the kitchen, Nicole looked up and whispered her thanks.

"You're welcome," Marcus murmured, unashamedly following the pair into the brick-and-oak kitchen and letting the door swing closed behind him.

Ovida parked Nicole at the wrought-iron table in the breakfast nook. "Can I get you something to drink, honey?"

Nicole glanced at the half-empty coffeepot on the counter. Marcus had noticed that wherever Ovida and Larry Cutler were, the coffeepot was kept in service. It seemed fitting that this girl, for she was little more than that, surely, should show a preference for the dark beverage.

Without being asked, he turned to the cabinet and took down a stoneware coffee mug. Then he filled it with strong, black coffee and carried it to the table, placing it gently in front of this dark-haired beauty. She was beautiful, he realized with a jolt. But very young.

"There's cream and sugar, if you like."

Smiling wanly, she shook her head, tugged off her worn red leather gloves and wrapped a slender hand around the mug.

"Thank you. Again."

"You're welcome. Again."

As she sipped, he pulled out a chair for Ovida and nodded her down into it.

"Now tell me, honey," Ovida urged, "what's wrong?"

Nicole glanced quickly at Marcus before dropping both hands into her lap in a gesture that bespoke both helplessness and frustration. Marcus pulled out another chair and sat, bracing his forearms against the glass tabletop.

"Forgive me if I'm intruding where I'm not wanted, but if there's a problem, I'd like to help. My name is Marcus Wheeler, by the way."

"Nicole Archer."

He smiled to put her at ease. "It's nice to meet you, Nicole. I take it that you know my sister Jolie."

Nicole shook her head. "I know she's married to Vince, that this is their house."

"If you know the Cutlers, then you must realize that, through Jolie, I'm part of the family now. You probably don't know that I'm also a minister."

Her slender, dark brows rose into pronounced arches.

"Really? You seem too...young."

Marcus chuckled. "That's good to hear today of all days." He leaned closer and confessed in a conspiratorial tone. "Today's my birthday. My twenties are now officially behind me."

"Happy birthday." Wrinkling her button of a nose, she added, "I didn't mean to crash the party."

"No problem." He folded his hands. "I'd like to help, if you'll allow it."

She sighed, braced an elbow against the tabletop, turned up her palm and dropped her forehead into it.

"There's nothing you can do. There's nothing anyone can do." Straightening, she shook her head. "I don't even know why I bothered to come here. It's just that..." She looked at Ovida, and fresh tears clouded her eyes. "You said this was where you'd be if I needed you."

Ovida reached across the table to squeeze her hand. "You did exactly right. Now, then, what's Dillard done this time?"

"Same old, same old," came the muttered answer.

"That man!" Ovida snapped. "Did he hurt you?"

Marcus stiffened as alarm and something he didn't normally feel, anger, flashed through him.

"Who is Dillard?"

"Nicole's father," Ovida divulged. "Dillard Archer's been mad at the world and living in a bottle ever since his wife died more than three years ago."

"He was never like this when Mom was alive," Nicole said, shaking her head. "He'd lose his temper once in a while, even put his fist through a wall a time or two, but now…" She bit her lip.

Marcus reached for the sheltering mantle of his professional detachment. For some reason that seemed more difficult than usual, but he managed, asking gently, "Is he abusive?"

Nicole bowed her head and whispered, "The worst part is the things he says sometimes, especially to my little brother."

"What's your brother's name?"

"Beau. He turned thirteen at the end of November."

An emotional age, as Marcus remembered all too well. The next question was, to him, all important.

"Has your father ever hit either one of you, Nicole?"

She sucked in a deep breath, her stillness indicating that she was deciding what to tell him.

"Not really. He's shoved us around a little, Beau mostly. I'm afraid my little brother hasn't learned when it's best to keep quiet."

Ovida shared a grim look with Marcus, saying, "Your poor mother's heart would break if she wasn't beyond such emotion, thank the good Lord."

"I just don't know what to do with him anymore," Nicole admitted tearfully. "I know he misses Mom, but we all do."

"Of course we do," Ovida crooned. "For her I'm happy, though. No more illness or pain. Just the peace and joy of heaven."

Nicole nodded, sniffing. "I believe that, but Dad doesn't."

Marcus sighed inwardly, unsurprised to hear that Dillard Archer was not a believer.

"Have you considered calling the authorities?"

Nicole shook her head, blurting, "I don't want him to go to jail!"

"It might be the only way to get him the help he needs."

"But what would happen to my little brother?"

Marcus knew the probable answer to that, but he needed more information to make an informed guess.

"How old are you?"

"Twenty."

So young, Marcus thought, *to be shouldering such responsibility.*

"Do you work?"

"Part-time. School doesn't leave a lot of time for work."

"You're in college then?"

"UTA."

He'd attended the University of Texas at Arlington himself, before seminary.

"Studying what, may I ask?"

"Early childhood education."

He smiled at that and heard himself saying, "We have a day care center at our church."

"Oh? I'd like to work in day care again, but waiting tables pays better, especially for part-time." She looked down at her hands, mumbling, "Dad's on disability because of his back, and that really doesn't go very far. If we hadn't used Mom's life insurance to pay off the house, I don't know how we'd make it."

"His drinking can't help any," Marcus pointed out gently, "and he isn't likely to quit on his own."

"Look," Nicole said firmly, "I promised my mom." Her beautiful brown eyes implored Marcus to understand. "I promised that I'd take care of them, Beau and Dad. Mom wouldn't want me to turn him in to the police."

"Nicole, your mother never imagined that your dad would fall apart like this," Ovida pointed out. "She wouldn't want you to risk yours or your brother's safety."

"It's not that bad," Nicole insisted. "It's just that I never know what's going to set him off, and he can say some really ugly things. I shouldn't let them bother me. I know it's the alcohol talking, but…" She sighed intensely.

"Don't make excuses for him, honey," Ovida advised, "and don't let him get to you."

She lifted big, wounded eyes to Ovida, whispering, "He said that Mom would be disappointed in me."

Ovida scoffed at that. "No way! Your mother thought the sun rose and set in you and Beau. Your father's the one she'd be disappointed in, not you. Never you, sugar. And no one knew Suzanne better than I did. I knew your mom from the time she was eleven years old. I was her Sunday School teacher. Trust me on this."

Nicole smiled wanly. "Mom always said you were the big sister she never had."

"Oh, and I loved her like a sister."

"He loved her, too, you know," Nicole said wistfully.

"I know," Ovida conceded. "I know. But that doesn't give him the right to behave this way."

"Would you like me to speak to him?" Marcus asked. "I think he needs to hear that God still loves him."

Nicole looked at him, wide-eyed, and shook her head. "I—I don't think he'd sit still for that. Maybe later, once he's calmed down."

"He'd have to be more open than the last time I tried to talk to him," Ovida warned sadly. "He threw me out of his house—me, who he's known for decades. He said God and church didn't do Suzanne any good and he didn't want to hear any more mealymouthed Bible-thumpers telling him it was for the best."

"Ah." Marcus nodded, understanding the problem exactly. He'd seen it before, a weak faith trying to believe that a desired outcome was the only right one, then shattering completely when God's will didn't follow the proscribed path. Jolie had succumbed to that kind of disappointment and doubt after Connie had reclaimed her son, Russell, but with prayer and patience and a willingness on Vince's part to be used by God, she'd come to see the truth. Marcus made a mental pact with himself to pray regularly for the Archers, starting now.

At his request, Nicole bowed her head and sat quietly while he spoke to God about protection for her and her brother and emotional and spiritual healing for Dillard Archer. Afterward, he spoke to Nicole about AlAnon, the support organization for the family and dependents of alcoholics, and she seemed interested in possibly attending a meeting, if her schedule permitted. Marcus promised to locate the nearest meeting for her, although it sounded as if she already had a pretty full timetable with classes and work and her family.

"Where do you live exactly?"

"Dalworthington Gardens."

"We're practically neighbors then. I'm at First Church in Pantego."

"I know that church," Nicole said, surprising and pleasing him. "I pass it on my way to school. I like the way it looks, sort of homey and old-fashioned, almost like its own little town."

Marcus felt his grin stretch to ridiculous proportions. Something odd shimmered through him, something he couldn't quite identify that snatched at his breath. He cleared his throat and said, "That's exactly the impression we were going for, a community of believers with the church at its center."

"But don't be fooled by the exterior," Ovida advised Nicole. "It's a powerful little church, a real asset to the city, and pretty cutting-edge when it comes to technology and worship."

"We do try," Marcus conceded. "It's been an exciting pastorate so far."

"You ought to visit, Nicole," Ovida urged. "You and Beau might like it there."

Nicole looked at Marcus, her warm brown eyes measuring him. "We might," she said, and then she dropped her gaze pointedly.

Marcus felt a jolt. That hadn't been *personal* interest he'd seen in her eyes, surely? No, of course not. To her, he must seem like the next thing to an old man, which, comparably speaking, he was. That seemed a particularly dismal thought.

As talk became more chatter than confession and hand-wringing, Marcus made himself sit silently, a mere observer now that the emotional crisis had passed. It was what he did, part of his calling. He was good at stepping up to the plate when called upon to bat and equally good at retiring once he'd taken his swing. He couldn't help wondering why this time it was proving so difficult.

Perhaps he should rejoin the party in the other room. He, after all, was the guest of honor. Yes, he should definitely excuse himself. Yet, he sat right there, listening as Ovida and Nicole talked of events in which he'd had no part and people whom he didn't know.

For some reason he couldn't tear himself away. Yet, this time, observation felt strangely like being on the outside looking in.

Was he suddenly so old, Marcus wondered, that he'd lost

touch already with such fresh-faced youth as this? If so, then surely it was past time for God to bring him a wife.

That wasn't too much for a man to ask on his thirtieth birthday, was it? Then again, hadn't he just told God that he'd be happy with those blessings already granted him?

He stared at Nicole's pretty profile, observing the animation with which she spoke, and knew that if his interest could be elicited by this mere *girl*, then he was in big trouble. Not only was she too young for him, she was entirely unsuitable.

A minister's wife did not dress in such eccentric fashion. She didn't bounce around in her seat and gesture broadly as if physically incapable of sitting still. And she sure wouldn't slide alarmingly coy looks across a table at a man she'd just met.

It struck him then how laughingly desperate he had become.

Nicole was little more than a child, whose life was, nevertheless, chock-full of stress and responsibility. At her age she probably batted her eyelashes at every male in the immediate vicinity without even knowing that she was doing it.

And he was a thirty-year-old fool who obviously needed to remember that his priority in life was his ministry. That ministry included helping emotionally beleaguered young ladies find the faith to make difficult decisions. If the opportunity arose, that was precisely what he would do for Miss Nicole Archer.

He had the unsettling feeling that such an opportunity would, indeed, arise and no understanding at all why that should alarm him.

Chapter Two

Nicole allowed both Marcus Wheeler and Ovida Cutler to escort her to the door, even though she knew it was an imposition for him. This was his birthday, after all, and the party had been going on without him for some time already. Still, she couldn't resist. He was so…calm. Serene, even. And gorgeous—in a very buttoned-down and conservative way, which, oddly enough, she didn't mind at all.

Once in the spacious entry hall, Nicole took some time to look around her, stalling the moment when she must actually leave. Western chic wasn't her thing, but the sheer proportions of the place were impressive, and she liked the colors and the rustic light fixture overhead.

She'd barely noticed her surroundings when she'd arrived. Her pain and desperation had blinded her to everything except the need to find a little reassurance, some measure of comfort. At times like that she missed her mother so much that she literally hurt. That was when she reached out to Ovida.

Lately, her father's drinking had escalated and she'd been reaching out more and more. Surely things would calm down soon, though. Her father seemed to cycle in and out of these ongoing rages.

He'd be surly and withdrawn for a while, then gradually would grow more belligerent until he began exploding over the smallest things. Finally he'd rage for hours, saying cruel, hurtful things to her and her brother. Eventually he'd drink himself into oblivion. Misery and apologies would follow the hangover. Then the cycle would begin again.

She hoped they were at the end of that ugly cycle now, but even if they weren't she still couldn't bring herself to follow the pastor's advice to call the police or even Family Services. She couldn't bear the thought of her father in detox or jail or her brother in foster care. Such a thing would have been inconceivable while her mother lived. Every time Nicole thought of calling the police, she'd picture her mother's face, see the sadness, disappointment and anguish in her eyes, and she couldn't do it.

No, she just couldn't see herself following the good minister's advice. That didn't mean, however, that Nicole wasn't glad to have met Marcus Wheeler. Far from it. Looking up now into his warm, moss-green eyes she felt safe, reassured, and not a little thrilled.

Who knew that ministers were this good-looking? Not to mention young.

Okay, he was a little older than the college crowd, but thirty wasn't exactly over the hill. Besides, she didn't fit in with that group all that well herself. She didn't fit in anywhere, truth be told. In some ways she felt aeons older than her friends. In others she felt like a complete innocent. They were into partying and carefree escapades. She was into her family and fulfilling her responsibilities.

For Nicole, it was all about making a future for herself and her little brother. She didn't have time for parties and dates. She'd be tempted to make an exception for someone like Marcus, though. All antique gold and polished bronze, Marcus was not only handsome, he radiated strength, gentle confidence and genuine concern. Surely such a man would be a good influence on her little brother.

At first, mortified to have broken in on a family gathering, Nicole was now glad that she had come here today. She'd found what she needed: the strength to go home again and put up with whatever awaited her there a little longer. On the way, she'd swing by the library and pick up Beau. Meanwhile, she owed this man, if only for his kindness.

"I'm sorry about interrupting your birthday party."

He shook his head, smiling as laughter spilled out of the living room. "Doesn't sound to me like you put a crimp in anything."

"Still, it was good of you to take time away from your guests to talk to me."

"It was my pleasure. I'll be praying for you."

"Thank you."

"We'll both be praying for you, honey," Ovida broke in, hugging her. "Think about what the pastor said, will you?"

Nicole nodded. She'd think about it, but she knew that she wouldn't call the authorities.

"I'd better go," she said reluctantly. "The library closes at nine."

"Hug that brother of yours for me," Ovida instructed.

"I will."

"And don't hesitate to reach out again if you need me."

"But if you should need another ally," Marcus interjected smoothly, reaching into his shirt pocket and producing a small card, "I can usually be reached at one of these numbers."

Ridiculously pleased, Nicole took the card and slipped it into her glove. She would definitely be calling on the young minister, just as soon as she could come up with a valid reason. With one last squeeze of Ovida's hand and a warm smile for Marcus Wheeler, Nicole slipped through the door that he opened for her.

He stepped outside onto the low front stoop and watched from beneath the tall brick arch until she was safely inside her old car. In his shirtsleeves against the frosty February temperatures, he continued to stand there while she cranked and cranked the starter on her rattletrap vehicle. Then, once the engine finally turned over, he lifted a hand in farewell before rejoining the party inside. It seemed a very gentlemanly thing to do.

Nicole smiled to herself as she drove off into the night, feeling the edges of his card against the back of her hand, where it nestled inside her glove.

Their paths would cross again.

Connie stirred honey into her herbal tea, tapped the spoon on the rim of the cup and laid it aside before slipping her forefinger into the dainty hole formed by the handle and lifting the hot, fragrant brew to her lips.

"So, find out any interesting tidbits about our unexpected guest at the birthday party the other night?" Jolie asked, lifting her straight, thick, biscuit-brown hair so she could lean back in her kitchen chair without trapping it.

Connie blew on her tea, then shook her bright gold hair. They'd both been curious about Nicole Archer. Something about that girl made a person sit up and take notice, something besides the wardrobe, which was even odder than those of the young women one saw on the streets these days.

"You know Marcus and his ministerial ethics," Connie said. "All I could get out of him is that her mother and your mother-in-law were friends."

"*Were* is the operative word," Jolie divulged, absently rubbing her swollen belly. "Mrs. Archer died over three years ago. Cancer. Ovida was her Sunday School teacher at one time, and the two stayed close over the years. Now Ovida's become sort of a surrogate mother for Nicole. Supposedly, Nicole's father drinks a lot."

Connie sipped from her cup and set it down again.

"I guess mothers-in-law don't have the same ethical concerns as ministers."

Jolie chuckled. Conversation turned to their plans for the upcoming weekend. Vince and Jolie planned to shop for the baby's room. Connie and Kendal were taking their children to a popular pizza arcade for the birthday celebration of one of their young friends.

"We may not stay long," Connie said. "It depends on how well Larissa does in that environment."

Little Larissa still suffered the occasional meltdown when overstimulated, but her conduct had improved by leaps and bounds in the ten months since Connie and sweet, placid Russell had come into her life. Still, Connie and Kendal were careful to monitor her environment and coach her behavior. They made a good team and, Jolie had to admit, were excellent parents.

Jolie no longer grieved or resented the removal of her nephew from her care. The way she looked at it, everything was as it should be. As God had wanted it to be. She could be Russell's aunt now without wishing she was still his de facto mom, and she again enjoyed the company and companionship of her sister and brother. Best of all, she and Vince were going to have their own child, who was even then turning somersaults inside her womb.

"Goodness, this boy's going to be an athlete of some sort. He's always in motion lately."

It was no secret that the Cutlers were football fanatics, and Jolie knew that Vince was dreaming of sitting on the sidelines to watch his son play. Connie opened her mouth to comment, but just then the doorbell rang.

"I'll go," she said, slipping out of her chair and waving Jolie back down into hers.

"Can't imagine who it is," Jolie murmured, arching her back to relieve an ache in her spine.

It was probably someone wanting to clean her carpet or sell her a magazine subscription. While she waited for Connie to return, she decided that she'd have another cup of herbal tea and rose to move to the kettle cheerfully steaming on the stovetop.

The tea bag was steeping when Connie appeared on the other side of the bar that separated the den from the kitchen. She was not alone.

"Do you happen to know where Ovida is now?" Connie asked, glancing meaningfully at the young woman at her side. "Nicole is looking for her."

Jolie shook her head. "I think she was going over to Sharon's, but that was hours ago." Sharon was the oldest of Vince's four sisters.

Nicole frowned. "I went by there," she said, "but no one was at home."

Jolie considered. "Obviously they went somewhere. That woman really ought to get a cell phone." She snapped her fingers. "Sharon's got one. Why don't I give her a call?"

Nicole brightened visibly.

"Would you mind? I don't usually work on Friday afternoons, but I've been called in to cover for another server, and I really need someone to pick up my little brother from school."

Jolie went to the telephone and dialed Sharon's number, but the cell went straight to voice mail. She left a brief message and hung up before turning back to Nicole.

"Sorry," she said, leaning against the counter. "Sharon isn't answering. She probably forgot to turn the phone on."

Nicole sighed and shifted her weight, one hip sliding out. Jolie glanced at Connie, who lifted her eyebrows, then studied the girl.

Girl wasn't exactly the right word. She was young, yes, and a little quirky with her dark hair twisted up on top of her head and sticking out in all directions. Fat, sleek tendrils of it hung down beside her face, which was really very pretty, no thanks to artifice.

Jolie didn't much like to wear makeup herself and considered that it would have been a crime to cover up Nicole's flawless ivory complexion. Nicole was really very striking, Jolie decided, despite the slender, fraying cropped jeans that she wore with clashing stripes.

Her oversize, rainbow-hued sweater was striped vertically in wide bands of vivid color, but the black-and-white stripes of the turtleneck that she wore beneath it ran horizontally, while her socks sported a diagonal pattern of yellow-and-orange bands.

It was enough to make an innocent observer dizzy.

Jolie cleared her throat and concentrated on Nicole's pretty eyes. They were almost leonine in their shape and size, and the slight tilt at the outer edges gave her an exotic air. It was the frankness in those warm brown eyes that most appealed to Jolie, however. They seemed to speak volumes, and one thing came through loud and clear.

This girl was worried about her brother.

"I could do it," Jolie said impulsively.

"Oh, Jo," Connie put in quickly, "you don't need to go out." She turned to Nicole. "I'll do it. Just tell me where his school is, and I'll drive by on my way home, pick him up and drop him off at your house."

Nicole made a face. "Actually, I don't want him dropped

off. I—I was hoping Ovida would take him home with her until I get off work. I mean, he's thirteen, he hardly needs babysitting, but…well, he spends a lot of time alone."

Jolie looked at Connie and saw the same conclusion in her gaze. Nicole didn't want her brother to go home because their father was drinking.

"Do you think," Nicole began hesitantly, "that your brother, Marcus, might…?"

"That's brilliant!" Jolie exclaimed. "Why don't we give him a call?"

Nicole lifted a shoulder, already backing away. "Maybe I'll just drop by the church on my way to work."

"Oh." Again Jolie traded glances with her sister, her instincts perking up. "That'll work. And if for some reason he can't help you, just ask him to give one of us a call."

"Thank you. I appreciate that," Nicole said, practically out of the room.

Jolie followed, trying to see her unexpected guest out. She barely got to the entry hall before Nicole opened the front door. "Thanks again. Everyone in your family is so nice."

"Think nothing…" The door closed before she could get the rest of it out. Jolie folded her arms consideringly before turning back toward the kitchen.

"She was certainly in a hurry," she told Connie as she reentered the room.

"Guess she had to get to work."

"Somehow I think it's more than that," Jolie said, sending her sister a droll look.

Connie set down her cup and folded her arms against the table. "I thought she seemed a little taken with him the other day. Not that he would notice."

"True." Sighing, Jolie lowered herself into her chair. "That's a big part of the problem, you know. He's just oblivious."

Connie shrugged. "Well, maybe a minister has to be."

"Maybe. On the other hand, how does he ever expect to find anyone if he doesn't at least open himself up to the possibility?"

Connie smiled. "Oh, the same way we did, maybe."

Jolie burst out laughing. "In other words, God will have to drop her on his head."

"Something like that." Connie grinned.

What neither of them said aloud was that Nicole Archer couldn't possibly be the one. Indeed, it went without saying. Just as well then, that Marcus would probably never even realize that quirky little Nicole was developing a crush on him.

"I don't get home until almost ten. The restaurant closes at nine on Fridays, but we have to clear out the electronic till and help clean up before we go."

"No problem," Marcus told her.

They'd met on the sidewalk in the midst of the church compound. He'd pulled in just ahead of her, having returned from the office supply store. His heart had leaped when her little jalopy had nosed into the space beside his dependable, late-model sedan and again when she'd clambered out to smile at him, costumed in the most outrageous stripes he'd ever seen. He could hardly look at her—and couldn't look away.

Nicole gusted a huge sigh of relief and turned those big, tilted eyes up at him. "Thank you so much. It's a huge weight off my shoulders. We need the extra money, you know, but right now Beau can't be home with…out me," she finished weakly.

It was cold out, but Marcus set the bag of office supplies on the hood of his sedan and leaned a hip against the fender, crossing his arms. "Have you given any more thought to what I said about calling the authorities?"

She shook her head. "It's just not an option."

"Nicole, it's not going to get better until he's faced with reality."

"Look," she said, skipping closer. "I'm less than two semesters away from graduation. Then Beau and I can afford to take off on our own."

"Just like that?"

"No, not...I mean, we're making real plans."

Marcus didn't have the heart to point out that their father might have a good deal more to say about that than either of them realized.

"Well, we can talk about this later. You just go on to work and leave Beau to me," Marcus told her. "Which school is it?"

Nicole told him the name of the middle school where Beau was an eighth grader and launched into directions. "You go out here and turn right." She pointed toward the street. "Then it's the third light—"

"I know it well," Marcus interrupted. "Several of our youngsters attend there, and some of our adult members are on the staff."

She clapped her gloved hands together. "Great! I'll call from work and let them know you'll be picking him up."

"Just have him wait in the office."

"You're sure you don't mind entertaining him for the evening?"

"Not at all."

She dug a toe into a crack in the pavement. "I thought maybe you had other plans or something."

"None. I'm looking forward to the company." He leaned toward her, aware that it wasn't a gesture he normally employed and a little puzzled by the urge to do so now. "Gives me a good excuse to play video games." She laughed, and the sound made him smile.

"As if any guy needs an excuse to play video games."

"Hey, you reach a certain age," he said with a helpless shrug.

"Puh-leeze." Reaching out, she gave his shoulder a little shove. "You're not exactly a grandfather."

His first impulse was to playfully shove back, but he kept his arms tightly folded, surprised by the discipline required to do so. "I'm not exactly a kid, either."

"Not exactly."

She didn't sound as if that was a bad thing. He didn't want to think about why. Instead, he reminded himself what his purpose was.

"I do have a favor to ask in return, though," he said.

She spread her hands. "Anything I can do. Anything at all."

"I'd like for you and your brother to attend church."

"Ah." She dropped her gaze and rocked back on her heels.

"You said you might," he cajoled.

She shined a blindingly bright smile on him. "I'd already planned on it."

"Excellent." He pushed away from the car and reached for the shopping bag. "This is what I call a real win-win situation."

"Yeah, well, don't be surprised tonight if Beau's not quite so…enthusiastic." She wrinkled her nose. "He is thirteen."

Marcus chuckled. "He doesn't like to be babysat."

"Exactly."

"Fine. I won't babysit him. I'll just pick him up, feed him and allow him to keep me company until I drop him off at your house."

"Oh, you don't have to do that. I'll pick him up."

Marcus shook his head. "No way. Not at that time of night."

"But I'm out at that hour all the time."

"Not if I can help it."

She rolled her eyes. "I'm not the thirteen-year-old."

"I'm aware of that. Nevertheless, I'd feel better if you'd go straight home after work."

Nicole flattened her mouth. It was a very pretty mouth, too pretty to appear stern. He smiled, and she threw up her hands.

"Oh, all right. But don't think I'm going to let you get away with treating me like a child, Marcus Wheeler, because I'm not."

"You are, however, young and female and too pretty for your own good." He snapped his mouth shut, wondering where on earth that had come from.

She had beamed before. Now her smile could have warned ships at sea.

He gulped and said, "I—I wouldn't let my mother wander around on her own late at night. In fact, if I could have stopped that, she might still be alive."

Nicole's smile softened. "It's terrible to lose your mom, isn't it?"

He nodded, suddenly swamped with emotion. "She died in an auto accident."

"I'm sorry to hear that."

"No sorrier than I was to hear about your loss. I was only seven when she disappeared. We didn't know she'd died for years." Now why had he told her that?

Long, slender fingers wrapped around his hand. Even through the leather of her gloves, he felt the heat of her hand.

"That's so sad," she said. "At least I had my mom until I was grown."

He almost snorted at that. She was barely grown now.

Barely, but grown.

Abruptly he stepped back. As if sensing that she'd made him uncomfortable, she swiftly turned away, saying, "I'd better run. Thanks again."

"Don't worry about it," he called after her.

She flashed him a smile and dropped behind the wheel of her car. That thing looked as if it was held together with baling wire and prayer. Another reason she ought not to be running around on her own late at night. He stood where he was until she managed to crank the engine to sputtering life and bully the transmission into reverse. Only as she drove away did he turn toward the office.

He hoped that restaurant where she worked made their servers wear uniforms. Otherwise, customers were bound to lose their appetites. He laughed at the memory of all those stripes as he pushed through the heavy glass door into the outer office.

Glancing at the clock on the wall behind his secretary's desk, he made note of the time. Ten minutes after three. He had plenty of time, but it wouldn't hurt to be in the principal's office waiting for Beau when the bell rang at four o'clock. Even as he deposited the bag on Carlita's desk and shrugged out of his overcoat, he told himself that he had known he would cross paths with the Archer family again.

He tossed the three-quarter-length tan coat over a chair, explaining, "I'm going out again in a few minutes. I just want to grab a few video games from David's office."

David Calloway was their part-time minister of youth. Marcus hoped to introduce him to Beau very soon.

"You shouldn't be here at all," Carlita reminded him in her tart, Spanish-tinged English. "It *is* Friday."

The single mom of four children and several years his senior, Carlita was prone to mother him a bit. He didn't mind. Having someone care about you was not an onerous burden.

He knew that Carlita and his sisters thought he worked too much, but he liked his work. Besides, some weeks emergency calls and visitation kept him out of the office, so Friday might be the only day he had to catch up on things, like picking up supplies he'd failed to have delivered with the regular monthly order.

Even as he rifled through the stack of video game discs on a shelf in David's tiny office, Marcus mused that he had no reason *not* to work. What use was a day off if it was spent alone? It was good to have the prospect of company, any prospect of company. Even if Beau Archer proved less engaging than his sister, Marcus would be grateful for the companionship.

It had been almost a year since Connie and Russell had moved out, but he still missed them. Not that he would have changed anything. They were happy as could be with Kendal and Larissa. It was just that he'd never been much good at living alone. The parsonage was small, but it could still feel lonely for one person.

In the early years after their mother had disappeared, he'd missed his sisters terribly, but at least he hadn't been alone. His foster parents had looked after a houseful of boys. Then when he'd first gone off to college he'd lived in a dorm, and after that he'd shared apartments or houses with various buddies.

He'd spent a few months on his own after the church had called him, but that had been a very busy time. Then Connie had gotten out of prison and she and Russell had come to live with him.

Those had been good months, especially after God had brought Vince into Jolie's life and spurred her to forgive him and Connie for removing Russell from her custody. Now the family was not only together again, it was expanding.

His sisters' happy marriages had seen to that. If it felt as though something was missing from his own life, well, he expected God to put that right one of these days, too. He was trying not to be impatient about it.

Unbidden, an image of Nicole Archer standing in his sister's foyer came to him, and he resolutely pushed it away. Nicole was an opportunity to minister, not a prospective spouse. The very idea was ludicrous for a number of reasons. Besides, she needed his help, not his desperate, misplaced attentions. She probably had a boyfriend, anyway.

The thought made him wince, and he resolved to put it firmly out of mind, unwilling to picture Nicole flirting and smiling with some boy and managing to do so just the same. He was forced to admit that he couldn't see her with a *boy*. Some guy like David was much more her speed. Thankfully, er, fortunately, the young minister of youth was engaged, a matter of no little irony to Marcus's mind.

Not even out of seminary yet and already engaged to be married. It was enough to make a mature, older man just a tad envious.

Marcus strolled past Carlita's desk, tossed on his coat, pocketed the game discs and moved toward the door again, saying, "I'm gone now. Have a good weekend."

"You, too, Pastor," she called as he pushed through the door.

The winter air was bracing, and the weather forecast predicted sleet in the wee hours of the coming morning. Marcus stood for a moment and inhaled deeply, clearing his head of unwanted thoughts. He hoped the prognosticators were correct about the timing of the coming sleet storm.

February always brought at least one ice storm to north central Texas, and it invariably shut down the entire Dallas-

Fort Worth Metroplex area for a day or more. For the sake of road safety, it was better that it happen on a weekend than a workday, even if it meant that church attendance would be down this Sunday.

Marcus let himself into his sedan and started up the engine, warm inside his coat. Lots of the kids around here routinely walked to and from school, regardless of the weather; Marcus was glad that Beau wouldn't be one of them, at least for today.

He was curious about Nicole's brother. Actually, he was curious about everything having to do with Nicole Archer. After only one meeting, he'd known that she was a very unusual young lady. Something about her had stuck with him since their initial meeting two days ago. In fact, he hadn't been able to get her out of his mind. That, no doubt, was because God was calling him to perform this service for her and her family, this and others to come.

Marcus was glad to do so. That's what his life, his calling, was about. God would take care of everything else in His own good time.

Chapter Three

When Marcus walked into the school, he was instantly recognized by the attendance officer and the vice principal, Joyce Ballard, who was a member of his church. He greeted both by their given names and stated his purpose for being there.

"I didn't realize you knew Beau," the vice principal observed nonchalantly.

A tall, thin woman, she looked older than her forty-something years and could be very stern, but Marcus knew that she genuinely cared about her young charges.

"Actually, we haven't met yet. I know his sister."

"Some of our parents could take a lesson from that girl," Joyce said.

"She does seem devoted to her brother."

"No doubt about it," the woman said, going back to the paperwork she'd been doing when he'd entered.

Marcus removed his coat and sat down to wait for the bell to ring. As she worked, the vice principal gave him the rundown on some of their church kids. One had done very well in a University Interscholastic League competition that week. Another had been out ill with a cold, and a third had recently won the lead role in a school drama. Marcus made the appropriate mental notes and was about to ask about another youngster when the bell rang.

Instantly, kids spilled out into the hallways. Noise swelled, happy voices punctuated the sounds of heavy footsteps and the slamming of locker doors. Rising, Marcus reached for his overcoat just as a group of youngsters swarmed into the office, talking loudly. Among them was a solemn boy with medium brown hair and dark brown eyes. The vice principal singled him out at once.

"Beau, this is Pastor Wheeler. Your sister sent him to pick you up."

Marcus stuck out his hand, saying, "Hello, Beau. I'm Marcus."

The boy hesitated, sizing up this newcomer. Marcus openly returned his regard, patiently keeping his hand out.

Beau's blocky build and squarish face had nothing in common with his sister's. Though of only average height at present, he was destined to make a big man. Only his coloring was similar to Nicole's, if reversed. Where her hair was dark and her eyes lighter, the opposite was true for Beau.

Unlike his sister's, his choice of wardrobe was mundane: athletic shoes, a maroon T-shirt that was a bit too small and faded, baggy jeans. What struck Marcus most, however, was the wariness in Beau's dark eyes. Marcus had seen that wounded, haunted, uncertain look before. He'd seen it far too many times, in fact, most often in the mirror.

Finally Beau shifted his bright blue backpack to the other shoulder and shook Marcus's hand. Marcus let his smile broaden.

After a farewell wave to the adults in the office, Marcus followed the boy out into the busy hallway. The boy didn't appear to have a coat, but Marcus said nothing, all too aware of the prickly pride of a thirteen-year-old boy whose par-

ents didn't live up to their responsibilities. Instead, he folded
his own coat over his arm and headed for the wall of doors
at the end of the hall. If Beau was going to suffer the cold,
Marcus would, as well, not that Beau seemed to notice.

The boy seemed uninterested in conversing. He sat
hunched in the passenger seat of Marcus's sedan, his attitude clearly wary and defensive. The only reply Beau made
to Marcus's explanation for why Nicole hadn't picked him
up and to the series of polite questions about what he'd like
to do that evening was, "I'm hungry."

So Marcus took him to the closest fast-food joint, where
he ordered a hamburger and a cola. Marcus said nothing
about the possibility of him ruining his dinner. He knew
from experience that boys the age of Beau could eat their
own weight three times a day and still be hungry.

When Beau pulled a couple of bucks out of his pants
pocket, Marcus politely ignored him, ordered a milk shake
and fries for himself, neither of which he really wanted, and
paid for everything. The food came quickly, and they carried it to a corner booth where they sat in silence for several
minutes.

Marcus picked a fry from a tiny paper bag and munched
it, turning sideways on the bench to stretch out his legs.
Having allowed the boy to eat undisturbed for some time,
Marcus adopted a nonchalant tone and prepared to gently
prod.

"So tell me about yourself, Beau."

"Like what?" came the doubtful reply.

Marcus said the first thing that came into his head. "Do
you have a favorite subject in school?"

The boy bit off a huge chunk of hamburger and studiously
chewed it. Marcus figured it was an excuse not to speak, but
then the boy surprised him.

Marcus discovered that Beau was an indifferent student

with a passion for music. He was not, however, in band classes, either because he couldn't afford it or he didn't like the band director. Or both.

"It's whack," Beau grumbled. "Mr. Placid doesn't like guitar. Says there's no future in it. Like there's a huge future in tuba and xylophone. Truth is, he just doesn't know squat about it."

Marcus was familiar with that term *whack*. In the parlance of the modern youth it meant the opposite of cool, but he had no intention of trying to demonstrate his grasp of current teen lingo. Kids were quick to spot a patronizing adult. Instead, he played it straight down the line.

"So you play the guitar, then. I'm envious. It's all I can do to follow along in the hymnal."

"My grandpa taught me when I was a baby," Beau said softly, and Marcus instantly picked up on the significance of that.

"Yeah? Does your grandpa live around here?"

Beau shook his head before explaining that his grandfather had died the same year as his mom.

"Tell me something good you remember about him," Marcus urged.

A light shone in Beau's eyes. The sullen, wary teenager had gone, and in his place sat a simple boy who had lost too much.

"He had this cabin up in Oklahoma. We used to go up there in the summertime. It's right on the river. You ever been on the Illinois River?"

Marcus shook his head and swung his legs around to sit facing the boy again. "No, I'm sorry to say that I haven't."

Beau began a monologue on an old canoe that they'd kept at the campground at the bottom of the bluff below the cabin and all the times he and his grandfather had taken it out.

"There's these pools, where the water's still, and that's

where you get the most fish," he said wistfully. "I wish I could go back there for good."

"What about your grandmother?" Marcus asked. "Doesn't she still live there?"

Beau shook his head. "She lives up in Seattle with my great-aunt. Her mind got bad even before my mom got sick, and she pretty much forgot everything. When Grandpa died, Nicole wanted to take care of her, but Aunt Margaret said she'd do it so Nic could go to college."

"That was good of your great-aunt."

"Yeah. She's pretty old herself."

Marcus wanted the boy to know that he was blessed despite all of his losses and problems, so he made a confession. "I don't have any great-aunts or anybody like that, and I don't have anything good to remember about any of my family except my sisters."

Beau furrowed his brow at that, asking, "How come?"

"My grandparents died before I was born. They didn't have any family except my mom. I never knew my dad's family or anything about them. My dad wasn't around much, and he split when I was about four. Then my mom took off a few years later and was killed in an auto accident."

"That stinks."

"It sure did. My foster parents tried to make things fun for the boys who lived with them, but there wasn't much money and my foster mom was crippled up pretty bad with arthritis. Besides, it was kind of hard to have fun without my little sisters there. All that's changed now, though." He sat back, aware that he had Beau's full attention. "Everybody's good now. My sisters are both married to really great guys. They both have nice homes, and I have a nephew and a niece with one more on the way. Plus, there are the Cutlers."

"You know the Cutlers?"

"My sister Jolie is married to Vince."

"No kidding?"

"That's how I met *your* sister."

"Nicole says the Cutlers are like a tribe. There are so many of them, and they've got all these rituals and stuff, like football, and everybody's always hanging out together. Man, that's gotta be bananas."

Marcus laughed. "Close." He pushed the milk shake over, saying offhandedly, "Want that? I'm not as hungry as I thought I was."

Beau drained his cola in one long swig and reached for the milk shake, asking, "So how come you're not married?"

Marcus was a bit taken aback. "Been wondering that same thing myself. Just haven't found the right woman yet."

Talk turned to other things. Beau never once mentioned his father, but he obviously depended on his sister for everything. Marcus hoped Beau knew how blessed he was in that sister of his, but he wasn't sure that a thirteen-year-old was capable of understanding how unique Nicole was.

Most young ladies her age were all about guys and friends and accumulating things, not providing stable homes for their younger siblings. Marcus understood her motivation better than most, but Beau likely took her somewhat for granted, which probably was as it should be. Someday, though, Beau would look back and understand what his sister had done for him. At least Marcus wanted to think he would, for Beau's sake as much as Nicole's.

Beau finished his "snack," including what was left of Marcus's French fries, and allowed Marcus to lead him outside. As predicted, clouds had swept in on a new pressure system, obscuring the sun and dropping the temperature into the twenties.

Marcus hustled the boy into the car and resumed his place behind the steering wheel. He started the engine and cranked up the heater, hoping that it wouldn't take long to warm up.

Beau's lack of a coat was troubling, and Marcus tried to think how to address the situation, finally coming up with a rather obvious approach. "Would you like to drop by your house to pick up your coat?"

Obviously alarmed, Beau exclaimed, "No!"

Knowing what he did about Dillard Archer, Marcus considered that response ominous, but he didn't want to judge the man unfairly. "Mind if I ask why?" When the boy pressed his lips together sullenly, Marcus explained, "It's too cold for you to be running around without a coat."

"Mine's dirty," Beau mumbled.

"A dirty coat is better than no coat, Beau," Marcus pointed out.

The boy suddenly erupted. "My dad threw up on it, okay? He was sloppy hungover and he barfed all over my coat this morning!" He turned his face away, ashamed.

Marcus surreptitiously fortified himself with a deep breath, his heart going out to the boy, and carefully chose his next words. "Your father's alcoholism is a real problem for you. I'm sorry about that. With my dad it was drugs."

Beau slid a curious look over Marcus. "Yeah?"

"He overdosed not long before my mom left with her boyfriend. She used it as an excuse, actually. She kept saying that she had to provide my sisters and me with a father, as if my dad had ever really been a part of our lives. I couldn't figure out how taking off without us was supposed to provide us with parents, anyway."

"My mom would never do something like that," Beau vowed.

"I understand she was a fine Christian woman," Marcus said softly. "You must be very proud of that."

ace to raise a family and boasted a large, double-car
that Marcus could easily covet.

arked his late-model sedan behind an aging pickup

anks for everything," Beau said, yanking open the
ger door and reaching toward the floorboard for his
ck.

n't see Nicole's car," Marcus pointed out.

parks in the garage when it's cold. Otherwise her
p won't start in the morning."

t wasn't surprising. "I'll just walk you to the door,"
s said, "I'd like to speak to her." In truth, he wanted
ure she was all right.

interior light of the car clearly illuminated Beau's
l gaze. "I could have her call you."

cus signaled his understanding with a smile. "I won't
nize your father, I promise, Beau, but I'm going to
ou to the door and be sure your sister arrived home
Okay?"

muttered something under his breath and climbed
the car. Marcus followed suit, and together they
l to the front of the house. A motion-sensitive light
on as they drew near the multi-paneled door, and
at once it opened. Nicole stood there, framed in the
oorway.

cus couldn't help smiling at her outlandish clothing.
ing about her propensity to costume herself like
s rather endearing. The stripes going in every direc-
l make him want to cross his eyes, but at the same
r some reason his heart seemed to climb up into his
nd lodge there. He knew he should say something,
smiled at him, and his mind went completely blank.
rds that seemed to roll so easily off his tongue from

Beau nodded, whispering, "Before she died, everything
was real good."

"It will be good again, Beau," Marcus promised. "I'm
living proof of that. Now about that coat…"

"He'll be drinking again by now," Beau said miserably,
shaking his head and staring out the windshield.

"Actually," Marcus said, "I was thinking about an old
coat I have that you can use. Want to go take a look at it?"

Beau hunched a shoulder in a seemingly unconcerned
shrug. Marcus took that for assent and headed for the parsonage.

When they turned into the church grounds, Beau seemed
surprised. Looking around him quickly, he exclaimed, "It's
almost like a town."

"A very small town perhaps," Marcus said, guiding the
car past the church offices and day care center.

He explained that the membership had needed to expand
the church but they hadn't wanted to abandon their beloved
old sanctuary. The solution had been to purchase, one by
one, the houses which had faced the original church on
every side.

The buildings were then renovated according to their assigned purpose and linked via covered walkways. In some
cases, two buildings had been joined by an addition to form
a larger space. Marcus pointed out the education building,
the fellowship hall, the youth department and the music
center. A house still undergoing renovation would soon
serve as a furlough home for missionaries and their families returning to the U.S. on leave or for some other reason.

As Marcus eased the sedan into the narrow garage of
the tiny parsonage, Beau pointed out that the "missionary
house" was much larger than the home occupied by Marcus.

"Well, maybe someday I'll get married and need the
larger house," Marcus said, unconcerned. "Then this house

will be the furlough house, although we might have to add a bedroom or two."

Marcus tossed his own coat over the counter that separated the small kitchen from the combined dining and living area, flipping on the overhead light as he did so. He'd forgotten that the place was so cluttered. A necktie, which went with the shirt draped over the back of a dining chair, lay in a snaky heap next to this morning's unwashed breakfast bowl and an empty milk carton. Books were stacked on the dining table. Today's newspaper had drifted off the old-fashioned, green vinyl sofa onto the floor, and Marcus wondered suddenly when he'd last vacuumed the sand-colored carpet.

Beau chuckled and commented, "Man, Nicole would send you to your room if she got a load of this."

Marcus sent him a bemused glance, bringing his hands to his hips before once again surveying the place. "She'd be justified, too."

He started gathering up his errant clothing. Beau leaned an elbow on the counter and parked his chin on the palm of his hand.

"What's for dinner?"

Marcus nearly dropped everything he'd gathered. They had just eaten, hadn't they? Growing boys. "Pizza?"

"I'll call it in!" Beau exclaimed eagerly. Marcus chuckled and pointed out the phone.

By the time he'd dumped his load and reached into his closet for the coat he had in mind for Beau, the pizza was on its way.

Made of quilted gray nylon with snaps up the front and ribbed cuffs, the coat was a couple sizes too large for Marcus, having once belonged to his foster father, which meant that it would swallow the boy. Marcus counted on the inexplicable teenage fixation with oversize clothing to make the coat acceptable to Beau, and it did exactly that.

"Über!" Beau exclaimed, pushing ⎵ expose his hands.

Marcus recognized the German word f⎵ keep it if you want," he offered. "I never ⎵

Beau looked pleased, then doubtful. "⎵ it. She says we have to do for ourselves."⎵

"I don't think she'll object."

Still unconvinced, Beau peeled off th⎵ across the chrome-banded, wood coffee ⎵

"Well, you can return it later, if you w⎵ lightly. "How about a video game?"

It was glaringly obvious long before th⎵ Marcus was no competition for the boy at⎵ seem to matter. As the pizza swiftly dis⎵ boy's mouth, Marcus silently marveled, ⎵ when he, too, had eaten like a human ga⎵ seemed long ago now.

When they finally turned off the game⎵ prised to find that the evening news was ⎵

"We've got to get you home!"

Beau didn't argue, just popped up and ⎵ rowed coat. Marcus grabbed his own coa⎵ ried out.

The winter night was brittle with cold,⎵ unexpectedly cleared away, leaving the c⎵ and glow against the pitch-black backdr⎵ Their breath puffed out in little fogs un⎵ up, which wasn't long before they reache⎵

A long, low, red brick ranch-style ⎵ lot at the top of a cul-de-sac, the home ⎵ Archer and their father had a welcomi⎵ grown shrubs, broken tree limbs and the⎵ box at the curb. Though an older home⎵

the pulpit were simply nowhere to be found. It was perhaps the scariest moment of his life.

Nicole smiled at Marcus and reached out a hand to her brother, who attempted to slip past her into the house. Only then did her mind register what her eyes were telling her.

"Hey, where'd you get this coat?"

Marcus coughed, cleared his throat and rasped, "It's an old one that I had in my closet."

She looked at Beau. "Where's your other coat?"

"In the hamper," Beau mumbled, turning to Marcus. "Thanks for everything."

"My pleasure."

Beau escaped into the house, his backpack bumping Nicole and rocking her sideways. She looked to Marcus with her brows arched in question.

He cleared his throat and croaked, "Uh, if he doesn't want it—the coat, that is—maybe you can give it to someone else. I never wear it."

"All right. Are you feeling okay? You sound like you're coming down with something."

He seemed flushed to her, but he shook his head. "No, no. I'm fine. Just—" he swallowed "—something in my throat."

"How'd it go with Beau?"

"Just fine." He looked down, and she felt a spurt of unease, but then he looked up again, a smile crooking up one corner of his mouth. "I have one question, though. Do you have to work a second job to feed him?"

She laughed. "Sometimes. I hope he didn't clean you out of groceries."

"Impossible. I didn't have anything in the house. We had pizza. And burgers." He grinned. "Fries. Milk shakes. Cookies…"

She rolled her eyes. "What do I owe—"

"Don't even say it," Marcus warned, holding up a hand. "I was really glad of the company."

A loud, slurred voice shouted from inside, "Shut that blasted door! You're letting out all the heat!"

Nicole immediately stepped outside, pulling the door closed behind her. She folded her arms against the cold and said, "Thank you. And thank you for the coat. He likes it. I can tell."

"Very fashionable for him," Marcus quipped.

"Obviously. I—I just don't want you to think that I routinely let him go to school without a proper coat. I have an early class on Fridays, so he rides with a friend. I can't imagine why he didn't take his coat. You know how kids are."

"Too well. Speaking of coats. It's too cold for you out here without one."

"I'm okay. D-Did he say anything about, you know, Dad?"

"Yeah, but listen, we can't talk standing out in the cold like this." Marcus glanced around, then took her by the arm. "Come on. Let's sit in the car."

Nicole let him tug her toward his roomy sedan. "Good idea."

He walked her swiftly around to the passenger side and handed her into the car's interior. It was still warm from the drive over but rapidly cooling. Thankfully, after taking his seat behind the wheel, he started the engine and switched on the heater.

"There. That's better." For good measure, though, he lifted his scarf over his head and draped it around her shoulders, spreading it out like a shawl, a narrow one but surprisingly effective, warmed as it was from his body.

He started to shrug out of his coat, but she put a stop to that. "I'm quite comfortable now, thank you."

"You sure?"

Beau nodded, whispering, "Before she died, everything was real good."

"It will be good again, Beau," Marcus promised. "I'm living proof of that. Now about that coat…"

"He'll be drinking again by now," Beau said miserably, shaking his head and staring out the windshield.

"Actually," Marcus said, "I was thinking about an old coat I have that you can use. Want to go take a look at it?"

Beau hunched a shoulder in a seemingly unconcerned shrug. Marcus took that for assent and headed for the parsonage.

When they turned into the church grounds, Beau seemed surprised. Looking around him quickly, he exclaimed, "It's almost like a town."

"A very small town perhaps," Marcus said, guiding the car past the church offices and day care center.

He explained that the membership had needed to expand the church but they hadn't wanted to abandon their beloved old sanctuary. The solution had been to purchase, one by one, the houses which had faced the original church on every side.

The buildings were then renovated according to their assigned purpose and linked via covered walkways. In some cases, two buildings had been joined by an addition to form a larger space. Marcus pointed out the education building, the fellowship hall, the youth department and the music center. A house still undergoing renovation would soon serve as a furlough home for missionaries and their families returning to the U.S. on leave or for some other reason.

As Marcus eased the sedan into the narrow garage of the tiny parsonage, Beau pointed out that the "missionary house" was much larger than the home occupied by Marcus.

"Well, maybe someday I'll get married and need the larger house," Marcus said, unconcerned. "Then this house will be the furlough house, although we might have to add a bedroom or two."

Marcus tossed his own coat over the counter that separated the small kitchen from the combined dining and living area, flipping on the overhead light as he did so. He'd forgotten that the place was so cluttered. A necktie, which went with the shirt draped over the back of a dining chair, lay in a snaky heap next to this morning's unwashed breakfast bowl and an empty milk carton. Books were stacked on the dining table. Today's newspaper had drifted off the old-fashioned, green vinyl sofa onto the floor, and Marcus wondered suddenly when he'd last vacuumed the sand-colored carpet.

Beau chuckled and commented, "Man, Nicole would send you to your room if she got a load of this."

Marcus sent him a bemused glance, bringing his hands to his hips before once again surveying the place. "She'd be justified, too."

He started gathering up his errant clothing. Beau leaned an elbow on the counter and parked his chin on the palm of his hand.

"What's for dinner?"

Marcus nearly dropped everything he'd gathered. They had just eaten, hadn't they? Growing boys. "Pizza?"

"I'll call it in!" Beau exclaimed eagerly. Marcus chuckled and pointed out the phone.

By the time he'd dumped his load and reached into his closet for the coat he had in mind for Beau, the pizza was on its way.

Made of quilted gray nylon with snaps up the front and ribbed cuffs, the coat was a couple sizes too large for Marcus, having once belonged to his foster father, which meant that it would swallow the boy. Marcus counted on the inexplicable teenage fixation with oversize clothing to make the coat acceptable to Beau, and it did exactly that.

"Über!" Beau exclaimed, pushing up the sleeves to expose his hands.

Marcus recognized the German word for *super*. "You can keep it if you want," he offered. "I never wear it."

Beau looked pleased, then doubtful. "Nicole may not like it. She says we have to do for ourselves."

"I don't think she'll object."

Still unconvinced, Beau peeled off the coat and laid it across the chrome-banded, wood coffee table.

"Well, you can return it later, if you want," Marcus said lightly. "How about a video game?"

It was glaringly obvious long before the pizza came that Marcus was no competition for the boy at all, but that didn't seem to matter. As the pizza swiftly disappeared into the boy's mouth, Marcus silently marveled, remembering well when he, too, had eaten like a human garbage disposal. It seemed long ago now.

When they finally turned off the game, Marcus was surprised to find that the evening news was just signing off.

"We've got to get you home!"

Beau didn't argue, just popped up and tossed on his borrowed coat. Marcus grabbed his own coat, and the two hurried out.

The winter night was brittle with cold, but the clouds had unexpectedly cleared away, leaving the city lights to sparkle and glow against the pitch-black backdrop of the starry sky. Their breath puffed out in little fogs until the car warmed up, which wasn't long before they reached the Archer house.

A long, low, red brick ranch-style built on a generous lot at the top of a cul-de-sac, the home of Beau and Nicole Archer and their father had a welcoming air, despite overgrown shrubs, broken tree limbs and the wildly canted mailbox at the curb. Though an older home, it appeared to be a good place to raise a family and boasted a large, double-car garage that Marcus could easily covet.

He parked his late-model sedan behind an aging pickup truck.

"Thanks for everything," Beau said, yanking open the passenger door and reaching toward the floorboard for his backpack.

"I don't see Nicole's car," Marcus pointed out.

"She parks in the garage when it's cold. Otherwise her old heap won't start in the morning."

That wasn't surprising. "I'll just walk you to the door," Marcus said, "I'd like to speak to her." In truth, he wanted to be sure she was all right.

The interior light of the car clearly illuminated Beau's worried gaze. "I could have her call you."

Marcus signaled his understanding with a smile. "I won't antagonize your father, I promise, Beau, but I'm going to walk you to the door and be sure your sister arrived home safely. Okay?"

Beau muttered something under his breath and climbed out of the car. Marcus followed suit, and together they walked to the front of the house. A motion-sensitive light flicked on as they drew near the multi-paneled door, and almost at once it opened. Nicole stood there, framed in the open doorway.

Marcus couldn't help smiling at her outlandish clothing. Something about her propensity to costume herself like this was rather endearing. The stripes going in every direction did make him want to cross his eyes, but at the same time for some reason his heart seemed to climb up into his throat and lodge there. He knew he should say something, but she smiled at him, and his mind went completely blank. The words that seemed to roll so easily off his tongue from the pulpit were simply nowhere to be found. It was perhaps the scariest moment of his life.

Nicole smiled at Marcus and reached out a hand to her brother, who attempted to slip past her into the house. Only then did her mind register what her eyes were telling her.

"Hey, where'd you get this coat?"

Marcus coughed, cleared his throat and rasped, "It's an old one that I had in my closet."

She looked at Beau. "Where's your other coat?"

"In the hamper," Beau mumbled, turning to Marcus. "Thanks for everything."

"My pleasure."

Beau escaped into the house, his backpack bumping Nicole and rocking her sideways. She looked to Marcus with her brows arched in question.

He cleared his throat and croaked, "Uh, if he doesn't want it—the coat, that is—maybe you can give it to someone else. I never wear it."

"All right. Are you feeling okay? You sound like you're coming down with something."

He seemed flushed to her, but he shook his head. "No, no. I'm fine. Just—" he swallowed "—something in my throat."

"How'd it go with Beau?"

"Just fine." He looked down, and she felt a spurt of unease, but then he looked up again, a smile crooking up one corner of his mouth. "I have one question, though. Do you have to work a second job to feed him?"

She laughed. "Sometimes. I hope he didn't clean you out of groceries."

"Impossible. I didn't have anything in the house. We had pizza. And burgers." He grinned. "Fries. Milk shakes. Cookies…"

She rolled her eyes. "What do I owe—"

"Don't even say it," Marcus warned, holding up a hand. "I was really glad of the company."

A loud, slurred voice shouted from inside, "Shut that blasted door! You're letting out all the heat!"

Nicole immediately stepped outside, pulling the door closed behind her. She folded her arms against the cold and said, "Thank you. And thank you for the coat. He likes it. I can tell."

"Very fashionable for him," Marcus quipped.

"Obviously. I—I just don't want you to think that I routinely let him go to school without a proper coat. I have an early class on Fridays, so he rides with a friend. I can't imagine why he didn't take his coat. You know how kids are."

"Too well. Speaking of coats. It's too cold for you out here without one."

"I'm okay. D-Did he say anything about, you know, Dad?"

"Yeah, but listen, we can't talk standing out in the cold like this." Marcus glanced around, then took her by the arm. "Come on. Let's sit in the car."

Nicole let him tug her toward his roomy sedan. "Good idea."

He walked her swiftly around to the passenger side and handed her into the car's interior. It was still warm from the drive over but rapidly cooling. Thankfully, after taking his seat behind the wheel, he started the engine and switched on the heater.

"There. That's better." For good measure, though, he lifted his scarf over his head and draped it around her shoulders, spreading it out like a shawl, a narrow one but surprisingly effective, warmed as it was from his body.

He started to shrug out of his coat, but she put a stop to that. "I'm quite comfortable now, thank you."

"You sure?"

"Absolutely. So what did Beau say about Dad?"

"He said he was 'sloppy hungover this morning,'" Marcus answered. "That's why his other coat's in the hamper."

She grimaced, not even wanting to know what that meant. She'd find out soon enough anyway. Tossing one end of Marcus's scarf across her throat, she inhaled. It smelled just as she'd imagined it would, just as she'd imagined he would.

"I thought he was just saying that so you wouldn't know that he left it home on purpose. His old coat's too small, and the other kids make fun of him because of it. You know how it is."

"Yeah, well, the way things are these days, too small could actually mean that it fits, not that these kids would see it that way."

She laughed. "True. I hate that we can't afford new things for him, but the way he's growing it's all I can do to keep him covered."

"There are worse things than not keeping up with fashion trends," Marcus said.

"That's the way I see it," she agreed sincerely, but then he got this big grin on his face.

"What?"

"Oh, nothing. I'm just glad to see that you have your priorities straight."

"Oh. Well, I'm glad you think so. Beau doesn't always agree."

"He's thirteen. I think agreement is a biological impossibility at this point."

She chuckled. "You're telling me! He's not a bad kid, though."

"I can see that. I meant it when I said I enjoyed his company."

"I'm sure he enjoyed your company, too, a lot more than he would have the Cutlers. They're wonderful people, but to Beau anyone over thirty is the enemy right now." Marcus winced, and she quickly reached out a hand. "I'm sorry. I didn't mean that literally. I just meant—"

"I know what you meant. Don't worry about it. Guess I'm just feeling my age these days."

"Well, it's not like you're arthritic or anything." Now she winced. "Are you?"

He laughed. "Not that I've noticed."

"Some young people are, you know. I mean, there's a girl in one of my classes with juvenile arthritis. She's stiff all the time, and you can, like, hear her joints popping when she moves."

"No arthritic joints here," he said merrily. "Not yet, anyway. Thank God."

"I'd better go in before I wind up with the other foot in my mouth," she muttered. And before her father took enough note of her absence to ask some awkward questions that she didn't want to answer.

"Beau's probably wondering what happened to you," Marcus agreed softly.

Reluctantly she removed the scarf from around her neck and offered it to him, but he shook his head.

"No, you keep it for now. You can return it on Sunday. Right?"

Nicole draped the scarf around her shoulders and tossed one end across her throat, smiling. "Right. I won't forget."

"Okay. See you then."

"See you then," she confirmed, opening the door and quickly hopping out. "Thank you, Marcus," she said just before she closed the door. "Bye."

He waved and put the car into reverse, but he just sat there with his foot on the brake until she reached the house.

"See you Sunday," Nicole whispered as she slipped inside. It wouldn't be wise to let her father find out what she was planning. He'd had a thing about church ever since her mom had fallen ill. But she knew that going was the right thing to do, if only because she'd promised Marcus. It wasn't only that, though. Her mother would want them to go, her and Beau.

For too long Nicole had catered to her father's anger on this subject. Somehow she'd allowed herself to fall into the trap of trying to appease him when she knew only too well that nothing could.

She hoped that Beau wouldn't put up a fuss. He probably wouldn't. She thought he'd go because he liked Marcus, but he was going even if she had to bully him. One way or another, Sunday morning was going to find them both sitting on a church pew again.

Her fingers slid over the soft wool draped about her shoulders. It took a moment for her to realize that the feeling growing inside her chest was hope.

It had always lived there. She couldn't have kept on keeping on otherwise. Suddenly it seemed to be branching out, though, and in some surprising directions.

Smiling to herself, she fairly danced down the hall to her brother's room.

Chapter Four

Nicole sat on the foot of her brother's bed and waited for him to get off the computer. He ended the game he was playing and swiveled around on the seat of his chair, one arm on the desk, the other draped over the chair's hardwood back.

"Where's Dad?"

"Asleep in front of the TV, probably."

"You mean he passed out in front of the TV," Beau corrected.

She didn't deny it, but she wasn't here to discuss their father or his drinking problems. She had another matter entirely on her mind. "So what do you think of the pastor?"

Beau shrugged and said nonchalantly, "I like him."

"Really? You're not just saying that because you think I want you to?"

"Chillax. I said I like him."

"So you wouldn't mind spending time with him again?" Nicole probed carefully.

"I'll kick it with the pastor whenever you want," Beau said, turning his chair around to straddle it and fold his arms across the top of the back. "He's easy to talk to, like one of the guys almost, not like he tries to *be* one of the guys, though."

"I know what you mean," Nicole said. "It's like he's really interested in you and what you have to say."

Beau nodded. Then he asked, "Doesn't it seem funny that he's not married?"

Nicole's heart gave a pronounced thump, but she kept her expression cool. She hadn't even considered that he might be married. Why hadn't she looked at his ring finger? Why hadn't she asked Ovida Cutler?

"How do you know he's not married?"

"He told me so."

"Oh? What did he say?"

"Just that he hadn't found the right woman yet."

"So he's looking, then?"

Beau screwed up his face, complaining, "I don't know. What're you asking me for?"

"No reason," she answered nonchalantly. "It's just that I promised him we'd try out his church this Sunday, and I wanted to know what you thought about him. That's all."

Dropping his chin, Beau sent her a pointed look. Clearly she wasn't fooling him. He knew she was interested in Marcus. She rolled her eyes as if to say she wasn't, and for some reason Beau chose to let it go. She wondered if that signaled approval or if it meant that he figured she had no chance of attracting Marcus's interest for herself.

She cleared her throat. "Well? Do you want to go to church on Sunday or not?"

He thought about it before asking, "What about Dad?"

"The way I figure it," Nicole said, "is that if he goes out on Saturday night, then he'll be sleeping in on Sunday morning."

"And he always goes out on Saturday night," Beau said matter-of-factly.

They stared at each other for several long moments, neither saying aloud what they both knew. It would be better if their father didn't realize they were attending church, at least initially. Maybe once he saw that it wouldn't interfere with his lifestyle, he would be amenable. That had proven the case with the issue of Nicole attending college.

For some time before she'd graduated from high school, Dillard had grumbled that Nicole should put any plans to further her education on hold until Beau was old enough to take care of himself. Wisely, Nicole had said nothing, and when the time had come to enroll she had not sought Dillard's permission. Instead she'd simply taken herself down to the university, signed up for classes and applied for every grant, scholarship and tuition aid she could find. She was halfway through the first semester before her father had realized that she was attending college and his life had not truly been impacted at all. Hopefully, it would be the same way when he found out that they were attending church.

On the other hand, it might turn out to be a one-time deal. Marcus Wheeler's church might not be to their liking. They might not go back. That's what she told herself anyway. In her heart, Nicole knew that regular attendance was definitely in her future. She missed going to church, but she hadn't seen any point in risking her father's wrath until now.

"You'd better try on your dress slacks," she told Beau, rising to her feet. "You'll probably have to wear one of Dad's shirts."

Beau nodded, shrugged and turned back to the computer, muttering, "Guess you'll be going through your boxes."

"Oh, yeah," she admitted. This occasion definitely called for something special.

She headed for the garage and the half-dozen boxes that

contained everything that was left over from her mother's and grandmother's closets. Nicole loved digging through them and wearing the clothes. Not only did it play to her personal tastes, it also saved her a lot of money on her wardrobe. Plus, it made her feel closer to those whom she missed most.

Luckily, retro was "in" right now, not that Nicole cared a fig for being in style. Some of the old stuff in those boxes was worth a good deal in resale shops, though. Once in a while, when money was especially tight, she'd pick out a piece to sell. Usually it was one of her grandmother's old handbags. Grandma Jean had claimed to have a handbag fetish. She'd accumulated dozens by the time she'd forgotten what the word *fetish* meant, along with so much else, including the family.

Dillard claimed that Jean was lucky because she couldn't remember the pain of losing her daughter and husband. Nicole didn't buy that philosophy, though. She was glad to remember. Every memory was a treasure to her, and she hung on to the memories much as she hung on to those boxes of old clothes.

It was too cold to go through her boxes in the garage, so Nicole towed them into her bedroom, one by one. A couple of them were actually made for garments, with poles for hangers. The rest were neatly stacked with smaller items. She knew exactly what each box held, but at times like this she would pull out every article and spread them around her colorful room, arranged by category. Once the contents of the boxes were properly displayed, Nicole would spend hours choosing what she would wear before lovingly packing it all away again.

On this occasion, she pulled everything out, then went to bed beneath an extra blanket of garments, leaving the decision-making process for the morrow. She wanted to relish this turn that her life seemed to be taking. Even if the ultimate destination was not what she hoped, she intended to enjoy the journey.

Marcus couldn't contain his pleasure when he looked out across his congregation on Sunday morning at the smiling faces of Nicole and Beau Archer. There were other visitors, as well, of course. The place was packed, in fact, as it often was of late. Even the tiny balcony section, reached via a narrow, winding staircase hidden in the back hall, was stuffed with bodies.

Marcus recognized several families whose children attended day care at the church and was glad that preparations were underway for adding a second morning service in the spring, even though it would mean more work for him. Meanwhile, all those involved in the actual production and execution of worship were busily planning what that second service would involve. At times, like this morning, the excitement was palpable as the church poised itself for that next big step forward.

As he moved into the pulpit, Marcus felt lifted up, his words imbued with a special power. Though he considered himself more of a thoughtful teacher than a spellbinding preacher, he seemed linked to his audience in an unusual manner that morning. It was as if he shared a special connection with every person present, and when all was said and done, the church had added three new families, numbering ten souls in all, to the membership roll. Through every moment, he was aware of the Archers.

Even as he stood at the vestibule door, shaking hands and sharing smiles and comments with the exiting throng, Marcus was keenly aware of Beau and Nicole Archer near the back of the line. Beau seemed somewhat hesitant when

Marcus paused to speak with him, but Marcus assumed that it had to do with his painfully awkward appearance.

Beau looked like a poster boy for the underprivileged, dressed as he was in a faded black tie and a white shirt which was considerably too large for him. The cuffs of his shirt sleeves had been rolled back several times to keep them from hanging over the boy's hands, and the collar was in no danger of choking him, despite the tightly knotted tie. To make matters worse, his charcoal-gray dress slacks were a little too short, showing a bit of white sock above worn black shoes. In addition, his shaggy brown hair slid haphazardly in several directions at once, despite having obviously been parted and wet-combed earlier. He held the coat Marcus had given him, clutched in both arms, like a security blanket.

Marcus knew he had to do something. He called over a couple of youngsters around Beau's age and introduced them. As the trio stepped aside to talk stiltedly among themselves, Marcus at last turned his attention to Nicole.

While Beau's attire branded him as a poor kid barely surviving in a harsh world, Nicole managed to look amazingly pretty in her odd getup. Considering the last two times he'd seen her, this outfit was fairly subdued, which was not to say conventional.

Her dark hair fell sleekly past her shoulders from beneath a yellow crocheted cap pulled almost to her delicately arched brows. The crochet was repeated in the ankle-length, purple vest that she wore over a slender, black, short-sleeved sheath, yellow stockings and knee-high, white vinyl boots. She clutched her red gloves in one hand and carried a familiar striped scarf folded over one arm with what appeared to be a royal-blue cape, though it could have been a voluminous coat arranged so that the sleeves were hidden.

Marcus couldn't help laughing. Not because she looked ridiculous—she didn't, oddly enough—but because something about her just inspired that reaction. It was as if the sun came out from behind drab clouds when Nicole appeared, as if color suddenly washed a black-and-white world with sparkling, breathtaking hues. Yet, no one could deny that she was a quirky character. Marcus saw the way that others looked at her, the smiles hidden behind coughs and throat clearings, the surreptitious glances and whispered comments. She seemed happily oblivious.

"That was great!" she gushed, rocking up onto her tiptoes as she held his hand. "Inspiring. Honestly!"

"Glad you enjoyed it. I'm delighted to see you and Beau here this morning."

"We'll be back," she announced, beaming.

"Wonderful. If you have a few minutes now, though, I'd like a word with you when I'm done here." A shadow passed across her eyes, dimming them momentarily. "Won't take long, I promise," he added quickly, then glanced pointedly over his shoulder at Beau.

"Oh, um, okay. Sure."

He directed her to a bench against one wall of the vestibule and made quick work of the few remaining farewells before joining her.

"As I said, I'm really glad to see you and Beau here this morning, Nicole," he told her. "I'm even happier that you plan to return, and I'd like to help Beau fit in, if I can."

"I'm sure once he gets to know people…" she began.

"Oh, absolutely," Marcus agreed. "If I could make one suggestion, though?"

Her slender brows drew together, and her voice carried a wary note despite her polite reply. "Of course."

"Let him lose the tie, or at least wear it loose and drooping." He touched his own neat Windsor knot and chuckled. "That's how our minister of youth wears his. Very cool, I'm told."

She made a face and relaxed. "I guess we were both thinking about the last time we attended church." Dropping her head she admitted, "It's been a long time, you know. Beau was just ten, and what was considered appropriate for a boy that age back then and what's considered okay now..." She waved a hand.

Marcus chuckled. "Yeah, I know. Some of the older folks complain when they see these kids with baggy pants and the shirttails out and hanging down to their knees, but I figure that this is their church, too, and they should be comfortable. That they're here is much more important to me than how they're dressed."

"I see what you mean."

"We do have standards," he went on. "We draw the line at T-shirts with slogans other than Christian ones and head coverings indoors for the boys. We don't even allow the girls to wear those backward caps that are so popular. Those so-called 'belly shirts' are absolutely forbidden, too, and we quietly monitor the length of skirts and, in the summertime, shorts. Otherwise, we pretty much try to go with the flow."

"Okay. I'll remember that," Nicole said. "I mean, it's bad enough that everything he owns is practically worn out. No reason he should stick out like a sore thumb, too."

Marcus bowed his head, fingering his chin, and said uncertainly, "Nicole, I could...that is, I'd be glad to—how should I put this?—front you some money on Beau's behalf."

She was on her feet and shaking her head before he got the words out. "Uh-uh. No way. Treating him to dinner is one thing, but buying clothes is something else."

"Think of it as a loan," he urged, but she was even more adamant in her refusal of that.

"Absolutely not. I couldn't pay it back, not for a long, long time, anyway." She folded her arms. "We've held out this long. We can hold out until I've paid next semester's tuition. After that we can start taking care of some of this other stuff."

He wanted to argue. It tore at Marcus's heart to see Beau going around so bedraggled because Marcus so vividly remembered being that boy. But he remembered, too, the pride that had gotten him through the worst of it, and well-deserved pride was better than new clothes. He wasn't thinking of the sort of pride that Scripture warned caused downfall but rather the pride that came from doing the difficult thing for the right reasons. Funny that Nicole should be the one to remind him of that.

"You're right," he said, rising to his feet. "Forget I mentioned it."

"That's okay." She smiled. "It just shows you care."

"Yes," he agreed unthinkingly. "Exactly. I do care."

"Thank you for that," she said, and then to his shock, she flung her arms around him in a hug.

For a moment Marcus froze, his arms trapped between them. Heat flashed through him, exploding into red blossoms on his cheeks. To his horror he realized that several of the kids were standing in the open doorway looking in at them, Beau in their midst, with none other than David Calloway in the background.

A couple of the teenagers giggled speculatively. Others seemed shocked. The minister of youth looked as embarrassed for him as Marcus felt. His throat burned and his face pulsed red by the time Nicole released him from what was surely nothing more than an impulsive display of gratitude, but he couldn't remember ever being quite so shaken before. He did his best to appear unconcerned, even casual. He said something about it being lunchtime and having to lock up before quickly turning away and immediately getting so busy that he didn't even see her leave.

Indeed, he didn't see much of anything after that. A red

haze seemed to fog his vision. He felt disoriented, tongue-tied, glaringly conspicuous. It must have been obvious, for when David finally joined him, he asked peremptorily, "You okay?"

"Sure," he answered, wincing inwardly because it seemed too loud. "Just trying to get out of here. As usual, my sisters are expecting me for lunch."

"Ah." David grinned. Fair and blue-eyed, he was an engaging young man, a bit on the small side, but good-looking in a trendy, polished way with his artfully spiked hair and designer attire. More importantly, he was very, very good at youth ministry. It wasn't his fault that he sometimes made Marcus feel as if he were teetering on the brink of old age. Like now. "I don't think I've ever seen her before," David went on thoughtfully.

"Who?" That was painting it entirely too brown, and Marcus knew it, but he was stuck now.

"Long, dark hair," David said, a twinkle in his eye that made Marcus want to drop through a hole in the floor.

"Oh, you mean Nicole Archer. The new kid's her brother."

"Hmm. I didn't get much out of him."

"It's a long story," Marcus said. "I'll tell you about it in the office tomorrow."

David nodded. "Must be interesting."

"Interesting but sad," Marcus said gravely. "The Archers are in a very difficult situation."

That doused the speculative gleam in David's blue eyes. "Is there anything we can do?"

"I don't know. Maybe. For now, just pray, I suppose. His name's Beau, by the way. Beau Archer."

"I'll add his name to my list," David said.

"Great. Now would you check that back door for me? I'm starving."

"Go ahead and take off," David said, hurrying away.

Marcus did, for once, as quickly as possible, but he couldn't seem to recover his aplomb. While he drove toward his sister's house, he kept thinking about that hug, and for the life of him, he couldn't figure out why it had flustered him so.

As a single man in ministry, he was acutely aware that his conduct must be above reproach. For that reason he had always been very circumspect in his dealings with females of all ages, especially the young ones, and that included Nicole.

Why, a full decade stood between them. And it showed. Anybody could see it.

That didn't really explain why that hug had sent him into a panic, though. It wasn't the first time such a thing had happened. Usually he just disengaged and kept a polite distance, and that was the end of it. He couldn't understand why this felt different.

Walking up the gently winding pavement toward Jolie's front door, a picture of Nicole climbing into her battered little car suddenly assailed him. He stopped in his tracks, remembering that he'd felt an odd kinship with her even then. It was as if he knew her somehow, although they'd never met before.

He hadn't even been aware of her existence before! Surely that kinship was nothing more than his ability to identify on an innate level with what she was going through. Wasn't it?

Yes, of course. It had to be. What other explanation was there?

"The explanation, my man," he told himself aloud, the thought coming to him in a flash of insight, "is that the devil always hits you hardest when you're at your weakest point, and you have got to stop feeling sorry for yourself."

That was it. This feeling of being alone in a world of happy pairs was clouding his judgment and muddling his emotions. He had no reason to be embarrassed by a public hug from a funny girl who simply needed a friend, and he had no reason for this maudlin lonesomeness, either. When the time was right, God would bring someone into his life. Until then he was just borrowing trouble by letting it prey on his mind.

He bowed his head right where he was and confessed his weakness to God, adding a petition for the Archer family before ending his silent prayer. Feeling better, he went inside to dinner and the warmth of his sister's home.

Nicole handed the paper bag and bucket of chicken to her brother before fastening her safety belt. The drive-through lane had been ten cars deep when she'd pulled up to the fast-food restaurant, and she hadn't wanted to burn expensive gasoline or waste precious time idling in line, so she'd parked and gone inside to place their order. Now the car was cold again. She started the engine and began wrestling the gearshift into reverse.

"Sorry, I didn't have enough money for all the sides you wanted, but I got the gravy, and we can make instant potatoes."

Beau shrugged and pulled a steaming biscuit from the paper bag. A yeasty odor immediately permeated the bare interior of the small car. The crystal rainbow that hung from the rearview mirror on a string reeled crazily as the transmission finally caught and the little jalopy lurched backward in an arc.

"'At's o-hay," he said around a mouthful of hot biscuit.

He gulped and shoved the second half of the biscuit into his mouth. Apparently it had cooled enough to allow him to actually chew, for he mauled it once or twice before swallowing this time.

As he reached for a second helping, Nicole mentally said

goodbye to her share of the hot bread. The kid ate as if constantly starving. She imagined that he'd be shooting up another couple of inches soon, which meant that his feet were going to get bigger, too.

That part of the equation worried her. He could wear his pants too short; with warmer weather coming on, she could always cut them off. As for shirts, he'd have to make do with Dillard's castoffs and cheap tees. But shoes were something else.

Beau detested secondhand shoes like those on his feet at that moment, and the cheap new ones, the ones she could afford, came apart within an appallingly short period of time. It was as if he wore them out from the *inside,* as if he steeped his feet in acid before he put on the things.

Anything durable enough to last longer than a few weeks was going to cost upward of sixty bucks. She could buy two or three pairs of the cheap ones for that, but in the end it would wind up costing her the same as the better ones. The only advantage was that she could parcel the money out in smaller portions. But Beau would be unhappy about it the whole time.

Sighing inwardly, she thought of the offer Marcus had made earlier, but she couldn't take his money, his or anyone else's. It was her job to care for her brother, hers and their father's, but she saw no point in dwelling on that. What Dillard did, Dillard did. She couldn't answer for anyone but herself. The thing was, she'd promised at her mother's deathbed to take care of Beau, and that's what she had to do. She'd realized early on that if she didn't stand firm, she'd be swept aside by those who thought youth automatically trumped responsibility, which was exactly why she couldn't reach out to the authorities as Marcus had suggested.

She pictured Marcus as he'd appeared that morning. The fit of his dark brown suit had been perfect. She'd have jazzed things up with a pink shirt and neon-green tie and socks, but the pale yellow and gold had been nice, too, especially with Marcus's coloring. The shoes he'd worn were positively elegant, gleaming, butter-soft slip-ons with tiny leather pleats across the toe box.

She wished Beau could wear clothes like that. Then again, even if she could afford to outfit him in such style, he'd only grouse about it. He wanted to be like the rest of the kids in their expensive, baggy, oversize gear. Nicole supposed it was understandable, even though she had never wanted to look like anyone else. It was much more fun to be one of a kind.

"So what'd you think?" Beau asked, having had his fill of hot biscuits or, perhaps, realizing that he'd better leave the rest for their dad.

"About church?"

"No, about traffic. Duh. The music wasn't as whack as I figured it'd be, and those kids said they're going to start doing a service with guitars and drums and everything."

"Really? That sounds like fun."

"Could be."

"So you liked it, then?"

"Yeah, I liked it."

"Me, too. Especially the sermon."

Beau snorted. "Especially the preacher, you mean."

Nicole shot him a startled glance but kept her tone nonchalant as she said, "What of it? You like him, too."

"But *I* don't want him for a boyfriend," Beau teased.

"I never said—"

"You were hugging him, Nic."

She fought the impulse to tighten her hands on the steering wheel and trained her gaze straight ahead. "I was just thanking him. You're making mountains out of molehills. Now, back to the sermon."

Beau snorted again, but he let the matter go, asking, "What was that Phillips thing he read?"

"Philippians. It's in the New Testament."

"I didn't get that part about dying being gain."

"It's about knowing that you're going to heaven when you die. See, it's like…" She had to gather together the right words to explain it to him. "Okay. We think this life is good because it's all we know. And there's plenty to like about it. Living is a good thing. But heaven's even better, so death isn't about losing this life as much as it's about gaining a better one. That's what it means."

Beau nodded. "I can get with that. I've always believed that Mom and Gramps were in a better place. It's getting left behind that stinks."

"I know, but even that's not all bad. It's not even mostly bad once you get over the worst part."

"That's Dad's problem, isn't it?" Beau said matter-of-factly. "He can't get over the worst part of missing Mom."

Can't or won't, Nicole thought, preferring to stick with the sermon, which had moved her. "Anyway," she went on, "that Scripture passage wasn't really about dying. It was about living the way we ought to."

"'Only conduct yourselves in a manner worthy of the gospel of Christ,'" Beau quoted, proving that he'd been paying attention.

Nicole smiled to show her approval. "Exactly."

She hoped Beau was thinking about the things that Marcus had said were part of worthy living, things like reading the Bible and praying every day, being honest and kind and "wholesome." She knew she was going to be thinking about that a lot. The honest part niggled at her because she and Beau were not being honest with their father about attending church.

What else could they do, though? If they asked, he'd say no. At least this way they'd get to go for a while.

Which meant that she'd get to see Marcus.

That thought made her feel even worse, because church shouldn't be about getting to see a guy you liked. Church was about worship. She remembered her mom saying that over and over again. Back then for Nicole church had been more about seeing her friends than anything else. Once her mother had fallen ill, however, church had become all about God healing her. Suzanne had realized it and said that shouldn't be the case. Nicole had wondered how it could be about anything else, and she remembered sitting in that pew next to her mom, her friends forgotten, pleading with God to spare her mother's life.

...to live is Christ, and to die is gain.

It was as if Marcus had been saying to her with his sermon that now she could put behind her the deaths of her mother and grandfather and live the rest of her life in a manner that would prove the reality and wonder of heaven. And that was just what she intended to do. As soon as she figured out how.

She smiled to herself, knowing exactly who could help her with that.

Chapter Five

Nicole handed two cans of soup to her brother and reached for the handle of the refrigerator door.

"Open these while I make us some grilled cheese sandwiches."

Beau turned one can in his hand in order to read the label, making a face. "Oh, man, I hate this stuff!"

"The other is chicken noodle," Nicole pointed out, slapping a stick of margarine onto the counter. Ignoring his second grimace, she bent over the deli drawer in the refrigerator, looking for the sliced cheese.

"Why couldn't we nab a pizza or something?" he whined, having gotten used to picking up dinner after church these past four weeks.

It had become their cover. On the one occasion when their father had actually been awake when they'd come in, he'd seen the food sacks and assumed they'd gone out for that and no other reason. The trouble was, carrying in fast food was expensive.

"I told you," Nicole reminded her brother, "I'm broke."

"Man, there's got to be something else here to eat," Beau

grumbled. Setting aside the soup cans, he shuffled over to the pantry and began poking around inside.

"Do not," said a raspy voice, freezing them in place, "try to tell me that you've been out getting lunch this time."

Her heart in her throat, Nicole made herself remove the sliced cheese from the drawer, close it and rise, giving the refrigerator door a gentle shove as she turned. Beau put his back to the counter and folded his arms defiantly. She carefully did not look at him. Instead, she fixed her father with a level gaze.

"No, we didn't go out to get lunch," she admitted calmly. "We're scraping the pantry today, but I get paid tomorrow, so no sweat."

Carrying the cheese to the counter, she took the remains of a loaf of bread from her grandmother's old-fashioned bread box, then reached into a cabinet for a skillet.

"So where were you?" Dillard demanded, pulling out a rickety chair at the equally rickety kitchen table. "And don't give me any guff about being broke and payday coming."

Well, what had she expected? This day had to come sooner or later. She was surprised that they'd gotten away with it this long.

Nicole turned to face him just as he lowered himself into the chair. He stretched out his long, thick legs, crossing his stocking feet at the ankles. He was a mess. The heel was out of one sock, and the hems of his jeans were ragged. His faded T-shirt had holes in it and looked none too clean. He hadn't shaved in days—or bathed, by the greasy look of his lank, untrimmed hair.

A much larger, older version of Beau, Dillard Archer still retained some of the heavy musculature that had once made Nicole believe that her daddy was the strongest man alive. His middle had given way to a pronounced paunch. By the way he held one arm across it, he was probably nauseous, and the furrow of his brow said that his head likely ached, too, all of which meant that he was hungover. But perhaps a little less hungover than normal, unfortunately.

Beau walked across the room to stand beside her, belligerence in his every move. She rubbed his arm soothingly, then took a deep breath, relief warring with dread. "We've been going to church."

Dillard's face wrinkled and bunched. "Now why would you want to do a fool thing like that?"

Nicole used her greatest weapon without a single compunction. "Mama would have wanted us to."

Dillard clamped his jaw and looked away. After a moment he lifted a hand to massage his temples with thumb and forefinger. "You'd better not be putting my money in the collection plate," he groused, "then expecting me to eat soup!"

Beau made a rude sound. Nicole sent him a quelling glance and figuratively bit her tongue. They all knew that Dillard routinely drank up nearly every bit of his small disability check. If she hadn't made sure that the electricity bill was debited from it and a portion automatically set aside to pay their property taxes at the end of every year, he wouldn't contribute to supporting the household at all.

Her heart pounding, Nicole carried the skillet to the stove and turned on a burner. Beau started rummaging around in a drawer, looking for the can opener, which was sitting in the dish drainer next to the sink.

"You two little idiots have really been getting up, pawing through the ragbag and hauling yourselves to church?" Dillard demanded in the acid tone that always meant he was spoiling for a fight.

Nicole was determined not to give it to him. "What kind of soup do you want," she asked calmly, "chicken noodle or tomato?" When he didn't immediately answer, she glanced over one shoulder.

Scowling, Dillard brought his hands to his hips, but then his shoulders drooped, and he rumbled, "Tomato, but put some sherry in it, for pity's sake." Nicole tried to keep her expression bland, but he saw her disapproval and immediately snapped, "It's how your mother would have made it."

"I remember," she said lightly, reaching toward the dish drainer, "but we don't have any cooking sherry."

She handed the can opener to Beau with a very pointed look. He was glowering, but he kept his back to their father as he opened the can and dumped the contents into a bowl. She concentrated on preparing the grilled cheese sandwiches, while Beau heated the soup in their old microwave.

After a moment, Dillard got up and shambled out of the room.

A minute or two later, Beau tapped her on the shoulder. When she turned her head, he pumped one fist in a gesture of victory. Nicole smiled, but she wasn't so sure that they'd won anything yet. Still, their father hadn't forbidden them to continue attending church, and that in itself was more than she'd expected. Maybe, as Marcus's sermon had asserted that morning, God really was at work in their lives.

Marcus watched as the enthusiastic young minister of youth drove away in his shiny red pickup truck. David was great with the kids, who met weekly on Wednesday evenings for Bible study and fellowship. Marcus liked to put in an appearance at those weekly meetings himself, and David seemed to welcome his input. The two of them made a pretty good team, and Marcus liked the young man immensely—and envied him almost as much.

David was cool, popular and had his life together. His parents came down from Oklahoma occasionally and stood around beaming with undisguised and fully-merited pride. He was engaged to a pretty, wholesome young woman from another solid family, who couldn't have been more fitted to the calling of a youth minister's wife, and they were happily planning a wedding that was apt to set her parents back several thousand dollars in another year or so. Marcus begrudged them not a bit of any of it. He just wanted some of that for himself, and he couldn't figure out where this unwarranted, unattractive and counterproductive discontent was coming from.

Crossing the square toward the parsonage, he cut through the parking lot and a corner of the lawn surrounding the sanctuary. Sand-colored grass crunched beneath his feet. February had gone, but the first day of March had brought only the slightest promise of spring. He dug his hands deeper into his coat pockets and hunched his shoulders against the frosty air nipping at his ears.

He admitted to himself that he was disappointed because Beau Archer hadn't attended the youth meeting this evening. Marcus had invited the boy personally on Sunday, but he'd mumbled something about Nicole having enrolled him in a computer program at the local library. Marcus figured she'd paid a fee and that Beau didn't want her to lose her hard-earned money.

Marcus knew that for Nicole it was probably more about keeping her brother away from their father than having him taught about computers. If he asked her, she might well drop the computer course so Beau could attend youth meetings instead, but should he?

He saw her in his mind's eye as he had last Sunday. He hadn't meant to look her up and down like that, but the long orange silk shirt with the slender, red cotton skirt under it could not be ignored, especially with that chain-link belt slung low around her waist. By the time his gaze had finished its upward journey, she was looking very pleased with herself, and no wonder.

With the sides of her hair swept back and caught loosely at the nape of her neck and the collar of that vibrant orange blouse turned up to frame her face, she looked like a particularly tasty piece of fruit. He'd had the distinct impression she'd cultivated that particular look just for him, and it wasn't the first time he'd gotten that sense about her.

She hadn't hugged him again, thankfully, but she had a way of brushing her hand down his arm that literally stopped his lungs from working. Then there was that little look she gave him from time to time, her pert chin tucked low so that her eyes appeared as big as full, tip-tilted moons. And unless he missed his guess, she'd taken to wearing lip gloss. At least he had this picture of full, shiny lips in his head that he couldn't seem to turn off.

Given all that and the way she'd started hanging around until everyone else had left the building so she could engage him in private conversation, he was fairly certain that Nicole was flirting with him. Now maybe *that* was something he should be talking to her about—if only he could bring himself to do it.

Bringing the subject up with her could do more harm than good. Besides, it might just be a figment of his tortured, overwrought imagination. Surely it was a figment of his tortured, overwrought—warped, self-centered—imagination. It *had* to be a figment of his imagination.

Marcus climbed the few steps and let himself into the house. The place felt as empty as a tomb. Switching on lights, he divested himself of his outerwear and tossed his coat over the low shelving unit that separated the entryway from the living area. He walked across the dining space and around the bar counter into the kitchen.

Opening the refrigerator door, he tried to turn his mind to dinner, but the contents of his larder left him uninspired. Finally, he took out a carton of milk and snagged a box of crackers and a jar of peanut butter from the cabinet. After plucking a clean spoon from a drawer, he carried the lot back into the living room, where he collapsed into the armchair and kicked off his shoes.

With only the television for company, he made a cursory meal, washing down the crackers and peanut butter with milk directly from the carton. Suddenly exhausted, he shut off the TV, put everything away and moved into the bedroom.

He got ready for bed and slid beneath the covers. Leaning back against the headboard, he reached for the Bible on his bedside table. After reading for a while, he closed the book and put it away. Folding his hands, he closed his eyes and prepared his mind for prayer, mentally reviewing the list he'd been constructing in his mind all day.

"Gracious Lord God," he whispered, "Creator of all things, Author of salvation, Fount of wisdom, I praise Your holy name. Forgive me for my shortcomings, all those sins I so thoughtlessly commit during the course of a day, the envy, the unkind thoughts, the irritations…"

The words dwindled away, and with them every thought in his head.

Blinking, he stared at himself in the mirror on the dresser opposite the bed. Everything looked perfectly in order, the covers smoothed and folded across his chest, the lamp shining down on the Bible on the bedside table. It was exactly the same picture he saw every evening, except for one thing: the look of panic in his own eyes.

He got out of bed and onto his knees. "I don't know what's wrong with me, Lord."

Yes, you do.

"What am I supposed to do? Tell me, please. What am I supposed to do?"

Your job.

Of course. And cravenly keeping his distance from Nicole Archer—and her brother in the process—just because he was lonely and couldn't seem to stop thinking about her was *not* doing his job. Marcus sighed and gave in. After all, he had no real excuse. What God willed, the Holy Spirit empowered, as he well knew.

With the impediment to his communication with God removed, he finished his prayers, got back into bed and turned out the light, settling down to sleep. But just as consciousness slipped away, a picture formed in his mind: Nicole in flaming orange, smile gleaming, brown eyes shining, a white veil floating about her dark head as she walked toward him, flowers clutched in her hands. He carried that incongruous image into his dreams and woke with it the next morning.

Maybe, he told himself with a groan, he needed a vacation.

By Friday Marcus had sufficiently steeled himself enough to do what he knew he should and decided how to go about it. He'd thought about calling the house, but he couldn't be sure how her father would react, and the very last thing he wanted to do was stir that pot. He could've waited until Sunday, but after what had happened the last time he'd pulled her aside for conversation there, that didn't seem a particularly wise move.

On the other hand, he knew right where she'd be about a quarter of four this afternoon. Plus, the street in front of the school seemed a perfect spot for a talk, public enough to be impersonal, private enough for a quick chat. Yes, that would do nicely.

So resolved, Marcus put in only a brief appearance at the office on Friday morning, much to Carlita's delight. If he hadn't known better he'd have thought his secretary liked having him out of the office. He knew, though, that her pleasure stemmed from genuine concern for him, and she was right.

Friday was his day off; he needed to learn how to relax and enjoy it. To that end, he spent the remainder of the morning sprawled on the couch watching old Westerns, a diversion in which he hadn't indulged in years.

After lunch he took himself off to perform several small, personal errands, things he'd been meaning to do for weeks, like having his tires rotated and purchasing some new socks. He got a haircut, too, and walked around a baby goods store trying to figure out what to purchase as a welcome gift for his namesake nephew's eventual entry into the world. All the while, his miserable little mind hummed with the knowledge that he would soon see Nicole again.

Just doing his job, of course.

The Bahamas sounded really nice right about then.

Nicole's head jerked up at the rap of knuckles against her car window, and then she laughed at the sight of Marcus bent at the waist, head cocked at an awkward angle, one hand cranking in a bid for her to roll down the passenger side window. Instead, she leaned over and opened the door.

"It falls off the track if I roll it down. Get in. Beau won't be out for some time. The bell hasn't even rung yet."

He dropped onto the ragged seat. "I had a car with a window that would fall off the track once."

"Yeah, what'd you do?"

"Drove around with the window open for months. It was on the driver's side, so that made it convenient for drive-through windows, at least."

"What about rain?"

"That was a problem. I learned to close an old raincoat in the door." He shook his head, remembering. "I kept hoping somebody would steal that thing so I'd have a good excuse to get a new one."

"A new raincoat?"

"A new car."

Laughing, she twisted sideways in her seat. "If you could afford a new car, why not just buy one and be done with it?"

"I couldn't afford the new *rain*coat," he said, mossy-green eyes twinkling, "but I was spiritually immature enough to think that if my car was stolen, the Lord would magically provide me with another. And, of course, whoever did would naturally need a broken-down old rattletrap of a car much worse than I did, which meant I wouldn't even have to report it." He closed his eyes and smiled. "Sweet justification. Unfortunately, the delusion disappears around the age of nineteen. At least it did for me."

Nicole laughed. "I can't imagine you being delusional at any age."

"I'm delusional now," he said, suddenly serious, "just about different subjects."

She could be just as serious as he could. "I don't believe that."

He looked away, smiling almost sadly, then looked back again and said, "I understand that Beau attends a computer class at the library on Wednesday evenings."

"He used to," Nicole answered, somewhat confused, "when I had a class on Wednesday evening." She was apparently no less confused than Marcus, who scratched his head.

He'd cut his hair, and she wished he hadn't. He had beautiful hair, and it would grow out again.

"Beau told me that he was taking a computer class when I invited him to youth group on Wednesdays," Marcus revealed.

"Ah." Nicole nodded, understanding now. "He didn't want

to tell you that there'd be trouble if Dad found out he was actually going to church *twice* a week."

Marcus's gaze turned inward suddenly. "I see." He sounded just the opposite, confused.

"I explained Dad's view of church."

"I—I guess I thought that was just for himself, that he was okay with you and Beau going to church now."

"I don't know if he's *okay* with it, exactly. I think it's more that he can't justify kicking up a fuss about it so long as it doesn't directly impact his life. See, Dad's always hungover on Sunday morning. He likes to stay out late with his drinking buddies on Saturday night."

"And he's home on Wednesdays," Marcus stated.

"Yep. That's one of his favorite TV nights."

Marcus sighed. "Maybe I could talk to him, get him to see reason."

Nicole straightened in her seat. "That's not a good idea. Let's just leave it as it is right now."

"You don't think Beau would benefit from Bible study tailor-made for his age group?"

"I don't think Beau would benefit from getting into it with our father. The two walk tightropes around each other as it is."

Marcus looked straight into her eyes, and it struck her suddenly that it had been a while since he'd done so. "Nicole," he said, "you have to think about calling—"

"Don't say it," she interrupted, yanking her gaze away. "There's no reason to call the authorities. Things are fine now."

"Now," he echoed pointedly. "But they won't stay that way. You know they won't, and I'm worried about you."

She bowed her head, delighted to hear that he gave her a single passing thought on any level. "I appreciate that, Marcus, more than you know, but I'll graduate at the end of the fall semester. Then…" She reached tentatively for his hand, willing him to understand from mere inference what she couldn't seem to come right out and say. "Then things will be different. Beau and I will move out and be free to go where we want…*see* who we want."

Marcus opened his mouth as if to argue that point, but then he blinked, and the next thing she knew he was climbing out of the car.

"Well, that's all I wanted to say."

"You don't have to go," she pointed out. "The bell hasn't even rung yet."

The bell rang, a loud, irritating, mechanical bleat that Nicole would have silenced without a second thought if she could have.

"Say hello to Beau for me," Marcus prattled cheerfully, and then he was striding away. She didn't even get a chance to suggest that he could do that himself in another minute or two.

Brow beetled, Nicole blew out a short breath. What was *that* about? Maybe he had an appointment he'd suddenly remembered.

And maybe the mere suggestion that she'd like to see him in a dating capacity at some point in the nebulous future had sent him running for the hills.

Disheartened, Nicole leaned her head against the window, frowning. Then the thought came that she had plenty of time in which to change his mind. It wasn't as if she was ready for any sort of relationship herself. With school and work and Beau, she barely had a social life, seeing her friends mostly in class. She could just imagine how her father would react if she started seeing someone—especially a minister! No, this wasn't the time for that, which meant, really, that nothing had changed. Yet.

But maybe one day. And in the meantime, Marcus could

very well get used to the idea. He cared, that was what she had to remember.

By the time Beau threw his backpack over the seat and plopped down beside her, she was smiling again.

Marcus dropped his head into his hands and groaned aloud. It wasn't that speaking to Nicole today had been a mistake. No, he hadn't mistaken God's intent there. He'd done what he should've done, and he'd learned what he'd needed to know, which was what had brought him to his knees at a time when he would normally be thinking about dinner and what he was going to do with his Saturday.

He could just as easily have gone to God in his own living room or his office, anywhere, really. But what he'd seen earlier in Nicole's eyes, what he'd felt in the touch of her hand, had rocked him right down to his soul, and he needed to be in God's house for this.

"I'm so sorry, Lord," he said, kneeling by the front pew. "I should've seen it coming. I did see it coming, I just didn't want to face it. Nicole needs a friend, someone to show her how to tap into Your power. She doesn't need to develop some silly crush on a man who's not right for her."

A man she's not right for, you mean.

"Yes, that, too. It's not just that she's young, she's spiritually immature, troubled, flamboyant… Lord, You know I want, need, a wife, and I've let that mess up my mind, interfere with my judgment. I understand that I'm called to help Nicole and her brother, and I'm committed to that. You'll take care of the other when the time is right. I believe that with all my heart. And I'll do my very best for them, just as I should. But please, Lord, in the meantime, is it too much to ask that Nicole not think of me in a romantic way?"

And that you not think of her in the same vein?

"Okay, I know that's the real problem here, so I'm asking

you now to just take these feelings away. She and I could never be a couple, and I can't allow her to think that we ever could. So please don't let her look at me in a romantic way. I'm walking a fine line here, already, and I need Your help in this. I need You to guide my feet, to keep me from slipping and falling."

Falling in love?

"Falling out of Your will."

The words of Hebrews flowed through his mind. *Let us hold fast the confession of our hope without wavering, for He who promised is faithful...*

Marcus knew in his heart of hearts that he had grabbed hold of the Lord with both hands and not let go. He could trust, then, that God would faithfully guide him. And yet, the fears that beat around inside his chest like manic butterflies offered no peace. He'd never felt so weak in the face of temptation before or seen so clearly the potential for harm.

Marcus set aside his sermon notes, aimed the remote at the music system and lowered the bass, head tilted to catch the shrill, discordant note that had bothered him for several seconds. The phone rang, and it was only then that he realized the sound was not part of the music that he routinely listened to on Saturday night as he made the final preparations for his Sunday sermon. That's what came from turning the sound up so loud.

Chuckling at himself, he switched off the system and reached with his right hand for the cordless phone resting on the table beside the chair. At the same time, from sheer habit, he checked the watch on his left wrist.

Nine forty-one on a Saturday night. It could be a social call, but not likely. He looked at the readout on the tiny screen in the telephone receiver. The name Archer had him suddenly sitting up straight.

For a moment he considered not answering, but then he shook his head in self-disgust. Of course he would answer. The Archers were now part of his flock, even if informally, and he truly cared about their welfare. He wouldn't allow his inappropriate feelings for Nicole to derail the right and proper functions of his office as her pastor. He punched the answer button with his thumb just as the phone rang again.

"Hello."

"Marcus, it's Nicole."

He leaned forward to brace his elbows on the arms of the chair, recognizing panic in the tone of her voice.

"What's wrong?"

"Is Beau there? Have you seen him? Have you spoken to him?"

"Whoa. Back up. Tell me what's happened."

She began to sob. "Beau's gone! I thought it would be all right. Like I told you, Dad often stays out all night on Saturdays. There's this bar he likes, these guys he knows there. So when my work called me to come in for another server, and Beau said he didn't mind, that he'd be all right on his own for a few hours…I thought…I thought…I shouldn't have left him!"

"Your father came home early," Marcus surmised.

"I don't know what happened!" she wailed. "Dad's obviously been in a fight, and Beau's gone!"

Marcus closed his eyes, sending up a brief, silent prayer before saying, "Let's think this through. Where might Beau go, besides here?"

"H-He has a buddy named Austin, but I didn't get any answer when I called his number. I guess he could try to get to Ovida in Fort Worth, but I don't really think he would. You're the only other one I could think of!"

"There has to be someplace else we could look," Marcus

insisted. "Where's his favorite place, someplace he talks about?"

For several heartbeats he heard only sniffing on the other end of the line, but then she gasped. "Tahlequah, our grandparents' old place in Oklahoma, but he wouldn't try to go there."

"Where you used to spend summers," Marcus said. "Yes, he's spoken of it to me. Are you sure he wouldn't try to get there?"

"The old cabin is barely livable," Nicole murmured, "but he is saying all the time how we could go there to get away from Dad. Y-You don't think he'd try something so foolish, do you?"

"I don't know," Marcus muttered, thinking quickly, "but it's all we've got. How far is it?"

"I'm not sure. Four, five hours by car."

Marcus rose to his feet and started gathering up his coat, wallet and keys, the telephone receiver trapped between his ear and shoulder. "Tell me how to get there. Maybe I'll come across him on the way."

"I should go with you," she insisted. "I can show you the way and keep an eye out for him at the same time. I'll meet you at the parsonage."

Marcus didn't argue. He knew it was the best way, but he didn't want her driving that old car in her state.

"I'll come to you." He stuffed his wallet and keys into his pocket and threw on his coat, heading for the front door because he'd left the sedan in the drive earlier. "I'm on my way now."

"Marcus," she whispered brokenly, "what if we don't find him?"

"We will," he assured her. "I promise you, honey, somehow we'll find him."

She was silent for a long, puzzling moment, but then she

whispered with silky, unnerving certainty, "I knew I should call. I knew you were the one."

Before he dared ask what she meant by that, she hung up.

Chapter Six

Marcus tossed the telephone toward the couch and reached for the doorknob. Just then he heard the scuff of footsteps on the concrete stoop outside. Yanking open the door, he surprised Beau just as the boy was about to knock.

"Thank God!" Marcus exclaimed, reaching out to pull the boy inside. "Your sister is scared out of her wits!"

Beau hung his head and hunched his shoulders inside his oversize coat. "I'm sorry," he mumbled, "I had to get out of there." He swiped at his face, sniffling, obviously embarrassed by his tears.

Marcus led him into the living room, shedding his own coat and divesting Beau of his as they moved. "I have to call her. She thinks I'm on my way to pick her up."

He dumped the coats, located the phone and made the call. "He's here. He's safe. I'll bring him—" She hung up before he finished his sentence, having declared she was on her way over. He shut off the receiver and laid it on a shelf. "She doesn't have a cell phone, does she?"

"Too expensive," Beau muttered with a shake of his head.

Marcus frowned, thinking of her driving through the night in a panic in her old car with no cell phone in case of an emergency, not that he could do a thing about it. "Tell me what happened."

"He came home early," Beau said glumly. "Some guy called him a drunk, and they got into it, so they threw him out of the bar."

"Which means he also came home mad," Marcus surmised.

Beau nodded and wiped his eyes with both hands. "He was screaming and yelling about everything he'd been through in his life and how nobody understands."

Marcus took the boy by the shoulders. "Did he hurt you, Beau? Did he hit you?"

"No. He shook me, though. Called me an ungrateful little—" He broke off. "I just didn't want him to drink anymore," he wailed. "His face was all beat up, and I just wanted him to put some ice on it and not drink anymore. But all he cared about was having another drink, so I yelled at him that the guy was right. He *is* a drunk!"

"And that just made him madder," Marcus pointed out.

Beau nodded miserably, shivering. "I know I shouldn't have said it, but it's true!"

Marcus sighed inwardly, aching for the boy. "How did you get here?"

"Walked."

He turned Beau toward the sofa and pushed him down onto it. "No wonder you're still cold. I've got cocoa. Would you like me to fix you some?"

Beau shook his head and leaned forward, elbows braced on his knees, gaze trained on the floor. "I'm okay."

Marcus sat down on the coffee table facing the boy. "I'm sorry this happened. I know what it's like when a parent disappoints you."

"As long as Nic's around, it's okay," Beau said in a small voice.

"But she can't always be there," Marcus pointed out gently.

"She's busy trying to make a better life for us and keep everything together," Beau said defensively. He looked up, anger drying his tears. "That's what makes me so mad. He lays around getting drunk and moaning about his back while she's out there working and going to school and trying to make everything all right! He wouldn't even have a hurt back if he hadn't been drinking on the job!"

"I understand," Marcus assured him soothingly, "but what *you* have to understand, Beau, is that your father is sick. He's literally ill, and until he faces up to that, nothing will change. But it's not hopeless. God has changed harder hearts than Dillard Archer's, I promise you."

Beau shook his head, muttering, "You don't know my old man."

"I don't know him personally," Marcus conceded, thinking of the sermon he'd prepared for tomorrow. "I didn't know St. Paul, either, but I know that God changed him."

The light of interest suddenly ignited in Beau's eyes. "How?"

Marcus settled in to tell the story. "Paul lived at the same time as Jesus. He didn't believe in a Messiah who would give His life to pay the sin debt for everyone else in the world, and he didn't believe in the resurrection. So far as he was concerned, Jesus was dead. Period. And he hated those who believed otherwise so much that he made it his work to eradicate them, to wipe them out. Then one day he was going to Damascus to arrest Christians there, and he met Jesus on the road."

"Like actually *met* Him?" Beau asked skeptically.

"In a light so bright that it blinded Paul," Marcus confirmed. "But Jesus told him that a man would come and take away his blindness. When he did, Paul believed, and instead of persecuting Christians, he became the greatest missionary of all time."

"Just like that?"

"Just like that."

"So it was a miracle."

"Exactly," Marcus said. "But that same miracle takes place every day, Beau, every time someone commits his or her heart to Christ. And that often happens because someone else has been praying. I've been praying for you and your father and your sister, Beau, and I'm going to go on praying that God will work that miracle in your father's life."

Beau seemed to think about this for several moments before he said, "Back when my mom was alive and we used to go to church all the time, it seemed like my dad believed then."

"Maybe he did and his anger at losing your mom won't let him admit it. Or maybe he was just going through the motions to please her, thinking that was enough. The thing to remember, Beau, is that Paul's life didn't get easier after he committed himself to Christ. In fact, it got harder. But he tells us in his writings that he didn't mind, because in Christ he found the ability to cope with his difficulties and to find happiness, even joy, in doing so. Do you understand?"

"I think so."

They talked for several more minutes before clasping hands and bowing their heads in prayer. Marcus began, but Beau soon picked up and poured out his heart. Oddly, as Beau talked to God, his tears dried, but Marcus found his own eyes beginning to fill. He heard in Beau's softly spoken entreaties and confessions his own voice, the voice of the boy he had once been—confused, buffeted by life, lost.

When the door opened, he knew that Nicole had just entered his house. Hearing her relieved gasp at the sight of her brother's bowed head, he glanced up and held out his hand in silence. She slid her small, cold palm against his. The silly woman had come out without her gloves. Bowing his head once more, Marcus tugged her close. Settling next to him on the coffee table, she gripped his hand tightly and bowed her head.

When Beau's conversation with God finally wound down, she said her own prayer of thanks, then slipped her arms around her little brother's neck. He groused a bit, but he did hug her back.

"I'm sorry, Nic! I shouldn't have gone off, but I just got so mad and I couldn't think what else to do."

"It's all right so long as you're safe," she told him, rising to her feet and taking him with her.

"Was Dad really mad when you got home?" he asked, pulling back.

She shook her head. "He was too drunk for that, but when I saw the bruises on his face and you were gone, I can't tell you how scared I was."

"I didn't do that to him," Beau quickly vowed.

"He got into a fight at the bar and came home angry," Marcus explained. Then he turned to the boy. "Beau, the next time that happens, I want you to call the police."

Beau cast a troubled glance at his sister before addressing Marcus. "But that'll just make him madder," Beau said uncertainly.

"And Child Welfare could very well step in," Nicole added skeptically. "I'd rather he do exactly what he did this time. Un-unless you don't want him coming here anymore."

"It's Children's Protective Services," Marcus corrected, trying not to sound exasperated, "and of course he can come here whenever he wants. That's not the point."

"I just don't see what good calling the authorities can do," Nicole argued.

"Nicole, this thing is just going to continue to escalate,"

Marcus warned. "Can't you see that? In the short time I've known you, your father's gone from saying hurtful things to getting into fights. The next time he uses his fists, it could be on one of you. I don't want to see that happen."

"But calling the police just makes it more likely to happen!" she insisted.

"Then call Family Services. They'll open a case file and—"

"No! They might take Beau away!"

Beau backed up suddenly, alarm rounding his eyes. "I'm not going anywhere!" he exclaimed. "I'm staying with you! Aren't I, sis? Aren't I staying with you?"

"Yes, of course you are," Nicole soothed, clamping a hand down on the top of his shoulder. "We said, remember? We promised Mom that we'd stay together, and we will. We are."

"It's only one more semester after this one," he told Marcus desperately. "Then Nicole will graduate and get a regular job, and we're going to move out into our own place, aren't we, Nic?"

"That's right," she answered soothingly. "Then once we're on our own, we can try to get Dad some help." *From a safe distance* were the unspoken words understood by all.

"And what if he doesn't let you take Beau?" Marcus asked softly, looking down into her upturned face. "He's the custodial parent, you know."

She looked like a deer caught in the headlights for a moment, wide-eyed and frozen with fear. He saw how truly young she was in that instant, little more than a child. But with such responsibilities! Then her expression hardened. Her mouth compressed into a tight line, and her chin rose, eyes flashing fire.

"We'll make it work," she said. "Even if we have to leave here, go far away where he'll never find us, we're going to do just what we've planned. It's the only way."

Marcus shook his head, truly fearing for both their sakes, and moved to the side, hoping to improve his perspective somehow. They still looked like two frightened kids doing their best in an uncertain and potentially dangerous situation. Both seemed downtrodden and weary. In fact, Nicole hardly looked like herself at all.

Maybe it was the subdued clothing. She wore blue jeans and a pilled gray sweater beneath an olive-green corduroy coat, her dark hair caught in a loose ponytail at the nape of her neck. Only the red leather shoes looked like something she would normally wear. Marcus sort of missed the color and vibrancy that he associated with Nicole. Then he saw the stamp of weariness around her eyes and mouth, and knew that arguing would only do more harm than good at the moment. Bringing his hands to his hips, he nodded in defeat.

"Do you think it's safe for you to go home tonight?"

She waved a hand dismissively, saying, "He's out like a light by now. He probably didn't even make it to bed. Trust me, when he's that drunk, he rarely does."

Marcus sighed. "All right. Then you'd better go. It's getting late, and I want to see you both in church tomorrow."

"We'll be there," she promised, turning Beau toward the door and giving him a little shove before looking up into Marcus's face. "Thank you. Again."

"Yeah, thanks," Beau chimed in from the entryway.

"I didn't do anything," Marcus protested, getting snared in those chocolate eyes.

"You always help when we need you," Nicole said softly.

"Of course," Marcus retorted impatiently, "but, Nicole, there's an old saying. God helps those who help themselves. And sometimes that's how it is. Sometimes we have to do the hard thing, take the difficult path, to get where we need to be."

"I understand, but just because it's difficult doesn't make it the right thing to do, Marcus."

He didn't know what to say to that. She was entirely correct and very possibly wrong. Either way, he was frightened for her, for them. He'd told himself long ago when he'd first found God that he would never deny his faith by being frightened again, but he hadn't realized then that he could be frightened for someone else. If only he could make her understand.

"The time may come when you don't have a choice," he warned her.

"But right now I do. In fact, since I met you, I have more choices than ever before. God bless you for that, Marcus."

She placed her hands on his shoulders then, rose up on tiptoe and pressed a kiss on his cheek at the very corner of his mouth. By the time his head cleared and he could get air back into his lungs, they were gone.

"It wasn't that troubles did not come into Paul's life," Marcus said, his voice ringing solid and true from the pulpit. "Indeed, the path Paul chose led to greater difficulties, but it also led to more joy. And Paul learned, as we must, to depend wholly on God for the answers to our problems, for there is not one detail of our lives that does not concern and interest our Lord."

Nicole looked down at the Bible in her lap as Marcus went on, his words calling to mind the troubles that her mom had known. Suzanne Archer had possessed a deep faith that had grown only deeper with her illness. Dillard, on the other hand, had always been somewhat ambivalent, and his ambivalence had hardened into anger as his wife's illness had progressed. Nicole vividly remembered his anguish on the day that they had received the diagnosis.

"Why you?" he had demanded.

Her mother's serene reply had been, "Why not me? Why should others be stricken with cancer and not me?"

Nicole could understand that sentiment. This life was not meant to be all good times and ease. That would be heaven, as Marcus had just pointed out. Looking at her own life, Nicole was even willing to concede that he was right about God providing solutions, too, even if sometimes the solution was simply to endure for another day or week or month or year. Thankfully, sometimes the solution was immediate.

Take the gas bill, for instance. She'd been so worried about paying it. February had been colder than usual, and their old house seemed to leak at every joint and corner. The bill, which was due next week, would undoubtedly be astronomical. But she'd prayed about it, and twice now she'd been called in to work extra shifts, and on weekends, too, when the tips were best. Catastrophe averted.

Even the fiasco with her father and Beau had turned out better than it might have. She shuddered to think what her impulsive little brother might have done if Marcus hadn't been available to him.

Crashing Marcus's birthday party was turning out to be one of the best mistakes she'd ever made. In fact, she was beginning to think that it might be part of God's plan for her life.

Her mom had believed completely that God always has a plan and a purpose for the lives of His children, and Nicole was starting to believe that, too. Except she still could see no purpose behind her mother's death, and the more she thought about that, the more it bothered her. Instinctively, she knew that this one question must be settled to her satisfaction before she could move forward, and she could think of only one place where she might find the answers she needed.

Immediately after the service she went straight to the pastor. "I need to speak with you."

"All right. About what?" He folded his hands and widened his stance as if settling in for a long conversation.

"I guess you could call it a spiritual matter."

"I see." Marcus nodded solemnly, his gaze flickering over those waiting to shake his hand. "Perhaps we'd best make an appointment then."

"An appointment." She was a little surprised by that, but the idea certainly had merit. "Yes, that will work."

"You can call the church office, and my secretary will find a convenient time for you."

At first she was taken aback by the formality, but then she realized that his office would be as private as his home or anywhere else they might meet. "Certainly. Good. I—I'll see you soon then."

She went out with a smile on her face, feeling as if a burden that she hadn't even known she was carrying had been lightened a bit. It was good to have someone to share things with, someone other than Ovida, who was good and kind and dear but who had her own family and concerns. If it should become more than that between her and Marcus someday, if he should come to see that he could depend on her, too, that they could be something more than friends, well… Prayers were answered every day, weren't they?

Marcus couldn't help feeling a certain excitement along with the trepidation that was fast becoming part and parcel of his dealings with Nicole Archer. He told himself that it had to do with his deep desire to help the Archers, but he couldn't be so dishonest as not to admit that it had more to do with his attraction to her and that kiss on the cheek, innocent as it had been. Something about Nicole intrigued him, which was, of course, a large part of the problem and exactly why he needed to inject a little formality and distance into the equation.

It was one thing to befriend the girl—which, he kept reminding himself, was exactly what she was—and another thing entirely to lead her on, even unintentionally. He meant to have a word with her about that, whatever the topic of discussion at this meeting.

Surely, that was why he felt as if insects were crawling beneath the surface of his skin and why the day seemed to creep by at a snail's pace, until suddenly he looked up and it was almost at an end. Alarmed, he rushed out into the reception area.

"Carlita, we do have Nicole Archer in our appointment book for today, don't we?"

"Five o'clock. Last appointment of the day," Carlita said, looking away from her computer screen. "I told you that on Monday afternoon."

"Right. I, um, I forgot."

He pinched the bridge of his nose between his thumb and his forefinger, feeling like an absolute idiot. For perhaps the thousandth time, he wondered what Nicole had on her mind. A spiritual matter, she had said. Such counseling was part of his job, and by some accounts he was actually good at it. Still, he sensed that he was courting disaster here. Gulping, he dropped his hand, becoming acutely aware of his secretary's furrowed brow.

"She's a young lady with a lot of adult responsibilities," he announced, wincing inwardly at the defensive tone of his voice. "I hope the appointment time is convenient for her."

Carlita rolled her black eyes, muttering, *"El loco!"* She pushed away from her desk, jabbed her fists into the indentation of her waist, and fixed him with her why-do-I-put-up-with-you glare. "What? You think I chose the time at random and kept it a secret. Of course, the time is convenient for her! That's the whole point of an appointment, isn't it?"

Marcus held up a hand, saying, "All right. Okay. I was just checking."

Carlita pulled her chair closer to the desk with a hand clamped onto the edge of the heavy, wood top, conceding, "She may be ten or fifteen minutes late because she has to get her little brother to the community center for a guitar lesson. I told her not to worry about it."

Marcus nodded and scrubbed a hand across his face. "I don't mean to be difficult. It's just that she's a sweet, troubled kid—"

"With an alcoholic father and a little brother who depends on her too much," Carlita said. "I know. Haven't you said it so many times already?" She smiled, adding gently, "But with your background you're just the one to help her."

Marcus tapped the tip of a forefinger against the edge of her desk, saying, "I pray so. I guess I do identify pretty strongly with her situation, although, by the time I was her age, my folks were both long gone."

"God prepared you in this, eh?" Carlita said. "So don't worry. It's not like you to have such worry."

She was right. It wasn't like him to worry. He hadn't worried like this since Connie had gone to jail, and he'd thought he'd learned the futility of the exercise then. If only Nicole would let Family Services take a hand with her father, he wouldn't *have* to worry. He could understand why she didn't want to, but it was almost the only way he could see for her and her brother to live safely. Almost.

There actually was another solution, one he couldn't help thinking about even though he didn't want to. The fact was that if Nicole had a husband, someone mature and sensible and settled, he could stand up for her and Beau. He could provide a stable home for them. If Nicole had a husband. Something he couldn't let himself think about.

"Sorry to bother you," he muttered, turning away from his secretary's desk and heading back to his office.

It wasn't difficult to keep himself busy for the next hour. Between the needs of the church and the day care center, the demands on his time had always been significant. The state licensing and oversight process of the day care center alone was almost a full-time job.

Nevertheless, he had always made counseling a priority, which was why he dropped what he was doing at precisely five o'clock and returned to the outer office. He was just in time to hear Carlita exclaim, "*Caramba!* I *like* this outfit."

A trill of bright laughter followed, and Marcus knew even before he clapped eyes on her that Nicole had outdone herself. Smiling, she stood with her arms outstretched, showing off the wide, pointed sleeves of the filmy, V-necked, madras print tunic that she wore over a purple turtleneck and bell-bottom jeans. Green platform sandals and purple socks encased her feet, while her long, sleek hair flowed straight from beneath the ribbed cuff of a bright yellow stocking cap with a hot pink silk flower pinned to the front.

She looked like something left over from the 1970s, with a touch of skater and a dose of shabby chic thrown in for good measure. Somehow it worked for her. In a funny way, Nicole was like walking, breathing art, and just looking at her never failed to make him smile, which was why he stood there now grinning like a blooming idiot.

She glanced up and caught him at it, beaming his smile right back at him. Marcus cleared his throat and made a show of checking his watch. "I, um, I understood you might be late."

"We got away from the house earlier than usual."

"I hope Beau wasn't inconvenienced."

She strolled toward him, stopping close and rocking up onto her tiptoes, as if barely able to contain her enthusiasm. Marcus had to remind himself to breathe.

"No, he likes a little extra time to set up," she said, her smile stretching even wider.

Marcus was having trouble following that. "I, uh, uh, set up?"

"For the lesson."

"Right. I—I knew he had an interest in music, but I didn't realize he was taking lessons."

"Oh, he doesn't *take* guitar lessons," Nicole said, tilting her head to one side. "He *gives* them to kids at the community center."

"Oh! That good is he?"

"Absolutely. It brings in a little extra spending money for him, too, though he doesn't charge nearly as much as an adult teacher would."

"I wonder if he's thought of trying out for the praise band we're putting together?"

"I'm sure he'd love that."

"I'll be sure to mention it to him then," Marcus said, pleased. Only then did he realize that he had rolled up onto *his* tiptoes in a copy of her exuberance. Abruptly, he slammed his heels onto the floor again and shot out an arm.

"My, uh, office is this way. First door on the right."

Still smiling, Nicole moved forward. Marcus swiftly stepped aside, catching sight of Carlita as she hunched her shoulders in question.

Nicole slipped past him into the hallway, allowing Marcus to address Carlita. "What?"

"I thought you said she was a child!" Carlita hissed.

Marcus glanced over his shoulder in time to see Nicole disappear into his office. Frowning, he turned back to his secretary. "I didn't say she was a *child.* I said she was young, which she is."

Carlita put her hands on her hips. "There is young, and there is *infancia."*

"She's not even twenty-one," he protested through his teeth.

Carlita threw up her hands, exclaiming, "I was a mother twice before twenty!"

"Will you keep your voice down?" Marcus insisted in a harsh whisper.

The hands went back on the hips, accompanied by a narrowing of the eyes. "You really are *loco."* With that she turned away, snagged her omnipresent coffee cup from the corner of her desk and stalked off toward the tiny break room, where they kept the coffeepot.

Marcus turned toward his office, muttering to himself, "I am not crazy. She's too young."

Nicole swiveled in her chair as he entered the small office, asking, "Who's too young?"

Had he actually said *too* young? "Oh. Um."

Blinking, he seriously thought about lying to her. That was not his way, though. In the end, he just shook his head and averted his gaze, edging past her to slip by the bookcase and around the desk in the corner. As he dropped into his chair, he glanced out the window at the church across the way, reminding himself why he was there. Somewhat more composed, he folded his hands at his waist and turned to face Nicole.

"Now then," he said in his best minister's voice, "what can I do for you?"

Nicole tilted her head and looked down at her hands, smoothing the hem of her tunic. "I want to ask you a question."

"All right. Shoot."

He was ready for any number of topics. Privately, he hoped that she was ready to talk about calling in Family Services to help her deal with her father's alcoholism. What she ultimately came out with, though, threw him for a loop.

"Why did my mother die?"

Initially, he must have looked like a blank slate sitting there. The subject was so unexpected that he couldn't seem to think beyond the obvious. He spread his hands. "I—I understood that it was cancer."

She gave her head a tight little shake and slid to the edge of her seat, leaning forward to lay one arm on his desktop. "That's not what I mean." She slumped forward, seeming to gather her strength as well as her thoughts before she looked up again. "On Sunday you said that God is concerned about every detail of our lives."

"Yes, I believe that's so."

"Well, it got me to thinking about something that my mom used to say."

"And that is?"

"My mom believed that God always has a plan, that there are reasons for everything that happens to us."

"I agree," Marcus said, leaning forward so that he, too, could brace his arms atop the desk. "I believe that God is intimately involved in the lives of His children, that He has a plan for each and every one of us. Now, of course, we also have free will, and we can choose to do things that are contrary to God's plan, and sometimes those choices have consequences that must be endured, at least in this life. But that, too, is a result of God's overall plan for us in that He created us with free will for a reason."

"That's what I'm talking about." She sat back and folded her arms. "I mean, if He has a reason for everything, then what reason could He have for letting her die?"

Now they had come to it.

Marcus nodded and linked his fingers together atop the desk blotter. "Let's be clear about something, Nicole. God did not cause your mom's illness."

"That's what Mom always said, too. Dad would get mad, you know, and she would tell him that God didn't give her cancer."

"That was a product of this world we live in," Marcus agreed. "But God does have power over life and death."

"And He chose to let her die," Nicole said simply. "I need to know why."

Marcus tried to decide how best to answer her, but in the end he could give her only one answer. Almost certainly it wasn't what she wanted to hear, but he could only give her what he had to give her and pray that it was enough.

"I don't know."

She looked stricken and disappointed at the same time.

Something welled up in him that he hadn't known for many, many years. Funny how something rooted so far in the past could feel so immediate and so familiar. Suddenly he remembered all the times he'd felt this way as a child, watching his mother sob over not being able to pay the bills or some boyfriend dumping her. Just as bad had been watching her manic elation when she'd embarked on some new romance and knowing that he and his sisters would once again be taking a backseat to her obsessive search for ever-elusive love.

But Nicole was not his mother. She was, in many ways, the exact opposite of his mother, and he was no longer that powerless, ignorant little boy.

On pure impulse, he reached across the desk and gripped her hand. Even as tears gathered in her eyes, a smile slowly curved her lips, and in that moment all his worry fell away. He knew that God had brought her here for this reason.

He was called to this, and he must not, could not, would not, fail her.

Chapter Seven

"I don't know," he said again, releasing her hand and sitting back. Words flowed into his brain. With them came the confidence that the Spirit upon Whom he relied was at work. Purposefully, he let the words leave his mouth. "There could be any number of reasons, Nicole, some of which we may never know, but I assure you, that it was not so your father could drink himself into an angry stupor every night. That is his choice, Nicole, his alone."

"I get that," she said softly. "What I don't get is what it was *for?*" She bit her lip, and when she spoke again, her voice quivered. "If I could believe there was a purpose for her dying o-or even that something good would come from it, then somehow I think I could…"

"Let it go?" he ventured gently. "Start to get over her loss?"

Nicole swallowed. "Maybe. Maybe it's just that it would make it easier to go on. Easier to *trust*. You know?"

"Well, then, let's look at it. Let's look at you."

"Me?"

"You." He spread his hands. "I was talking about you earlier when I said, 'She's too young.' And you *are* too young for the responsibilities you bear. On the other hand, I don't know anyone else your age who cares for someone more than you care for your brother. Certainly, I know of no finer example of sisterly love than you."

She brightened. "Really?"

He was grinning again, and couldn't do a thing about it. "Most twenty-year-old college girls are busy partying and chasing boys," he went on. "You're making a home, working, caring for your family, getting an education, trying to do the right things. Maybe you wish you could be that carefree party girl, and I would certainly wish an easier life for you, but who you are is just a delight. And I have to wonder if you'd be that if you hadn't had to take on a more responsible role."

She sat there for a moment, just staring at him. Then she whispered, "Wow."

Pure joy beamed straight into his heart. "And there's Beau," he said earnestly. "Would your relationship with him be what it is if your mom had lived? Most brothers and sisters argue and feel a little jealousy even when they really love each other, but you and Beau... I've never seen siblings who were closer. Even my sisters and I weren't able to be that close."

Nicole leaned forward slightly, her beautiful eyes sparkling. "I'll tell you a little secret," she confessed. "When he was about three until he was maybe nine, I thought Beau was the biggest pain who ever lived."

Marcus chuckled. "And I'm sure it was mutual."

"Oh, yeah!" She wrinkled her nose. "I guess I was a little spoiled back then." Suddenly, a look of wonder came over her face. "You know, I really wouldn't want to be that girl again." As the realization settled over her, she put her head back and laughed.

Marcus enjoyed her pleasure, but he wasn't disturbed

when she sobered and a thoughtful expression once again overtook her face.

"When Mom got sick," she said, "Beau became so precious to me. It's awful that it took that, isn't it?"

"It's just the way it is," Marcus said. "I'm glad that Beau was there to fill a place in your heart, because I'm sure your father grew more angry and distant."

"Yes, he did. But he used to be a good dad, you know."

"Maybe he will be again, if he can get past being angry at God."

She bowed her head as if in contrition. "I guess maybe that's part of the reason I'm here. I think…" She sighed, then forthrightly admitted, "I was pretty mad myself for a while. Then I sort of got over that, but I just…I don't know… pushed God away, I guess."

"And now you're ready to renew your commitment," Marcus surmised gently.

"*Now* I am."

A great sense of satisfaction swept through him, and he rocked forward in his chair to address her. "Would you like to know how to start that process?"

"Yes."

"You start with confession. You start by telling God what you've just told me."

"That's it?"

"That's how you start. After that, it's a matter of making God a real priority in your life by daily taking time to pray and read the Bible and worship. It's like anything else you want to change. You have to behave your way into a closer relationship with God."

She nodded her understanding, and then she sucked in a deep breath. He noticed a certain softness about her, a new sense of ease, and his soul rejoiced because he felt that he had given her, or at least led her to, what she needed.

He reached across the desk for her hand again, asking, "Would you like me to pray with you?"

She clasped his hand tightly. "Yes, please."

They spent some time talking to God, first him and then her, and then him again. Afterward, she rose to leave, wiping happy tears from her eyes. He came around the desk to walk her out, but she stopped him before they reached the door, a hand on his shoulder.

"You know something else, something I'm really, really thankful for?"

"What's that?"

"You," she said, holding his gaze with hers. "I'm just so glad that you're a part of my life now."

He smiled, and somehow his hand found hers. "I'm glad, too."

"You've made a real difference for us, Marcus."

"That's what I'm here for. I want to help. That's the only reason I suggested you contact the authorities concerning your father."

She squeezed his hand. "I know." The hand on his shoulder slid around his neck as she leaned into him, going up on tiptoe to press her face into the curve of his shoulder and hug him. "Thank you for caring."

He couldn't seem to speak past a sudden lump in his throat, and he was literally unable to stop his free arm from curling lightly around her waist. After a long moment, she lowered herself to her heels, loosening her embrace, and then he was gazing down into her face, a face that seemed to come closer and closer, even as it tilted back, her chin lifting.

Suddenly he realized that he was about to kiss her!

Galvanized, he jerked back, cracking his elbow against the bookshelf behind him. White-hot pain flashed up his arm all the way to his shoulder.

She reached for him, exclaiming, "Are you all right?"

He jerked even farther away. "Ow! I mean, sure. Uh…" He grabbed the tingling joint in question, desperately searching for rescue from his own folly.

"Beau!" he exclaimed. "Wh-what time do you have to pick him up?"

Nicole stared, goggle-eyed, for several seconds before reluctantly checking the cheap watch with its worn leather band on her wrist. "Yeah, I have to go, but are you sure you're okay?"

"Of course!" he insisted too brightly, forcing his hands to his sides, though one of them felt disturbingly numb still. "I'll walk you out."

She wrinkled her brow, but then she turned and moved through the door into the hallway. Marcus intentionally lagged a step behind, relief and dismay mingling within him.

What on earth was wrong with him? Had he lost what little sense he'd had? And where were his ministerial ethics? He couldn't go around kissing, or even almost kissing, those who came to him for counseling!

He managed to keep a straight face as Nicole took her leave, but he avoided Carlita's all-too-perceptive gaze, heading at once back to his office. Closing the door, he walked around his desk and sank into his chair, squeezing his eyes shut. Sighing richly, he bent forward and rested his forearms on his knees, dropping his face into his hands.

"Lord, forgive me," he said, and what followed was a long confession of unruly desires, envy for those happily married, indulgence in self-pity and a lack of control. He would do better, he promised, if only God would remove the temptation from him.

When Carlita tapped on his door to say that she was leaving for the day, he didn't open it, only called through it that he would see her tomorrow.

"Tomorrow's your day off," she reminded, the door muffling the volume but not the sternness of her voice.

A day off, he thought. Maybe that was what he needed right now. It certainly wouldn't hurt. Maybe he'd even get a little perspective.

"Monday, then."

"Right," she muttered doubtfully, but she went away, and he went back to his problem.

The hour was bordering on seven before he came to some unsatisfactory conclusions. One: Obviously he couldn't be trusted around Nicole Archer! Two: Until he got these ridiculous impulses under control he simply couldn't minister personally to the family. It wouldn't be prudent.

That concession made him sick at heart, but what else could he do except keep his distance from the Archers? He wouldn't abandon them completely, of course, but hereafter someone else would have to fill the role of personal rescuer.

Ovida Cutler was the logical choice. Her relationship with the Archer family went back for many years, decades, even. He didn't know what he was thinking to have interfered in the first place. He'd been warned in seminary about the tendency of many ministers to try to save or aid everyone who crossed their paths, the result being burnout or ethical lapses. Though often born of a genuine desire to serve others, the overinvolved minister sometimes began to serve his own need to be of service rather than the needs of others. Marcus felt that he might be suffering from a touch of that. Certainly he was overstepping the bounds of good, effective ministry.

Time to back off. Definitely. He saw no alternative. What had almost happened today could not be repeated.

Glum but resolved, he went home to his lonely little house and a cold, solitary evening.

"Hello."

Nicole smiled at the sound of his voice. "Marcus! I thought for a moment that Carlita was mistaken and you weren't at home, after all."

"I, uh, I'm doing some cleaning."

"Ah. The dreaded housework," she teased. "I know how you guys hate anything remotely having to do with actual neatness. I, on the other hand, actually enjoy straightening up—when I get the opportunity to do it, which admittedly isn't often." She sighed. "Oh, well. In a way, that's why I'm calling. I have to go in early to the restaurant again. Would you mind picking up Beau from school? He'd love to hang out with you again, or 'kick it,' as he would say."

A short pause followed, then, "Nicole, I'm sorry. I'm afraid I can't. Why don't you call Ovida? I'm sure someone in the massive Cutler clan would be happy to have Beau this evening."

Surprise and disappointment made her pause to actually look at the telephone receiver, as if that might tell her why his voice sounded so odd. Carefully placing the receiver against her ear again, she asked, "Marcus, are you all right?"

"Oh, yes. Just busy."

Impersonal, she decided suddenly. That was the tone she was hearing. Or might it be distraction? Of course, if he was very busy, that would be it.

"Okay. I understand. Thanks anyway."

"Goodbye, Nicole."

"Bye."

She barely got the word out before he hung up. Nicole slowly replaced the receiver in its cradle on the kitchen wall, her lip clamped between her teeth. Then she shook her head.

No matter what was going on with him just then, she could trust in Marcus's intentions. If he couldn't help them out, then he undoubtedly had good reasons. So he had sounded odd. So what? Whatever the problem was, she was sure that it was important. She and Beau weren't the only people in the world with troubles, after all. In fact, compared to some people, their troubles were small, indeed.

Picking up the phone, she dialed Ovida's number. Unfortunately the phone rang and rang without answer. Finally, the machine clicked on. Nicole left a brief message, and then began dialing other Cutler numbers. After several calls, she reached Donna.

The baby could be heard wailing in the background, and Donna herself sounded exhausted. It seemed that the Cutlers had been hit by a twenty-four hour stomach virus that had spread through the family like wildfire.

"One of the drawbacks of being a close family, I guess," Donna said with a chuckle and a sigh. "Vince is so worried about Jolie getting it that he's planning a little jaunt down into the hill country over the weekend with Connie and Kendal and their kids."

Nicole kept her voice light as she asked, "Any idea when they're leaving?"

"This afternoon, I think."

Grimacing, Nicole conceded defeat. "Well, I hope y'all get better real quick. Tell your mom not to worry about us. We'll be praying for you."

Donna thanked her and got off the phone. Nicole dropped the receiver back into its cradle, idly watching the old-fashioned cord coil and knot as she tried to decide what to do.

Beau had a couple friends whose parents she might call, but one of the moms worked and Nicole had no idea how to reach her at her job. The other friend didn't exactly have a stellar home life himself. His parents seemed to scream and argue all the time, and they didn't care who was around to witness it. As she chewed over the problem, her father came into the room.

"What's going on?"

Nicole straightened away from the wall. "Oh, uh, I've got to go into work early."

"That's good. Little extra money won't hurt, will it?"

"No, it sure won't."

He flattened a hand against his belly, and she noticed that he was wearing a clean T-shirt. His hair looked freshly shampooed, too, although he could use a good shave.

"Well, don't worry about us," he said. "I'll scramble up some eggs or something for supper."

Nicole bowed her head, trying to think her way around the immediate problem. True to form, Dillard had been easing up on the booze lately. She guessed they were cycling out of the bad phase and into a good one. In fact, they'd passed a pretty pleasant night the evening before. It had almost seemed like old times, everybody sitting around the television for an hour or two.

Usually, after she and Beau retired to their individual rooms, Dillard would sit up late into the night, watching television and drinking himself into a stupor. Last night, however, he'd shut off the television well before midnight. She knew because the sudden silence had actually awakened her. She'd sat up in bed, blinking at the clock and thinking that it must be time to get up until she'd heard him on his way to his room.

Maybe her dad was on the upswing again. If so, surely he could be trusted to spend one evening with his own son. It wasn't as if Beau needed constant supervision, after all. This might even heal the breach that had opened the night that Beau had fled to Marcus.

Nicole took a deep breath. "Okay, Dad. Um, actually,

there's some mac and cheese in the pantry. You might try that with the leftover chicken in the fridge."

Dillard shrugged. "Yeah, whatever. Don't worry about it."

"All right. I'll just get my things and take off then."

"Hey," he said as she slipped past him.

Nicole froze, suddenly tense. "What?"

"Don't you have a class this afternoon?"

Relaxing, she wheeled around to face him. He really was more sober than usual. For a moment there, he'd actually sounded like a real dad.

"Yeah," she said. "But it's an easy A for me. I can skip without hurting my grade average, and the money's more important right now."

He just nodded and turned back into the kitchen. Feeling suddenly lighter than she had in some time, Nicole hurried to her room and gathered up her things. Then she stopped by Beau's room and penned a quick note, which she left on his desk, suggesting that he concentrate on his homework that night instead of putting it off until Sunday evening. That ought to keep him out of his father's way. Just in case.

Confident she'd done the best she could under the circumstances, she went out to the car and headed off to work.

Dillard was sitting alone in front of the TV in the darkened living room nursing a drink when Nicole came in later that night. She figured Beau had already turned in or simply stayed out of their father's way. Dillard did little more than grunt at her when she walked past on her way to her room, but she saw the dirty dishes in the sink and knew that he'd made them some sort of dinner, at least.

She was tired, and her feet hurt, so she peeked in at her sleeping brother and went on to bed herself. In the morning, she rose and wandered out into the small hall bath that she shared with Beau. She was washing her hands and looking for the towel that normally hung from the ring next to the sink when she saw the hole in the wall beside the door.

Gaping, she backed up a step. Only when water dripped from her hands onto her bare feet did she jerk and actually start to think. Quickly she turned off the water and went back to studying the hole in the wallboard. It only took a moment to realize what had happened. Just to be sure, she curled her hand into a fist and slipped it into the jagged hole.

Oh, Lord, what have I done?

She tore out of the room and down the hall, practically falling into Beau's bedroom, the doorknob grasped firmly in one hand. "Beau!"

He rolled over, then sat up, grumbling, "What time is it?"

"I don't know." Swiftly crossing the room, she dropped onto the side of his narrow bed. "Are you all right?"

He hung his head.

Going up on one knee, she clamped her hands onto his upper arms. "Answer me, Beau! Are you all right?"

Silently he pulled his hand from beneath the covers and presented it to her. Nicole gasped. The knuckles were skinned, bruised and swollen. She had no doubt now who had put that hole in the bathroom wall. Tears blurred her eyes.

"What happened?"

Beau suddenly yanked his hand away and flopped back on his pillow, declaring, "I hate him!"

Nicole picked up his injured hand and cradled it in her own. "Don't say that, Beau. Hating him hurts you more than him."

"I don't care! I hate him anyway. I wish he had died instead of Mom!"

"Beau!"

He yanked away from her again and rolled onto his side,

weeping as she hadn't seen him do since shortly after their mother's death. "I don't care," he wailed in a small voice, repeating it again and again.

Grimly, Nicole insisted, "Let me see your hand again."

Beau scrubbed his uninjured hand over his face and shifted onto his back, presenting the injured knuckles.

"Can you move your fingers?"

He made a fist, then straightened his fingers out flat.

"At least it's not broken. Does it hurt?"

He shook his head, and Nicole breathed a sigh of relief.

"Did you do anything for it last night?"

"I put some antibiotic cream on it," he muttered sullenly.

Nicole nodded approval. "Okay. Well, let's try some ice and a couple aspirin, then, but first I want to know what happened."

Beau folded his arms, but after a moment he started to talk. He'd wanted to watch a certain music program on TV, but Dillard had been intent on watching some "stupid" movie that he'd apparently seen many times. The disagreement had escalated into a shouting match, and Dillard had resorted to the name-calling and put-downs that had become his norm. This time he'd sneered that Beau ought to stop dreaming about something that would never happen, specifically a career in music. He'd even degraded Beau's talent and intelligence. In frustration, Beau had locked himself in the bathroom and put his fist through the wall. Dillard had promptly drunk himself into unconsciousness. Not wanting to upset his sister, Beau had hopped into bed and pretended to be asleep when he'd heard the car in the drive.

Nicole mentally kicked herself, but she didn't let Beau see how upset she was. Instead she went into the kitchen, prepared breakfast and made an ice pack with a zipper bag and a kitchen towel.

They ate breakfast in Beau's room, while he iced his

hand, Nicole entertaining him with an account of a precocious toddler who had dumped a bowl of salad on his head at
the restaurant the night before. She left him to dress, moving
into the kitchen to add their breakfast dishes to those already
stacked in the sink and headed to the phone. Lifting the receiver from the cradle, she slipped out into the garage for
privacy, leaving the door cracked to accommodate the cord.

Her first call was to Marcus, but he didn't answer, so next
she dialed Ovida. Her mother's old friend answered on the
second ring, and after ascertaining that Ovida was feeling
better, Nicole began to tell Beau's story.

"Bless his heart," Ovida said after hearing the whole tale.
"I understand his frustration, but Nicole, he can't go around
punching holes in the wall."

"I understand that. I just don't know how to help him deal
with his frustration in a healthier way."

"Of course you don't. He needs counseling, honey, professional counseling. You probably do yourself. I would in
your position."

Nicole dismissed the part about herself. The only counseling she needed concerned how to help her brother, but
she didn't bother arguing the point. "I don't know how to get
him the kind of counseling he needs," she said. "You know
we can't afford to pay."

"I'll ask around," Ovida said. "I know there are programs.
I'm just not familiar with them. Someone at church has to
know."

"Marcus," Nicole said. "He'll know."

"Yes, I dare say he will," Ovida agreed.

Nicole closed her eyes and sent up a silent prayer of thanksgiving, feeling that she was halfway to a solution already.

"Nicole," Marcus said, not quite able to meet her eyes
as he moved toward the panel of light switches beside the

sanctuary door, "forgive me, but I don't have time to visit today."

He'd realized that she was waiting for the building to empty so that she could meet with him privately, and he'd been racking his mind for a way to avoid her. It shamed—and in a strange way, angered—him that he'd just lied to her. And for nothing, apparently, as she simply followed him as he went about his routine for closing up the place after the morning service.

"I know you're very busy. I tried to reach you yesterday, but this is really important. I need your advice. About Beau."

He stopped in the middle of the center aisle and turned to face her. Advice he could give. If he'd known that was all she wanted, he'd have answered his phone yesterday. But he hadn't. He hadn't even turned on the answering machine. He'd just sat there with his head in his hands and stared at the caller ID, telling himself that he had to keep his distance.

"You remember that I called you on Friday," she began.

"Yes."

"Well, I called Ovida as you suggested. That is, I tried to, but the Cutlers were all sick. They've been passing around this stomach thing."

Marcus blinked. Before she'd left town, Jolie had said that a flu was going around, but he hadn't realized that it had laid low the entire Cutler family. The back of his throat began to burn. "Go on."

She did so, telling him how things had been with her father lately and why she had elected to leave Beau alone with him, and then how the evening had devolved into ugliness and, finally, the violence of a fist through a wall. Marcus listened in horror, guilt welling inside him. This was his fault! He'd let his own lack of control interfere with his ministry, and Beau had suffered for it!

"The thing is," Nicole was saying, "I don't know where to find it."

He shook his head, realizing that he'd missed something important. "I'm sorry. Find what?"

"Counseling," she said, tilting her head in obvious confusion. "Counseling for Beau."

"Of course." He gave himself a mental smack between the eyes.

"Like I told Ovida, we can't afford to pay, but she says there have to be programs available."

"There are," he informed her. "Our denomination provides psychological counseling for those in need on a sliding fee scale."

She rocked up onto her toes and back down again, a pleased expression on her face. "I knew you'd have the answer."

He couldn't look at her anymore. In her vivid green dress with its flounces and ruffles worn beneath a large, bulky shawl crocheted in zigzag stripes of rust and black and red, her dark hair braided and lying across one shoulder, she looked like a refugee from a vintage clothing store window.

Utterly adorable.

Completely trusting.

Guileless.

Unconsciously dangerous to his peace of mind.

Too young. Too *everything* for him.

Gulping, he gave her the unvarnished truth. "It may not be as simple as it sounds. Spiritual counseling and psychological counseling are two different things. As a minister, I can counsel Beau as long as your father does not expressly forbid it, but a psychologist will need written permission up front."

Nicole set her teeth and pressed her lips into a grimace. "I didn't count on that." She thought about it and finally shook her head. "I'm not sure I can convince Dad that Beau needs this."

Guilt and responsibility weighed heavily upon Marcus's shoulders. "I'll speak to him," he decided firmly.

"Oh. I—I don't know," she hedged. "That might not be such a good idea."

A part of Marcus wanted to accept that and simply walk away, but a larger, stronger part of him wouldn't, couldn't. "It's either that or inform Child Protective Services and let them get him the counseling he needs."

"How would they manage it without Dad's permission?" she asked warily.

Marcus worked his jaw side to side, wishing he could fob her off with evasions and half truths, but she deserved better than that, especially from him. "They'd have to remove Beau from your father's custody."

"Foster care."

"They couldn't leave him in the house with his abuser."

"Dad didn't bust his knuckles," Nicole argued. "Beau did that to himself."

"In reaction to your father's verbal abuse. The end result is the same, Nicole. Don't you see that?"

"But if Beau learns to control his temper, it won't happen again! That's the point!"

Marcus sighed. "CPS won't see it that way. They'll conclude, and rightly so, that the behavior will escalate on both ends until someone is seriously injured."

She backed away, shaking her head. "I can't let them take Beau! I promised my mom. It was practically the last thing I said to her! Don't you get it?"

"But if it's best for Beau—"

"It's not! Staying with me is best for Beau. Counseling would help, yes, but not at the cost of being separated." Her expression turned pleading, wounded, and Marcus saw in her achingly lovely eyes the girl who had lost so much more than a member of her family. Her mother's death had been the death of the family as a whole. "We're all either of us has," she whispered.

Marcus swallowed, unable to argue against that even though he knew intellectually that his way was best. "Leave it to me, Nicole. I'll do everything in my power to convince your father to allow Beau to receive counseling."

Doubt and fear stamped her face, but in the end she relented. "I'll be praying that you can convince him," she said forlornly.

Marcus linked his hands together to keep from reaching out for her. He wanted desperately to hug her close and give her comfort, but he didn't dare. He didn't trust himself to let it end there. How, he wondered, had he so completely lost his way?

"We'll both be praying," he said quietly.

Chapter Eight

Marcus placed the consent form in a black leather portfolio, checked to be sure that it also contained an ink pen and got out of the sedan. He carried the portfolio up the walk to the battered front door of the Archer house, sending up a prayer with every step.

Only a week or two ago the evening would have carried a decided bite. It was still cool, but he'd put away his overcoat in favor of a lightweight jacket. Tonight he wore jeans and a sport shirt with it.

He'd thought long and hard about the impression that he wanted to make, but without knowing Dillard Archer personally, he really couldn't make an informed judgment. He was prepared to be friendly but firm, approachable but authoritative.

Ringing the bell, he then knocked for good measure. The door opened a few seconds later, and Nicole stood before him, her pretty brow furrowed with worry.

"Marcus, I'm not sure about this."

"It has to be done, Nicole."

She leaned closer, whispering, "He's drinking."

"He's an alcoholic, Nicole. When he's not drinking, he's

sick." She bowed her head, and he gently pressed on. "You asked me to wait until you were home. Then you asked me to wait until after dinner, but you can't ask me to wait until he's sober because he never is completely sober. You know I'm right."

"Just don't be surprised if he doesn't agree."

"I'll be surprised if he does," Marcus admitted, "but we have to try. *I* have to try. For Beau's sake."

Nodding, she backed out of the doorway and motioned for him to come inside. Marcus stepped up into a narrow, tiled entry.

A small, dark dining area lay on his right, separated from the tiny foyer by a halfwall. The polished rosewood table-top gleamed in the gloaming light of a tall bay window that overlooked the front walk. On the left, the paneled living area could be seen through a short row of uniformly spaced spindles running from ceiling to floor. The heavy, old-fashioned, pleated drapes had been drawn, and as no lamps had been switched on, the only light came from the flickering television screen. Outside it was twilight, but in the Archer household it was already deep night, or so it seemed to Marcus.

Nicole led him toward the sagging recliner placed dead center of the floor in front of the TV. The rest of the furniture, with the exception of a small side table, had been pushed back against the walls. As he followed Nicole, Marcus glanced around at it, noting a mundane off-white sofa suite strewn with faded afghans and quilts.

"Dad," Nicole said over the sound of the television, her voice containing twin notes of studied nonchalance and ragged uncertainty, "there's someone here I'd like you to meet."

A large, squarish head swung around. "What?"

"Dad, this is Marcus Wheeler."

Archer pitched sideways in his chair, craning his neck, and staring at Marcus. He let out an undignified snort, lifted a beer can in salute and turned back to his television program.

"She doesn't have time to date," Archer announced loudly.

Astounded, Marcus felt heat flush his neck and face. Anyone with eyes in his head could surely see that he was too old to be dating Nicole. Wasn't he? Yes, of course, he was. Archer was just too drunk to know that, which didn't bode well for this mission. Embarrassed and deflated, Marcus dared not even look at Nicole.

"Dad, he's not here for that," she said in a cringing tone.

"I'm here about Beau," Marcus volunteered, stepping closer.

Dillard leaned forward, craning his neck again. "Beau?"

Marcus walked around in front of the recliner and went straight to the point. "Mr. Archer, your son needs psychological counseling."

Dillard's mouth cracked a wry smile. "Say what?"

Marcus wanted to sit face-to-face, but the nearest seat was a couple yards away. He had no choice but to stand. Holding the portfolio in front of him, he widened his stance slightly. "I'm concerned about Beau's level of frustration."

"Frustration?" Dillard scoffed. "Buddy, let me tell you about frustration. *I* have frustration. He's a kid. What does he know about frustration?" He shook his head and looked past Marcus to the television, muttering, "Frustration! Where do they get this stuff?"

"I understand that you're dealing with your own issues," Marcus said smoothly but firmly, "but my concern at this point is for Beau. I want your permission to take him for counseling. If you desire counseling, it can be made available to you, also."

Dillard glared up at Marcus for all of five seconds, then he calmly set aside his beer and rose to his full height, which was a couple inches taller than Marcus's own six feet. He was a big, beefy man going to fat but still strong enough to cause Marcus serious injury, although in that moment Marcus would have welcomed the excuse to try to pound some sense into the man. As coherent as he sounded, however, Marcus could now see that Dillard was well on his way to complete inebriation. The way he swayed slightly and the sour gust of his breath told Marcus that much. He wasn't the first sober-sounding drunk whom Marcus had encountered.

"Just who do you think you are?" Dillard demanded. "Coming in here spouting off about frustration, telling me my kid needs counseling! Who are you to be taking my boy anywhere?"

"I am your son's pastor," Marcus said flatly, "and his friend."

Dillard glared for several seconds longer, but then he put his head back and laughed. The action toppled him backward into his chair, which rocked alarmingly. "His *pastor*," he sneered. "We got no use for your kind here, *Pastor*. Go peddle your lies somewhere else."

"I'm peddling no lies, only genuine concern."

"Take your concern and stick—"

"Daddy," Nicole interrupted in a soft tone that Marcus was sure she'd perfected as a tool of distraction long ago, "Marcus is here to help."

"I don't need his help!" Dillard growled. "I don't want it!"

"This isn't about you," Marcus said heatedly. "This is about Beau!"

"Your god means nothin' to me!" Dillard roared. "So *you* mean nothin' to me! What do you know about me and mine anyway?" He grabbed the beer can and drained it,

then shoved back in his chair. With a loud creak, the recliner flopped back, rocking wildly. Dillard seemed not to
notice that the thing could collapse with him. He was too
busy sneering at Marcus. "Your god's done nothin' for me,
so I'm doing nothin' for you!"

Marcus clamped his jaw, trying mightily to moderate his
tone. "This is not for me. This is for Beau."

Suddenly Dillard turned on Nicole, snarling, "Get him
out of my face, girl, or so help me he's gonna regret it!"

She grabbed Marcus by the sleeve, tugging insistently, her
big eyes imploring him not to argue further. Marcus sighed
inwardly. Obviously he wasn't going to make any headway
with Dillard tonight. He let Nicole lead him away. Dillard
grumbled behind him, and when Marcus looked back over
one shoulder he found the man fishing another beer from
the cooler stashed beneath the side table, his chair tilting
precariously side to side as he maneuvered.

Resigned to failure, Marcus quietly followed Nicole into
the hallway that bisected this portion of the house. She made
another quick turn into the kitchen, pulling him along with
her. The lights blazing overhead were almost too bright
after the gloom of the living room. Marcus glanced around,
taking in the faded wallpaper and mottled green counter-
tops.

The pecan cabinets were scratched and dull, the dinette
set rickety and scraped. Nevertheless, the room possessed
a cheery neatness. Yellow ruffled curtains hung over the
window above the sink. The center of the small, round table
held a pretty glass bowl of bananas, while a colorful set of
canisters took center stage on the longest counter, and a red
ceramic rooster looked down on it all from atop the refrigerator. A blue-enameled stew pot sat between the burners
on the olive-green stove. This was Nicole's room, the heart

of her home, and it evoked a certain longing in him that he was quick to suppress.

"Where's Beau?" he asked softly.

"I asked him to stay in his room. I haven't told him about the counseling for obvious reasons."

Marcus nodded grimly. "I haven't given up."

"Dad's not going to change his mind," Nicole warned, shaking her head.

"Maybe not, but God can change the situation, Nicole. You have to believe that."

"I know. I do know. That's what I'm counting on."

"If you were to call Family Services," Marcus pressed carefully, "they would see to it that Beau and your father both get the counseling they need."

She was shaking her head long before he got through the sentence. "We've been through this. I can't risk them taking Beau into foster care."

"But, Nicole, something has to change. You can't go on living like this."

"Better like this than separated from my brother!" she hissed.

A door opened somewhere down the hallway. Nicole lightly touched Marcus on the forearm, warning him with a glance. He nodded and pasted a smile on his face. Beau entered the room a few moments later, carrying an empty glass. His eyes widened at the sight of Marcus.

"Hey! What are you doing here?"

Marcus clapped a hand on his shoulder in greeting. "Talking to your sister."

Beau's gaze slid from Marcus to Nicole, clearly speculative. "What about?"

Nicole ruffled his hair, saying glibly, "Mind your own business. Want some more milk?"

Beau grinned, and Nicole widened her eyes at him in

some silent message. "Yeah, if it's got banana and chocolate in it."

Nicole rolled her eyes, but she took the glass from him and motioned him toward the table. "Sit down." She moved to the cabinets. "You, too, Marcus."

Beau went around the table and pulled out a chair, plopping down into it with no obvious concern for its stability. Marcus followed suit, but a bit more gingerly. Nicole took down a blender and went to the refrigerator.

"We call it a poor man's milk shake," she told Marcus, carrying a tray of ice back to the counter. "It doesn't keep very well, so you'll have to help us drink it."

Marcus watched her walk toward him, noticing for the first time that she was garbed rather mundanely in jeans and a splotchy blue sweatshirt, her sleek, dark hair held back by a white knit headband. It was something of a disappointment. He sort of missed the more interesting costumes that she usually wore.

"Okay," he said.

As she drew near, she laid a hand on his shoulder, then leaned past him to pluck a banana from the bowl. Peeling it, she carried the fruit back to the blender. When she went to the pantry for cocoa powder, he made himself focus on Beau, asking lightly, "So, how have you been?"

"Okay."

Marcus quickly searched his mind for a sustainable topic of conversation and came up with, "Tell me about these guitar lessons."

Beau launched into his favorite subject, ignoring the noisy whine of the blender. Beau taught three kids, one of them as old as he was. None had access to guitars of their own and shared Beau's old acoustic model. It was basically a tale of poor kids, Beau included, eager for a chance just to indulge the dream of escaping hardship through music and fame.

"My friend Austin's got an electric," Beau went on happily, "and, man, I can make that baby sing. When Nic and I get out on our own, I'm gonna get me one. I am so crunk about it."

Marcus laughed. "I'd love to hear you play." He didn't have to ask twice. Beau was already on his feet and heading for the door.

Nicole carried three glasses of light brown slush to the table, saying, "Now you've done it."

"No, really," Marcus said, eyeing his glass warily, "I'd really like to hear him play."

She took the chair to his left, her own beverage in her hand. "We have a straw if you'd like."

A straw, Marcus mused, wondering if she literally meant one straw. He reached for his glass. "No, that's all right." The first sip surprised him. He lifted an eyebrow and went back for more. "Not bad."

Nicole laughed and leaned back, her feet braced against the spanners between the legs of Marcus's chair. He fought the urge to slip his hand down around her ankle.

"Mom always put vanilla extract in it," Nicole told him, wrinkling her nose, "but it's too expensive."

"I like it this way," he said, taking another drink.

Beau reentered the room just then, a blond guitar strung around his neck with a leather thong. It was obviously old. The wood had lost much of its original luster, and the brand name was partially worn away, but his eagerness was palpable. He took his chair, paused long enough to gulp down about half of his drink and began strumming.

"I tuned her up earlier," he explained. Nevertheless, he made a tiny adjustment before downing another long swig of his drink, wiping his mouth on his shirtsleeve and setting to work.

Marcus saw that the knuckles of Beau's right hand were

scraped and scabbed, but it didn't seem to hinder his playing. In fact, Marcus required only moments to realize that he was in the presence of true talent. The boy's nimble fingers flew over the strings. Closing his eyes, Beau poured his heart into the music, which filled the room and those in it with unexpected richness.

It wasn't a song that Marcus recognized, but he knew he would never forget so much as a note of it. Indeed, they seemed to swell inside Marcus until he felt ready to burst with the ethereal beauty of the sound. When the last chord was strummed and faded into memory, Marcus felt himself wanting more. Then suddenly Beau launched into a rollicking, bluesy number that put a smile on Marcus's face. This one he recognized as a classic.

"My word," Marcus breathed, sharing a glance with Nicole, who smiled with supreme satisfaction.

He found his feet tapping along in time with Beau's. And then the sound morphed into the riffs and rills of solid rock. This, it became obvious, was where Beau's heart lay. The boy shifted to his feet and moved with the execution of the music, dipping and swaying, forward and back, gliding side to side as the music took him where he made it. When he was done, Beau dropped into his chair with a plop, as if his strength had left with the music.

Marcus was dumbfounded. He couldn't find words to express his appreciation, but his mind whirled with possibilities. Finally a coherent thought crystallized and popped right out of his mouth. "I have to introduce you to Leanne."

Beau slid a knowing look at Nicole, asking, "That the lady who plays the piano at church?"

"Leanne Prist, our director of music," Marcus clarified, nodding. "She's going to want you to provide special music and, of course, join the praise band we're putting together."

Beau shrugged and picked up his glass, sitting back. "Sure."

Marcus grinned. His time here hadn't been wasted, after all.

He looked at Nicole and caught his breath. Her brown eyes glowed with some emotion that shimmered through him, tingling in his extremities and clogging his throat. For a long moment, he literally could not look away. Then Beau rose, stretching and saying that he was going to bed. He started toward the door, and Marcus realized that in another moment he would be alone with Nicole.

He could not, dared not, allow himself that luxury. How long, he wondered, even as he planned his getaway, would he have to carry this cross before God took these dangerous feelings from him?

Marcus glanced at his watch. "I'd better be going, too," he said smoothly, picking up his glass for a final swallow as he rose to his feet.

Nicole slipped out of her chair and placed a stilling hand on his shoulder. "I'll walk you out. Just hang on a minute, will you?" With that she quickly left the room.

Beau met Marcus's gaze openly. "She wants to be sure Dad's out of it before you go. Does he even know you're here?"

"Yes," Marcus answered tersely.

"I had my headphones on," the boy said matter-of-factly. "Did he yell at you? Tell you to get out?"

"We had a few words."

"Don't take it personally. He's like that with everyone."

Marcus nodded. "I'm not worried about that. I am worried about you. Your sister said you put your fist through the wall."

Beau's gaze slid away, and he shrugged. "No big deal.

He made me mad is all. Said I've got no talent, only stupid dreams."

"He's wrong," Marcus declared quietly. "You have great talent, but you can't go around busting up things, Beau. You'll destroy your hands, if nothing else. Think about that. How will you play with busted fingers?"

Beau grimaced and whined, "I know, but I can't help it."

"Beau, listen to me," Marcus said urgently. "You and your sister need assistance, professional aid from people trained to deal with these types of situations. I'm sure if you asked her to call Family Services she would."

"It'll just make everything worse," Beau insisted. "I won't punch the wall anymore, honest."

"That's not the point, Beau."

"Dad's out of it," Nicole said from behind Marcus, adding sternly, "and we've already had this discussion."

Marcus sighed. Why couldn't they see that he just wanted to protect them? This was no way to live, tiptoeing around a sharp-tongued drunk. Perhaps he hadn't resorted to physical abuse yet, but Marcus did not doubt that he would unless something changed.

He bid Beau a final good-night and followed Nicole from the room, racking his brain for some way to convince her that his way was best. As they passed the living room, Dillard's snores could be heard over the sound of the television. Marcus marveled that Beau's music hadn't awakened him. Obviously the man was far drunker than he'd realized.

They reached the front door, but instead of standing aside, Nicole opened it and walked through, obviously angry. He had a pretty good idea what was coming, so he merely followed her out and pulled the door closed behind him. Folding her arms against the chill, she stepped out of the shadow of the eaves and turned on him.

"That was low, Marcus, trying to turn Beau against me."

"I wasn't doing that. I just need to make you two understand the reality of your situation."

"Don't you think I know! I live with it every day. Every day. I'm just trying to make the best of a bad situation here, and so far we haven't done too badly."

"So far," he tossed back at her, "but what if next time your father takes his fists to your brother? What then?"

She seemed small and vulnerable, standing there with her head bowed. "We'll just have to cross that bridge if we come to it," she muttered. Then she lifted her chin to a stubborn angle. "But so far we haven't, and I intend to keep looking for a way around."

Marcus put his hands to his head. Couldn't she see that she was running out of options? How could he protect them, he wondered bleakly, if she wouldn't let him?

Perhaps he should call the authorities himself. Even if she never forgave him, at least she and Beau would be safe. How he would live with their anger and disappointment, he didn't know, but what else could he do?

And it might even be for the best.

If she never spoke to him again, he couldn't give in to these inappropriate impulses. If he was going to fail, he might as well fail safely.

"Everyone fails sometime," he told himself, not realizing he'd spoken aloud until he heard the scuff of feet as she shifted closer, reaching out a hand to place it gently against his chest, over his heart.

"Please don't," she begged softly. "You did your best, and truly I didn't expect any other outcome."

With a groan, Marcus closed his eyes, fighting the need to drop his arms around her and pull her close. "I'm not the one in need of comfort here. I'm just sorry that I couldn't help."

She laid her head against him, tucking it neatly beneath his chin. "We just need to find another solution is all."

There is another solution, whispered *a small voice in his mind.* And it meets everyone's needs.

Startled, Marcus let the thought come. She needed someone who could legally stand up for her, someone to help her shoulder responsibilities that would have crushed a lesser individual by now, someone CPS wouldn't hesitate to recommend as a guardian for her brother. A husband.

Someone like Marcus, who himself needed a wife.

Appalled, he shook his head. She was not the wife he needed.

True, it could be done. So easily. She was over eighteen and wouldn't need permission to marry any more than Marcus would. He could convince her. He knew he could. Marriage to him would get her and Beau out of this house and away from Dillard. She could finish college without working herself half to death. Marcus wasn't wealthy by any means, nor would he ever be, but he could provide her and Beau with everything they would ever need. They would be a real family. Marriage would solve everything. For her.

There was nothing to prevent them from marrying. Except his commitment to live in God's will.

He was a minister. He had a calling that he could not doubt. He needed a woman called to be a minister's wife, a spiritually mature, sedate, retiring individual to whom his congregation could relate and look for guidance and aid. He needed a woman who understood the challenges and limitations of his position, a partner in ministry. A young, ebullient, quirky almost to the point of eccentric *student* would never fit the bill, however much he might want her to.

He couldn't escape the fact that Nicole Archer was not the woman for him. No matter how beautiful she was or how much she lit up his heart simply by walking into the room, no matter how much she needed and deserved rescuing, no matter how much he wanted to be the one to do it, marriage between them just wasn't appropriate. And he couldn't believe he had to tell himself that!

Suddenly he wanted desperately just to walk away. Run, truthfully, so far and so fast that he could forget he'd ever met Nicole Archer and her brother. But he couldn't do that, either. His calling demanded otherwise. He couldn't give up, not on Nicole and Beau and not on the ministry to which he was called.

Now all he had to do was figure out a way to manage one without destroying the other.

After a moment, he gently extricated himself and took his leave, but there would be no escape from the fearful ideas that crowded his mind. Not now. Not for him.

God help him.

Nicole closed the door to her bedroom and put her back to it. The red shawl that she'd draped over the lamp on her bedside table cast a dim, rosy glow over the cheap French Provincial furniture. It corresponded fittingly with the warm glow around her heart.

She ought to be steaming, considering what Marcus had done tonight, urging Beau to call the authorities the minute her back was turned, but she couldn't stay angry with him. He tried so hard to do what was best, and like most men he couldn't conceive that what he thought was best might not be. Her mother used to say that her father couldn't help it if he saw the world through the eyes of a man. That's why they needed wives, after all. And Marcus was no exception.

Because he considered every situation carefully—she never doubted that he prayed diligently over every issue— Marcus naturally assumed that the first answer he hit upon was necessarily the right one. He didn't understand yet that her perspective was every bit as valid as his.

She knew that in Marcus's world calling Family Services and letting them deal with her father was only reasonable, but in hers it was tantamount to dumping her problems on them when she'd vowed never to do so. It wasn't that she didn't see his point or that his point didn't have validity. It wasn't even that she couldn't see a time or a circumstance when his solution would make more sense than hers. It was just that they hadn't gotten there yet, and God willing, they never would.

That didn't mean that Marcus wasn't the sweetest, dearest man on earth anyway for trying so hard to help them.

She peeled off her robe and dropped it over the chair beside the door wandering over to the bed and plopping down. Tired, she fell back against the pillows and stacked her hands beneath her head, considering. If her life wasn't so complicated right now, she'd go after Marcus Wheeler so hard he wouldn't know what hit him, even if he did think she was too young.

Wrinkling her nose, she rolled onto her side, tucking her hands beneath her cheek.

She wasn't too young. She understood why he thought that, though. A minister had to be a sober, responsible sort, which just meant that he needed brightness and childlike enthusiasm in his life more than most others did. He wouldn't see it, of course, precisely because he was sober and responsible. Nicole, on the other hand, made a concerted effort to seek brightness and hold on to all the innocent enthusiasm she could for as long as she could.

She wished she could give that to Marcus.

"He's a good man," she whispered, only realizing at the last moment that she was talking to God. "He deserves all the good things in this world, and I'd give them to him if I could, but I can't, so You'll have to do it. Please."

After a few more moments, her prayer fell back into its usual pattern, filling with her concerns for her father and her brother and the knife-edge of ruin against which her family seemed continually to dance.

"Just help me hold it together a few more months," she pleaded. "I'm not asking for miracles, just a few more months. Then Beau and I can head out on our own."

What would happen to her father then? she wondered.

"He's the one who needs the miracle," she said. "Save it for him, if You please. All I need is just a few more months."

It never occurred to her to ask for more than time or that anyone else would be asking for more on her behalf.

She slid beneath the covers and snuggled down to sleep, remembering what it had been like to lay her head on Marcus's strong shoulder, if only for a moment.

Chapter Nine

"I'm not having any of your charity or anything else!" Dillard Archer exclaimed. "And stay away from my daughter!" With that he slammed the door in Marcus's face.

"Charity!" Marcus fumed, whirling away to stomp toward his car. He was offering the man psychological counseling, not alms, for pity's sake.

No wonder Beau was putting his fists through walls. Dillard was as stubborn as he was unreasonable. The man considered it *charity* to get his son the counseling that he so obviously needed!

After much prayer and thought, Marcus had come back here today on his lunch hour hoping that he'd have a better result by speaking with the man when he was sober, albeit hungover. He'd felt that he had to give it one more shot before he took the next step. He should have known that he would fail. Again. But desperate men took desperate measures.

And even if it is charity, Marcus thought angrily, *his pride shouldn't trump Beau's emotional pain.*

But Dillard seemed incapable of thinking of anyone

except himself: *his* pride, *his* loss, *his* prejudice, *his* anger. He wouldn't even let Marcus into the house to plead his case.

As for staying away from his daughter, Marcus had already come to the same conclusion. Again. Which both simplified and complicated the matter greatly.

Nicole needed help. The Archers needed help, the kind of help that only Family Services and the weighty authority of the state could give them. How was he to convince her to take the necessary steps, though, if he couldn't even trust himself to sit down in a quiet place with her?

Marcus knew he'd run out of options. The ridiculous notion of marrying the girl aside, it had become painfully clear that Dillard could not be moved to do what was best for his children, not by an individual, at any rate. What was just as painfully obvious was that Marcus wouldn't have to worry about getting too close to Nicole if he availed himself of the only viable solution he could see.

He didn't kid himself. The personal consequences of taking such an action would be grim, but it would be best for everyone all the way around. Given another choice, he'd have gladly taken it, but he couldn't put his own considerations ahead of what was best for Nicole and Beau. That would make him no better than Dillard.

Besides, he thought bleakly, if Nicole never spoke to him again, that would remove temptation from him as nothing else could. Accepting her anger and disappointment as the price he paid for doing what was right could well be the most loving thing he could do for her.

After unlocking the driver's door, Marcus tossed the portfolio containing the unsigned permission waiver onto the bench seat of his sedan and followed it inside. He gripped the steering wheel with both hands, steeling himself for what he was about to do.

"Lord, if this is what it takes, I'm more than willing, but

if it's possible, for her sake more than my own, let her forgive me. Help her understand why this is necessary. I don't expect her to look at me ever again with that hero worship in her eyes, but that's just as it should be, surely. Amen."

He reached into his breast pocket and took out his mobile phone. As he thumbed through the preprogrammed numbers, he took in a deep breath. He had tried it her way, and it hadn't worked. He could only assume, then, that the one remaining credible option was the one he should take.

The name for which he was searching popped up. Jonathan Bertrand was a friend from seminary who had found his calling with the offices of Child Protective Services. Having grown up in the CPS system, Marcus was all too aware of how difficult a career in social service must be, and he had long admired his friend's dedication in the face of thankless tasks, red tape and heartbreaking situations. He was grateful that he had this resource, sorry that he had to use it.

Grimly resigned, Marcus dialed the number and waited for the answer, expecting to leave a message on Jonathan's voice mail. Instead, he reached Jonathan himself.

Having risen through the ranks of CPS caseworkers to a position of supervisor, Jonathan was uniquely placed to take immediate action. After hearing Marcus's version of the Archers' story, Jonathan was prepared to send one of his field agents to make an unannounced visit to the Archer home the very next evening. Satisfied, Marcus ended the call.

If his stomach felt tied in knots as he drove back to the church, he bore it with as much resigned grace as he could muster. What point could there be, after all, in holding out against the inevitable? Whatever befell he was bound to reap a whirlwind in this situation.

The confirmation of that dreary fact came almost forty-eight hours later. He was heading back to the office from the day care center via the covered walkway that connected the buildings when Nicole's car turned the corner in front of him.

She didn't park outside the administration building. She didn't even bother to put the car in a space, let alone turn it head in. Instead she simply swerved to the curb next to him, threw the transmission into park and bailed out with the motor still clanking.

She was dressed in black from the jaunty beret parked atop her head to the boots on her feet, including a turtle-neck sweater of thin knit and a gauzy, ankle-length skirt composed of ruffled tiers. The color perfectly portrayed her mood.

"How could you?" she cried, her hands fisted at her sides. "You knew we didn't want CPS brought in!"

Marcus didn't bother pretending that her accusations were unfounded. Neither did he defend himself.

"I made sure they came when you would be there. I didn't want them talking to Beau or your father without you."

"Oh, they came, all right, some silly little woman with ex-cruciatingly good manners and no idea when she was being snowed!"

Marcus's heart filled with dread. "What do you mean?"

"You spoke to him," Nicole pointed out sharply. "No one who doesn't know him will even realize he's drunk unless he gets up and starts bumping into things! How was she to know that he'd keep his cool until she'd gone?"

Marcus winced. She was right. He should have thought of that. He should have warned Jonathan that Dillard could maintain precise speech even when scarcely conscious.

"What happened?"

She parked her hands on her hips and glared at him. "He exploded. He smashed Beau's stereo for punishment!"

Marcus briefly closed his eyes. "Was Beau hurt?"

"Physically, no. But Beau doesn't know when to keep his mouth shut, so I wound up between him and Dad's belt!"

Suddenly Marcus was too angry to breathe, but he didn't know who he was angrier with, Dillard or himself. Finally, he got out what felt like the most important words he'd ever spoken. "Did he hit you?"

She looked him square in the eye. "No."

"Did he touch you at all?"

Her gaze dropped. "Just to try to shove me out of his way. When I didn't budge, he backed off."

Marcus forced air into his lungs, held it until his heart slowed and expelled it again. "I'll buy Beau another stereo," he vowed, but Nicole dismissed that with a slash of her hand.

"What's the point? Dad will just smash it the next time he's angry. I had to hide the guitar to keep him from destroying that, and he tore up *my* room looking for it!"

Gulping, Marcus said, "I'll talk to him. I did this. His anger should be directed at me, not you. I'll make him see that."

She folded her arms, her chin set at a stubborn angle. "You will not. He already suspects it was you who turned him in, and if he finds out for sure he'll forbid us to attend church. He probably will anyway."

Marcus shook his head, confused and contrite. How could this be? Had he sacrificed her goodwill, her friendship, even his ministerial position in her life for nothing? Calling CPS had been for the best. Hadn't it? It had to be.

"They have a case file now. The next time they won't be fobbed off so easily. It'll work out in the end," he promised, but the look on her face smashed him to bits inside. It was like a hot poker in the chest.

Her big eyes welled with tears, and her stubborn little chin began to quiver while the rest of her features remained wooden.

"Yes, it will," she agreed in a thin, trembling voice. "But there won't be any next time, Marcus. I promised my mom, and I'll do whatever it takes to keep that promise." She stomped her foot then. "But none of that has anything to do with the fact that I trusted you and you betrayed me!"

Marcus closed his eyes. "I had no choice."

"And for what?" she went on. "It didn't change a thing."

He popped his eyes open. "It would have if you'd told them the truth. But you pretended everything was fine, didn't you?"

"What else was I going to do? Hand my little brother over to them, forget every promise I've ever made?"

For nothing! he thought. He couldn't have done this for no good at all. And she hated him now. Was that what it had been for, so she would hate him because he wasn't strong enough to ignore the way she looked at him? "I didn't know what else to do!" he said helplessly.

She was already sliding back into her rattletrap car, as if she hadn't even heard or just didn't care anymore. The tires screeched as she whipped a U-turn and left the same way she'd come in.

Marcus put his head back, sheer agony writhing inside his chest.

"I didn't know what else to do," he repeated, which was no comfort at all. All he could do now was try to put it right somehow.

He pulled his cell phone from his pocket and quickly found Jonathan Bertrand's number. This time he did have to leave a message, and nearly an hour passed before Jonathan returned the call. He explained that he'd taken the time to speak personally with the investigating agent. She'd reported that the Archer home seemed safe, clean and comfortable despite its slightly run-down condition.

"God knows she's seen much worse," Jonathan commented, and Marcus knew that was solely because of Nicole's efforts.

Jonathan went on to read aloud the caseworker's notes. She had found Dillard Archer lazy, self-involved and somewhat crude but neither abusive nor dangerously inebriated. She'd written that Nicole obviously had assumed a major role in the life of the family, and that since Nicole seemed trustworthy and responsible, Beau was of an age to assume some personal accountability and neither of them had made any complaint concerning their father's behavior, it was the caseworker's opinion that no further action on the part of the county or state was necessary. Jonathan concurred.

Feeling sick, his heart pounding with dread, Marcus explained what had happened after the caseworker had left the Archer house.

"Will she swear to that?" Jonathan asked. "Because if she will, I'll send my agent back out there right away. I expect she would at least recommend anger management classes for Mr. Archer."

Anger management classes would be a start, Marcus admitted, but only that, and he knew without a doubt that Nicole wouldn't cooperate.

"Beau might under the right circumstances," Marcus speculated aloud.

Unless one of them did, Jonathan's hands were tied. Marcus groaned inwardly, thanked him and got off the phone.

He was in no mood for the agitated mother of two who greeted him the moment that he stepped foot back into the office, but it was his job to deal with such minor problems as a toddler with a tendency to bite, and he did so with as much patience and diplomacy as he could muster. Only later did he have time to sit down, bow his head and beg God to show him where he'd gone wrong.

After much more prayer, he decided that he'd been somewhat precipitate, that he'd done it as much for his own sake
as Nicole's or Beau's. He still believed that involving the
authorities was best for them and that he'd had a responsibility as a member of the clergy to report the abuse, but his
motives had been selfish.

At least he'd accomplished one thing. Neither Nicole nor
Beau would likely ever speak to him again. That might well
have been the point of the whole exercise. Perhaps that was
what God intended.

He'd prayed to have the temptation removed, after all, and
so it had been. He didn't have to worry about a romantic relationship developing between himself and Nicole anymore.
If ever she'd had a crush on him, that was surely finished.
He should feel relieved.

He felt as if he'd lost his best friend, as if color had
drained out of the world, leaving it a pale, pallid version of
what it might have been.

It was best, no doubt, but it wasn't happy, and he couldn't
help feeling that he ought to try to make amends. If he and
Beau could just remain friends, he might still be able to help.

It was the only recourse he could think of and little
enough, considering how it had turned out. Sick at heart,
he accepted this half measure as all that was left to him, and
for the first time in more years than he could even remember, he had to fight back tears.

Nicole looked at the brown paper bag that Beau had
dropped in her lap and folded her arms. The bag should
have been empty, but obviously it wasn't. Unfolding the top,
she checked inside. All the original contents were there, with
the exception of the cookies. Sighing, she handed the bag
back to him and fixed him with a questioning glare.

"Care to explain to me why you only ate cookies for lunch?"

Smiling smugly, Beau dug into the bag, removed the peanut butter sandwich and began peeling back the plastic wrap, clearly preparing to eat it. "I didn't eat cookies for lunch," he said cheekily. "I ate them in study hall."

"So you skipped lunch," Nicole surmised, quickly seizing the wheel and driving forward as the line of cars ahead of her moved.

"Nope. I ate a chili cheese dog, onion rings and a side salad with buttermilk dressing." He bit off a huge chunk of the sandwich and apparently swallowed it whole.

"Chew your food," Nicole instructed automatically, looking both ways before pulling out into the street that ran in front of the school. "And where did you get the money to buy a chili cheese dog, let alone onion rings and… You ate a side salad?"

"Mmm-hmm. Wi bu-urmil drezin."

"Don't speak with your mouth full," she scolded mildly. "Now answer my question."

He gulped, smacked his lips and said, "I had lunch with Marcus."

She brought the car to a stop at the red light on the corner and turned her head to gape at her brother. She still hadn't forgiven Marcus for calling the authorities, but deep down she knew she wasn't going to hold it against him forever. He'd only done what he thought was best. The fact that he was wrong, at least to her mind, did not negate his intentions, and she couldn't deny the relief that she felt at knowing he hadn't completely abandoned them to their fate.

"So Marcus came to the school for lunch," she said, looking away again.

"Yep, and brought lunch with him."

Nicole faced forward and lifted a hand to her hair, trying to appear nonchalant. "What did he have to say?"

Beau finished the sandwich and reached into the bag for the pretzels she'd packed for him that morning. "He's worried about us, and he feels bad about my stereo." Beau turned big, pleading eyes on her. "He'll replace it if you'll let him."

"Beau."

"I know. It's not really his fault Dad broke it, but if I wait for Dad to replace it I'll get old and grow hair in my ears before I can listen to my music again."

He started crunching the pretzels, and Nicole found herself on the verge of smiling. She quickly disciplined her pleasure as she pulled away from the light.

"Marcus shouldn't have called CPS."

"I know. I told him that."

"And what did he say?"

Beau poked around inside the paper bag for a moment, long enough for her to know that he was stalling.

"Beau, what did Marcus say when you told him that he shouldn't have called CPS?"

Beau looked up and reluctantly said, "He wanted me to tell CPS what Dad did after that lady left. He said if I would, they'd probably send Dad to anger management classes."

Nicole rolled her eyes. "Anger management. Like that'll help the next time he's too drunk to see reason. You told Marcus you wouldn't do it, didn't you?"

"Sure I did."

"If he bothers you about it again, I want to know."

"Aw, Nic. He's just trying to help," Beau said.

She shifted in her seat. "Yes, well, he always tries to help. He just has to learn that we sometimes know best. Not everyone fits the standard protocol."

"What's that?"

"Never mind."

Shrugging, Beau worked on the pretzels for another block or two. Then he reached into the bag for the apple. Lightly polishing the apple on his pant leg, he asked, "Think I could go to youth group at church tonight?"

Nicole bit her lip. "I don't know, hon. Dad's liable to be home and sober enough to notice."

Beau sighed. "Yeah, that's what I figured, too. Think we'll be able to make it on Sunday?"

She'd thought about not going at all or finding another church, but once her anger had subsided somewhat, she'd known that she would do neither. Still, things could get a lot trickier now.

"Maybe. I can't promise, though."

Beau nodded his understanding. "I can meet the music director some other time, I guess."

Sadly, Nicole couldn't offer more hope than that. Dillard could stop them from going to church if he really wanted to, and she had no doubt that he would if he were sober enough to think of it. They'd have to be very careful from now on.

She watched Beau bite into the apple, wishing that she could give him the same carefree, untroubled life that other boys seemed to experience. At least she could keep his life from getting any worse, and that's what would happen if she lost him to the foster care system. Couldn't Marcus see that? Didn't his own experience tell him that was the case?

On one hand, she wanted to be angry with Marcus. He'd had no right to call CPS, knowing how she and Beau felt about it. On the other, she knew that he'd done it because he cared about them. That was something she couldn't forget. She only hoped that with time things would get back to normal. In the meanwhile, she'd do the best she could.

Seemed as if that was what she'd been doing ever since her mom had died.

One more semester to go, she told herself.

Surely they could hold out for that long. Maybe she shouldn't skip the summer, though. She'd meant to work full-time in order to scrape together the tuition for her final semester, but maybe she could manage full-time work and summer school, too.

She shook her head. The summer semester was short, and Beau would be out of school. She dared not leave him on his own every day in the house with their dad. They'd just have to keep on keeping on as they were—and pray for the best.

Marcus clasped the hand that Nicole offered.

"I'm so very glad to see you," he said, casting a glance around the church foyer. He nodded at someone behind her, and his manner grew slightly more formal. "We've missed having you and Beau at services."

She let her hand fall, knowing that they were being observed. They had nothing to hide, she and Marcus, but she was astute enough to realize that it wasn't wise for Marcus to show more interest in one member of the congregation than another. Besides, she wasn't quite ready to completely forgive him.

Still, it was wonderful to see him. She smiled, realized that she was standing on her tiptoes and quickly lowered herself again.

"It's been difficult to get away lately," she told him, sure he would understand.

"I'd like to talk to you about that if you have time," he said meaningfully, glancing down the line of those waiting to shake his hand.

She knew what he was asking her to do, and despite everything she would have liked to hang around until they could speak privately, but she dared not. Her father had stumbled in and fallen into bed around four in the morning, but he'd wake up when he got hungry. She and Beau were already taking a chance just by being here. If their father woke before they got back home, he'd know where they'd been, and while he hadn't specifically forbidden them to attend church, he suspected that Marcus was the one who had called CPS.

They couldn't give him the slightest pretext to lower the boom. She shuddered to think what he'd do if ever he knew that Marcus had been meeting Beau regularly for lunch at school.

"I'm sorry," she said, leaning in close. "I just can't. Not yet. Maybe in a few more weeks."

"This is the first time you've been here in a month," Marcus whispered urgently. "Beau won't tell me what's going on, and I can't help worrying when you don't show up for church."

The woman behind Nicole nudged her slightly, and she straightened away from Marcus saying loudly, "Wonderful sermon. I look forward to next time."

Marcus nodded stiffly and reached out for the other woman's hand. Nicole strode swiftly for the exit, signaling Beau to leave his acquaintances and join her. They hurried around the church, across the street and between the administration and day care buildings to the car parked at the curb on the street beyond. The church parking lot had a tendency to bottleneck, and they didn't have the time to spare.

In truth, it had been foolish of her to take the time to greet Marcus personally when she could have slipped out another door, but she hadn't been able to resist. Now they had to rush. She broke speed limits getting home, holding her breath all the way, only to walk into the kitchen and find her father sitting at the table. He held his head in one hand, nursing a cup of coffee with the other.

Dillard jerked at their sudden halt, as if the squeaks of

their shoes on the worn vinyl flooring pained his head. Nicole reached out a hand to keep Beau in his place, her heart in her throat. Dillard slid a narrow-eyed glance over them and turned back to his coffee in glum silence. After a moment, he spoke.

"So did you make plans for lunch or what? I'm starving here, or don't you care?"

Nicole handed Beau her purse and Bible and motioned for him to leave them. At the same time that he slipped from the room, she walked across the floor to the counter and the slow cooker atop it. The spaghetti with meat sauce that she'd put into the freezer last week had gone into the cooker as a solid lump before she'd started dressing for church this morning. With luck, it would just about be ready. She'd intended to put together a salad, but opening a can of green beans would be quicker, and at this point, quick was definitely the better option.

A few minutes later, when she set Dillard's plate in front of him, he looked up and growled, "Don't think I don't know where you've been or that I can't put a stop to it."

She said nothing to that, merely asked, "Have you taken anything for your head?"

Dillard closed his eyes, muttering, "I forgot to get the aspirin before I sat down." He opened his eyes and looked up at her beseechingly. "Will you get them for me, baby?"

Nicole's heart turned over. He was a pathetic loser drunk, but he was still her dad, and no matter what, she loved him. She'd take the first opportunity to get away from him, but that didn't mean he wouldn't always be her dad. For today, at least, that seemed to matter.

"Sure, Daddy."

Absently patting his shoulder, she went to get the painkillers, silently breathing a sigh of relief. Maybe things would get better for a while again. As Marcus had said in his sermon today, God really did have the power to change lives, and maybe, just maybe, He was already beginning to change her father from the inside out.

Chapter Ten

Nicole hung up the phone, carefully assessing the situation.

It had been a couple weeks of relative peace and normalcy. Dillard hadn't again threatened, even obliquely, to forbid her and Beau from attending church. In fact, he'd said nothing at all about it. He'd had little to drink, gone to bed at a decent hour and been downright pleasant most of the time, sometimes even joking and teasing with them. As a result Beau was content and relaxed. Still, she wasn't quite ready to trust that all would be well if she left Beau and her father alone together again.

Beau shambled into the kitchen just then, his backpack slung over one shoulder, humming as he fingered an invisible guitar. Catching her pensive expression, he stopped.

"What?"

Nicole smiled, thrilled to see him so happy. But how long, she wondered, would it last? Another day? A week? She dared not hope for forever at this point, but didn't that demonstrate a lack of faith on her part? She'd been thinking a lot about that. Only last Sunday Marcus had said from the pulpit that asking God to fix your problems and then not trusting Him to do so was tantamount to denying His ability and right to direct our lives.

She missed Marcus deeply. He hadn't tried to talk to her again since she'd rebuffed him a few weeks ago, and his greetings, while perfectly polite, were strictly impersonal. He continued to spend time with Beau, but if he even thought about her, she certainly couldn't prove it. Nevertheless, she trusted his teachings. Perhaps it was time she stepped out on faith.

"I've got another chance to work a few extra hours," she said to Beau. "The restaurant just can't keep fully staffed on Fridays." Some people, it seemed, actually had social lives.

"That's cool," Beau commented offhandedly, walking over to the counter to pick up his lunch bag.

"You think it'll be all right then, even after last time?"

Beau turned and met her gaze. "Don't worry," he said. "It'll be fine. Besides, don't we need the money?"

"You know we do."

"Well, then."

She bit her lip. Old habits died hard. "I could call Ovida and Larry Cutler. You haven't seen them in a long time."

Beau made a face, complaining, "You know I'm not as tight with them as you are. They're old folks, and besides I'm not some little bitty baby anymore."

"Marcus, then. You've been eating lunch together a couple times a week. I'm sure he wouldn't mind."

"Listen," Beau said emphatically, "it's okay." He lowered his voice, adding, "And I don't think Dad would like it if we called Marcus."

"Has he said something?"

Beau hitched up one shoulder. "Not really. But the other night when you got up and left the room, he asked if you were still seeing Marcus."

"Seeing? As in *dating?*" Where, she wondered, had he

gotten an idiotic idea like that? It must be more obvious than she realized how much she liked Marcus—and less obvious how little he thought of her.

"That's what it sounded like," Beau confirmed. "I sort of blurted that I was the one Marcus was having lunch with all the time, and Dad looked—I don't know—hurt, I guess. Then I thought he was going to get mad, but instead he got, well, nicer."

Nicole lifted her eyebrows. "Really? Hmm." It almost sounded as if their father was a little bit jealous of Marcus. Perhaps he regretted having alienated his son. Was it really possible that God had begun to soften his heart? "So you think it'll be all right if I go on to work and leave you two here alone together?"

"Yeah, I think so. In fact, I want you to. It could be fun, just us guys. You know, the way it used to be when you and Mom would go off together. If Austin's mom can't give me a lift after school, I'll even catch the bus home."

Nicole widened her eyes comically. "Now that's a first."

The bus ride was long and monotonous, and some kids chose to entertain themselves by picking on others. Beau had been an occasional target, so they tended to avoid that particular district service. Beau was older now, though, better able to avoid trouble and defend himself if the need arose.

"I'm not saying I'll make a habit of it," he warned.

Nicole suppressed a smile, put away her fears and gave in. Her little brother was growing up. And maybe it was time not only to exercise her faith but also to give their dad the benefit of the doubt. She picked up the drawstring bag that contained the things she'd need for the day and slung it over one shoulder.

"Well, what are you waiting for?" she demanded teasingly. "Or maybe you want to ride the bus *to* school."

"No way!" Beau exclaimed, heading for the door.

Nicole laughed and followed him out. Maybe, just maybe, the long, gloomy winter of their lives was finally coming to an end.

Nicole heard the shouting the moment she got out of her car. In an instant the hopeful dream in which she had passed the day vanished like so much smoke in a gale. Dropping her bag on the garage floor, she darted through the narrow laundry room and into the kitchen, discerning at once her father's voice coming from the living room.

"I am your father!" Dillard roared. "And I'll teach you to watch your mouth!"

A loud, sickening *thwack* followed, and Beau cried out. Gasping, Nicole lurched for the doorway, only to draw up when the horrific sound came again. She had no doubt what was transpiring. Her father was taking his belt to Beau. She knew as well that she could do nothing to stop it, not physically anyway.

In hopes of defusing her father's anger, she called out cheerily, "I'm home!"

"Stay out!" Beau screamed, as the leather belt whistled through the air again.

"Disrespectful little idiot!" Dillard bellowed.

Nicole ran for the phone. For an instant, her finger hovered over the key pad as she wondered frantically whom to call. Marcus was her first thought, but she greatly feared that would only incite Dillard to greater violence. Besides, Marcus's solution would be to call the cops. She realized in that instant that Marcus had been right all along. She had only one real option now. Perhaps it had always been so, and she just hadn't wanted to face it. Sobbing, she punched in the numbers 9-1-1.

After choking out the reason for her call and answering what seemed like endless, pointless questions, she hung up and rushed to the living room, which had gone eerily quiet. For a moment, the heap of bodies on the floor seemed as still as death, but then Beau gasped and began to struggle beneath the much greater weight of their father.

Nicole lurched forward, seized Dillard by the shoulder and tipped him sideways, literally rolling him off her brother. Dillard groaned and muttered something unintelligible. Apparently he had passed out. Beau pushed up into a sitting position, drew his knees close and rested his forearms atop them, dropping his head into his hands.

"I'm sorry!" he wailed. "I'm so sorry. I didn't mean to argue with him!"

Nicole went to her knees and pulled his hands away from his face, which showed clear signs of bruising. The marks of a belt were visible on his forearms and the backs of his hands. He gasped out the details of his fight with their father.

Dillard had wanted to go out for dinner, but he'd been drinking steadily for hours, and Beau had known that he was in no shape to get behind a steering wheel, so he had refused to get into the truck with him. The argument had escalated from that to this.

Nicole cast a despairing glance at her father, who had begun to snore as if comfortably tucked into his bed. Thank God he'd passed out when he had. Otherwise, she shuddered to think of what damage he might have done.

At least Beau hadn't gotten into that truck with him, but why, oh, why had she trusted in the fragile peace that had arisen within her crippled little family? She had the awful feeling that things were only going to get worse before they got better. Her instincts were proven right not a minute later when the police arrived. They were not alone.

As soon as two uniformed officers had swept into the house and declared it secure, a tall, slender gentleman with prematurely gray hair entered and went straight to Beau, looking him over with a practiced eye. An African-American, Linus Eversole introduced himself as the local police department's Child Advocate. Though probably only somewhere in his late thirties, Mr. Eversole had an air of caring, world-weary wisdom about him, and he quickly assessed the situation with self-assured expertise, asking a few, seemingly casual questions and listening with focused intent.

Emergency medical technicians arrived in an ambulance and one pair promptly carted off her father, while another made a thorough evaluation of Beau's injuries. Eversole quietly conferred with the officers before firmly but gently steering Nicole into the hallway, where he explained that her father was being transported under arrest to an Arlington hospital where it would be determined if his blood alcohol level was sufficient to be toxic. Beau would also be leaving, with Mr. Eversole himself.

"I'll follow you," Nicole said, looking around for her bag and only belatedly remembering that she'd dropped it in the garage.

Linus Eversole laid a consoling hand on her arm and looked her square in the eye. "I'm sorry," he said, "that won't be possible."

The bottom seemed to drop out of Nicole's stomach, but she refused to accept the inevitable without an argument. "Wh-what do you mean? How will he get home?"

"Beau won't be coming home, Miss Archer, unless or until this can be proved a safe environment for him."

"B-but it is safe!"

"Circumstances have proved that is not the case, I'm afraid."

"You don't understand," Nicole argued frantically. "I've been taking care of my brother since our mom died! A-and with Dad gone, everything will be fine."

"I'm sorry," Mr. Eversole said again, "but even if your father is remanded to treatment, which I expect to be the case, he'll eventually return here, and that could place your brother in danger once again. So I'll be taking Beau to an emergency shelter. In a few days he'll be placed with a foster family until such time as the court can ascertain—"

"No!" Nicole cried, but Eversole went on calmly.

"If your family can be reunited." He patted her shoulder kindly, adding, "Reunification is always our ultimate goal."

"When?" Nicole demanded. "How soon?"

"A few months, most likely," he hedged carefully.

Nicole put her hands to her head. It was her worst nightmare come true, the very thing that she'd most feared. Beau would feel crushed, terrified and betrayed. And her father! She knew how angry he would be and whom he would blame. How had this happened? What about the promise she'd made her mom?

"But why can't he just stay with me?" she begged. "I won't leave him alone again, I swear."

"Miss Archer," the Child Advocate interrupted, "let's be frank. You're twenty years old. If you were thirty, after what's happened here tonight I'd still remove Beau from your care."

"But later?" she asked tremulously.

Eversole adopted a milder tone. "Please understand that Beau's welfare must be our only concern. Should your father prove unfit even after treatment, he would still be free to return to this house. Therefore, Beau must not."

"We'll go somewhere else," she promised.

"I'm afraid you'll have to meet a very high standard of proof to convince a court that you are capable of giving Beau the guidance and support he needs," Mr. Eversole told her, shaking his head.

She stared at him, horrified beyond words. He patted her shoulder and bowed his head to look into her tear-ravaged eyes.

"Do you need medical care? Were you injured?"

She couldn't seem to do anything more than shake her head.

"You'll be safe here tonight," he told her, "but you may not want to be alone in the house. Maybe you have a friend you can stay with?"

A friend? she thought. The first person who came to mind was Marcus. She knew there were others, but in that moment, she couldn't conjure up a single face or name besides his, and suddenly she wanted desperately to see him.

"You'll want to speak to your brother before he leaves," Linus Eversole said, turning and walking back into the living room. Nicole followed him robotically.

The EMTs had gone. Only one police officer remained, a woman with long blond hair fashioned into a thick plait at the nape of her neck. She held Beau by one arm as if to prevent his escape, but her eyes showed a sort of steely compassion.

Nicole went straight to her brother, took his hands in hers and cleared her throat, but her voice still trembled noticeably when she said, "You have to go with Mr. Eversole, Beau. I'll see you tomo—" She broke off and amended, "Soon. Very soon."

"I don't want to," he insisted, sounding panicked. "I have to stay with you!"

"I know," she said, trying and failing to smile. "We'll be together again soon. I'll talk to Marcus. He'll know what to do. But right now you have to go with Mr. Eversole."

Murmuring words of encouragement, Eversole steered Beau through the door with both hands. At the last moment, Beau turned his head, looking over his shoulder at Nicole with both fear and accusation in his eyes.

"It's going to be okay," she whispered, tears rolling down her face, but Beau was gone, and she was not at all convinced that her own words were true.

The officer stayed behind to ask her more questions, all of which Nicole answered, but then she had one of her own.

"What if we don't press charges? What will happen then?"

She was told that it was out of her hands. The state would press charges against their father on Beau's behalf. Apparently, having given statements, neither Nicole nor Beau had anything more to say about that part of it, which meant that Beau was now a ward of the state. Nicole was still crying about that when the other woman pressed a card into her hands, promised that someone would be in touch and took her leave. The moment the door closed behind her, Nicole ran to her car in the garage, just one thought in mind.

She had to see Marcus. Now.

In some ways the trip to the parsonage seemed to take forever, and in others it passed in the blink of an eye. She couldn't remember afterward how she'd actually gotten there, only that she seemed to have been traveling for a very long while. As she ran up the walk to the steps, she didn't think about the lateness of the hour or the possibility of being turned away. She only thought about Marcus and the need to see him. She didn't even wonder what help he might have to offer her or whether he could offer her any help at all. She only knew that in this moment of acute distress his was the face she most wanted to see, and she didn't bother to even wonder why.

Nicole ran to him without question or forethought, like a homing pigeon winging its way back to safety by instinct and nature alone. Despite her anger at Marcus in the past, despite the fact that she hadn't shared a single private word with him in weeks, her need of him was the most real thing in her world at the moment.

Marcus had just set aside the novel he was reading and turned out the bedside lamp when he heard the sound of a car in the drive. Telephone calls at this time of night were not terribly unusual, given how many medical emergencies seemed to arise after 11:00 p.m. Visitors were. Not much thought was required to realize that something was wrong.

He was out of bed, hastily but decently clad, by the time the first blow fell on his door. Flicking on lights as he passed through the house, he threw the dead bolt and opened up without even checking the peephole to see who was on the other side. It didn't matter who was there, only that someone needed his help. Unsurprisingly, that someone turned out to be Nicole, who literally fell into his arms, sobbing incoherently.

Every protective instinct he'd ever possessed rose swiftly inside him. Wrapping his arms around her, he guided her quickly into the living area, kicking the door closed behind them.

"What's wrong?" It didn't take much imagination to figure that her father was involved. "Did he hurt you?"

She was shaking her head when he dropped onto the sofa with her. "B-Beau," she gasped. "They t-took him!"

"Who took him?"

"P-police! E-Eversole."

Marcus knew Linus Eversole well, and just the mention of the name told him much. Linus was a dedicated advocate for children, a stern but caring man with excellent judgment who routinely tended to err on the side of caution.

Letting out a breath that he'd been holding much too long, Marcus tucked her head beneath his chin and gently rocked her, crooning comfort and gradually pulling the full story out of her. As she spoke, she calmed. By the time the facts had been disclosed, it was obvious that her very fine brain had started to function with its usual sharpness again.

"This is exactly why I didn't want to call the authorities," she stated hotly, emphasizing the thought with tiny pecks of her forefinger against one knee as she sat facing him on the end of the couch.

"You did the right thing," he assured her. "Your father didn't give you any other choice."

She brushed that aside with a sharp shake of her head. "The important thing now is getting Beau back. Tell me how."

Choosing his words very carefully, Marcus outlined what was going to happen and how she could petition the court for physical custody of her brother. "In other words," he summed up, "you have to prove that, as family, you are the most capable supervisor of your brother's welfare, despite your youth and this incident. I, of course, will speak to Child Protective Services on your behalf."

She reached for his hand and squeezed it at that, saying, "I'll do anything. I'll drop out of college and get a full-time job, if I have to."

"I'm not sure that's the best approach," he told her, unable to resist the urge to reach out and smooth back a strand of hair that had fallen forward and tangled in her damp, spiky eyelashes. It slipped through his fingers like dark silk. "You're too close to the end to think of quitting now, and I suspect that CPS would be better impressed if you got that degree."

"But I can't leave Beau with strangers that long!"

"You may not have to," he argued gently. "Listen, if worst comes to worst, I'll have myself certified as a foster parent and get Beau placed here."

Crying out, she literally launched herself at him, throwing her arms around his neck and rocking him back. His own arms closed around her reflexively.

"Thank you! Thank you! Oh, Marcus, I love you! I'll love you forever!"

He heard those final words with horror. Her declaration of love necessarily brought any expression of affection, however innocent, to a screeching halt. Marcus wasn't at all sure just how "innocent" his affectionate feelings were, anyway. Desperate to put distance between them, he all but shoved her away. Leaping to his feet, he tucked his hands safely into the rear pockets of his jeans.

Nicole's brow furrowed. Then understanding sent her warm chocolate gaze to her lap. She nodded as if to say that she'd gotten his message loud and clear. He felt an instant of relief, but when she lifted her head again what shone in her eyes made his breath catch in his throat. It was his worst nightmare and his fondest dream, and he felt immediate recoil along with the sharpest yearning imaginable.

"Nicole, I—"

"It's all right," she interrupted, giving her head a truncated shake. "I understand."

"I'm not sure you do," he began determinedly. "You're a lovely young woman, operative word here being young."

"I'm not *that* young, Marcus. I know how I feel."

He let that pass, pressing on with what had to be said. "It's not just your youth, Nicole. It's…" This was more difficult than he'd realized, but he took a deep breath and plunged on. "A minister has to be careful who he loves, Nicole, r-romantically, that is. He just can't casually involve himself with anyone."

"No one said anything about involvements, casual or otherwise," she pointed out, just an edge of testiness in her tone.

"What I'm trying to say is that a minister's spouse is

called by God just as surely as a minister is. A-And there are certain...*qualifications* necessary to the calling."

"Qualifications I obviously don't have," she said, lifting her chin and waving a hand as if completely unconcerned by this.

Marcus hurt for her, but he couldn't deny that he believed her correct in this. He licked his lips, trying to find words that wouldn't bring her greater pain.

"You're a lovely, vibrant—"

"Too vibrant, you mean," she put in, darting a glance at him.

"In ways, perhaps," he said carefully, "not that I'd have you change for the world. It's just, you are who you are, who you should be."

"And not for you," she murmured, looking away. "Yeah, I get it."

"I'm sorry," he whispered.

She swiped a hand across her eyes, huffed a deep breath, and shot a bleak smile at him. "No apology necessary."

He wanted to cry for her, and he wanted her out of there before anything else was said that they'd both surely regret.

"It's late," he said softly, pausing to clear his throat. "You need to get home and rest."

Nodding, she rose to her feet and slowly moved past him toward the door. It was only then that he realized she was wearing a hooded purple sweatshirt with the sleeves cut out over a red T-shirt and stirrup pants tucked into yellow galoshes. He was quite certain that it hadn't rained in days; yet he found the getup strangely charming. Nevertheless, it only pointed up the fact that Nicole Archer was not the woman for him. Imagine a minister's wife who wore yellow galoshes as a fashion statement!

He walked her to the door without actually walking *with*

her. When she paused and whirled around to face him, he literally skittered backward, his heart thumping.

Her gaze searching his, she quietly asked, "Aren't we going to pray?"

He couldn't believe he'd had to be reminded. "Of course! Absolutely." Bowing his head, he linked his hands together and put forth what he hoped was a pointed, eloquent prayer for peace of mind and healing, as well as guidance for those whose decisions could reunite brother and sister.

Nicole added her own spoken prayer to his, pleading for her brother's quick return home. She asked, too, that her father's alcoholism would be dealt with successfully, and she finished by thanking God for Marcus and all that he had meant to the lives of her and her brother. Marcus felt a stab of guilt at the latter. His mind was still reeling, and he was beginning to understand that he might have made a rash promise earlier.

It was much heavier of heart that Marcus returned to his solitary bed a few minutes later.

Nicole let herself into the darkened house and tiredly slung her bag onto the kitchen counter. She didn't bother to turn on a light. The dark suited her mood better, and she could navigate her childhood home with equal ease day or night, but the house now felt strangely alien, as if her presence alone was not enough to make it home. She stood a moment simply to gather her thoughts before she began the journey to her bedroom.

Two conclusions stood out. One, when she'd picked up that phone and dialed 9-1-1, she really hadn't had any other option. Even if she'd known that her father would pass out before he could do Beau any further harm, she'd still have made the call. That didn't mean she was happy with the results. She could say the same thing about her second conclusion, which was that, despite everything, she loved Marcus Wheeler with all her heart.

Sadly, Marcus didn't feel the same way about her. That much was painfully obvious, but it changed nothing, really. No matter what he felt—or didn't feel—for her, she loved him. Deep down, she'd known it for some time, but in the back of her mind she'd assumed that he would discover it for himself when the time was right. Now she knew there wouldn't be a right time for them.

It hardly seemed to matter at the moment, but she knew that the numbness overlaying her heartbreak wouldn't last forever. She was right about that. After falling into an exhausted, uneasy sleep, she woke sobbing hours later. Curling into a fetal position, she wept for every loss—her mother, her brother, Marcus, even her father. Grief literally swamped her. At length, she began to fear it would drown her. That was when she began to cry out to God.

Day came. She didn't even think about getting up or going to class. Instead, she sprawled on her face and spoke into the mattress as if she were speaking straight into God's ear. Eventually, she began to hear—sense, really—His answer.

There was no going back from here. All she could do was deal with what she had. Like it or not, keeping her promises now meant dealing with the state, so that's what she would do.

She faced a few other unhappy facts. For one thing, she and Beau might have to live apart for some time. That didn't mean she would abandon him. Quite the opposite. She'd work every moment for reunification, and in the meantime she'd spend every possible minute with him.

Loving Marcus was another fact of her life, unchanged by the knowledge that Marcus didn't love her. So be it. She felt how she felt; his feelings were his business. She happened to think that she'd make a fine minister's wife, so long as that minister was Marcus, of course. But what difference did it make when he didn't feel the same way? He owed her nothing, least of all an emotion he didn't possess. On the other hand, she owed him much. Not only had he done his best to help them, he'd been proven absolutely right in his arguments and warnings.

She had what she had, and she had to learn to deal with it. She came to one other conclusion, then, and this one at least gave her some comfort. What God willed, He would give her the strength and acceptance needed to live with. All she could do was to go on fighting for what was left of her family, knowing that the outcome rested solely in God's hands.

Marcus tossed and turned throughout the night, deeply troubled. No matter how he looked at it, he couldn't convince himself that following his heart was right. Nicole was not the woman for him. Oh, he could see them together well enough, with entirely too much ease, in fact, but he couldn't see Nicole as a pastor's wife.

As he'd told her, it wasn't just her youth, which time would remedy soon enough. It was her exuberance, her flamboyance, her eccentricity, none of which he would see changed. Nicole was who she was, perfect and whole as God had made her, but not right for the difficult role of a minister's wife. Therefore, it only stood to reason that she couldn't be for him. He'd known it all along.

He couldn't help asking himself what would happen to her fledgling faith after this, though. Would she blame God as her father had blamed God for her mother's death? Marcus couldn't bear the thought of that. Yet, what could he do about it?

No one could sustain another's faith. That, ultimately,

was the personal responsibility of every individual. But, as an old seminary professor of his had used to say, a pastor could go a long way toward destroying the faith of another. He very much feared that he had become just such a pastor to her.

It seemed to him that whatever he did, he was bound to fail in this situation, and he supposed that was just recompense for his inability to control his wayward heart. By offering to take Beau, he had put himself into a no-win situation. He couldn't depress her hopes for the two of them and at the same time maintain a close personal relationship through his care of her young brother.

How could he bring Beau into his house and deny Nicole easy, frequent access? Yet, under the circumstances, how could he maintain any but the most cursory contact with her? He thought of the past lonely weeks when he'd tried to do just that, and something inside him shriveled with dread. It came down to this: rescind his promise to take Beau or risk becoming more involved with Nicole than was wise for either of them. Either way, his ministry suffered.

Morning came with Marcus no closer to resolving the debate with himself. He finally concluded that he would have to go outside himself for another perspective. Perhaps a female perspective was what was needed here. Fortunately, God had given him excellent resources in that regard.

As soon as it was decently acceptable to do so, he called his sisters and invited himself to breakfast at Jolie's house.

Chapter Eleven

Marcus shoved a hand through his hair. "I can't believe I let it come to this."

"Hey," Jolie said, reaching across the table to clasp his hand with hers. "You haven't done anything wrong."

"That's right," Connie added, returning to the kitchen table with a fresh cup of coffee. "All you've done is try to help and be yourself."

"That doesn't matter. What matters is what I do about Nicole."

"What do you want to do?" Jolie asked.

Closing his eyes, Marcus sighed richly and said, "The right thing." He didn't say what he wished the right thing could be.

"Do you know what that is?" Connie asked softly.

Marcus looked down at his hands. "Yes. That is, I—I think so. The real problem is that I just don't see how I can possibly take custody of Beau and derail this...this..." He couldn't bring himself to say the word *infatuation*. What he'd seen in her eyes last night deserved something more than that, which made it all the worse.

"I don't think you can," Connie said after a moment. "If

you take custody of Beau, you're just going to wind up hurting Nicole even more in the long run."

"I agree," Jolie said. "Unless, that is, you *want* to encourage her."

Marcus shot her an appalled look, exclaiming, "No! No, of course I don't *want* to encourage her." At least he didn't want to want to encourage her.

"Then I think you have to back out of your offer to take Beau," Jolie said gently.

"I know that you've given your word," Connie added, "but in this case, it's only wise not to invite more misunderstanding."

Reluctantly, Marcus agreed. "You're both right. It's the only solution, but I feel so guilty because I know she'd rest easier if he was with someone she could trust, someone she's familiar with."

"Let me talk to Ovida and Larry," Jolie suggested. "I'm betting they'll offer to step in, but if they don't, I'll ask them to consider it."

"That sounds like a reasonable solution," Connie said brightly.

Marcus thought about it and really couldn't see any better answer. Finally, he nodded. "I'd appreciate it if you wouldn't say anything about my situation to the Cutlers though. I don't want to embarrass Nicole. She doesn't deserve that."

Jolie glanced at Connie before aiming an understanding smile at her brother. "Sure. Don't worry about it. I'll be very circumspect."

That, Marcus realized, was all he could really do for Nicole in this. He only hoped that she and Beau would be more enthusiastic about this idea than he felt himself.

Jolie absently rubbed her distended belly, specifically that spot where little Aaron Lawrence liked to kick his mommy.

As May approached, with the baby's delivery scheduled for late June, it was getting very crowded in there, but Jolie wasn't thinking about that at the moment. What she was thinking spilled from her lips the moment Connie walked back into the room, having seen their brother on his way.

"Do you think we gave him the right advice?"

"I think we gave him the only advice, and I think he knows it, too."

"That's it, though," Jolie said, wrinkling her nose. "Marcus knew perfectly well what he had to do, yet he came to us for affirmation. Makes me wonder if he really wants to do it."

"Well, of course, he doesn't *want* to do it," Connie said.

"Yes, but what if he doesn't want to do it because he cares for her more than he wants to admit? I mean, what if she's the one?"

Connie stared at her as if she'd grown a second head. "The one? For Marcus?" Folding her arms, she pursed her lips in consideration. "I don't see it. A minister's wife must be sedate and mature. Nicole is…well, Nicole. I mean, she's adorable, but she's just not *suit*able."

Jolie leaned back, trying to ease the tingle in her rib where the little rascal had gotten in a particularly smart blow, and looked up at her baby sister. "You said that about someone else not so long ago, as I recall. You."

Connie shrugged helplessly. She *had* thought that about herself. Of course, she had. How could an ex-con—no matter that she wasn't guilty of an actual crime—be a suitable wife for an upstanding man like Kendal Oakes? Yet, she no longer doubted that God Himself had picked her for Kendal and vice versa. Still, Kendal was a financier, not a minister.

"I trust," she said, "that God will work it out. Don't you?"

Jolie smiled. "Yes. You know I do. All I'm saying is, don't be surprised if it doesn't work out like we think it should."

"I'm sorry," Marcus said, standing in the middle of her living room. "I should never have made that promise."

Nicole looked stunned. Her eyes were swollen and red, her mannerisms listless and slow. She wore drab sweats and her hair hung in a tangle down her back. He wanted nothing so much as to take her in his arms and tell her that everything would be okay, but instead he slid his hands into the pockets of his pleated slacks, cringing inwardly with shame for having gone back on his word.

What else could he do, though? He'd prayed and prayed for an alternative solution, and he just couldn't see anything between risking romantic involvement with Nicole and this difficult course of action.

"But I've already told Beau that he would be with you," she said in a small, perplexed voice.

"I'm sorry, Nicole," Marcus said again, feeling helpless. "I'm just not comfortable with the arrangement now."

"Because I'm in love with you," she surmised softly.

For a moment Marcus couldn't seem to breathe. He felt splintered, one part glad, one part appalled, one part proud, one part frightened, one part certain, one part doubting. He couldn't think what to say at first; then he simply said, "Yes."

"I know you don't feel the same," she told him, beseeching him with her gaze. "I don't expect anything from you."

Except that I keep my promise, he thought miserably. All her expectations, it seemed, were for Beau, and that almost convinced him that moving Beau in with him wouldn't be courting disaster. Then she showed him the folly of that with one whispered thought.

"Of course, if you should change your mind then—"

He brought a hand up swiftly, cutting her off. She bit her lip, and he used the hand to bracket his temples with thumb and forefinger, swallowing. "It's best if we limit our contact, I think. You and me, I mean. I want to be here for Beau. I intend to be here for Beau, but…"

"You'd rather not see me," she said for him.

Something clinched inside his chest. He looked down at his feet. "I think that's best."

Nicole sighed, walked over to the sofa and collapsed onto it. Marcus hesitated, then went over and lowered himself onto the edge of the love seat that now sat perpendicular to the end of the sofa in the middle of the living room floor. Leaning forward, he braced his elbows against his knees and clasped his hands together.

"I know you're disappointed," he said, "but we've worked out a solution to keep Beau from going to a foster home that you don't know or trust."

"We?"

"Myself, a fellow named Jonathan Bertrand, who's a supervisor at CPS, and the Cutlers."

Nicole sat up a little straighter. "Ovida and Larry?"

Marcus nodded. "They've volunteered to get themselves certified and take Beau."

Nicole swallowed and nodded. "At least I won't have to tell him that he's got to stay with strangers."

"I'll speak to him about it if you prefer," Marcus offered, but she shook her head, slipping him a glance from the corners of her eyes.

"Better let me."

"You think he'll be angry?" Marcus surmised.

"He's already angry."

"Angry with me, then," Marcus clarified.

She carefully avoided his gaze. "I—I'd just rather he didn't know about…"

Marcus swallowed, the back of his throat burning. "I understand."

She looked up sharply. "Do the Cutlers know why you backed out?"

Marcus shook his head. "No, only that Beau needs a place to stay and that you and he both would feel better if it was with someone you know and trust."

Nicole seemed relieved about that, and he was glad that he could give her that much, at least. He glanced around the living room, commenting, "You've moved the furniture."

"Yes, among other things."

"I like it."

"I still have work to do before the official home visit," she said, lifting her chin. "I called Julia Timmons first thing this morning and asked her advice about that."

"Julia Timmons?" he asked, curious.

"She's the caseworker who came by that time you called CPS."

"I see. I hope she's been helpful."

"Yes."

"I'm glad. I've felt bad about that, but maybe it was for the best, after all."

"Maybe so. I like to think that God's working everything out, you know, and that she's part of it, even though it didn't seem that way at the time."

Marcus heaved a great, silent sigh of relief. "I'm so glad to hear you say that. I may have failed you, Nicole, but God never will."

"You haven't failed me," she insisted, leaning forward and copying his position. "It's not your fault that you don't feel the same way I do."

It was as if a hot poker prodded him. He shot up to his feet without even realizing he was going to do it. "Please don't try to absolve me from responsibility!"

"There's no responsibility to be absolved from," she declared. "It's no one's fault, Marcus. It just *is*. I would change it if I could, you know, for Beau's sake, if nothing else, but I realized a long time ago that what can't be changed has to be endured."

Endured, he thought, twisting with an emotional agony unlike any he'd ever felt before. How much was she supposed to go through in her life? That he had given her one more disappointment to be suffered was a pain that *he* would have to live with, which seemed both just and at the same time terribly unfair.

"I'm sorry," he told her. "I—I really just have to go now."

She rose to see him out. He fairly bolted for the door. Once there, though, he found he couldn't leave without offering her something in parting.

"You must know," he said, standing in her open doorway with one hand firmly gripping the knob, "that I wish you only the best." She managed a weak smile, and his chest tightened. There was a heaviness behind his face that he didn't immediately identify with tears until he turned his back on her. "You'll be in my prayers," he told her, and then he walked resolutely away.

"Goodbye, Marcus," she whispered, pushing the door closed behind him. His face was wet with regret by the time he reached his car.

The first day of May was gloriously beautiful with the kind of perfect weather that made sunlight seem crystalline and the air as soft as velvet. The vegetation had turned a green so deep and rich that it hurt the eyes, and the sky was the clearest blue. Birdsong could be heard even where there were no trees, and the great Metroplex area of Dallas-Fort Worth seemed to be at peace with itself. It seemed ironic that such a day should be the stage for one of the most horrific moments of Nicole's life.

She sat beside her brother in the small, informal courtroom and bit her lip as he threw himself facedown over the great blond table and sobbed his heart out, while the judge, a kindly middle-aged woman who wore a lace collar with her black robe, swept from the room.

"It really is for the best," Julia Timmons said gently about the judge's decision to place Beau with Larry and Ovida Cutler until Dillard was judged to be a fit parent or Nicole finished college and was employed full-time.

Short and plump and somewhere in the vicinity of thirty, Mrs. Timmons stood in her ill-fitting suit, clutching her briefcase in one hand, and offered Nicole a crumpled tissue. Until that moment, Nicole hadn't even realized that she was crying, too. All that had happened had left her so numb and drained that she was barely even aware of her surroundings anymore.

Logically, she had known that she was taking a risk by pressing for a quick decision, especially since she couldn't afford legal representation, but Beau was so unhappy with the situation that she'd felt she had no other option. It wasn't as if the Cutlers hadn't done everything in their power to make him comfortable in their home. It was just that it wasn't his home. Except that now it had to be.

Ovida was trying to comfort Beau, and he was ignoring her, ungrateful brat that he had become lately. But Nicole couldn't really blame him. Their lives had been turned upside down and inside out. She'd be angry, too, if she could muster the energy. Sighing, she leaned forward and slipped her arms about her brother's torso, tugging him back into an upright position in his chair.

"It's all right," she said softly, keeping her mouth close to his ear. "It isn't as if we aren't going to be seeing lots of each other. We're both safe, and you're getting the counseling that you need."

"I don't want stupid counseling," Beau grumbled, sniffing and wiping his eyes with the back of his hand. "What does that guy know anyway?"

"More than you think, I'm sure," Nicole told him. "Besides, it won't be that long. This semester ends in a couple weeks, and the new one starts in a month. I'll be finished by the end of the summer."

Provided I can come up with enough money to get enrolled and don't flunk anything, she added silently. Fearing this very outcome to today's proceeding, she had arranged to take more than a full course load during the short summer semester. Instead of taking the summer off to work, she would instead finish her degree early, provided she could come up with the tuition, didn't fail any of her classes and could find an internship.

It was going to be a formidable amount of work, but she dared not cut back on her hours at her job. Things were tight financially as it was. Nevertheless, there were only so many hours in a day. She didn't know how she was going manage, but she had to try, for Beau's sake. The sooner she was out of school, the sooner she could convince the court to name her as his guardian.

If she could find an internship that paid, that would help immensely. If not... She couldn't bear to think of disappointing Beau again, but all she could do was her best and trust God for the rest. Meanwhile, Beau was safe with the Cutlers, if not happy, and her father was drying out, by mandate of the court and courtesy of the state of Texas, in a hospital in Terrell. At least she didn't have to worry about him right now.

If only Beau could be reconciled to living in the Cutler home, everything would be easier, but he complained that he

felt lost amongst the multitude of Cutlers and that Larry and
Ovida were "too old." Worse, he'd had to change schools, so
he didn't even have his two best buddies around anymore.
He even complained that the Cutlers' church was too big.

Nicole knew exactly how he felt. Truthfully, she still felt
like a stranger in the big Fort Worth church where she went
with the Cutlers on those Sunday mornings when she could
manage it. She was at fault, she knew. The services were
fine, better than fine, really. She just didn't belong. She belonged where Marcus was, and she suspected that Beau felt
the same way. Marcus Wheeler seemed to have left a huge
hole in both their lives.

It hurt terribly that he hadn't come to the hearing today,
but she shouldn't have expected it. She'd told herself not to
expect it. Yet, somehow she had.

Beau didn't understand why Marcus hadn't taken him.
Nicole had tried to explain that it was her fault, but because
she hadn't given him any of the details, Beau was not exactly accepting of that. She didn't know what she could do
about it. She didn't know what she could do about anything
anymore.

Sometimes she felt like snapping at Beau that her life
was no picnic, either. She hated being alone in the house.
She missed him. She missed Marcus. She missed church.
Oddly, she missed her mother more than before. She even
missed their father.

It was so bad that at times Nicole worried that if Beau did
adjust to his new surroundings, they would grow apart. Of
course, she wanted him to be happy, but Beau was all she
had, and she was beginning to understand that she wouldn't
have him forever.

Beau would grow up. One day he'd even get married.
Nicole felt suddenly as if time was running out, but how
could that be when autumn still seemed so very distant?

* * *

The month of May was nine days old when Marcus could no longer stay away. He didn't dare go to Nicole, but he couldn't convince himself that he didn't bear a certain responsibility to the Archers, either. So he went to Beau.

When Ovida let him into her chintz-upholstered house, he could hear the television playing softly in the den. The Cutler siblings had banded together to purchase a big-screen set for Larry the Christmas before last, the very Christmas when Vince had proposed to Jolie, and it had become the family joke that Larry really liked to demonstrate his appreciation for that gift.

Marcus wondered if Beau found as much to like on TV as his foster father did. Apparently not, since Ovida walked him back to the boy's bedroom.

"How's it going?" he asked on the way.

She shrugged, frowning. "I know we're a couple of old fuddy-duddies compared to Nicole, but he won't even give us a chance." She sighed, adding, "Ah, well, it hasn't been that long. The counselor says some anger and bitterness is to be expected at this stage."

"I hope you know what a good thing you're doing," Marcus told her.

"Well, our intentions are good," she conceded wryly, "but we'll have to wait and see what the results are."

"God has a plan," Marcus assured her.

"He surely does," Ovida replied. "Now if we can just keep from mucking it up."

Marcus felt that he'd already done that.

They stopped in front of a closed door. Ovida tapped with her knuckle, then opened up and stuck her head inside.

"You have company, hon."

"Nicole?"

The desperate sound of it tore at Marcus's heart. Marcus knew just how the boy felt.

He hadn't been able to keep from looking for her on Sunday, even though he'd known she wouldn't be there. They must keep a certain distance, but the thought of never seeing her again was alarmingly painful. He'd tried to convince himself that in a few more weeks or months her feelings would fade and they could begin to gradually rebuild their friendship, but he didn't really believe it. He knew somehow that they would never be simply friends, which meant that they would never be anything again. That, undoubtedly, made his being here pretty stupid, but he couldn't figure out how not to be.

"Hello, Beau," he said, pushing the door wider.

For an instant, hopeful welcome lit the boy's eyes, but it quickly dimmed, leaving him sullen and resentful.

"What do *you* want?"

"Beau!" Ovida scolded mildly.

Sensing that would do more harm than good, Marcus sent her a loaded smile, asking, "Could you excuse us?"

Reluctantly, she nodded and went on her way. Marcus didn't wait to be invited in, he simply stepped into the room and closed the door behind him. It was rough going for the next hour or so.

Fort Worth wasn't so far away from Dalworthington Gardens, but it might as well have been the moon. Beau complained about school and having to leave his friends and not being able to give guitar lessons at the community center anymore. Nobody at the immense youth group at the Cutler's church was friendly, he claimed, and who wanted to watch sports all the time or play golf or dominoes or do any of the other stuff that Larry and Ovida Cutler did?

"At least my granddad played the guitar and went fishing," Beau huffed, folding his arms mulishly.

"And it doesn't matter to you at all that Larry and Ovida have opened their home so you don't have to live with total strangers?"

"They wouldn't have to if you had," Beau accused. Then suddenly tears filled his eyes.

Marcus took that as his due. He sat down next to the boy and looped an arm around his shoulders, knowing how lost and confused Beau must feel. Marcus remembered so well how he'd felt after he and his sisters had gone into foster care. The adjustment had been agonizing but unavoidable.

Yet, there had been other options for Beau. If Marcus had taken him, he could have stayed in his old school and carried on with his life pretty much as usual.

"I'm sorry, Beau," Marcus said earnestly. "I let you down."

The boy turned his face into the hollow of Marcus's shoulder and sobbed, "Why did this have to happen?"

Marcus couldn't answer that, so he talked to Beau about his own problems in adjusting to life without his mom and sisters. He spoke, as well, about Jolie's rebellious cynicism and Connie's neediness, which had landed her in an abusive relationship and, eventually, jail.

"What's that got to do with anything?" Beau wanted to know. "Me and Nic aren't you and your sisters. We're old enough to take care of each other."

Nothing Marcus said, no correlation that he was able to draw, made any difference with Beau. Finally, Marcus simply advised Beau to give his own situation time, but he could tell that didn't go over very well, either. Thirteen was too young to appreciate the fleetness of time, and Beau's judgment was heavily colored by his anger. He had a lot to be angry about.

"Yeah, I know," he grumbled. "Wait until Nicole gets out of school."

"You don't think you'll go back home after your dad gets out of rehab?" Marcus asked.

Beau just rolled his eyes. "He doesn't care about us, and I'm not giving him another chance to beat me."

Marcus couldn't blame the boy for feeling that way, but he was praying that Dillard would get sober and realize the value of being a father before it was too late. That, it seemed to him, would be best for everyone, but only God and Dillard could make it happen. Marcus chafed at his own helplessness. Right now, praying seemed to be about the only thing that he could do, and for the first time it didn't seem like enough. But it was either that or inflict his rejection on Nicole daily. Or marry Nicole and take Beau into the house with them.

He was shocked by how appealing that idea was.

Appealing but completely inappropriate.

He could see it quite clearly, the three of them in his little house, Beau in Connie and Russ's old room, he and Nicole in his. He smiled, thinking about what she must go through to get herself dressed in the mornings. How did she ever come up with those outrageous costumes?

His smile died, because though he could so easily envision making a place for Nicole and Beau in his house and heart, he couldn't see Nicole standing next to him at the sanctuary door, demurely shaking hands as people filed past them.

"How is she?" he heard himself ask, fearing that really might be why he'd come.

Beau shrugged. "How would I know? She's working and in school all the time, and when she does come over, she doesn't tell me nothing because she doesn't want me to worry. I guess I might as well get used to not seeing her, 'cause she's trying to finish up early by going to school this summer. Then in the fall, we'll get our own place."

The more he talked about that, the more Marcus realized that Beau was holding on to the picture of what he wanted the future to look like, not realizing how it resembled the past he'd described to Marcus.

"Me and Nic could go to Tahlequah," he theorized, "and live on the river. It wouldn't take much to fix up that old cabin, I bet."

Marcus didn't bother explaining how unlikely such a move would be, especially if the courts did not deem Nicole an adequate custodian for her brother. Instead, he promised to return soon, prodded Beau into joining him in a short prayer, and left before Ovida could invite him to stay for dinner.

Marcus didn't think he could handle that. He probably deserved to sit across the table from a determined-to-be-miserable Beau, but he just didn't have the heart for it.

Lately, Marcus grimly admitted to himself, he just wasn't very good at his job. But he would do better. He had to. Otherwise, what was the point in anything?

Please, God, he prayed, *help me do better.*

It had become his personal litany, and it was starting to take on the feel of desperation.

Chapter Twelve

Big whoop, Nicole thought morosely, sitting across the desk from her academic advisor. That pretty much summed up Nicole's enthusiasm about the possibility of landing one of the two—count them, one, two—paid internships remaining on the advisor's list of unfilled summer positions.

They were the same words that Beau had used about the end of the school year, which was exactly one week away. He hated the Fort Worth school, but apparently he hated the prospect of a "do nothing" summer even more.

Nicole figured Beau's chances of having an exciting summer were far stronger than her chances of landing one of those internships, but she had to try. Besides, as she'd often reminded herself lately, anything was possible with God.

"This one's a plum," the advisor said. A brusque, sixty-something woman with short, steel-gray hair and ink-stained fingertips, she slid a sheet of paper across the desk for Nicole. "It's only minimum wage, but because they have a preschool and kindergarten they offer classroom as well as day care experience. I can't imagine why it's still open, frankly. It's usually one of the first to fill."

Nicole leaned forward hopefully. Classroom and day care

experience, as well as a paycheck. *Please, God,* she silently prayed. Then the words printed on the top of the page leaped out at her: First Church Pantego Day Care. She sat back with a stifled gasp, closing her eyes.

"What is it, hon? Something wrong?"

"No, um, I know that church, that's all."

The advisor reached for the phone, chirping, "Excellent! Familiarity always helps." She began pecking in numbers.

Nicole sat forward again. "Oh, uh, I—"

The advisor stalled her with a lifted index finger, her attention centered on the telephone receiver pressed to her ear. After a moment, she smiled.

"Hello, Carlita! It's Linda Marsh, with the Early Childhood Development department at UTA. Any chance you're ready to start interviewing for that summer internship? I have a candidate who says she's familiar with your program." She nodded at Nicole, conveying Carlita's answer to her question, then went back to the conversation. "Her name's Nicole Archer. You know her? Excellent!" The advisor consulted Nicole's schedule and added, "She's available Thursday afternoons for an interview."

Mrs. Marsh covered the mouthpiece with the palm of one hand and addressed Nicole. "Is tomorrow good for you?"

"Yes, but—"

"Tomorrow at three," the woman said into the telephone, jotting the date and time on the top of the sheet of paper in front of Nicole.

Nicole felt her heart sink. It was department policy not to schedule more than one interview at a time in order to give everyone an equal shot at the positions available. Since there were always more applicants than paid internships—half a dozen early childhood development students waited in the outer office at that very moment—it was only fair, but in this case it undoubtedly meant that Nicole had just lost her best shot.

"Now," Mrs. Marsh said, hanging up the telephone and folding her arms against the top of the desk as she swept her gaze over Nicole, "let's talk about the interview. Wardrobe is one of the best ways to make a good impression."

Nicole made a pretense of paying attention as the adviser droned on about what not to wear, which pretty much covered everything Nicole owned, but she was only listening with half an ear. What difference did it make when the pastor at First Church Pantego was only going to take one look at the name of the applicant and strike it from the list? Still, she reminded herself as she folded the paper and tucked it into her bag, she had to show up for the interview. Otherwise, she wouldn't get a chance at an internship next semester. Those were the rules.

Maybe Marcus didn't have anything to do with the hiring at the day care center? Besides, chances were she'd at least catch sight of him while she was there. It was embarrassing how much she missed just looking at him. Meanwhile, her hopes for finishing her degree this summer and gaining custody of her brother by fall were melting. Her only hope now was that the judge would take into consideration that the internship was just a formality and accept her finished transcript as proof of her degree.

If that didn't work, she'd file for custody when she turned twenty-one in October. That was better than having to tell Beau that it would be at least the end of the winter term before he could come home with her.

It would work out, Nicole told herself. She had to believe that God was in control of the situation. Because she hadn't found any other way to cope.

Marcus laced his fingers behind his head and leaned back in his desk chair, smiling at Nina Upconn, or "Miss Up," as the day care staffers fondly referred to her. Marcus could never be sure if the nickname referred to her cheerful attitude or the short, dishwater blond hair which always stuck up somewhere, giving one the impression that she'd fallen out of bed the very moment before meeting.

At thirty-nine, Nina was not a Miss. Indeed, she was married and the mother of two teenagers. She was also a cheerful improvement over the last director of the day care center, whose negative attitude toward his niece, Larissa, and her admittedly challenging problems had led to a mutually agreed upon departure. Given, Nina wasn't the most efficient director the day care had ever enjoyed, but she was beloved by all, which was why Marcus tended to cut her a good deal of slack.

"I know I should have taken care of this already," she was saying about the hiring of a summer intern, "and I do appreciate you helping to expedite the matter by agreeing to simultaneous interviews."

"No problem," Marcus replied.

The usual routine was for the day care director to interview prospective interns on her own, weed out those she didn't like and arrange for Marcus to interview the front-runners. Then the two of them would make the final selection together. This way would work just as well, though.

They'd interview the prospects together over the next two days, compare notes and make a firm decision by Monday. With seven applicants so far, it made for two full days of interviews, but Marcus didn't mind. He'd always preferred keeping busy. More so now than ever. It helped keep his mind off other things. Like Nicole.

Why, he hadn't thought of her in, oh, maybe half an hour, Marcus realized ruefully. He'd begun to accept the fact that she would always be in his thoughts, but that brought him uncomfortably close to questioning God's intent. Or his own interpretation of it. As much from habit as conviction, he pushed the thought away and concentrated on the job at hand.

The two morning interviews went well enough if one discounted an irritating habit of smacking gum and a bad case of spring allergies. The first applicant after lunch was the lone male in the group. He was obviously more interested in the business end of things than the healthy development of children, but Marcus commended him for taking an in-the-trenches approach to learning the field before turning him down flat.

Then Nina handed Marcus the résumé for the next applicant and his heart stopped. For long minutes, he couldn't think, let alone digest the information printed on the sheet, but he didn't have to. He knew everything relevant there was to know about Nicole Archer.

True to form, she'd taken a unique approach to selling her abilities. The résumé was printed on vivid yellow paper with purple ink and a border of baby dolls and toy fire trucks against a background of rainbow stripes. Marcus quite liked it. The whole situation had a feeling of inevitability about it, and in one blindingly stupid and shockingly impulsive moment, he decided that if she walked in wearing anything approximating a normal outfit, he'd hire her on the spot.

She came in wearing red overalls, a tie-dyed T-shirt, candy-cane-striped socks and those ridiculous yellow galoshes, her hair up in pigtails. He could have wept. Instead he surprised himself by laughing and that seemed to put her at ease.

The happiest hour he'd known in weeks passed in the blink of an eye, and he knew Nina was going to pick Nicole before it was half over. He didn't have the heart to gainsay her, though he tried to talk himself into it that night, praying long and hard about the matter.

Friday's interviews were mere formalities. Marcus left it

to Nina to inform Nicole of their decision and sternly told himself that his contact with her would be severely limited. He suspected even then that he lied. On Sunday at church, Nina informed him how ecstatic Nicole had been, and he couldn't help smiling at the day care director's description of the scene.

"I thought she was going to fly right out of the room. She sprang up on her tiptoes and threw out her arms. 'Thank God!' she exclaimed." Nina chuckled and then she sighed. "Now all Nicole has to do is scrape together four hundred bucks to cover the cost of her books." Nina shook her head, revealing a patch of hair that stuck out at a forty-five degree angle from just below her crown. "That sweet kid. Do you think we could use the two hundred dollars we have remaining in our scholarship fund to help her? I know it usually goes to a graduating high school senior, but I think need should trump age, don't you?"

Marcus reached into his pocket for his wallet, nodding in agreement. "Here's the other two hundred," he said, marveling at how impulsive he'd become of late. It was his personal benevolence fund, the money he kept on him specifically for those in need whom he came across in the normal course of things. "Just don't tell her it came from me personally."

Nina literally snatched the cash from his hand, beaming ear to ear. "I like that kid!" she exclaimed. "I can't wait to work with her."

Me, too, thought Marcus. *Me, too.* Yet, he'd never stood on more dangerous ground ministerially.

Or was it that things were finally going right? Had he been wrong about this all along? Was that why God had suddenly thrust her back into his life like this?

He'd prayed repeatedly these past weeks that God would remove his feelings for Nicole and bring him someone else, someone more suited to his position, and he couldn't figure out why that wasn't happening. He was trying to be patient about it, and really, in an odd way, he was in no hurry.

He'd come to realize that his feelings for Nicole would not be easily dismissed, and some part of him so treasured those feelings that he was reluctant on several levels to let go of them. Yet, he sincerely wanted God's will in this. Anything less would be sheer disaster. He just didn't know anymore what God's will was.

He wasn't as certain now as he had once been that Nicole wasn't who God intended for him.

True, she didn't fit his idea of what a minister's wife should be, but was his interpretation of what God wanted in a minister's wife truly God's ideal? Or was it something he, Marcus, had made up from assumptions and arrogance? He didn't know anymore.

What he did know was that God is not a god of confusion. He never sets out to perplex and frustrate His children. Besides, Marcus seemed to have done that well enough all on his own. Perhaps it was time to forget his assumptions, set aside certainty and simply wait for God to make His will known.

Marcus felt something then that he hadn't even realized he'd been missing for a while. Hope.

Nicole slipped the sales receipt into her wallet and picked up the shopping bag with the heavy textbook inside. This was the last one, and the only one she hadn't been able to find as a used book. Still, she had $7.74 left over, enough for a ticket to the movie matinee this afternoon and a treat from the concession stand. Beau could pay his own way with the allowance that the Cutlers were giving him from the monthly stipend they received from the state.

Nicole wished nothing but blessings on Larry and Ovida Cutler. Instead of using the rest of the state money to pay

Beau's living expenses, as it was intended, they had opened a savings account for him, calling it his college fund. How Beau could remain so ungrateful and downright bratty she didn't understand, but so far as Nicole was concerned things were finally looking up.

Not only had Marcus not blackballed her, she'd landed the internship *and* a scholarship from the church to help buy her books for the semester. She'd already started the part-time job and loved the work, especially as it meant she saw Marcus every day.

Oh, it was only glimpses, to be sure. They hadn't actually spoken, and she didn't expect that they would. It was easier, frankly, if they kept their distance. Once she started classes again, on the first Monday in June, exactly one week from today, she wouldn't have very much time to think about him, so it was a good thing that she'd be carrying such a heavy load. Yes, she could definitely see the hand of God at work.

If only Beau could be happier about his situation, she could face the grueling summer ahead with an almost light heart, but he wouldn't even try. As she drove them both to the theater that afternoon, she remarked that they had never used to go to the movies. Beau grumbled that he didn't care about that, though he seemed to enjoy the movie itself well enough. Still, he whined when she dropped him off at the Cutlers' house.

"You're juicing me, Nicole. Don't you see that?"

Nicole sighed. "How have I 'juiced' you, Beau? Where's the betrayal in this? Things are going according to plan, if you haven't noticed."

"Something will mess it up," he grumbled, yanking on the door handle. "We'd be better off in Oklahoma."

It had become a recurrent theme with him. They could run off to Oklahoma, live in their grandparents' tumble-down old cabin and hide from the state of Texas indefinitely.

How he expected them to support themselves, let alone get him enrolled in school, was something he dismissed out of hand. Shaking her head, Nicole watched him trudge up the walk to the Cutlers' neat, boxy house. Ovida appeared in the doorway. Nicole waved and drove away, determined to be optimistic.

When she pulled into the driveway at home, she was struck by something odd. Her father's old rattletrap truck, which still sat nose-in almost against the garage door, seemed to be parked a few inches farther to the right than she remembered, but she dismissed the notion at once. The thing couldn't have moved by itself, after all.

Since it was warm out, she left the car parked next to the truck and let herself into the house through the front door, carrying her purse and the heavy textbook in its plastic shopping bag. She dumped everything on the kitchen counter and went to the refrigerator for a drink of cold water from the pitcher that she kept there during the warmer months.

The pitcher was empty. Only her father ever emptied the pitcher without refilling it before returning it to the refrigerator. Her heart skipped a beat, and that was when he spoke.

"You moved my furniture."

Nicole jumped and whirled around. Her father stood in the doorway to the hall, leaner than she'd last seen him and cleanly shaven. She clapped a hand to her chest, trying to still her galloping heart. One part of her was pleased; another was horrified.

"Daddy."

Dillard folded his arms and put his back to the door frame. "Long time no see, Nicole."

She ignored the razor sharpness of his tone. He was her father. She wanted to be glad to see him. "You look well."

"No thanks to you," he said bitterly. "Do you have any

idea what they put me through? Does it matter to you that I have a record now?"

"Daddy, please," she began. "I had no other choice."

He threw up one hand, exclaiming, "No other choice but to have me arrested! How's that?"

"You took a belt to Beau!" she pointed out.

"I didn't know what I was doing," he argued, as if that were an excuse. "And he wasn't even hurt. I asked, and they told me he had some bruises." He mimicked someone else then, saying, "'But that's not the point. Sobriety is the number-one goal.' They made me out to be some kind of monster!" He pointed a finger at her. "You made me out to be a monster. This is all *your* fault."

For the first time in a very long while, she lost her temper. "This is *your* fault, Daddy! I didn't pour alcohol down your throat and put a belt in your hand!"

"No, you called the cops!" he roared. "Now your brother's living in some foster home, and I'm branded a child abuser for the rest of my days! How do you think your mother would feel about that, Nicole Suzanne?"

"No better than she'd feel about you drinking yourself into oblivion and abandoning us!" she threw back at him.

"I never abandoned you!" he roared.

"Yes, you did!" she shouted right back. "Every time you opened a bottle and crawled inside it!"

He looked stunned, as if she'd struck him, but then his anger hardened into resolve. "Well, then," he said, suddenly as cold as he'd been hot the moment before. "You sure as shootin' don't want to be sharing a house with me."

Nicole felt the air leave her lungs in one sharp *whoosh.* "What do you mean?" He couldn't mean what she thought he did—except that he did mean it, of course.

He folded his arms again, saying calmly, "Your brother's

not here and not likely to be for some time, so it seems to me you don't have any right to be here, either."

"You're throwing me out?"

He hung his thumbs in his pockets and glared at her. "Isn't that what you did to me? Or tried to. But you forgot that this house and everything in it belongs to me."

She stared at him, barely able to believe it. "You're throwing me out." It was a statement this time, a statement he didn't refute.

After a long moment while the world turned upside down, Nicole numbly picked up her purse and the shopping bag. She saw the rest of her textbooks sitting in a neat stack on the kitchen table. She lurched over to them, gathered them up and turned blindly for the door, knowing that whatever happened this would never again be her home.

Her impulse was to go straight to Marcus, but the moment she realized where she was heading, she turned the car in another direction. Realizing that it would be upsetting to Beau, she didn't even consider going to the Cutlers in her present state. Instead, she just drove around until she could get hold of herself. It was some time before she could even begin to think rationally. When she passed a gas station, she realized that she was wasting precious fuel and pulled over. Calming finally, she tried to take a dispassionate look at things.

It shouldn't have surprised her that her father had come home. She'd been told that the program to which he'd been sent would last four to six weeks. It was thirty-five days since that awful night, exactly five weeks.

She had expected that he'd blame her. Yet, for some reason she'd convinced herself that once he was sober he'd actually be reasonable again. The anger was still there, though, and she'd begun to realize that until he dealt with his anger toward God, he would never be able to face life.

That was one lesson she supposed she ought to thank him for teaching her. At the moment, however, she was having a difficult time thanking him for anything.

Pushing away the hurt of his rejection, she rubbed her forehead and tried to take stock of her options. They were extremely limited. In the end, she went to her friend Kattie.

Kattie, short for Katrina, was a server at the same restaurant as Nicole. Two years older, she'd worked for a while before starting college and was able to afford a small studio apartment in an aging building near the campus in Arlington. At various points in the past, she'd tried to convince Nicole to share a larger apartment with her, but Nicole had always refused because she'd had Beau to worry about.

Kat was surprised to see her. Nicole didn't often stop by. As soon as she heard her story, Kattie offered to let Nicole camp out with her. She only had a twin bed to sleep in and was locked into a lease for another five months, but she offered Nicole her broken-down old couch. Nicole took it. What else could she do?

She couldn't bring herself to impose further on the Cutlers. They hadn't taken both Beau *and* her to raise. Going to Marcus was out of the question. Besides, she found that she didn't want anyone else to know what had happened just yet. Beau would have to know eventually, of course, but at the moment she was too embarrassed to talk about it. She was embarrassed for her father, embarrassed for herself and embarrassed for Beau. What kind of people lived the way they did?

It was time to live a different way. From now on, she determined, life would be lived on her terms. That meant with some dignity.

She wished she'd thought to pack some personal items before she'd walked out of her old life, but Kattie loaned her what she could. Kat's long, bone-thin frame didn't correspond too well with Nicole's shorter, shapelier one, but Nicole couldn't make herself go back to the house and beg her father for her own things.

For starters, she was afraid of what she might find. If her dad was drinking again, she didn't want to know. If he wasn't, that could be even worse. It was easy to justify and excuse the behavior of a drunk, not so easy to dismiss the considered words of a sober man.

She could make do. She was good at making do. Besides, she found much to be thankful for in this. At least she didn't have to worry about Beau. He was safe with the Cutlers, safer even than he had been with her. Meanwhile she would pray that her father would come to the Lord and keep going forward. She'd stick to the plan and trust God to work it all out. That, she realized, was what her mother would want her to do. One day, even Beau would see that the Lord God never abandoned His own.

Marcus stood outside the classroom door and peeked through the window set into the top half of it. Nicole sat cross-legged on the floor, holding a picture book open on her lap, while a scattered group of four-year-olds listened spellbound to every word she read. Suddenly feeling a presence at his side, Marcus stepped back, tempering his smile. Nina Upconn folded her arms knowingly. It wasn't the first time she'd caught him watching Nicole.

"Pastor," she said.

Marcus cleared his throat. "How is she? I mean, how is she doing?"

"Still doing fine," Nina told him, the glint in her eye said that she saw more than he wished her to.

He fought against blushing and adopted a caring, paternal tone. "She seems different lately. The clothes, I think."

"Mmm, more subdued," Nina concurred. She waggled an eyebrow. "Not her usual style."

So Nina had noticed, too. Well, of course she had. Who with functioning eyeballs wouldn't?

"Any idea why?" Marcus asked, faintly troubled.

Nina shook her head. "None. She just suddenly started wearing jeans and white T-shirts every day. Occasionally she wears something a little more colorful, but now that I think about it, it's always the same two or three things."

"Grass-green shirt, bright yellow tank," he said.

"Mmm-hmm, and once in a while a purple paisley print skirt."

"Sometimes she wears them all together," Marcus noted, smiling at the thought of her in yellow and green over purple paisley.

"And sometimes mixed with jeans and the white T-shirt," Nina confirmed.

"But always with the red shoes," Marcus murmured.

It was as if she only had the two outfits, but Marcus knew better than that. He'd never seen Nicole in the same outfit twice before the past couple of weeks. He knew because everything she wore was utterly unforgettable. Even now.

He wondered if he should speak to her about it, but the very thought made his heart pound and his palms sweat. It had been that way for some time, so he kept avoiding her, afraid of what he might say if he didn't.

"I've noticed you're dressing normally for a change. What gives?" Very endearing.

Or how about, *"I'm praying that I've been an idiot and misinterpreted God's will, but I'm still waiting to find out"?* Yeah, that would take care of everything.

Of course, he could always just declare the truth. *"I'm very much afraid that I've fallen in love with you, too. Now I'm trying to figure out what to do about it."*

He just wasn't ready for that. Yet. And he didn't know if he ever would be. Better to keep his mouth shut, which meant keeping his distance. Problem was, he didn't seem to be doing that very well, either, judging by the number of times he found himself standing where he was at the moment.

Even as Marcus took his leave of Nina and walked back to his office, he mused that it hadn't been so very long ago that he'd begged God for a wife, and now he was afraid to even think the word *wife*. Because when he thought about marriage, his next thought was invariably of Nicole. Maybe that was his answer. He just didn't know.

Whatever the answer was, Marcus was starting to think that God would have to smack him upside the head with it. Otherwise, how could he ever know that his own desires were not leading him astray?

"How've you been?" Marcus asked, keeping his tone bright.

Beau barely acknowledged his presence, shrugging as he picked out a desultory tune on the guitar. Stifling a sigh, Marcus tugged on the legs of his slacks and sat next to the boy on the sofa in the Cutler den. Ovida and Larry had gone into their bedroom and shut the door to give them privacy. Marcus didn't waste any time beating around the bush.

"Ovida and Larry are worried about you, Beau. You should have made the adjustment by now. Can't you see that they're doing everything they know how?"

Beau slammed the guitar down on the cushion beside him and slumped back. "I don't want them to do anything. I just want to go live with my sister!"

"Everybody understands that, Beau."

"Nobody understands anything!" Beau declared in a

strangled voice. "Not even Nicole! We were always going to get our own place anyway, so why not now?"

Marcus shook his head. "You know that isn't reasonable, Beau. Even if the court would allow it, Nicole can't afford—"

"But she's already got her own place!" Beau complained, folding his arms sullenly. "It's supposed to be with me, but instead she's moved in with someone else, and she says they don't have room for me."

For a moment Marcus couldn't do anything but stare at Beau. What he'd said just didn't compute. "I don't understand. Why would she move in with someone else?"

"She can't stay at the house with Dad," Beau told him, spreading his hands.

Marcus caught his breath. "Your father's back?"

Beau glanced at him worriedly. "Yeah, and he's been coming around here, even though he's not supposed to."

Marcus blinked. "I see." And he really was beginning to. Nicole was wearing the same two outfits all the time because that's all she had to wear. He wondered if Dillard had even given her a chance to pack a suitcase before he'd tossed her out. He was on his feet before he even realized he'd meant to be. "I'm sorry, Beau," he said. "I have to go."

Beau threw up his hands. "Go on," he said. "What do I care?"

He cared. Marcus saw it in his eyes. "I'll be back soon," he promised. "Just try to be patient a little longer."

"But what if they give me back to him?" Beau whispered, his greatest fear revealed.

Marcus wanted to tell him that wouldn't happen, but he couldn't. Instead he said, "Everything's going to work out. You'll see. God has it all under control."

Beau snorted. "That's what Nicole always says."

"Does she?" Marcus smiled to himself. "Well, she's right. Maybe you should start listening to her."

Maybe they should both start listening to her.

Chapter Thirteen

"I have something for you," Marcus said. "Could you come by the house when you're through here?"

Nicole bit her lip. She'd counted on having an hour or so to read before class, but it wouldn't be the first time she'd gone to class unprepared lately. Besides, it wasn't like Marcus to seek her out, let alone invite her over to his house. It had to be something important. She nodded and glanced over her shoulder at the children on the playground.

"I'm done here at noon."

Of course, he'd know that. He smiled, nodded and walked away before she could ask what was going on. She supposed she'd find out soon enough. Part of her was thrilled that he'd taken this step; an older, wiser part knew better than to get her hopes up. Marcus was a friend, nothing more. She turned back to the children in time to stop a particularly precocious little boy from jumping off the top of the jungle gym.

The rest of the morning passed in a blur. Nicole was dimly aware that she wasn't firing on all cylinders lately. The lack of sleep was getting to her. The long hours at school, the longer hours on her feet waiting tables and the all-too-fleeting ones when she tried to study didn't leave much time for sleep. The utter lack of privacy and the uncomfortable sofa at Kattie's didn't help, either. Some mornings it was all she could do to drag herself out of bed in time to get to the day care center by six.

She yawned as she climbed the few steps to Marcus's front porch. The door opened before she got to it, and Marcus stood there looking at her with what felt like mild rebuke.

"What?" she asked, stopping where she was.

He waved her in, saying nothing as he turned away from the door. She followed, curious and now a little timorous. Was she in some sort of trouble? If so, she wasn't sure she could handle that.

He led her into the living area or, rather, to it. The space was filled by a number of large boxes, *familiar* boxes.

"My things!" she exclaimed, turning to him with a dozen unspoken questions.

"You should have told me," he scolded mildly, bringing his hands to his hips.

She shook her head. "That he put me out? What good would that have done?"

Marcus lifted a hand as if it should be obvious. "You'd have had your clothes for one thing."

Nicole looked around her again, touched but troubled. What did she do now?

"Marcus," she said, "I appreciate this. I really do, and God knows I'll be glad to have something else to wear, but I don't have anyplace to put this!"

He blinked at her. "What do you mean? Don't you have a place to stay? Beau said—"

"I have a place to stay," she answered quickly, "but it's tiny, just a studio apartment. I don't even have a closet of my own." She flapped an arm helplessly. "I can't take all this. Kattie would have a cow!"

"Kattie is your roommate?" he ventured.

Nicole nodded. "It's her apartment."

"Ah, so she gets all of the closet?"

"What there is of it."

"Well, that is a problem," he said, folding his arms and lifting one hand to grasp his chin between thumb and forefinger. He shrugged. "Guess you'll have to leave it here."

"Oh, like you've got room for it."

"It can go in my garage. It was in your garage, I mean, your father's garage, until last night."

"Are you saying you have room for it in there?" she asked hopefully.

"For now. I don't put the car inside unless it's cold and wet. It's too small."

Nicole frowned. "Well, I guess I don't have a choice at the moment. I'll have it out before winter, I promise, even if I have to rent a storage locker."

"Don't worry about it," he told her. "Just take what you need for now, and the rest will be here when you're ready for it."

Nicole nodded, sudden tears welling into her eyes. She gulped. "Thank you for this, Marcus. I was afraid he might destroy everything or give it away."

"I don't think so," Marcus mused. "Oh, he seemed angry, yes. Gruff, certainly. But...I don't know...hurt, too, I think."

"Was he drinking?" she asked warily.

"I don't think so, but we didn't talk long. I told him I'd come for your things, and he led me straight to the garage, then he went back into the house, and that was it. I knocked on the door to tell him that I'd have to go borrow my brother-in-law's pickup truck to get everything, but he ignored me.

He didn't answer the door again when I went back, so I helped myself and left again."

Nicole considered the information. "Larry Cutler doesn't think he's drinking, either. My dad's been going over there, trying to see Beau. Of course, the Cutlers haven't let him, but it worries Beau all the same."

"I know."

"Do you think he can get Beau back?" she asked worriedly.

Marcus bowed his head. "I don't know. Maybe. Not right away, though."

"How long do you think we have?"

He shrugged. "Six months, maybe. Don't hold me to that, though."

"Six months," she whispered, thinking that she'd be out of school and more gainfully employed by then. She closed her eyes in a quick prayer.

"I can ask," Marcus said, "try to get a better idea for you. I have friends at CPS, you know."

"Would you?"

"Absolutely."

"Oh, thank you, Marcus. For that and this." She flipped a hand at the boxes. Then she looked him in the eye and said what had needed saying for some time. "And thank you for the internship."

He shook his head. "Now that wasn't my doing. Nina does the hiring at the day care center."

"With your approval," she said. "Nina told me."

He inclined his head. "You were the best candidate. Nina saw that. I agreed."

"You didn't have to agree," she argued softly.

"Yes, I did," he responded simply.

Nicole looked away. No doubt he thought he owed her somehow, just because he didn't feel for her what she felt for him. It was nonsense, but she didn't argue with him; she was too grateful. Instead, she looked over the boxes, deciding which one to look in first. That was when she realized there were more boxes than there should have been.

"These two don't belong," she said, pointing out two smaller ones she'd never seen before.

"Funny you should say that," Marcus commented, "because I could swear those two weren't there the first time I looked in the garage."

"But they were when you came back with the truck?" she asked.

"Right."

Nicole shifted one of the boxes and opened it. Only moments were required to recognize the contents of the dresser and closet in her bedroom. It looked as if her father had dumped the dresser drawers one by one, but some care had been taken to create order with what had come from the closet. She was somewhat surprised. Dillard had never put himself out this much for someone else since her mom had died. Nicole sat on the floor, considering, but then she shrugged. What difference did it make? She had only to remember what had happened the last time she'd trusted that he'd changed.

Marcus crouched next to her. "Something wrong?"

"Nope." She indicated the two boxes from her bedroom, saying, "I'll take these two. They'll fit in the back of my car."

Marcus shifted, grasped the first box in a bear hug and rose. "If you'll give me your keys, I'll come back for the other in a minute."

"No need," she said, getting up to gather in the second box herself. "We'll get these in the car, then I'll help you move the rest out to the garage."

"Deal."

They carried the boxes out and stowed them in the tail of her hatchback. They just fit, which meant that her much-abused little car had now become a rolling closet. She just hoped it didn't become a closet broken down on the side of the road. Lately the engine coughed more than it chugged, but since she couldn't do anything about it, she elected to put it out of mind.

After helping Marcus shift the boxes from his living room to his tiny garage, she checked her wristwatch and saw that she just had time to get to class.

"I have to go," she said, heading back into the house.

"No time for lunch?" he asked, following on her heels.

She looked back over her shoulder in surprise. "No. Not today. But I hadn't planned on taking time to eat anyway."

He stopped her with a hand on her arm as she moved around the kitchen counter and toward the entry. "What had you planned on taking the time to do?"

"Read," she answered shortly, moving away again. "I'm behind. But I'm sure I'll catch up."

"Nicole, I'm sorry," he apologized, coming after her. "I didn't mean to usurp your time like this."

"It's all right, Marcus," she said, pausing long enough to smile at him. "Those things out in your garage belonged to my mother and grandmother. It's worth it to know they're safe."

"They'll be here when you're ready for them," he told her again, "and it doesn't matter when that is."

"Thank you, Marcus."

He shook his head. "I'm just glad to help. I want to help, you know."

"I know."

The fact that he hadn't brought Beau to live with him didn't change that. That Beau wasn't with Marcus now was her fault, not his. She understood, even if Beau didn't, that Marcus had only done what he thought best in that situation.

Marcus always did what he thought best. Sometimes she disagreed with him, but she couldn't fault him for following his conscience. It wasn't as if he just did the easy or convenient thing. He hadn't kept her from getting the internship, after all, and he certainly could have. Now he'd saved her things for her.

Where Beau lived at the moment would be a moot point, anyway, if the court sent Beau back to their father. She gulped, afraid to think what might become of Beau if that happened.

It wasn't that she didn't want to believe her father had quit drinking for good—nothing could please her more—but unless she was there to know for sure, how could she rest easily once Beau was back in that house with their father? Provided, of course, that Beau could even be persuaded to go back.

She very much feared what Beau would do if told he'd have to go back to live with his father. He'd taken off once already, and he talked a lot about how easy it would be for the two of them to get away now, openly advocating that they do so.

She prayed that Marcus was right about it taking six months or more for the courts to make a decision. Maybe by then she'd have a fighting chance to persuade everyone that she was the better guardian for her brother. If not… *If not* was too worrying to even think about.

Marcus found her the next morning sitting out in the empty playground behind the day school during her morning break. Perched atop the picnic table sheltered beneath the dubious shade of a pin oak, she had a textbook opened on her lap. She wasn't studying, however. Instead, she was staring off into space, her elbows resting on the knees of her folded legs.

Marcus noticed that she was wearing neon pink flip-flops and khaki capris under what appeared to be a straight, sleeveless, flowered sundress. She'd twisted her hair up on top of her head. Sort of. A great deal of it was falling down in wisps that floated around her face. He couldn't help smiling.

"Finally catching up on that reading?"

"What?" She turned her head to look at him, surprise quickly shifting to delight. "Not so you'd notice," she amended wryly, closing the textbook and laying it aside.

"Can I sit down then?"

"Sure."

She scooted closer to the edge of the table as he stepped over the bench. Straddling it, he sat sideways, the white elbow of his shirtsleeve resting on the edge of the table. He could see the question in her eyes.

"I talked to my friend at CPS."

She leaned back, bracing her upper body weight against her stiffened arms, palms flat against the tabletop. "And?"

He hated to give her this news, but she needed to know, and he'd rather do it than leave this difficult job to someone who might not try to reassure her.

"Your father's filed to regain custody."

She sat up straight. "Already? It's too soon, isn't it? Surely they'll need more time to figure out if he's going to stay sober."

Marcus nodded, reaching for her hand. "That's what Jonathan said. No one's rushing to judgment, Nicole. They want to be as certain as they can be that Beau will be safe with him. The thing is, though, he's likely to get visitation pretty soon."

Nicole caught her breath. "Beau isn't going to like that."

"I understand," Marcus said, squeezing her hand with his, "but he may not have a choice. Don't worry, though, the visitation will be supervised, at least in the beginning."

"You don't understand," she said, blinking rapidly. "Beau's liable to do something foolish when he hears this."

"Beau's already been foolish, if you ask me," Marcus commented, "not that you did. I just wish he wouldn't punish Ovida and Larry for how this has all turned out."

"I know." She stretched one leg over the bench where he sat and slid it to the ground before standing, adding, "especially when it's all my fault."

"It is not," he refuted instantly, rising to follow her as she wandered over to put her back to the trunk of the tree, her arms folded, head bowed. "None of this is your fault. How could you even think it? You've devoted your whole life to your brother's welfare since your mother fell ill. You know you have."

She swiped at her cheek with one hand, brushing back a strand of hair. "But I'm the one who called the police that night."

"You had no choice."

"But I'm still the one who did it," she insisted, digging her toe in the dirt. "And he blames me. I know he does, just as he blames me for him winding up with the Cutlers."

"We both know *I* am the one to blame for that," Marcus stated firmly.

She shook her head. "No, you wouldn't have had to beg off if I hadn't put you in a difficult spot." She sniffed, and that's when he realized she was crying.

He curled his fingers beneath her chin and tilted her face up. The tears streaming from her eyes clutched at his heart. He didn't know what possessed him to do it, but somehow it seemed like the only thing to do. He pulled her into his arms, and then she was sobbing against his shoulder.

"Hey, don't. Shh. It's all right."

"I—I know," she whispered brokenly. "I keep trying to count my blessings, you know, but I just feel so alone!"

"You're not! You're not," he assured her, holding her close.

She gulped, sniffed, and gulped again. Then she pulled back slightly and looked up at him.

There it was again, that look that always hit him like a sledgehammer. It humbled him, the love that he saw there behind those damp, spiky lashes, a love so strong that it could forgive anything: loss, abandonment, broken promises, dashed dreams.

The next thing he knew he was kissing her and her arms had stolen up around his neck.

He had never felt such trust, such rightness, and he was mentally kicking himself for everything he'd thought and said and done right up to this moment when she suddenly jerked away, clapping a hand over her mouth.

"Marcus, I'm so sorry!"

"Sorry," he echoed stupidly, the world whirling to a stop around him. She covered her face with her hands, and he tried desperately to marshal his thoughts, babbling, "No, no, I take full responsibility. I was—"

Kissing her. He'd been kissing her. He could hardly believe it.

"I don't know what happened!" she exclaimed.

He frowned. How she could've missed it, he didn't know, but just in case she had, he told her. "We kissed."

"I know that! I just don't know, er..." She closed her eyes, color flooding her face. "Marcus," she pleaded, "c-could you please just go away!" She turned her back on him then and bowed her head against the tree. "Please," she whispered.

He stood there for a moment, uncertain what to do or say. Then he realized that he was reaching for her and snatched back his hands. He racked his brain…and couldn't think of a thing to say. It was as if that single kiss had emptied his head.

After a moment, unable to think of anything else to do, he spun on his heel and walked away, straight through the building and out onto the covered walkway that led to his office. Every step of the way, he asked himself what he should do now.

Marry her.

As before, the thought rocked him right down to his socks. This time, however, it brought with it only a sense of certainty and relief, so that when he finally reached his office, he closed the door and went straight to God.

He'd already prayed about this until he was sick of his own thoughts, but he had no need to ask God to take these feelings from him now and no reason to think that he should. What he had need of now was confession, an apology even.

"Forgive me, Father. I just didn't understand. I admit I've been an idiot. It was my birthday. I asked for a wife, and Nicole walked through the door." He laughed, elated and appalled and hopeful and wary all at the same time. "It just seemed too easy. I—I guess I made it so difficult because… that's how my life's been." He closed his eyes. "I'm sorry. I should have known. What difference does it make how she dresses or how old she is in years when there's such goodness and sweetness and beauty and…" He spread his arms, looked up to the ceiling and said humbly, "Thank You."

After a moment, he walked around his desk, stood in front of his chair and took a deep breath before letting it out again and sitting down. So now what did he do?

Ask her to marry him, yes, obviously. Or, more accurately, *convince* her to marry him. He didn't doubt for a moment that's what it would take at this point because no matter what he said now, after what he'd said before, she was going to think that this was about rescue, about making up for not taking Beau when he should have.

He shook his head. That kiss hadn't been about rescuing anyone, but he wasn't sure she'd realize that. She thought that kiss was her fault! As if fault even needed to be assigned.

No, he couldn't have her thinking that he would marry her out of pity or a misplaced sense of responsibility or for any other reason except that he loved her and she was the woman God had made for him. Nicole deserved better than to think—or to have anyone else think—that any man would marry her simply as an altruistic gesture.

So how did he convince her? He shook his head. Oh, man, if ever he'd needed a female perspective, he needed one now.

He was still trying to figure out how to explain this all to Jolie when he arrived at her house in west Fort Worth. He hadn't even bothered to call first or even to explain to Carlita where he was going when he left the office. He did ring the bell, but impatience quickly got the better of him, so after a moment, he simply opened the door and walked in, thanking God that she was obviously home.

"Jolie? Jo?"

Just as he got to the end of the entry hall, he saw her coming through the den toward him, her enormous belly leading the way. She looked ready to pop, though her due date remained almost three weeks away yet.

Jolie took one look at him and demanded, "What's wrong?"

"What's wrong?" He threw up his arms. "I'm an idiot, that's what's wrong! Correction. I *was* an idiot. Now I've got it figured it out. Mostly. Sort of, anyway. The thing is, how do I convince her?"

"Her?" Jolie echoed. Then she smiled. "I take it we're talking about Nicole Archer again."

"Who else?"

"Who else, indeed." She slid one supportive arm under her belly and placed the other hand on the top of it before turning to waddle back toward the couch and collapse upon it. "Okay. So what happened?"

"I kissed her," he announced, moving to stand in front of her. "To be perfectly fair, she kissed me, too."

"And since you don't want to marry her…" Jolie began, only to fall silent when he shook his head.

"I *do* want to marry her."

"But you don't think you should?" Jolie ventured carefully.

"I know I should," he corrected smoothly. "Like I said, I was an idiot before."

Jolie blinked. "I see. And the problem now is?"

"Exactly what I said. How do I convince her?"

"She needs convincing, does she? I thought she was in love with you."

"She does. She is. At least I think she is." He frowned, considering. Then he smiled, nodding. "Yes, she is, I'm sure of it. The problem is, after what I said before, she may not believe me when I tell her that this isn't about me feeling guilty and trying to fix all her problems. Although I do and God knows I would if I could."

"Well, why don't you then?" Jolie asked.

"Fix everything, you mean?"

"Sure, if you can."

He sat on the coffee table in front of Jolie. "I'm not sure I can now. It may be too late."

"You won't know until you try, will you?"

He leaned forward, wrapping his arms around as much of his sister as he could manage. "I love you," he whispered, "and that's one lucky kid in there. One very large kid." Grinning, he sat back again.

She made a face. "I love you, too, and I think we can safely say he takes after his father."

Marcus laughed. "At least sizewise."

"Let's hope in more ways than just the one," Jolie commented. Then she tilted her head. "Before you go running off to fix Nicole's world, can I ask you something?"

"Anything."

"Why are you so convinced you should marry her now? Before you didn't seem to think she would make a proper minister's wife."

"What *is* a proper minister's wife, Jo?" he asked. "Do you know?" She shook her head. "Neither do I," he admitted. "Maybe there isn't any such person. Or maybe it depends on the minister."

Jolie smiled. "That sounds right to me, but what about your congregation?"

"I don't know," he admitted, "and I'm not sure I care."

The truth was, he liked Nicole exactly as she was, naive exuberance, ridiculously flamboyant clothing and all. He could see himself all too easily at seventy, shaking his head over some outrageous pink-lamé-and-flowered-nylon nonsense. And loving her all the same. Because that was the fact of the matter.

He loved Nicole Archer. He loved everything about her, her devotion and her determination and her sweetness and her faith in God—and in him.

He should be so selfless, so slow to condemn and blame, so quick to forgive and excuse. Maybe the minister could learn something from that "unsuitable" young lady, such as not to jump to conclusions and be so quick to assume that he knew the mind of God.

Maybe his congregation could learn from her, too, if they'd just give her half a chance. Somehow he thought they would. In fact, he was pretty ashamed for not having realized it sooner. The congregation had never been the problem; it was always him.

But that was the past. The future was Nicole, and he had a pretty good idea now how to prove it to her, though it was going to take divine intervention to make that happen. Well, he knew Who to ask for that.

Marcus rose, bent to place a kiss in the center of his sister's forehead and straightened. Jolie winced and pressed a hand low against her belly.

"Something wrong?" Marcus asked, frowning.

"Yeah, I'm nearly eight-and-a-half months pregnant, and your nephew's dancing on my bladder," she cracked. She let her head fall back against the couch. "Only a couple more weeks to go!"

Marcus smiled. "Hang in there, sister mine. You'll be a mommy before you know it."

"I just have one favor to ask," she said. "Don't get married until after the baby comes. I simply cannot attend a wedding like this."

Marcus laughed and started for the door. "No promises, sis." He looked back over his shoulder and winked. "But I'll see what I can do."

"I'll say a prayer for you!" she called as he opened the door.

"Ditto!" he returned as he stepped through the doorway.

He closed his eyes and did just that. He'd like a healthy nephew brought into this world right away, please, and a wedding as soon after as he could manage it, but he'd settle for a solution to Nicole's problems.

Her happiness mattered more to him now than his own or anyone else's. And he knew who held that key. Whether or not he could pry it out of Dillard Archer's stubborn fingers was up to God alone.

Chapter Fourteen

"Someone to see you, hon."

Nicole looked up from her position on the floor, where she sat drilling a circle of four-year-olds on the alphabet via a game with flash cards. Beau stood in the doorway next to Millie, whom everyone referred to as "the gatekeeper" at the day care center. No unknown person got by Millie without proper identification or, apparently in this case, a very long face.

Nicole knew immediately that she wasn't going to like whatever was going on, starting with how her brother came to be standing in her classroom. Then again, this hadn't been the best of mornings so far, anyway. She hadn't slept well last night, despite being dog-tired. She just couldn't get that ridiculous kiss out of her head.

She still couldn't believe she'd kissed Marcus yesterday. Talk about dumb. Whatever she said or did after this, he was going to assume that she was throwing herself at him—and she wasn't entirely sure he'd be wrong.

Casting a wary look at her brother, she rose to her feet, ruffled a couple of heads and asked, "Thank you, Millie. Can you watch this bunch for me? I'll be as quick as I can."

"Take your time," Millie said, moving into the room and leaving Nicole to shepherd her brother out into the hallway.

"What's wrong? How did you get here?" she demanded at once.

Beau shook his head, hissing, "We don't have time for that. We gotta go! We don't have a choice now."

Nicole folded her arms, saying, "You're not making sense, Beau. I can't leave. I'm working here. Then I have a class this afternoon and work again tonight at the restaurant. Now how did you get here?"

"I hitched a ride," he told her shortly, insisting, "I had to!"

"Beau! Ovida's going to be out of her mind. You can't just take off like this!"

"Dad came to the Cutlers' this morning," he said anxiously, grabbing her forearm. "He said he's going to get me back, no matter what. Then the caseworker called. He's going to get visitation, Nic. What's to keep him from taking off with me?"

Nicole leaned against the wall, momentarily closing her eyes. She'd known this would happen. "It's supervised visitation, Beau. You won't be alone with him."

"I don't care! It's the first step in sending me back to him. I heard what the caseworker said to Ovida. I was listening in on the telephone, and don't tell me I shouldn't have because I had to. Nobody tells me anything."

"That's not true."

"Yes, it is! Please, Nic, let's just go now before it's too late!"

"Had Dad been drinking when he came by this morning? Was he hungover?" she asked.

"I don't know! I didn't talk to him. Larry didn't think so, but what if he stays sober just long enough to convince a judge to send me home again? What then?"

"That's a long way off, Beau. I know because Marcus

looked into it. I'll have my degree well before Dad can regain custody. We can take off as soon as I graduate, if we have to."

"Let's just go now," he pleaded, "and you can finish your degree next semester the way you originally planned, just not here."

"It's not that easy to transfer, Beau," Nicole told him. "Now come on, we have to call Ovida and let her know you're safe." She took him by the arm and started down the hallway.

"No!" He planted his feet and yanked his arm free. "We have to get away before anyone finds out!"

"Beau, we've discussed this. I can't just pick up and leave everything I've worked so hard for now."

Beau folded his arms mulishly, muttering, "I thought you cared about me. I thought you were going to take care of me."

"I do! I am! But the best way to do that is to finish my education, get a good job and—"

"You care more about that dumb degree than you do about me," he accused.

"I do not! How can you even think that?"

"Just forget it," Beau said, turning away.

"No." She caught him by both shoulders and physically turned him back the way they'd started. "You're coming with me. We're going to talk to Marcus. Maybe he can convince you. But I'm telling you right now that we're going to be sensible and responsible and do all the right things. Do you hear me, Beau Leonard Archer? We're going to do this the way *Mom* would want."

That seemed to take the fight out of him, at least momentarily, but just in case, she didn't take her hands off him as she marched him down the hall, out onto the walkway and next door to the administration building. Even after they pushed through the heavy glass door into the outer office, she kept one arm around him.

"Hello, Carlita. We'd like to see Marcus, please, and would you call Ovida Cutler to let her know that Beau is safe with me?"

"Sure thing." Eyeing Beau with blatant curiosity, the plump secretary buzzed Marcus on the intercom. "Nicole's here."

Marcus appeared mere seconds later, a smile on his face. "Hi. You must've been reading my mind. I was just wondering—" He broke off when he realized that she wasn't alone. "Beau. This is a pleasant surprise." He glanced at Nicole, who had a hard time meeting his gaze.

She'd give anything if she could take that kiss back. Except that it was likely to be the only one they'd ever share and it had been rather nice. Oh, this wasn't helping at all!

"Maybe you'd better come into my office," Marcus said, and Nicole nodded.

They followed him, Nicole prodding Beau to get him moving. Marcus perched on the edge of his desk and waved the two of them down into the pair of chairs facing him.

"What's up?" he asked without preamble.

"You know that possibility we were discussing yesterday morning?" Nicole asked.

Marcus looked from her to Beau and back again. "I think so, yes."

"Well, Beau's heard it, too, and he did just what I was afraid he'd do. He took off."

"Ah." Marcus laid a fingertip against his nose.

"My dad's going to get custody of me!" Beau erupted. "And Nicole won't do anything about it!"

"That's not fair," Nicole and Marcus said at the same time.

Surprised, she looked at Marcus, only to find him looking

at her. He switched his gaze back to Beau and bent forward slightly, bracing his hands on the edge of the desk beside his hips.

"Beau, I've never seen a sister as devoted as Nicole is to you. She's killing herself to graduate a semester early just because you don't like temporarily living with two perfectly nice people like Ovida and Larry Cutler."

Beau folded his arms and slumped until his chin was pressed into his chest, broodingly silent. Marcus sighed and shrugged apologetically in Nicole's direction.

"This isn't right, Beau," he went on. "You should be doing everything you can to ease your sister's mind, not worrying her like this."

Beau just folded his arms tighter and sank lower in his chair.

"Save your breath, Marcus," Nicole said, casting a look at her brother from the corner of her eye. "He wants what he wants when he wants it, and nothing else matters."

Beau grimaced and pushed up straighter in his chair again. "I just don't want to go back with him," he muttered.

"Not even if he's stopped drinking and is willing to do whatever it takes to put his family back together?" Marcus asked, looking at Nicole.

"Will he?" Beau mumbled, sounding half hopeful and half scornful.

Marcus switched his gaze back to the boy. "I don't know," he admitted. "Maybe someone should ask."

Nicole considered that. "I'm not sure it's a good idea. He can say anything now, but what's to keep him from starting to drink again once Beau's home with him?"

"What's to keep him from snatching me and disappearing?" Beau demanded.

Nicole couldn't quite imagine that. Their father had never shown that much interest in either of them. She didn't know if Beau was genuinely afraid of being abducted by his father or if he was using it as a scare tactic to try to get his own way.

"Has Dad said something to make you think he would do that?"

"You don't think he'd do it just out of spite?" Beau demanded. "What's to stop him?"

Nicole turned to Marcus, worried now. "Maybe it's time he left the Cutlers, went someplace where Dad wouldn't know to look for him. Could you arrange that with CPS?"

"No!" Beau cried before Marcus could answer.

Confused, Nicole sat back. "But if you're frightened—"

"I'm not going to strangers! You promised."

"With me, then," Marcus offered.

"Oh, I don't think that's a good idea at all," Nicole hedged. "I—I mean, nothing's changed that kept us from doing that to begin with."

"Everything's changed," Marcus said.

If he really thought that, though, then he was mistaken. Nicole knew better, and after what had happened yesterday, so should he. Before she could find a diplomatic way to point that out, Beau flatly announced, "I'm staying where I am."

Exasperated, Nicole threw up her hands. "What is this? First you can't wait to get out of there, and then you're staying no matter what!"

"At least I know what to expect there," Beau muttered, ducking his head.

"What's best for you, Nicole?" Marcus asked. "Where do you think he should be?"

Nicole sighed. "I'll never know for sure he's safe unless I'm with him no matter where he is. At this point it would almost be easier if we could just both go back home, like before."

Beau stiffened beside her, but Marcus ignored him, asking, "Is that what you want?"

She glanced at Beau before admitting, "Not really, no. I mean, it's going backward, isn't it?"

"What *do* you want?" Marcus asked.

"A place of our own," she answered immediately, "somewhere safe. To be able to pay the bills. That's all."

Not all, she admitted privately, but it would have to do.

"Really?" Beau asked, turning toward her.

"That's what I've been working for all this time, Beau," she pointed out.

Beau looked down, seeming to think about that.

"I'd still like to speak to your father," Marcus said, "unless you object, not only to assess his intentions but also to let him know that there's someone else on your side."

Nicole thought about that. "I'm not sure he'll talk to you."

"Can't hurt to try. You never know. He might be reasonable at this point."

"Marcus," she said. "I know you want to help, but this isn't your problem."

"Oh, I disagree," he countered. "It's very much my problem."

"I don't see why."

He glanced at Beau, shrugged and said, "Still, I want to try to make him understand that it's best for you to care for Beau. If he's willing to let you, then maybe there's a chance to heal this family."

"I don't suppose it would hurt to know exactly where he stands," she said at last, "but frankly I don't hold out much hope that he'll listen to you."

"At least I'll have tried," Marcus said. "We can then go on from there."

Carlita tapped on the open door then and stuck her head into the room. "The Cutlers are here."

"Already?" Nicole said in surprise. "I didn't mean for them to come after him."

"I couldn't reach them by phone," Carlita explained. "Apparently they figured this is where he would go and had already started out."

It made sense. "Tell them we'll be right out, would you?" Nicole said.

Carlita nodded and left.

Nicole looked to her brother, prodding gently, "Beau."

Sighing dramatically, he got up and dragged himself toward the door. "Fine. Just remember what you said."

"About us getting our own place?" she clarified. "I haven't forgotten and I won't."

"We already *have* a place. You know, Grandpa's cabin," Beau said, "and we're going there when you graduate. Aren't we, Nic?"

"We'll see. I have to have a job, Beau. If it's not there, we'll find someplace."

Beau frowned, but he didn't argue, just set his jaw mulishly and went out to face the Cutlers. Nicole rose to go with him, but Marcus stopped her with a hand on her wrist.

"Before you leave, can I at least ask where you're living?"

"I'm staying with a girlfriend right now, but it's just temporary."

"I mean that I'd like the address."

She crooked up one corner of her mouth in a wry smile. "You already have it. I submitted a change of address right away. It's on my employee record."

Marcus nodded, shamefaced. "Nicole," he began, "about what happened yesterday—"

She winced and shook her head. "Let it go, Marcus, please. To tell you the truth, I've got enough on my mind just now without getting into that."

He subsided reluctantly. "All right, if that's what you want. For now."

Nodding, Nicole didn't tell him that if they never mentioned that kiss again it would be too soon for her. The last thing she needed was to humiliate herself like that again.

She also didn't mention that she could foresee a time and a circumstance when taking off with Beau might be the wisest course, but only if it began to look as though their father might actually regain custody. Until then, she'd stick to the plan, such as it was.

True, she was practically living out of her car—Kattie simply didn't have room even for the few things Nicole had taken from Marcus's—but at least she had a place to sleep. It was awkward, but she didn't think Kattie would toss her out, especially since she was paying a good portion of the rent now.

Meanwhile, Dillard had to know that if he had any hope of regaining custody of his son, he'd have to toe the line. She had to trust that. She had to trust that God wouldn't put her brother back into a dangerous situation without her being there to protect him. And this time she'd do a better job of it.

She turned toward the door, saying, "I have to see Beau off and get back to work."

Marcus didn't try to stop her again, and she told herself that she was glad. But glad or not, it was undoubtedly for the best. She just wished that for once what was best was not also what hurt most.

Marcus worked hard to cover all his bases before the week's end. He spoke to Jonathan at Child Protective Services again and then to a family law attorney recommended by his brother-in-law Kendal, who had arranged cross-adoptions for his and Connie's children.

He even convinced Beau's therapist to speak with him, shamelessly claiming the position of Beau's pastor. Since he'd recommended Beau for the denominational counseling service, he wasn't questioned on that. The psychologist was too ethical to give Marcus specific information, but he agreed that Marcus's proposal would be beneficial for Beau and willingly signed an affidavit to that effect.

Marcus had to wait for the attorney to draw up the necessary papers, and that was the most difficult part of his plan, but he used the time to pray diligently. Specifically, he needed to be very certain what he should say to Dillard Archer. He didn't want to threaten Dillard if he could help it. He had to consider the man's immortal soul, after all.

It was important to make Dillard understand that his best chance of healing his family was in letting Nicole take on responsibility for Beau. Marcus meant to help her do that by proving to the satisfaction of the courts that she wouldn't be shouldering that responsibility alone. Even if she wasn't convinced that marrying him was the right thing to do, he intended to make a commitment to her and Beau on paper. Financial support, legal support, emotional support, spiritual support—whatever it took.

Of course, Dillard could fight them in court if he chose, but Marcus intended to stack the deck against him by every legal and ethical means at his disposal. The optimum solution would be for Dillard to willingly choose what was best for his family. Only then could he even begin to win back the trust and devotion of his children. Marcus's most solemn prayer, however, was that in making such a choice, Dillard would open his heart to God. True healing could come from no other source.

The restaurant where Nicole worked was one of a popular Mexican food chain that stayed open from 11:00 a.m. to

11:00 p.m. on Saturdays. Nicole spent almost every minute of those twelve hours on her feet. The tips, fortunately, were worth it.

Exhausted, she managed to drag her aching body back to Kattie's apartment before midnight, thanking God that it was on the ground floor of the aging building. She hadn't even taken time to change out of her work uniform, and once she reached the apartment she simply crashed on Kattie's lumpy couch in her black pants and white shirt. Kattie came in around three in the morning from a night on the town with some of the other girls from work. Nicole woke just enough to pull a pillow over head to block out the light and went back to sleep.

Bleary-eyed, she tried to make herself get up and dress for church when the alarm went off, but she just couldn't manage it and fell back asleep. She woke suddenly, sitting up on the sofa, half-dressed but somewhat refreshed. A glance at the clock told her that morning services were already underway. An urgent knock at the door revealed why she'd awakened at all.

Kattie mumbled from the bed, "You're closest, you have to get it."

Nicole got to her feet, wearing her wrinkled shirt from the night before and a chiffon skirt she'd put on for church when she woke earlier, and went to the door, expecting some chum of Kattie's. She did *not* expect to find Larry Cutler standing there. For a long moment, she wasn't sure that she just wasn't imagining Larry's broad, stocky form, wire-rimmed glasses and thinning gray hair. Then he spoke.

"We tried to call but figured the phone must be off the hook."

A sound had Nicole looking over her shoulder at the bed. Kattie gave her a sleepy, apologetic shrug as she groped for and found the cordless telephone receiver beneath the bed-covers.

"Sorry," she said, punching a button and dropping the receiver back into its charger.

A deeper concern had taken hold of Nicole, though. She looked back to Larry, who seemed distinctly uncomfortable standing there beneath the second-story balcony. Sheer terror threatened, pushing the fog from her sleepy brain.

"What's happened to Beau?"

"I guess that means he's not here," Larry deduced, frowning.

"Not here?" Nicole echoed, stepping closer. "Isn't he with you?"

Larry rubbed his furrowed forehead, saying, "He wasn't in his room when I went to get him up for breakfast, and we figured he most likely came here to you."

Panic sweeping over her, Nicole blurted, "I haven't seen him!"

"Where else would he go?" Kattie asked, tugging Nicole's attention her way again. She was sitting up now, holding a pillow to her chest. Shoving short, streaky brown hair out of her face, she asked, "Do you have any idea where to look?"

Nicole closed her eyes, imagining the worst. "What if Dad grabbed him? Beau's been afraid of that."

"I don't think so," Larry said. "The CPS caseworker came by yesterday afternoon. Apparently Dillard's doing everything they're asking of him. He's enrolled in parenting and anger management classes, and he's taking unscheduled tests every few days to prove that he's not drinking. Why would he do all that unless he planned to regain custody legally?"

Nicole beat back her surprise, sharpening her focus on the most pertinent facts. "Did Beau hear that?"

"Yeah, but I can't say he was reassured," Larry admitted

dryly. "Kept saying that he didn't care and didn't believe it. He was so rude at one point that Ovida sent him to his room. Later, when I went in to say good-night, it was obvious that he still had a burr in his blanket. He doesn't trust your father, and I don't blame him, but it's not entirely rational. The counselor keeps saying to just give him time, but I'm not so sure that's going to work, frankly."

"Beau is more like Dad than he would care to admit," Nicole murmured, thinking. "Has anyone contacted Marcus? Maybe Beau went there."

"Marcus is in the middle of services," Larry pointed out. "We did try, but he'd already left the house, and his cell went to voice mail. We called Austin, that buddy of Beau's, but his mom says they haven't seen him."

Well, that about covered it. There could only be one other place where her stubborn, willful little brother would head, and Nicole knew as well as she was standing there that he'd taken off for Oklahoma on his own. He'd probably been planning this as a backup if she wouldn't go with him.

Of course! She snapped her fingers. That's why he'd been so desperate to stay with the Cutlers after these months of complaining about it! He wasn't reconciled to the familiar. He'd wanted to stay because he knew that he could get out of there whenever he wanted to. He'd proved that already by slipping away once before and hitching a ride to the church in Pantego. Now he was trying to get to Oklahoma. The little goof was forcing her hand.

"I think I know where he's headed," she said, turning back to Larry. "In fact, I'm sure of it."

"Where? Just tell me where. Better yet, come with me," Larry urged, holding out a hand to her. "Show me the way. We'll bring him back together."

Nicole stared him, her mind whirling. If they tried to drag Beau back here, he would hate them all, and next time he ran away, it wouldn't be to Oklahoma. Next time she wouldn't have a clue where he'd gone or any way to protect him.

Besides, what if their father did regain custody? That was looking more and more likely all the time. Even if by some chance she could be convinced that Beau would be safe with him, Beau would never be, not without a lot of hard work on her father's part. And one thing Dillard wasn't known for was hard work.

Whether he was forcing her hand or not, she had no choice but to follow Beau and try to make the best of it. Even if what awaited in Oklahoma turned out to be as difficult and unpleasant as she feared, she saw no other way now.

Maybe it was always going to come to this anyway. As badly as she hadn't wanted to admit it, she was falling farther and farther behind in school. Two jobs and a heavier than normal academic load were just too much for her under the present circumstances.

She thought of Marcus and knew that the farther away she was from him the better. What had happened the other day just proved it. Staying around would only leave her open for additional humiliation and rejection. She just didn't think she could take any more rejection.

Finally, she shook her head. "No. I'm sorry, Larry, but no. This is something I have to do myself."

Larry frowned, obviously troubled, and seemed to sink in on himself. "Are you sure?"

Suddenly she saw him as Beau might, aging and gray, his once-solid frame shrinking, sagging, his hair thinning and no longer dark. He was still a man to be trusted and admired, but he must seem as old as the hills to her thirteen-year-old brother, and certainly no match for their father who, despite his drinking, was twenty years younger and a bigger man.

She thought with longing of the possibility that her dad really was trying to turn his life around. He was doing what the courts said he must, in order to be the father he hadn't wanted to be before. But even if he did everything that everyone asked, it would be a long time before they could trust him again, if ever. Beau especially.

"This is the best way," she said firmly, "maybe the only way."

Mr. Cutler shook his head, saying, "I don't like the sound of this."

Nicole smiled with rueful understanding. "I know," she told him softly. "I know. But don't you see? It's out of our hands now."

Larry stared at her, his craggy face softening to resignation, and she knew that he understood what was happening here. "Ovida's going to be upset, but you've always had a good head on your shoulders. We know you'll do what's best."

"I'm sorry that we've been such a trial."

"It's just that we care so much."

"I know, and thank you," she told him with heartfelt sincerity. "You and Ovida have been wonderful to us ever since Mom died, and I'm more grateful than I can tell you. But you've done all that you can. Please try not to worry, and say a prayer for us, won't you?"

"Of course," he said. Then, "You'll be in touch?"

They both understood that this was goodbye. "As soon as I can."

He stood there for a moment longer before sliding his hands into the pockets of his khakis and turning away. Nicole closed the door and began gathering up her things, determined to find her brother and make sure that he was safe even if it meant turning her back on everything she'd worked for here.

God knew she couldn't have kept on the way she'd been going much longer anyway. Her weary, aching body told her that much. Besides, catching up with Beau was going to take the rest of the day, provided the little knucklehead had done what she thought he had. She wouldn't give up all hope of graduating just yet, but taking care of her little brother was her top priority. School would just have to wait.

She began to silently pray that Beau managed to make it to Tahlequah. Hitching a ride to Pantego from Fort Worth was one thing; making it all the way to northern Oklahoma was something else. Yet, she felt certain he would make it.

If she got to Tahlequah and he wasn't there, she'd be forced to call the police, but not yet. She'd done that once before and Beau still hadn't forgiven her. Besides, every instinct she possessed told her that he'd had carefully laid plans in readiness for some time now.

As she hugged Kattie goodbye and threw her few remaining things into the car, she told herself that she was doing the right thing.

Of course, Ovida or even her father might call the police. Even if that happened, though, she and Beau had a good chance of getting where they were going without being caught. After that…well, it was all up to God, anyway.

With a heavy but resolute heart, she stopped at the first ATM she came to and cleaned out her bank account. Armed with that and nothing more than a tall cup of coffee obtained via a drive-through, she set out.

By the time she reached Interstate 35 and aimed north, she was weeping, her thoughts having turned to all that she was leaving behind. She thought of the Cutlers, her friends at school and church and the day care center, neighbors, even her father. She thought of the diploma that wouldn't be hers at summer's end, family photos she might never see again, the house where she had grown up.

Most of all, she thought of Marcus, who had been so appalled at her unthinking declaration of love and yet had tried in every way possible to help her. She would never stop loving him, so it was undoubtedly best that she put as much distance between them as she could. As long as he was near, she would just keep embarrassing herself as she had twice already.

If she wasn't going to be near him, she might as well be in some tumbledown old cabin on the Illinois river outside of Tahlequah as anywhere else, not that she expected to stay there. The place was a mess, and her father would surely think to look there for them at some point. Until then, they'd be together, and eventually they'd find a safe place. And she would have kept her promise to her mom.

Maybe in a few years when Beau was older and no longer subject to the vicissitudes of Child Protective Services they could come home to Texas again. Maybe not. What would be the point anyway?

She wiped her eyes and looked forward resolutely. From now on she would only look to the future. There was nothing to be gained by looking back.

"God has a plan," she said aloud, more desperate than ever to believe it, more determined than ever to yield to it.

No matter that it wasn't the plan she had thought it to be, her job as a child of God was to sublimate her desires to His will. Marcus had taught her that, and her mother before him. She wouldn't falter now just because her heart was breaking. She would see this through, and somehow she and her brother would come out on the other side, better than before, stronger than before, wiser than before.

And happier. She had to believe that, now when she had never felt so bleak.

"God has a plan," she whispered again, praying that losing her little brother as well as everyone else who had ever meant anything to her, including Marcus, was not part of it.

Chapter Fifteen

After many hours of prayer, Marcus had put himself to sleep on that Saturday night only to awaken in the black hours of Sunday morning with the rarest sort of pure and certain knowledge blanketing his mind. God had once again made wisdom from foolishness.

All this time that he'd been struggling against his own assumptions and calling it God's will, God had been preparing him. His own failures and faults had become the pathway to understanding, hopefully not only for him.

It was all so clear now. He'd begged God for a helpmate and then been quite sure that the only woman who truly delighted him could not possibly be the answer to his prayer. She hadn't fit his carefully constructed vision of what God intended, so he'd fought not to be affected, no matter how often or unmistakably God had thrust her into his path. There she'd been all along, the answer to his every desire, and he'd done his best to push her away. How stupid could a man be?

Just thinking of Nicole made him smile, and he never felt more firmly grounded, more sure of himself, more truly the man he wanted to be than when he was with her. It was afterward that he'd always started to question and assume and doubt.

He hadn't been just a fool; he'd been an ungrateful fool! In truth, the only difference between him and Dillard Archer was the saving grace and unbound wisdom of Christ Jesus, and because of that Marcus knew now what to say and how to say it.

Only Dillard could make the decisions that would set everything right, of course, for God so valued the personal choices of people that He would not violate their gift of free will. Now Marcus could only do his part and trust God to soften Dillard's heart. Hopefully, with weeks of sobriety behind him and time to think, rattling around in that empty house by himself, Dillard would be at his most receptive.

His mind full of the words he would say, Marcus had gone back to sleep, enjoying a truly untroubled rest, and risen early to meet his morning's obligations with a cheerful heart and calm assurance. Standing in the pulpit now, he looked out over the congregation and saw that Nicole wasn't there. He was disappointed but philosophical.

Perhaps it was for the best. This day's work must be done with finesse and dedicated concentration, and she could turn his mind to butter and his mouth to mush as no one else could. Besides which, he knew he'd have a difficult time keeping his intentions to himself, and he didn't want to disappoint her if he failed.

He greeted every congregant and shook every hand with smiling patience, knowing that Godly obligations must come first in any scheme. Once the building was empty, he left David to lock up and ran home to change into casual clothing before heading off to his sister's as expected, Connie's this time, this being Jo's monthly Sunday with the Cutlers. He no sooner walked through the door of Connie's magnificent home, though, than she thrust the telephone at him.

"Call Jolie's cell. She needs to talk to you. And it isn't the baby, I've already asked."

He never got to dinner. Connie had it on the table by the time he'd spoken with Jolie, Ovida and finally Larry, but Marcus couldn't have choked down a single bite by then. Not only was his stomach tied in knots, he knew that God had made other plans for this day.

"I'm sorry, sis. I have to go," he said, handing the cordless telephone to his bewildered brother-in-law and turning to hug the kids in their highchairs.

Larissa ignored him, busy as she was trying to feed Russell in his high chair, who in his laid-back fashion as usual, was perfectly content to allow her to do so. They were beautiful children, Larissa with her curls and Russ with his flame-red hair.

"Marcus, I couldn't help overhearing," Connie said, stripping off her apron. "Are you sure about this?"

"Going after Nicole? Absolutely. But I have something I have to do first."

Connie stared at him for a moment, standing there in her lovely home with her tall, quiet husband at her side, a worried expression on her face. "Jolie saw it first," she said, "but I'm not sure I really believed you were in love with her until now."

"Believe it," he said.

"It doesn't seem to fit," Connie murmured, "but God always knows best." She glanced meaningfully at her husband.

"How right you are," Marcus said.

She smiled and came to him with open arms. "Be happy."

He would if everything worked out the way he hoped. "Pray for me," he said, hugging her tight before he went out.

Half an hour later, he was standing on Dillard Archer's doorstep. Dillard didn't seem pleased to see him; neither did he appear particularly surprised. Without a word, he backed away, left the door standing open and turned to go into the living room. Marcus took that as an invitation and followed, closing the door behind him.

The first thing he noticed was that Dillard had left the furniture the way that Nicole had rearranged it. The second was an open book facedown on the seat of the recliner. Dillard picked it up and laid it aside, but not before Marcus had seen the title and recognized it as popular layman's work on the science of addiction.

"Might as well sit," Dillard rumbled, waving a hand desultorily as he dropped into his chair.

Marcus took a seat on the sofa and crossed his legs.

"I guess you're going to tell me what a jerk I've been and how this is all my fault," Dillard grumbled. Marcus inclined his head, spreading his hands, but before he could say anything, Dillard went on. "Well, don't bother." He looked away, snapping, "Don't you think I already know?"

Surprised, Marcus cleared his throat and leaned forward. "Okay," he said slowly, "now that we've established your responsibility in this whole fiasco, what are you going to do about it?"

Dillard turned sad, agonized eyes on him, muttering, "Everything I can, but you don't know how hard it is. My kids hate me, and I want to just drink that away!"

"They don't hate you," Marcus told him. "They're *afraid* of you, and *not* drinking is the only way to change that."

Dillard rubbed his chin, thoughtfully. It was cleanly shaved, Marcus noted, and the hand that rubbed it was steady and strong.

"Even if Beau could forgive me," he said in a deep, thick voice, "Nicole never will."

"I think you might be surprised," Marcus told him.

Dillard snorted at that. "Why should she? I've done nothing but make her life harder." He looked away, adding softly, "And all she ever did was make mine easier. I never knew how much I depended on her."

"She's the dependable sort," Marcus said with a smile, "dependable, caring, smart, forgiving. She's forgiven me more than once, and I didn't even have to ask."

"You?" Dillard retorted, frowning. "What does she have to forgive you for?"

Marcus smiled wryly. "Believe it or not, sir, you and I have made some of the same mistakes where your daughter is concerned. We've both underestimated her, to our detriment, and she's the most loving, forgiving person I've ever known. Oh, and beautiful. Did I say beautiful? Not to mention unique, determined. Unforgettable, really."

Dillard's mouth twisted, but then he rubbed the hollow of his temple with a forefinger. "Figures it would be you," he said. "I always knew someone would look past that crazy wardrobe of hers someday. I just didn't expect it to happen this soon. Then again, she's mature for her age."

Marcus chuckled. "She sure is, which is why I intend very soon to ask her to marry me."

Archer flattened his mouth, but then he sighed morosely. "She really won't be coming home then."

"If she does," Marcus said, "I hope it won't be for long."

Dillard nodded, the motion heavy with resignation. After a moment, his gaze grew pensive. "She's just like her mom, you know. Suzanne was my rock, and after she was gone, Nicole became the only person in the world I could depend on, including myself. I don't know what I'd have done without her. Drank myself to death, I guess. Instead of taking care of her and her brother as I should have, I just tried to drink away my pain and let her deal with everything." He narrowed his eyes. "I don't know when it changed, when the drinking became the pain and not the remedy. Now I've lost them all," he said bitterly, "my whole family."

"I said I want to marry her, not take her away from you," Marcus pointed out dryly.

"Same thing," Dillard mumbled, "even if I have already blown it."

"No, it's not the same. And all Nicole needs is a reason to trust you and some time. I'm sure of it."

"What about the boy?" Archer asked in a gravelly voice.

"That may take a little longer," Marcus warned.

Dillard tucked his chin in disappointment, asking, "And what happens in the meantime?"

"If everything works out as I hope," Marcus told him forthrightly, "Nicole and I will marry, and Beau will live with us."

"I see."

"Until you can prove to everyone's satisfaction that you're capable of being a father again," Marcus added pointedly.

Archer sat up very straight, both feet firmly planted on the floor, his hands gripping the arms of his chair. "Do you really think I can?"

"Yes, Mr. Archer, I do."

Hope sparked in his eyes. "Might as well call me Dillard," he mumbled, obviously turning the possibility over in his mind, "if we're going to be related."

Before Marcus could point out that their hoped-for future relationship was far from guaranteed, the other man suddenly drilled him with a very direct gaze. "How?" he demanded. "How can I get my family back?"

Marcus paused before saying, "Are you asking the man who wants to marry your daughter or the pastor?"

A muscle began to quiver along the lower ridge of Dillard's jaw. He looked down at his hands. "Maybe both," he said in a strained voice, his brow furrowed.

Marcus decided that it was time for a gentle prod. "Aren't you tired of being angry at God?" he asked softly.

For a moment, Dillard glared at him, but then a sort of weariness seemed to come over him, a tacit agreement with Marcus's assessment. "When my wife was sick," he said wearily, "I begged, I bargained, I raged. And Suze kept telling me, 'God will heal me, Dill. It just may not be in this world.' And I thought, what good is that? I just couldn't see any reason or hope in that." He shook his head. "But lately I've been thinking about something a fellow said to me in rehab. I was too mad to really think about it then, but—" he waved a hand "—I've had some time since, you know?"

Marcus nodded his understanding. "And what did this fellow say, Dillard?"

The other man leveled his gaze. "He said maybe I couldn't find any comfort in that because deep down I was afraid that I wouldn't be joining her in the other world where she's well."

"It doesn't have to be that way," Marcus said. "Because God's always willing to forgive."

"Even me?" Dillard rasped with acute hope.

Marcus clasped his hands together, momentarily bowing his head. *Thank You, God! Thank You!* When he lifted his gaze once again to the man whom he very much hoped would be his father-in-law, tears of joy stood in his eyes.

"Even you."

Marcus found her as the sun sank low against the horizon, trudging alongside the narrow road that wound through the craggy hills east of Tahlequah, dressed in a fluttery ankle-length skirt of orange organza and a white shirt that looked as if she'd slept in it. Since he'd passed her old car broken down on the side of road some miles back, he wasn't surprised, only relieved.

She stopped where she was, holding her long, dark hair up off her neck with one hand and looking so tired and bedraggled that he wanted to cry for her. Instead, Marcus put the car in park, got out and took her into his arms.

She leaned into him, asking wearily, "How did you find me?"

"Your father gave me a map." He felt her stiffen. "Come on," he said, moving her toward the car. "I'll explain as soon as we find Beau."

She let him help her into the passenger seat, then looked up at him with tears in her eyes. "What'll I do if he's not at the cabin?"

He brushed her hair back from her face and smiled. "Aren't you the girl too wise to cross bridges until she comes to them?"

"I'm not smart enough to stop and think," she scoffed in a trembling voice, "let alone wise."

"Oh, yes, you are," he told her, "wiser than you know. Now, how much farther?"

By her estimation, they were within ten miles of the cabin. According to the odometer on the dash, it was less than eight. Marcus turned where she told him and eased the car down the narrow, overgrown trail to the edge of the bluff, where the cabin perched, overlooking the Illinois River below.

It was a pretty pathetic sight. The roof had fallen in on one side, and the glass was broken out of the visible windows. The front door appeared to be missing. Its best feature was a familiar guitar stacked atop a familiar backpack on the ground-level porch right next to the space where the door should have been.

Nicole was out of the car and calling for her brother before Marcus had shifted the transmission into park. The boy appeared in the open doorway almost instantly, his dirty face streaked with tears. Even as Nicole gave a small cry and ran toward her brother, Marcus reached into the glove box for the papers he'd stored there before setting out, just as Beau fell into Nicole's arms, sobbing.

"It's all ruined. Rain got to the furniture. Even the floor's fallen through."

"I knew it couldn't be good," she said, surveying the damage over the top of his head.

"What're we gonna do?" he asked. "It was our last hope. There's nowhere else to go."

"Oh, Beau, this was never going to work anyway," she told him. "I thought for a minute that it might myself, but then I realized that as determined as Dad is, he'd just come looking for us."

"He never would," Beau insisted bitterly, wiping his face and adding more streaks in the process. "He'd have given up quick enough. He always has."

"I don't think that's likely to be the case anymore," Marcus said, coming to stand beside them. "I spoke to your father earlier today. He's a changed man in many ways."

Beau snorted. "I'll believe that when I see it."

"Maybe this will help," Marcus said, shaking open the folded papers and holding them out.

Beau squinted at them, frowning, but Nicole was quick to take them in hand. "What's this?"

He let her read until he got the first gasp, and then he began explaining the situation to Beau. "Your father's signed papers asking the court to grant your sister full custody of you."

"Where did you get these?" Nicole exclaimed, shuffling the documents.

"I had a lawyer draw them up," he answered before going back to his explanation to Beau. "Your therapist has en-

dorsed the deal, too, and CPS will be making the same rec-
ommendation."

Nicole gave him another gasp just then, demanding,
"Why are you pledging financial support?"

Marcus turned to face her, smiling as if his heart wasn't
threatening to break out of his chest. "That's just a fail-safe
plan," he said, "in case you won't agree to marry me."

Her eyes went wide. Beau whooped. And she dropped
like a stone, sitting down hard in the dirt.

"Nic!" Beau cried, dropping beside her.

Marcus was already there, on his knees, gathering her
up. "Nicole, are you all right? Sweetheart, say something!"

She clutched the papers to her chest and wailed, "Why?"

He cupped her face in his hands and laid his forehead
against hers and said, "I love you, more than you can even
imagine."

She threw her arms around him. "I love you, too!"

Marcus laughed, the sweetest relief imaginable washing
through him. "I'm taking that as a yes."

"Yes! Oh, yes!" Suddenly she jerked back and shook a
finger at her brother. "Let that be a lesson to you, Beau
Archer! God does look out for us!"

Marcus couldn't have agreed more.

God was good. God was so good.

They married one month and three days later on the
twenty-second of July. Marcus got a friend from seminary
to perform the service at First Church Pantego, where each
of his sisters had married before him. His sisters both cried.
The baby, however, just three weeks old, slept peacefully
through the whole thing in his mother's protective arms.
Truth be told, Marcus himself shed a tear or two while
repeating his vows, so overcome with joy was he. Nicole

beamed through it all, from the very first moment she appeared in the doorway on her emotional father's arm.

She wore her mother's wedding dress. Marcus secretly found it a little too conventional for his tastes, but he knew how Nicole valued those things of her mom's and grandmother's, and since he valued her above all else in this world, whatever she wanted was fine with him. Marcus couldn't imagine a more beautiful bride anyway.

The wedding wasn't entirely conventional, of course. Beau, along with Nicole's friend Katrina, served as his sister's attendants while Marcus's two brothers-in-law stood up with him. And the reception took place in the vestibule, with Marcus standing at the back of the sanctuary shaking hands and smiling much as he did on Sunday following service. Except this time, his bride was at his side. He couldn't believe how right that felt.

The whole thing was done with a minimum of fuss and expense, frugality being Nicole's middle name. A fine trait for a minister's wife. Though, in truth, Marcus wouldn't have quibbled if she'd maxed out the credit cards and drained his bank account. A fine sentiment for a husband who knew his greatest blessings were not material.

During their month-long engagement, Marcus had moved from the old parsonage to the newer, larger house in the compound. Beau had kept him company, while Nicole had gone home to her father. Dillard had made great inroads during that time, and Marcus foresaw the day in the not-too-distant future when Beau would happily move back into his old bedroom.

Beau didn't know that Dillard was secretly making trips to and from Oklahoma to repair the cabin. The damage was significant, but not as bad as it had appeared. The building was still sound, and Dillard meant for the repairs to be a gift to his children, a material acknowledgment of the good times in the past and the grief he had finally laid to rest. Marcus had fronted him the money, but he was paying it back from the earnings of his new job.

While Dillard had rejoined the workforce, however, Nicole was taking some time off. She would finish her degree in the fall, work for a time in the church day care center, and then they would think about starting their own family. Marcus sensed that his ministry would deepen and broaden in ways he couldn't even grasp yet.

After it was all over, Beau happily went off with the Cutlers to give the new husband and wife some privacy. Nicole watched the last of their guests leave the building, then she followed along with Marcus as he shut up the place.

"Have you ever noticed," she asked suddenly, "that when you look back at something you can see the hand of God at work?"

He smiled warmly. "Oh, yes."

"It's a shame we can't see it at the time, isn't it?"

"Maybe we're not meant to," he said after a moment's thought, "at least not all the time, because He's teaching us what to look for."

"True," she agreed sagely. "God's plans are always perfect, after all."

"Perfect," he agreed, opening his arms.

Husband and wife were of one mind on the subject, as they would often be, for God's plans are indeed perfect and beautiful and imbued with a love so strong that it defies even the understanding of the most wise among us.

* * * * *

Dear Reader,

God wants only good things for us, and He's faithful to hear and answer our prayers. Sometimes the answer isn't what we want it to be, but we have the comfort of knowing that it's always for our best. What amazes me is that often our prayers are answered with such abundance that we can't believe God really means it! That premise is at the heart of Marcus and Nicole's story, *A Love So Strong,* but two others are also at work here.

Have you ever made a promise that you ultimately couldn't keep? I have. Eventually all worked out, and it was better for everyone than my original plan would have been, but not being able to live up to my word was an agonizing—and humbling—experience. I just had to accept that God's will ran counter to my promise. That experience is at the core of Nicole's personal story, but another bit of personal growth informed Marcus's.

Part of being a Christian is wanting to do God's will. Unfortunately we often assume we know what that is and have a hard time getting our preconceptions out of the way in order to understand what God is really saying. Thankfully, no matter how difficult we might make it for ourselves, God is patient, and He honors and blesses our desire to understand and do what is right.

My prayer for you is that you have that desire and are blessed with the greatest reward this life has to offer: love.

Arlene James

WHEN LOVE COMES HOME

Therefore, let those also who suffer according to the will of God entrust their souls to a faithful Creator in doing what is right.
—1 *Peter* 4:19

Victoria, I know you are too small to read or even understand this yet, but the place you hold in my heart is immense, and it's never too early to say, "I love you." Granna

Chapter One

Grady frowned across the desk at his older brother and fought the urge to fold his arms in an act of pure defiance. It wasn't just that Dan expected Grady to spend Thanksgiving traveling for business but that he expected him to do it with Paige Ellis.

Pretty, petite Paige made Grady feel even more hulking and awkward than usual. It didn't help that Dan might have just stepped out of the pages of a men's fashion magazine. Slender and sleek, his dark hair having long since gone to silver, Dan served as a perfect contrast to his much larger—and much less dapper—younger brother. Dan was elegant, glittering silver compared to Grady's dull-as-sand brown.

Dan's white shirt looked as if it had just come off the ironing board, while Grady's might have just come off the floor. The navy pinstripes in Dan's expertly knotted burgundy tie perfectly matched his hand-tailored suit. Grady's chocolate-brown neckwear, on the other hand, somehow clashed with a suit that he'd once thought brown but now seemed a dark, muddy green.

The only thing the Jones brothers seemed to share, besides their parents and a law practice, were eyes the vibrant blue of a perfect spring sky. Grady considered them wasted in the heavily featured expanse of his own square-jawed face.

"It's not as if you'd enjoy the holiday anyway," Dan was saying.

Grady grimaced, conceding the point. Okay, he wasn't eagerly anticipating another chaotic feast at Dan's place in Bentonville. Why would he? A fellow couldn't even watch a good football game without one of his three nieces or sister-in-law interrupting every other minute.

"I didn't say I wouldn't do it," he grumbled. "I said the timing stinks."

No one wanted to spend a major holiday flying from Arkansas to South Carolina, but for Grady the task seemed especially disagreeable because it involved a woman and a kid.

Grady did not relate well to women, as his ex-wife had been fond of pointing out. She had contended that it had to do with losing his mother at such a young age, and no doubt she was right about that. He always felt inept and stupid in female company, never quite knowing what to say. As for children, well, he hadn't known any, except for his nieces, and he'd pretty much kept his distance from them. These days their adolescent behavior made him feel as if he'd stumbled into an alternate universe.

Besides, family law was Dan's forte, not Grady's. Give him a good old bare-knuckle brawl of a lawsuit or a complicated legal trust to craft. Even criminal defense work was preferable to prenups, divorces and custody cases, though he hadn't done much criminal defense since he'd left Little Rock. After his marriage had failed he'd come back home to Fayetteville and the general practice established by his and Dan's father, Howard.

"The timing could be better," Dan agreed, "but it is what it is."

Grady made a face and propped his feet on the corner of his brother's expansive cherrywood desk with a nonchalance he definitely was not feeling. "You're the attorney of record," he pointed out. "You should do this."

Dan had worked every angle on this case from day one. By rights, he ought to be there at the moment of fruition. But Dan had a family who wanted him at the dinner table on Thanksgiving. And Grady had no feasible excuse for not stepping in, even at the last minute.

"Trust me," Dan said, "Paige isn't going to complain."

Paige Ellis had doggedly pursued her ex after he'd disappeared with her son nearly three and a half years ago. Now the boy had been found and was waiting in custody of the state of South Carolina to be reunited with his mother.

Grady was glad for her. He just wished he didn't have to be the one to shepherd her through this reunion. The petite, big-eyed blonde made Grady especially uncomfortable, despite the fact that they hadn't exchanged half a dozen words in the three years or so that she'd been a client of their law firm.

"You'll want to look this over," Dan went on, plopping a file folder a good two inches thick onto the desk next to Grady's feet. "All the pertinent paperwork is ready. You should probably take it with you when you inform Paige about her son."

Grady bolted up straight in his chair, his feet hitting the floor. "Now hold on! The least you can do is deliver the news."

Dan turned up both hands in a gesture of helplessness and rocked back in his burgundy leather chair. "Look, I'd love to deliver the good news, but this needs to be done in person ASAP, and Chloe has a jazz band program at three."

Grady knew without even looking at his watch that it was at least half past two in the afternoon now. No way could Dan get to Nobb, where Paige Ellis lived, and back to Bentonville, where his daughters went to school, by three o'clock. If he skipped out on Chloe's performance, Dan's wife, Katie, was liable to skin him alive. Katie wasn't shy about demanding that Dan make his family a priority. Grady didn't understand how his brother could be so disgustingly happy in his marriage, but he was fond enough of Dan to be glad that it was so.

After a few more minutes of discussion, Grady sighed in resignation, gathered up the file folder and strode back to his office, grumbling under his breath. Just thinking about Paige Ellis made him feel even more hulking and plodding than usual.

Thanks to an expensively outfitted home gym, he was in better shape than most thirty-nine-year-olds, but that didn't keep him from feeling too big and too clumsy. Standing a bare inch past six feet in his size twelve shoes, his square, blocky frame hard packed with two hundred pounds of pure muscle, he wasn't exactly a giant, but he'd felt huge and oafish since puberty, when he'd dwarfed the other boys. In the company of some delicate, feminine little creature like Paige Ellis, he felt like a lumbering monster.

Entering his office, Grady turned down the lights, crossed the thick, moss-green carpet, dropped the folder onto his desk and switched on a lamp. He sat down in his oversize brown leather chair, tilted the bronze shade just so and opened the folder. He began thumbing through the notes and documents, scanning the material and jotting down notes as he went.

His ability to read quickly and comprehend completely was his greatest asset and brought in a considerable amount of income in consulting fees. Other attorneys knew that

Grady by himself could accomplish more in the way of research than a roomful of clerks. Consequently he spent a good deal of his time alone at his desk.

Grady reached the end of the last page in the file. After making a copy of his notes for the folder, he tucked it into the file and carried the whole thing to the office of Dan's terribly efficient personal secretary.

Janet was none too fond of Grady. She stared at the file that he placed on her desk, then looked up at him, her pale pink frown seeming to take issue with his very existence.

"What is this?"

"Case file."

She blinked at him, her lashes too black and clumped together. "I can see that it's a case file, but why are you giving it to *me*?"

"You're Dan's secretary."

She let out a long-suffering sigh and narrowed her eyes at him, her lips compressed into a flat line.

Janet had given up complaining that Grady didn't have his own personal secretary, but she made her displeasure known by grudgingly performing those tasks which he did not perform for himself or push off on the young receptionist. Grady had made a halfhearted attempt to find a male secretary at one point, but without success. He'd gotten by with a part-time male law clerk from the University of Arkansas School of Law. Having no personal secretary was an inconvenience, but he had no desire to stutter and stammer his way around a strange female.

Janet flipped open the file folder and checked the contents for herself. "Ah. The Ellis file."

Grady's face heated.

Without a word the secretary handed over the necessary warrants and writs that would be required to prove identities and custody assignments to the South Carolina authorities.

She also passed Grady a map and a pair of printed sheets showing the next day's available flights to and from South Carolina via the regional airport and Tulsa, some ninety minutes away. Then she immediately rose and carried the folder into the back room, where it would be swiftly and efficiently filed.

Donning a camel tan cashmere coat that reached mid-calf, Grady took the elevator down to the parking lot and a cold, drizzling rain, briefcase in tow. He slung the briefcase on to the seat of his Mercedes and followed it, resisting the urge to huddle inside his coat until the heater started blowing warm air.

While navigating the forty-some miles between Fayetteville, Arkansas, and the tiny community of Nobb tucked into the foothills of the Ozarks to the northwest, Grady mulled over what he would say to Paige Ellis, much as he would have thought out an opening statement. He found the Ellis place on the edge of the village just past a pair of silos and a big, weathered barn. A dirt lane snaked upward slightly between gnarled hickories and majestic oaks, past tumbledown fencing and rusting farm implements to a small, white clapboard house.

After parking his sedan next to a midsize, seven-year-old SUV in dire need of a good washing, Grady stepped out of the car. A scruffy, well-fed black lab got up from a rug on the porch and lumbered lazily down the steep front steps to greet Grady with a sniff.

Dan had judged it best not to call before arriving, and Grady hadn't questioned that decision. Paige Ellis worked from her home as a medical transcriptionist and kept regular hours, so she was apt to be available on any given weekday. Suddenly, though, Grady wondered if it was too late to warn her that he was about to descend upon her. Then the dog abruptly opened its yap and did that for him.

The seemingly placid dog howled an alarm that could have put the entire nation on alert. The lab couldn't have been more vociferous if Grady had shown up wearing a black mask and hauling a crate full of hissing cats.

Feeling like a felon, Grady hotfooted it to the house, practically leapt the steps leading up to the porch and skidded to a halt in front of the door, which needed a coat of white paint. He saw no bell, but a brass knocker with a cross-shaped base had been attached to the door at eye level and engraved with the words, As for me and my house, we shall serve the Lord.

Somehow Grady was not surprised to find this evidence that Paige Ellis was a believer. Dan and his family were Christians, active in their local church and given to praying about matters, as was his father, but Grady himself was something of a secret skeptic. He didn't see any point in arguing about it, but he privately wondered if God even existed. If so, why would He let so many bad things happen, like his mother's death and Paige Ellis's son being abducted by her ex-husband?

With the dog still barking to beat the band, Grady reached for the knocker, but before his hand touched the cool metal, the door yanked open. There stood an old fellow with more balding head than sooty, graying hair. Slightly stooped and dressed in a plaid shirt, khakis, suspenders and laced boots, his potbellied weight supported on one side by a battered cane, he swept Grady with faded brown eyes recessed deeply behind a hooked nose that had been broken at least once. Apparently satisfied, he looked past Grady to yell at the dog.

"Shut up, Howler!"

To Grady's relief, the aptly named dog seemed to swallow his last bark, then calmly padded toward the porch.

"Matthias Porter," the old man said, stacking his gnarled hands atop the curved head of his cane. "Who're you?"

Grady had at least four inches and fifty pounds on Porter, and that cane wasn't for show, but the way the old fellow held himself told Grady that he was a scrapper and the self-appointed protector of this place. Grady put out his hand, aware of the dog moving toward the rug on one end of the porch.

"Grady Jones. I'm here to see—"

"Jones," the older man interrupted, "you're Paige's attorney, ain't you?"

Grady nodded. "Actually, my brother, Dan—"

Porter didn't wait to hear about Dan or anything else. Backing up, he waved Grady into the house, saying, "I don't shake. Too painful. Arthritis in my hands. And you're letting in cold air."

His ears still ringing from the dog's howling, Grady stepped forward and found himself in a small living room. He took in at a glance the braided rag rug on the dull wood floor, the old-fashioned sofa covered in a worn quilt, the yellowed shade on the spotted brass lamp next to a broken-down recliner and a wood-burning stove that filled a corner between two doors. A shelving unit stood against one wall at an angle to the recliner and couch. In its center, surrounded by books and numerous photos of a young boy, sat a combination television-set-and-VCR.

Grady knew that the search for Paige Ellis's son had been expensive. If the condition of this house and its furnishings were any indication, the search had required every spare cent that she could scrape together. Feeling out of place and too big for the space, Grady watched Matthias Porter hobble through a door and disappear into a hallway. He had no idea who Matthias Porter was, but it didn't matter. Standing there like an overgrown houseplant, the handle of his briefcase gripped in one fist, he waited with a strange combination of dread and anticipation for Paige Ellis to show herself.

Paige looked up from the computer screen as Matthias entered the room, her fingers automatically typing out the words that continued to drone into her ears. The interruption was sufficiently unusual, however, to have her shutting off the recording a moment later.

Matthias had been a great comfort since he'd moved in nearly two years ago, and he never interrupted her work with anything trivial. Beneath his gruff, somewhat aloof exterior, he was really very sweet and considerate, not to mention protective. She tossed the headphones onto the desk.

"What's wrong?"

"Dunno. But something's up. You got company."

"Who is it?"

The answer knocked her back down into her chair. "Jones."

Her heart thudded heavily. Vaughn. This could only be about Vaughn. Why else would her attorney arrive here unannounced? *"Lord, please let this be good news,"* she prayed, gulping. She looked up at Matthias. "Did Dan Jones say why he's here?"

Matthias shook his head. "Not Dan. Big fella. Says his name's Grady."

Grady Jones was Dan's brother and law partner. She could see even less reason for *his* presence. As curious as she was shaken now, she stood up to her full five feet height and moved woodenly around the desk that occupied almost all of her tiny office.

The room was really nothing more than a screened-in back porch roughly converted with plywood, batts of insulation and plastic sheeting. When Matthias had moved in, she'd refused to even consider taking over Vaughn's bedroom, so this had become her only option.

Paige tugged at the cardigan that she wore with jeans and a flannel shirt and led the way down the hall to the living room, smoothing her fine, yellow blond hair en route. The last cut had been a bit too short and shaggy for her taste, but the stylist had insisted that the wispy ends feathering about her triangular face made her chin look less sharp and brought out the soft green of her eyes. Since her large, tip-tilted eyes already dominated her slender face, Paige wasn't so sure that was a good thing, but it was too late now to worry about it.

Matthias skirted the stove and went into the kitchen as Paige greeted Grady Jones, offering her hand.

"Mr. Jones."

He backed up a step, before slowly reaching out to briefly close his large, square palm around her small hand. Her heart flip-flopped. She'd seen him often around the office in Fayetteville when consulting with Dan, but they'd rarely spoken. A big man with even, masculine features, he reminded her of a bear standing there in that expensive tan overcoat, a wary bear with electric-blue eyes.

"Can I take your coat?"

"Oh, uh, that's all right," he said, shucking the long, supple length of it and draping it over one arm.

"Won't you have a seat then?" She gestured toward the sofa.

Nodding, he backed up to the couch and gingerly folded himself down onto it as if worried he might break the thing. For some reason she found that endearing. She perched next to him, crossing her ankles, and waited until he placed his briefcase at his feet and dropped his coat onto the cushion beside him.

"What's going on?" she asked warily.

"First of all," he said, his voice deep and rumbling, "I want you to know that Dan would have come himself if possible."

She swallowed and nodded her understanding, afraid to ask what was so important that her attorney's partner and brother would come in his stead. Fortunately, Grady Jones didn't keep her in suspense.

"It's good news," he stated flatly. "We've found your son."

She heard the words, even understood that her prayers had finally been answered, but for so long she'd accepted disappointment after disappointment, while trusting that this day would eventually come. Now suddenly it had, and she sat there too stunned to shift from faith to realization.

Then Grady Jones began to explain that Vaughn had been picked up from school by child welfare officials in South Carolina, where his father was being held under arrest after an alert state trooper conducting a routine traffic stop, had recognized him from one of the many electronic flyers they'd distributed to law enforcement agencies around the country. Finally, the realization sank in.

Vaughn was safe and waiting for her to come for him! At last, at long last, her son was coming home!

Clasping her hands together, Paige did the only thing she could think to do. She closed her eyes, turned her face toward the ceiling and thanked God.

"Oh, Father! I praise Your holy name. Thank You. Thank You! Vaughn's coming home!" She began to laugh, tears rolling down her face. "He's coming home. My son is coming home!"

Grady Jones cleared his throat. Paige beamed at him. With two bright spots of color flying high in his cheeks, he looked down. That was when she realized that she was gripping his hand with both of hers.

* * *

She was crying and laughing at the same time. How was a man supposed to react to that? Grady wondered. Displays of emotion always unnerved him. He'd been uncomfortable before; now he wanted to crawl into a cave somewhere. Racking his brain for something, anything, to say, he came up blank, which left him feeling even more hopelessly inadequate than usual.

She suddenly released him, jerking her hands back into her own lap as if he'd snapped at them with his teeth. He felt a fresh flush of embarrassment, but at least his brain began to work again. After a few moments he realized that certain matters had to be addressed. He opened his briefcase and extracted documents, explaining each in detail.

The first would allow the Carolina authorities to release information which would help prove the boy's identity and had already been faxed to the appropriate party. The next proved her identity. Another granted her custody in the state of Arkansas. The fourth proved that such a grant both superseded and complied with Carolina law, and so on. The last document was a charge filed against Nolan Vaughn Ellis for interference with the lawful physical custody of a minor, allowing the state of South Carolina to hold him until such time as the issue of jurisdiction could be settled. Finally came the flight schedules.

"We assumed you wouldn't want to wait until after the holiday to be reunited with your son," Grady told her matter-of-factly.

"I'd go right this minute if I could!" she declared, wiping at her eyes with delicate, trembling fingertips.

He thought of the fresh, lightly starched handkerchief in his pocket, then he looked into her eyes and promptly forgot it again. Those enormous eyes, sparkling now with happy tears, were a soft, muted sea green. He was vaguely aware of the perfect cupid's bow of her dusky pink lips and the adorable button of her nose, but up close like this he couldn't get past those big eyes. Her long, brown lashes, spiked now with her tears, seemed gloriously unadorned. She put him in mind of a sprite or a fairy, her sunny yellow hair wisping at the nape of her neck and around her face. The delicate arch of her pale brows proved that the blond shade was completely natural.

Grady gulped and forced his mind back to the issue at hand.

"Uh, that's, uh, why I'm here instead of Dan. Th-the holiday, I mean. Dan has to consider his family, you understand, but I have no obligations of that sort."

She tilted her head as if trying to figure out why that should be the case. After a long moment she said, "I see."

He winced inwardly, feeling as if she'd looked him over and found the reason why he, unlike his brother, was alone and unattached.

"You, um, you just tell me which of these times works best for you," he mumbled, flushing with embarrassment yet again.

Smiling slightly, she took the printed flight schedules into her small hands and bent her head over them. The edges of the paper trembled. Realizing that she was very likely in shock, he felt duty-bound to point out that the flights leaving from Tulsa were considerably cheaper than those leaving the regional airport.

She nodded and after several seconds said breathlessly, "Early would be best, wouldn't it?"

"If we hope to get there and back in the same day, yes, I'd say so. Plus, they're an hour ahead of us on the East Coast, and we could have lots of legal hurdles to jump before we can bring a minor back across the state lines."

"Well, then, the 5:58 a.m. flight is probably best."

Grady nodded, mentally cringing at how early he'd have to get up to have her at the airport in Tulsa before five o'clock in the morning as security rules dictated. Might as well not even go to bed. Except, of course, that he had to be alert enough for a two-hour drive to the airport in Oklahoma.

"Can you be ready to leave by three in the morning?" he asked apologetically.

She nodded with unadulterated enthusiasm, handing over the papers. "Oh, yes. I doubt I'll sleep at all, frankly."

"I'll be here for you at three, then."

"No, wait," she muttered thoughtfully, drawing those fine brows together. "You'll be coming from Fayetteville, won't you?"

"Yes."

She smiled, and he caught his breath. She literally glowed with happiness.

"Then I'll come to you," she told him. "It'll save time."

Grady frowned. "I couldn't let you do that."

Her tinkling laughter put him in mind of sleigh bells and crisp winter mornings.

"You forget, Mr. Jones," she said with mock seriousness, "that you work for me. Shall we meet at your office? Say, three-thirty? That's cutting it fine, I know, but I can't imagine we'll encounter much traffic along the way."

Her plan would save him over an hour all told, but he just couldn't handle the thought of her being out on the road alone at that hour.

"I'll pick you up here," he insisted.

She blinked, then she smiled. "I guess I'll see you here at three in the morning."

Only then did it occur to him that he might have explained his reasoning instead of just growling at her. Confounded, he snapped the papers inside his briefcase once more and got to his feet, muttering that he had to go.

She popped up next to him, asking, "How can I thank you?" Then next thing he knew, she'd thrown her arms around him in a hug.

"N-no need," he rumbled, his face hot enough to incinerate.

"Please thank your brother for me, too," she went on, tucking her hands behind her and skittering toward the door.

Grady had heard the term "dancing on air" all his life; this was the first time he'd actually witnessed it.

He ducked his head in a nod and stuffed one arm down a sleeve, groping for his briefcase. Getting a grip on the handle, he headed for the door, still trying to find the other armhole of his coat.

"Mr. Jones," called a rusty voice behind him.

He froze, looking back warily over one shoulder, his coat trailing on the floor. Matthias Porter stood next to the stove, beaming, his eyes suspiciously moist. Grady lifted his eyebrows in query.

"I'll see she gets some rest," the old man promised. "Don't you worry none about that."

"Very good," Grady muttered.

Paige opened the door, and he charged out onto the porch. The dog pushed itself up on to all fours and assaulted his eardrums with howling, multioctave barks, the top end of which ought to have shattered glass.

"Howler, hush up!" Matthias Porter bawled from inside the house, and the fat black thing dropped back down onto its belly as if it had been felled with a hammer.

"Thank you again!" Paige called. "Try to get some rest."

Grady scrambled for his car in silence, desperate to get away, but once he was behind the wheel and headed back down the rutted drive, he found that the day was not so gray as it had seemed before. He thought of the happy glow that had all but pulsed from Paige Ellis's serene eyes, and he couldn't help smiling to himself.

He suspected that he'd never again think of Thanksgiving as merely a turkey dinner and a football game.

Chapter Two

Paige sighed with pure delight and settled comfortably onto the leather seat of the Mercedes. She couldn't stop smiling. She suspected, in fact, that she'd smiled in her sleep, what little of it she'd managed to get.

Matthias had insisted that she retire to her bed immediately after dinner, and she had done so simply to humor him. Surprisingly, she'd actually slept a few hours. When the alarm had gone off in the dead of night, she'd awakened instantly to dress in a tailored, olive-green knit pantsuit, her excitement quietly but steadily building.

Her parting with Matthias, who had insisted on getting up to see her off, had been predictably unemotional. He, more than anyone else, knew what this meant to her, but his pride didn't allow for overt displays. Paige understood completely. For a man with nothing and no one, pride was a valuable thing, a last, dear possession.

When they'd heard the vehicle pull up in the yard, Matthias had practically shoved her out the door, rasping that she'd better call if she was going to be returning later than expected. After almost falling over Howler, Paige had climbed into Grady's sumptuous car, where a welcome warmth blew gently from the air vents.

Excitement percolating in her veins, Paige unbuttoned her yellow-gold wool coat and removed her polyester scarf before securing her seat belt. Grady Jones had been right to insist that she not drive herself to his office. She was much too anxious to manage it safely.

"Coffee?" Grady offered as he got them moving. He nodded toward a tall foam cup in the drink holder nearest her.

His voice and manner were gruff, but she didn't mind. Even if it had been a decent hour and she hadn't been on her way—at last!—to her son, Matthias had taught her that gruff was often just a protective mannerism. Besides, it had been thoughtful of Grady to provide the coffee, so even though she rarely drank the stuff, she put on her sweetest smile and thanked him.

"There's sugar and cream in the bag," he said, indicating the white paper sack between them.

"Black's fine," she assured him, unwilling to risk trying to add anything to a cup of hot coffee in a moving vehicle. Saluting him with the drink, she bade him a happy Thanksgiving.

He inclined his head but said nothing, concentrating on his driving. She noticed that his drink holder contained a metal travel cup emblazoned with the logo of a Texas hockey team. She'd seen the same logo on a framed pennant in Dan Jones's office. The brothers apparently shared an interest in the game. They seemed to share little else, other than their occupation.

Besides the obvious physical differences, Dan was friendly and chatty with a quick, open smile, while Grady struck her as the strong, silent type. She felt oddly comfortable with him, safe, though she sensed that he did not feel the same ease in her company. Perhaps he was a loner, then, but a capable one judging by the way he handled the car, and a thoughtful one, too. He'd brought her coffee, after all.

Smiling, she sipped carefully from her cup and found that the beverage was much less bitter than Matthias's brew. Then again, what could possibly be bitter on this most thankful of Thanksgivings?

They traveled for some time in silence while she nursed her coffee and stared out the window. Unsurprisingly, she looked fresh and eager, her big, tilted eyes glowing. That just made Grady feel even more worn and rumpled than usual and did nothing to improve his mood. He knew he ought to say something, but as usual he couldn't think of anything that seemed to make sense.

Somewhere along the turnpike southwest of Siloam Springs, she pointed out across the dark hills and valleys, exclaiming, "Oh, look! Christmas lights."

Grady turned his head and saw a two-story house outlined in brilliant red. "Little early," he rumbled without thinking.

"It is," she agreed, "but aren't they pretty?"

He didn't say anything. Red lights were red lights, so far as he was concerned. He suggested that she might want to get some sleep. "It's still an hour or more to Tulsa."

"I'll sleep once my son's tucked in his own bed again," she commented softly, and they fell back into silence.

After a few minutes, he reached for his coffee and was surprised when she said, "So you're a hockey fan?"

"Hmm?"

"It's on your travel mug."

He glanced at the item in question, drank and set the travel cup aside. "Right. Yeah, I like most sports."

"Me, too."

That surprised him. "Yeah?"

"Uh-huh, I'm really hopeful about the Hogs's basketball season, aren't you?"

Surprised again. "Football's more my thing."

"Oh, that's right. You played corner for the Hogs football team, didn't you?"

Surprised didn't cover it this time. "How did you know?"

"I looked you up on the computer right after my first appointment with your brother."

"You looked me—" His gaping mouth must have appeared comical, for she laughed, and the sound of it brightened the interior of the night-darkened car.

"I have a propensity for trivia, sports trivia in particular. The name sounded familiar to me, so I looked it up."

Grady worked at shutting his mouth before he could mutter, "I don't think that's ever happened before."

"Oh, you might be surprised," she told him. "There are some big sports fans around. My father was one of them, you see, and having only daughters, he literally pined for someone to discuss statistics with. My older sister, Carol, wasn't interested. She lives in Colorado now."

"And you were? Interested, I mean."

"Very. I much preferred sitting in the living room with Dad discussing RBIs and pass completion rates to washing dishes with Mom in the kitchen." She laughed again.

"So it was more an attempt to get out of your chores than a real interest in sports," he surmised.

She shook her head. "No one got out of chores in our household. I just like knowing things. Information is powerful, don't you think?"

Did he ever. "Key to my success as an attorney," he heard himself say, and then when she asked him to explain that, he did. She asked a question, which he answered, and before he knew what was happening they were in Tulsa.

He quickly became consumed with finding a parking spot in the crowded terminal lot. As a consequence, it didn't hit him until he was dragging his briefcase out of the backseat of his car that he'd just spent over an hour in conversation with a woman talking mostly about himself—and he had enjoyed it!

The thought literally froze him in place for a moment. Then Paige Ellis tossed her plaid scarf around her neck and tucked the ends into the front of her bright gold, three-quarter-length coat, looking more polished and lovely than a woman in cheap clothes ought to. Grady shook himself, recalling that she was in an emotional stew at the moment and probably wouldn't remember a word that had been said between them. Her distraction had no doubt led to his own.

Feeling somewhat deflated, he trudged toward the terminal. She fell into step beside him. It had apparently rained in Tulsa the evening before, and little glossy patches of damp remained along the pavement. Paige failed to see one, and the slick sole of her brown flat skidded, so naturally Grady reached out to prevent her from falling. Somehow, she wound up in his arms. She beamed a smile at him, stopping the breath in his lungs. After that he couldn't seem to find a way to let go of her, keeping one hand clamped firmly around her arm until they were safely inside the building.

Thirty minutes later as they moved from check-in to the passenger screening line he began to worry that arriving a mere hour ahead of their departure time had been foolishly shortsighted. Thanksgiving, after all, was the busiest travel day of the entire year.

Paige chattered about first one thing and then another. His fear that they might not make their flight was reason enough not to interrupt her ongoing one-sided conversation about... He lost track of what it was about. But it allowed him to worry for them both, then to be relieved when they walked onto the plane and into their seats with minutes to spare.

When she reached for the in-flight magazine, he knew a moment of mingled relief and disappointment. Apparently, she thought he would be interested in an article, for she began a running commentary on a piece about the latest in computer technology.

Grady remembered his brother saying that because he lived with four women he heard at least 100,000 words per day. At that moment, Grady didn't doubt Dan's assessment. But surprisingly Grady found himself interested. Afterward, they found themselves discussing her work.

Paige Ellis, it turned out, was a marvel of ingenuity and self-discipline. Not only was she a self-taught medical transcriptionist, she had her own cottage industry. By means of a small business loan, she had supplied state-of-the-art computer transcription equipment to four other women, all of whom worked out of their homes and were paid by the hour. By concentrating on doctors in the smaller communities around Fayetteville, Paige had garnered the lion's share of the transcription contracts in the area. Due to the lower costs of her business format, she was able to undercut her competition substantially.

"Thank the good Lord," she declared happily, "I will have the time I've been dreaming about to spend with my son before it's too late." She laughed, and then, to Grady's shock and dismay, she suddenly began to cry.

For Grady it was like being pulled out of a comfortable chair and thrust on to a torture rack. He didn't know what to do or say, so he just sat there like a deer frozen in the headlights and listened to her.

"He's eleven now. Eleven! I've missed *four* birthdays!"

Grady already knew from reading the case file that Nolan Ellis had ostensibly taken the boy for a two-week camping trip at the end of June, three-and-a-half years earlier. It was to have been Vaughn's birthday gift from his dad, and they were to have returned before the boy's actual birth date of July 1. The camping trip, of course, had been a ruse meant to give Nolan a two-week head start to disappear, and it had worked like a charm. Only as she'd sat alone hour after hour, she told him, waiting to light the candles on Vaughn's birthday cake, had Paige begun to realize that the two weeks of her son's absence might well turn into a lifetime.

The particulars of the divorce were likewise already known to Grady, though the Jones firm had not handled it. That, in his opinion, was most unfortunate, something she matter-of-factly confirmed as the story spilled out of her.

High school sweethearts, she and Nolan had married young. By the time their son had reached the age of four, Nolan had decided that he didn't want to be married, after all. Resentful over his "lost youth" and the burden of family responsibilities, he had simply walked out.

Even more shocking, the divorce papers had alleged that Nolan might not be Vaughn's father. Angry and hurt, Paige had signed without even consulting an attorney. Only later did she realize what Grady, or any other halfway competent attorney, could have told her: she had, in effect, signed away her and Vaughn's right to financial support.

She'd realized her mistake when she'd transcribed notes concerning a case in which one of her clients, a medical lab, had been called upon to verify paternity so that child support could be levied. After hearing Paige's story, a helpful lab technician had arranged for Vaughn to be tested and had also recommended an attorney who dealt with paternity cases. When Nolan predictably resurfaced several months before Vaughn's eighth birthday, Paige had been ready. She'd hit Nolan with a court order, proved that he was Vaughn's father and been awarded substantial monthly child support.

Nolan had been livid, but he'd seemed to calm down fairly quickly.

"I did think he might disappear again after the court decision went against him," she said, sniffing, "but after he stuck around for a while, I started to believe that he really wanted to be a father to Vaughn. That's what my little boy wanted, and who could blame him? Every little boy wants a daddy. I never dreamed Nolan would take Vaughn and disappear."

"It's not your fault," Grady said, wondering when his arm had come to be draped about her shoulders.

"I can't help wondering if he's missed me," she whispered.

"Little boys want their moms, too," Grady assured her.

"Do you really think so?"

Grady realized suddenly that all this chatter was a product of her emotional state, so when she turned that hopeful, tear-stained face up to him, what else could he do but tell her about his own experiences?

"I know so. I was six when my mom died, and nothing's been quite right in my world since."

How on earth they got from talking about losing his mom to talking about his divorce, he would never know. At some point he started telling her how his marriage had fallen apart.

"So, she left you to marry your boss," Paige clarified sharply, both surprising and puzzling him.

Embarrassment and pain roiled in his gut, but he'd come so far already that he didn't see any point in pulling back now. "Technically he was her boss, too, since we both worked for the same Little Rock law firm."

"And how did that come about?" Paige wanted to know.

Grady shrugged. "I asked them to hire her."

Paige folded her arms at this. "So let me get this straight.

First she refused to stay in Fayetteville and join your family's practice."

"There aren't any opportunities for advancement in a small family partnership," he explained.

"Then, the firm in Little Rock hired *you*, and wanted you bad enough to take *her* in the bargain. Right?"

Eventually he nodded. "Right."

"So she used you to get into a firm she couldn't have gotten into on her own, then she left you for someone with more power and prestige." Paige threw up her hands, exclaiming, "Well, at least she stayed true to form!"

"T-true to form?"

"It's obvious, isn't it? She manipulated you, and when she found someone else who could offer her more, she traded up."

He was so taken aback by the idea that for a moment he couldn't even give it proper thought. Paige must have taken his silence for censure, for she suddenly wrinkled her pert little nose, sighed and muttered, "Okay, I shouldn't be judging, but such selfishness gets to me."

His family had hinted at the same thing, that Robin had left him for his boss not just because the man was elegant, affable and downright loquacious but because she was greedy. It hadn't made sense at the time. His bank account was hefty enough, after all. Since then he'd avoided thinking about it because it was too painful.

Now, after several years, he could see things from a different perspective. Robin had used him. That didn't make the hurtful and numerous accusations she'd thrown at him any less true. Did it?

He shook his head. Robin was correct about him being inept with women. Had she not pursued him, he doubted that they'd have ever gotten together. One-on-one with a woman, his tongue stuck to the roof of his mouth and his mind went completely blank. The more attractive he found her, the worse it was.

Usually, he amended silently, glancing sideways at Paige.

It was nuts to think that he might be any different with Paige. If his poor communication skills and emotional ineptness were not enough, there was his clumsiness. Okay, maybe once he'd been fleet of foot and a force to be reckoned with on the athletic field, but those days were long gone. That he'd been able to discuss them, even briefly, with Paige Ellis had been terribly flattering, which had led to hours of conversation. The fact that he'd enjoyed those hours so much suddenly made him seem especially pathetic.

None of this meant anything to Paige, after all. She was an admitted sports freak; he'd allowed her interest in the fact that he'd once played college football to become more personal than it was surely intended to be.

Disturbed, Grady let his seat back, mumbling that they had a long day ahead of them, and closed his eyes. She agreed with him and curled up in her seat, but she did not sleep. He knew this because he didn't sleep, either.

They changed planes in Atlanta, and on that last, short leg of the trip, he avoided personal conversation by discussing business, beginning with a particular form that she needed to sign. He'd mentioned it before, but she'd been in too much shock to really understand at that time.

"In other words," she said, after he'd gone over the whole thing once again, "if I sign this, we'll be pressing charges against Nolan in South Carolina as well as Arkansas. Is that correct?"

Pleased that she'd grasped the concept this time, he reached for an ink pen. "Exactly."

"But I'm not sure that's what I ought to do."

His hand stopped with the slim, gold-plated barrel of the

ink pen still lodged within the leather loop provided for it. "I beg your pardon?"

"I'm not sure I want to prosecute Nolan."

Grady's tongue seemed to run away with him. "Why on earth not?" he demanded. "The man kidnapped your son!"

The spike-haired lady across the aisle turned a curious gaze on them, and Grady realized he'd raised his voice.

"You think I don't know that?" Paige said with some asperity. "Believe you me, I know what it's like to miss your child with every fiber of your being, minute by minute, hour after hour, day after day after week after month.... And I realize that I'm about to do the same thing to Nolan that he did to me. The pain of that may be punishment enough."

"That's not the point," Grady told her urgently, doing his best to keep his voice down. "This is about protecting you and Vaughn."

"That *is* the point," she insisted, sliding into the far corner of her seat and folding her arms. "I can't let this be about retribution, and right now, for me, it is."

"I don't understand."

"I don't expect you to. Suffice it to say that I've been seeing a counselor for some time now, and she, along with my Christian ethics, warn me against seeking any sort of vengeance."

"What about what's best for your son?"

"I think this is what's best for my son," she stated firmly. "Nolan is his *father*. Do you think he wants his father punished? I don't think so."

"I would," Grady insisted. "Knowing he kept me away from my mother, I surely would."

Paige shook her head. "You only say that because you can't see the other side. You haven't been a parent. You don't know what it means to put the welfare of your child first. I'm sure Dan would understand what I'm trying to say."

That stung, far, far more than it should have. She was correct, but that didn't keep Grady from feeling great alarm on her behalf. As far as he was concerned, allowing Nolan Ellis to walk around free was a reckless and frightful thing for this woman and her son. His every instinct screamed for prosecution on every possible level, but all he could do was point out the legal loopholes that she would be leaving open if she failed to follow his advice.

She listened, but he could tell that he wasn't convincing her. Frustrated, he searched for a way to compel her to accept his reasoning.

"No one would blame you if you locked him up and threw away the key!"

"That's beside the point."

"Then what is the point?"

"Doing the right thing."

For a moment he could only stare at her, wondering if she was for real. "This *is* the right thing."

She stared back and finally said, "I'll pray about it." With that she turned away from him.

Confounded, Grady watched her bow her head and retreat into herself. He'd made his best case, giving her good, solid legal advice, but he might as well have saved his breath. Obviously they didn't communicate as well as he'd thought.

This wasn't the first time his legal advice had been rejected, after all, not by a long shot, but he'd never been more disturbed about it.

Popping his seat back again, he folded his arms and shut his eyes, determined to finally catch a few minutes of rest or at least some peace.

Both would prove to be in very short supply.

They touched down at the Greenville-Spartanburg International Airport at a quarter past eleven that morning.

After renting a car, they drove to the Greenville County Sheriff's Department where Vaughn waited, having spent the previous night in a group foster care facility. Grady had not pressed Paige for a decision about prosecuting Nolan, which was good since she truly didn't know what she was going to do.

Now that the moment to see her son again—after three years, six months and one day—had finally arrived, Paige was so nervous she felt ill. Pressing a hand to her abdomen and surreptitiously gulping down air in an effort to settle her stomach, she walked through the heavy glass door that Grady held open for her. They met briefly with a polite, efficient uniformed officer who checked their paperwork and led them through a narrow hallway to a private conference room.

Her heartbeat grew louder and the knots in her stomach pulled tighter and tighter with every step that she took, so that by the time Grady paused with his hand on the plain, brushed steel doorknob, she could barely breathe.

"Ready?" he asked softly.

Reminding herself that Vaughn might be ambivalent at first, she pulled her spine straight and nodded. As that heavy, metal door swung inward, she began to tremble. Grady pushed into the small, crowded room. She practically ran over him, suddenly so eager that she could not contain herself.

Everything registered at once: pale walls, pale floor, pale, rectangular table flanked by lightweight metal chairs with blue, molded vinyl seats. A green-and-white bag with some team logo printed in red sat in the center of the table, stuffed so full of clothing that it couldn't be zipped. Two women— one young, white and plump with a brown ponytail, the other African-American, slender and slightly older—occupied two of the chairs on the near side of the table.

Across from them sat a boy, a stranger, who shot abruptly to his feet.

Paige's first thought was that they'd made a mistake. This could not be her son. He stood at least as tall as her own five feet, with no trace of the bright copper-blond hair that had crowned her baby boy. Instead, the thick, fine locks falling haphazardly over his brows, tangling with the thick lashes rimming his warm brown eyes, was a rich auburn. Then he tossed his head defiantly, and she caught a glimpse of a jagged scar just above his right eyebrow, the scar he'd gotten tumbling headlong off the porch into the shrubbery.

"Vaughn!"

How she got around the table she didn't know, but when she threw out her arms, he flinched and backed away. She'd been told to expect this, and yet disappointment seared her trembling heart. Sucking in a deep breath, she forced her feet to slow.

It was like approaching a feral animal, once domesticated but now wild. He seemed uncertain, but she sensed that he definitely recognized her. Carefully, her lips quivering, she slipped her arms around him. Perhaps it wasn't wise, but she had to, *had to,* hold him, if only for a moment.

"Mom," he whispered in a voice she would never have recognized and yet somehow knew.

Only with great effort did she manage not to sob, but stopping the tears completely was impossible. She smiled through them, cupped his slender, oval face in her hands, pulled it gently forward and laid her forehead to his as she had so often in the past.

"Thank You, God. Thank You. Thank You."

Chapter Three

Vaughn let her hold him for a time, but then the two women at the table introduced themselves, and he pulled away. The young one was a caseworker with Child Protective Services, the other a Victims Services agent with the county sheriff's office. After making themselves known, they seemed content to sit back and observe, leaving Paige to focus once more on her son.

He had backed into the corner of the room, his arms tightly folded across his chest. It was not a good sign. Paige tried not to take offense. It was only to be expected. He'd spent the last three-and-a-half years with his father. He was bound to be confused. She couldn't help noting that he was a handsome boy whose shoulders were already broadening, and now that she got a good look at him, she realized something else.

"You look like my dad."

He frowned. "No, I don't. I look like *my* dad."

"You're built like Nolan," she agreed quickly, aware that she was tiptoeing through a minefield here, "and you have the same coloring, but that's my father's chin and nose you've got." He bowed his head, as if rejecting anything she might say. Paige gulped and searched for some way to meaningfully engage him. "Do you remember your grandfather?"

Vaughn snorted, glancing up at her sullenly. "'Course. I wasn't *that* little when he died."

He'd been five and inconsolable. The memory of how he'd cried for his grandpa wrenched her heart. Had he cried like that for her? She wouldn't ask, for both their sakes.

Chairs scraped back as first the Child Protective Services caseworker and then the Victims Services agent rose. "I think we've heard all we need to," the VS agent said, her dark face parting in a smile that was half congratulatory, half sympathetic. "You should have some paperwork for us."

"The desk officer has it," Grady replied.

"Yes, of course." She stepped forward and addressed the boy. "You take care, Vaughn. Happy Thanksgiving."

He did not so much as acknowledge her words. The CPS caseworker skirted the table and hugged him.

"Cheer up, honey. It's going to be okay." He nodded glumly, but didn't speak. She patted his shoulder and turned to Paige. "Happy Thanksgiving."

"A very happy Thanksgiving," Paige murmured, clasping the woman's hand. "Thank you both from the bottom of my heart."

"Just doing our jobs," she said.

The two women quickly exited the room. The instant the door swung closed, Vaughn all but attacked. "What happens now?"

"We're going home, son," Paige said gently. "I thought you knew that."

"I know I gotta go with you," he declared, his voice breaking with the weight of his emotion, "but it's not my home, not anymore. What I mean is, what happens to my dad?" He started to cry. "They got him in jail! He always said you'd put him away if you found us. That's not right! He doesn't belong in jail!"

"Don't worry," she urged, pulling him into her arms again. She couldn't let herself be hurt by his concern for Nolan. What counted now was putting Vaughn's fears to rest. She knew what she had to do, had known how it would be. Taking a deep breath, she firmly stated, "I have no intention of pressing charges against your father."

"That may not be wise," Grady warned, but she shook her head at him, convinced that she was right in this.

As much as she believed Nolan had wronged her and their son, as much anger as she'd carried with her over their separation, no good would be served by punishing Nolan legally.

"Does that mean they'll let him go?" Vaughn asked hopefully. "I'll leave with you if they'll let him go."

"You'll go with her anyway," Grady pointed out to Vaughn, pitching his voice low. "You don't have a choice. Paige, you need to think about this."

"I have thought about it."

"We need to consider this carefully," Grady argued.

"My mind's made up, Grady."

"For pity's sake, Paige!" Grady Jones erupted, and that triggered Vaughn.

"It's none of your business!" he shouted at Grady, then rounded on his mother. "What's he got to say about it, anyway? Just 'cause he's your boyfriend or something, that doesn't—"

"He's *not* my boyfriend!" she exclaimed, grasping the boy by the tops of his arms. "He's my attorney."

"*One* of your attorneys," Grady corrected smartly.

"*One* of my attorneys," she snapped, glaring at him over her shoulder.

Vaughn shuffled his feet and bowed his head, muttering, "It's still none of his business."

"It's not his decision, but it *is* his job to advise me," Paige pointed out calmly.

"For all the good it does," Grady muttered.

Paige ignored him, looking to her son, who asked, "So Dad can go home?"

"I can't say what the South Carolina authorities will do," Paige told the boy, "but your dad won't stay in jail because of me, Vaughn, I swear it." Sliding one arm around his shoulders, she turned to face Grady. "Can the South Carolina authorities keep him if I don't press charges?"

Grady clenched his jaw and looked away, but then he answered. "No."

"What about the state of Arkansas?"

He fixed her with a level stare. "They may want him held for failure to pay child support."

She could feel Vaughn trembling beside her and lifted her chin. "What if I speak in his favor, petition for leniency on his behalf? Forgo the back payments?" Grady was so clearly appalled by the mere suggestion of her intervention that she felt her temper spark.

"That would not be wise," he rumbled.

"That is not an answer to my question."

"You haven't thought this through," he insisted.

She took that to mean that her intervention on Nolan's behalf would likely result in him doing no time. She turned back to her son. "I'll keep him out of jail," she promised.

Vaughn slumped with obvious relief. Paige put on as bright a face as she could manage and announced, "Our plane doesn't leave until almost three, so Mr. Jones made lunch reservations for us at a hotel downtown."

Vaughn put on a sullen face and grumbled, "I'm not hungry."

"No? But it's Thanksgiving, and you love turkey. I know you do. Especially the drumstick." He made a face at that, and she supposed that his delight with drumsticks at Thanksgiving dinners past seemed babyish to him now. She quickly went on, changing the subject. "We should be home before nine this evening."

He lifted his head, looked her in the eye. "My home's in South Carolina."

She felt her heart drop, but swallowed down the part that seemed to have lodged in her throat. "But Nobb's your home, too," she said softly. "You'll see that if you just give it a chance. I've missed you so much, Vaughn, more than you can possibly know, and we're going to work everything out, I promise."

He said nothing, just ducked his head, sighed and dragged his feet toward the door with all the enthusiasm of a condemned prisoner on his way to the gallows. Pushing aside her heartache, Paige reminded herself that this was to be expected. Only God knew what adjustments they had in store for them, but then only God could make them a family again.

Grady determined that he would not let his own dissatisfaction with Paige's decision not to prosecute her ex-husband color the meal. He was furious with her, worried about her and just generally disgruntled, but after an hour or so in the boy's icy, hostile company, he decided that *his* mood was definitely the brighter of the two.

Paige, for all her quiet joy and steely determination, could not lighten the atmosphere. Nevertheless, she tried, commenting gently on the quality of the food and the service, remarking what a treat it was not to have to cook Thanksgiving dinner for herself, asking quiet, neutral questions about Vaughn's life, most of which he answered with as few syllables as possible.

Did he like school? Sometimes.

What was his best friend's name? Toby.

Favorite junk food? Barbecue potato chips.

Last book he'd read? Didn't know.

She appeared to take no offense at his sullen, almost belligerent replies. When the meal arrived she prayed over it, simply bowed her head and began, as if it was perfectly normal.

"Father, we have so much to be thankful for today. I cannot thank You enough for bringing my son back to me. You have heard my prayers, and I know that You will continue to do so. Give each of us wisdom now, Lord, as we work to make of our lives what You would have them be, and bless the Jones brothers for all that they have done on our behalf. Amen."

As she spoke softly, Grady looked around the room self-consciously, while Vaughn sprawled in his chair, glaring at him. Grady noted with some surprise that several other diners had also bowed their heads.

The meal crept by with Paige pretending not to notice that Vaughn wasn't eating. She did try to deflect his glower from time to time, without much success. Grady fumed, uncertain just what the boy's problem was. The crazy kid seemed to blame him, Grady, for his father's problems!

Didn't he understand how lucky he was to be back with his mom? At his age Grady would have done anything, *anything*, just to share one more meal with his mother. In Grady's opinion, Vaughn Ellis should be on his knees, kissing his mother's feet instead of worrying about his self-centered father, and it was all Grady could do not to tell him so.

As soon as the meal was finished and Grady paid the check—determined that this was one part of the trip that wouldn't find it's way onto Paige's bill—Vaughn demanded to see his father. Paige turned troubled, pleading eyes to

Grady, and he found himself almost sorry that he hadn't had the foresight to arrange any such thing. Almost.

He shook his head. "Can't be done, not on this short notice and a holiday."

"I'm sorry, Vaughn," she told the boy sincerely, an arm draped lightly about his shoulders. "You can call him later."

Grady shook his head at that, at a complete loss. Didn't she know what Nolan would do if she gave him just half a chance? He'd already absconded with her son once. Did she think he wouldn't do it again? Grady decided that he was going to have a long talk with his brother about this once he got home. Maybe Dan could make her see reason. What it would take to reach the boy, Grady couldn't even imagine, but he was glad that he wasn't in Paige's shoes. This, he thought morosely, should have been such a happy day, not tense and silent and barely civil.

The ride to the airport was gloomy at best. Sitting in the backseat with her son, who seemed determined to ignore her, Paige didn't even try to make conversation. They had to visit a shop in the airport in order to purchase a second bag and get the boy's clothes safely stowed for the trip, but when Paige began to repack his things, Vaughn elbowed her aside, grumbling that he would do it.

She backed away, her arms locked about her middle as if she was trying to hold herself together. Grady found himself at her side, his voice pitched low.

"He doesn't know what he's doing right now."

She flashed a wan smile at him. "I expected it to be difficult," she said softly, "but I thought my son would at least be glad to see me."

"Well, sure he is," Grady insisted, though they both knew better.

Her eyes gleamed with liquid brilliance, brimming with a kind of bittersweet pain that made Grady want to howl. "I don't know him anymore," she whispered brokenly. "I don't even know my own son."

"You'll get to know him," Grady rumbled, squeezing her fingers quickly. "It'll be okay," he told her, wishing for an eloquence he'd only ever found inside a courtroom.

Her smile grew a little wider. "You're a good man, Grady Jones."

His heart thumped inside his chest. Vaughn rose from his task then, sparing Grady from having to find a reply. He pointed toward the ticket counter, muttering that they had to get the boy checked in for the flight, and walked off in that direction. Only later, when the flight clerk was ready to receive the boy's luggage, did it dawn on Grady that he'd left Paige and the kid to manage the bags.

He was still mentally kicking himself for that a half hour later when they arrived at the departure gate, having passed through security. The place was surprisingly crowded, and Grady frowned. Weren't these people supposed to be home eating turkey? He concentrated on finding seats for them in the waiting area, then parked himself against the nearby wall.

Paige had bought Vaughn a couple of magazines in which he'd shown interest at the store, but the brat shook his head mutely when she offered them to him. Deflated, Paige shot a resigned look to Grady, and it was all he could do not to shake the kid. Grady tried not to watch the careful way in which she approached the boy, as if he were a wounded animal, but he couldn't seem to take his eyes off them, and every time her son rebuffed her, his temper spiked a little higher.

By the time they were finally able to board the flight, Grady was gnashing his teeth. What was wrong with the kid? Didn't he see how unfairly he was treating his mother? She hadn't created this situation; his father had.

Only after they changed planes in Atlanta did Paige again try to communicate with her son. She asked gentle question after gentle question and received in reply only shrugs and sharp glances from the corners of his eyes. When she began to talk about her plans for Christmas, explaining what she and Matthias had discussed, Vaughn finally deigned to speak.

"Who's Matthias?" he demanded, screwing up his face.

Paige smiled. "Didn't I say? Matthias Porter is our boarder."

"What's that?"

"Well, he rents a room in our house."

"So we're poor?" Vaughn surmised caustically.

"No, we're not poor. We're not rich but certainly not poor."

"Then how come you're renting out rooms?"

Paige looked down, and for a moment Grady thought she'd tell the kid how much money she'd spent finding him. Instead she said, "Matthias had nowhere else to go. He's elderly but too healthy for a nursing home and too poor to live on his own."

"What happened to his family?"

"I don't think he had much. His wife died, and he was left all alone," Paige told the boy softly. "Like me."

Vaughn looked away at that. "I'm sorry," he said, his voice like shards of glass, "but if you've got Matthias now, why don't you let me go back to Dad? Or else he'll be all alone!"

Grady saw the naked pain on her face, even after she squeezed her eyes shut, whispering, "Oh, Vaughn."

A moment later she reached up and pressed the boy's head down on her shoulder. He let it stay there, but he wasn't happy about it. In fact, looking at them, Grady didn't think he'd ever seen two more miserable people in his whole life.

He'd have given his eyeteeth if he could have somehow made it better.

It had never occurred to him that Vaughn wouldn't be eager to return to his mother, that the boy might actually prefer his father. Didn't the kid realize that his father had literally stolen him from his mother?

Grady began to understand that finding her son had been a beginning for Paige rather than simply the end of her search. Her waiting and wondering was over, but now she had embarked on a long, new, difficult journey with her son, and that trip promised to make this one look like a romp in the park.

It was dark when the plane landed in Tulsa. Vaughn perked up a bit when he saw the Mercedes, asking his mom, "This yours?"

"No," she answered evenly. "It belongs to Mr. Jones."

Vaughn's manner was almost derisive as he climbed inside, as if she had somehow proven herself a failure in his eyes by not owning the car. Grady had to bite back the impulse to point out that Vaughn's precious dad had been picked up in a four-year-old truck with a crease in the tailgate.

As chatty as Paige had been on the drive from Arkansas, she was that silent on the long drive back from the airport in Oklahoma. In fact, if a single word was spoken during the first hour, Grady remained unaware of it. Vaughn leaned into a corner of the backseat, crossed his arms and feigned sleep, while Paige sat beside him and bowed her head. Every time Grady looked into the rearview mirror, there she sat with her head bowed, as still as a statue. He began to think that, unlike Vaughn, she really had fallen asleep. Then Grady saw her lips moving and realized that she was praying again.

She looked up at the sigh that gusted out of him, and their eyes seemed to meet in the mirror, though he doubted that she could actually see him. A small, tender smile curved the corners of her mouth before she looked away again. He couldn't imagine that her smile was for him, but it kept him looking at her in the mirror when he should have been concentrating on his driving.

Eventually Vaughn sat up and complained that he was hungry. Considering that he hadn't eaten his Thanksgiving dinner, Grady wasn't surprised. At Paige's request, Grady found an open drive-through at one of the little towns that they passed along the way to Nobb. Vaughn ordered a burger, tater tots and a drink that looked like it could fill a fifty-five-gallon drum. Grady didn't say anything about the kid eating in his car, though it was not something Grady normally would have allowed.

Vaughn had wolfed down the food and was sucking air through his straw by the time Grady turned on to Paige's drive. For the first time, the boy showed some interest in his surroundings. The house came into view, and for an instant Grady thought he saw something pleasant in the boy's reflection in his rearview mirror before Vaughn sat back and remarked derisively, "Hasn't changed a bit."

Grady held his tongue, recalling perfectly well that the address given on Nolan's arrest record had been that of an apartment complex in Curly, South Carolina, a small town on the outer edge of Greenville County. He heard Paige murmur that she'd had the back porch remodeled into an office, but Vaughn didn't ask why as Grady parked the vehicle and got out.

The big black dog came down from the porch to greet them, and Grady assumed that his car was now familiar enough that the animal wouldn't bother barking. The thing hadn't let out a peep when Grady had arrived in the dark that morning, but no sooner did Vaughn step out of the Mercedes than the dog sat back on his haunches and lived up to his name, throwing back its head and slicing the air with yips and yowls and some sounds Grady had never before heard a living creature make.

Vaughn clapped his hands over his ears, while Paige attempted to scold the dog into silence. Light spilled out of the front door. Matthias appeared, and as before a command from him shut off the awful cacophony.

"Howler!"

Subdued now, the dog's pink tongue lolled out of its mouth as it waited eagerly for Vaughn to pet it. Instead, he stomped toward the house, leaving his mother to retrieve the bags that Grady pulled from the trunk of the car. Matthias came down the steps toward the boy, a smile—or at least what passed for a smile—on his craggy face.

"Don't mind old Howler," the old man said. "He's all alarm and no guard."

Ignoring Vaughn's scowl, he stuck out a hand, but the kid twisted past him and all but ran into the house, slamming the door behind him. Matthias stood for a moment, gazing toward Paige, who sighed. She seemed tired and sad. Finally, the old man turned and made his painful way up the steps and back inside.

Paige turned to Grady. "I tried to prepare myself," she said, and he heard the trembling uncertainty in her voice. "Knowing intellectually how difficult it might be and going through it are two different things, I guess."

He wanted to tell her that time would heal all wounds, that the worst was past her, anything to make it better. But what did he know? As she'd pointed out earlier, he had no experience as a parent and no hope of it. She likely would not appreciate words from him, anyway, so he just hoisted the bags and muttered, "I'll carry these in for you."

"No," she said, taking them from him, "you've done enough. Thank you. With all my heart, thank you."

He shook his head, shocked by the urge to hug her. Instead he asked, "You going to be okay?"

She smiled tremulously. "Oh, yes. My son is home. He isn't happy about it, but I knew he might not be, and I really have tried to prepare myself to deal with it."

"I don't know how anyone could prepare themselves for this."

"I've been seeing a Christian psychologist for the past two years."

"Didn't know there was such a thing."

"Oh, yes. Why wouldn't there be?"

He shrugged. "Just never thought about it."

"I wanted someone who shares my beliefs. My pastor recommended her."

"Ah. Makes sense, I guess."

"Dr. Evangeline's been very helpful," she said. "I'm really not surprised by Vaughn's behavior."

Just disappointed. Heartsick. Weary. She didn't have to say it. Grady saw it in the droop of her slender shoulders, the tilt of her head, the dullness of her beautiful eyes.

Grady looked to the house, escaping the weight of her emotions by wondering what might be going on in there. "I guess."

Her gaze followed his, and she whispered, "I can't help wondering what Nolan's told him about me, though. I mean, how did he explain taking him away from me?"

Grady hadn't thought of that. "Well," he said slowly, "any number of ways, I guess."

"And none of them good," she muttered, adding wistfully, "he was barely eight when they disappeared, just a little boy. He wouldn't know what to believe or what not to." She looked to the house again. "Now he's almost a teenager, and I have to accept that there's no making up for lost time. He has to learn how to have a mom again."

It occurred to Grady that he and Vaughn had something in common: they'd both been denied their moms at very young ages. Suddenly Grady thought of the last time he'd seen his own mother.

No one could have guessed that day as she'd dropped him off at school that she would never make it back home. To his shame, he'd shrugged away the kiss that she'd pressed to his cheek as he'd gotten out of the car, and he hadn't looked back or waved a farewell even though he'd known that she would watch him all the way through the door of the building.

He'd never seen her again. When his dad had shown up at the school later that morning with his brother sobbing at his side, Grady had known that something awful had happened, but he'd never expected to hear that his mom was gone forever. He hadn't believed it. Sometimes he still didn't believe it.

Grady didn't tell any of that to Paige. He had never told it to anyone. It was just something that he lived with. Suddenly Vaughn didn't seem like such a brat. No doubt the kid was terribly confused right now. Remembering what that was like, Grady hoped that the boy would soon come to see how lucky he was to get his mom back.

Clearing his throat, he said that Dan would probably be calling her in the next couple of days. She thanked him again, and then there was nothing left to do but get back into the car and head home alone.

He should have been relieved, and on one level he was. It had been a long, trying day. Still, he couldn't help feeling that he was abandoning Paige.

His last sight of her was in his car's left side mirror. Bathed in the rosy glow of his taillights, she stood there alone with a bag grasped in each hand, a small woman with a big job before her.

If he'd been a praying man, Grady would have said a prayer especially for her. As it was, he fixed his gaze forward and drove home, even more troubled than the last time he'd done so.

Chapter Four

Paige listened to the door slam and dropped down onto the sofa, sighing inwardly.

Nothing she'd done or said in the past month had made her son the least bit happy. He'd hated his room on sight. Too "babyish."

She'd rearranged everything and bought new linens and window treatments, keeping her regret buried as she'd put away the boy he'd been, all the things she'd treasured to remind herself that he was real and belonged in this place. He hadn't seemed particularly pleased once the changes had been made, but given how often he retreated to his room in a huff, he must have felt more comfortable with his personal surroundings than before.

Today's huff had to do with his impending return to school. Or perhaps it was the gifts he'd received yesterday for Christmas. Or the "do nothing" environment of Nobb. It was all tied up together somehow.

She'd kept Christmas low-key, realizing that it might not be the celebration for him that it was for her. Recalling the dreary Christmases she'd spent without him, she tried not to dwell on the fact that this one hadn't quite lived up to her expectations. He'd spent most of the day bemoaning the fact that he was missing out on a hunting trip his father had promised him.

Before noon on this first day after Christmas he'd declared the video games she'd bought him "boooring," the radio-controlled car "junk," the clothes "lame." Then he'd complained that he didn't have anyone to do anything with.

Realizing that she was not yet *someone* to him, she'd made the mistake of suggesting that they invite over a few of the kids from church. He'd rolled his eyes, already having made known his feelings about church, which according to his dad was for "weaklings and nut jobs."

She wondered if Nolan had always thought that, even during the years that he'd attended with her, starting when they were dating in high school. After Vaughn's birth Nolan's church attendance had grown increasingly sporadic, until it finally ceased. Once that had happened, the divorce had quickly followed, but Vaughn didn't need to know that.

Or did he? She wasn't sure, and since she wasn't certain, she kept her mouth shut. Everything she believed told her that it was wrong to point out Nolan's faults to his son. Yet, she wanted him to understand the importance and value of regular worship. Reminding herself that if she was confused, then he must be even more so, she held on to her patience. And her convictions.

Because Vaughn had nixed inviting over any of the youth from church, she had wondered aloud if he might want to call some particular friend from school. He'd laughed aloud at her idea of contacting one of the boys from his class, declaring that those who didn't attend the local church were even "dumber" and "hickier" than those who did. In fact, the whole school was "stupid," he'd declared, and he wasn't going back after the first of the year.

Paige had quietly but firmly refuted that, which had sent him slamming into his room.

Their counselor, Dr. Evangeline, had strongly recommended public school for Vaughn. Paige's first impulse had been to hold him out until the start of the new semester, giving them a chance to get to know one another again, but Dr. Evangeline had insisted that Vaughn needed the socialization, needed to find replacements for the buddies he'd left behind in South Carolina. When the doctor had pointed out that because of state attendance standards, keeping him home those three weeks between Thanksgiving and Christmas vacations could cause him to be left behind a year, Paige had been convinced.

She constantly fought the impulse to hold him close and never let go again, so it had been difficult to take him down on the Wednesday after Thanksgiving and enroll him in the Nobb Middle School, which was part of the large, wealthy Bentonville district. He'd hated it from day one.

He hated Dr. Evangeline, too, a fact he'd made known during their first joint session with her. It hadn't been pretty. Since then he'd repeatedly said that a "guy" would do better, understand more, "actually listen, maybe."

Paige worried that Vaughn had a problem with women in general, starting with her. He not only disdained the psychologist to the point of rudeness, he disliked his female teachers—though the lone male in the group hardly fared any better—complained that the husband of the couple who taught his mixed Sunday school class deferred too often to his wife, and made sure that Paige knew how far short she fell of the Nolan ideal in parenting, running a household and everything else.

In short Vaughn hated everything and everyone in Arkansas, including her. Maybe most especially her. Those sentiments had grown darker and more vocal over time, especially since Dr. Evangeline had suggested that Vaughn should not be allowed contact with his father at least until he settled into his mother's household again. That, more than anything else, had enraged Vaughn.

Now Paige no longer knew what the right thing to do was. She only knew that her son resented not being allowed to call his father and that it was just one item on a very lengthy list.

Matthias limped into the living room, his cane thumping pronouncedly on the hardwood floor with every step. The weather had turned sunny and mild, but his arthritis had not noticeably improved. That had nothing to do with the frown on his weathered face, though.

"It ain't my habit to give advice unasked," he announced, "but I'm makin' an exception here and now."

Resignation weighing heavily on her, Paige crossed her legs, denim whispering against denim. "Go ahead. Say it."

"It's time to tie a knot in that boy's tail."

"And how would you suggest I do that, Matthias? Take a belt to him?" They both knew that was out of the question.

"Stop letting him walk all over you. Ever since he's been here you've bent over backwards trying to please, but the world just ain't ordered to his liking. We know who he's got to thank for that, even if he don't. Maybe it's time he was told."

She shook her head. "I don't think it's wise to run down his father to him. That's Nolan's game, and it's bound to backfire. It's bad enough that Vaughn's life has been turned completely upside down without me trying to turn him against his dad."

"He can be glad it ain't up to me," Matthias mumbled, heading back into the kitchen where she had a pot of stew bubbling on the stove and corn bread baking in a cast-iron skillet. "I'd show him upside down."

Paige closed her eyes and fought the bleakness of despair with the only tool she had. *Lord, help me do what's best for my boy,* she prayed silently. *Show me what needs to be done and give me the strength and patience to do it. Help him understand how much I love him, how much You love him, and thank You for bringing him home to me.*

She could only trust that one day Vaughn would be thankful, as well.

"Happy New Year."

"Hmm?" Grady turned away from the window, a cup of coffee in hand to find his brother standing in their father's kitchen, grinning.

"What'd you and the old man do last night, party until the wee hours?"

Grady snorted. "Hardly. I might have been the youngest one here, but I went to bed as soon as the ball dropped in New York."

"Party pooper," Howard groused, coming into his kitchen with one arm draped around his daughter-in-law's shoulders. "Look what Katie brought us."

She slipped free of Howard and carried the enameled pot with its glass lid in sight of Grady before placing it on the range.

"Spaghetti?" Grady noted, surprised.

Katie turned her dentist-perfect smile on him. "You're not superstitious, are you, Grady?" Katie asked.

"Black-eyed peas are just more traditional."

She scrunched up her nose. "Never could stand them."

Grady shrugged, wondering if Paige Ellis would serve black-eyed peas on New Year's Day. He immediately regretted the thought. She should have been out of his head long ago. But at odd moments like this, she suddenly sprang to mind. He couldn't imagine why.

After the long debriefing he'd had with his brother on the Monday after Thanksgiving, Grady had refrained from asking Dan if he'd heard from her. Other than being pestered more than once by Janet to submit his billing report and expenses from the trip to South Carolina, the case had not been mentioned again except in passing. Grady couldn't help wondering what the last six weeks had been like for Paige, though.

Had the boy come around? Was he walking the woods that surrounded her old house with that dog at his heels, pretending at some childish fantasy? Did he gaze at his mother with worshipful eyes now and grimace halfheartedly at the way she babied him? Had he made friends with Matthias?

"Where on earth are you?" his father's voice asked.

Grady realized with a jolt that the conversation had carried on around him. He shook his head, gulped his coffee and said that he needed a good rest in his own bed tonight. He couldn't for the life of him remember why he'd started sleeping over at his dad's on New Year's Eve, anyway. Except, of course, that he never had anywhere else to go, and Howard always claimed to need help with the party he routinely gave. He'd started doing that about the time Grady had gotten divorced.

They were a matched pair, Grady and his father, despite the thirty years between them, both big and square-built with deep, rumbling voices and hands and feet the size of platters. Both alone.

"Do you know what your problem is?" Howard asked, and Grady just barely managed not to roll his eyes.

"Here it comes," he groaned.

He didn't really resent his father's lectures. His father's concern for him was a good thing. They had never discussed those difficult early years after his mother's death when the distance between them had seemed to stretch into infinity.

But it was after his divorce, that he'd discovered how firmly his father was in his corner.

"Your problem," Harold said, ignoring Grady's irreverence, "is that you spend too much time alone."

"And you don't?"

"That's different."

"I've been alone four years, Dad. How about you? More like thirty-four, isn't it?"

"Thirty-three. But I've had my family. When are you going to start one, Grady?"

"As soon as some woman throws a rope around him and drags him back to the altar," Katie said drolly.

"That's pretty much what the last one did," Dan noted.

"I blame her for this," Howard announced gruffly.

"You blame Robin for everything," Grady pointed out. "It's not her fault that I'm no good with women."

"She certainly didn't help things," Howard grumbled.

"Listen," Dan said in an obvious effort to change the subject, "we're throwing a football party in a few weeks. I want you both to put it on your calendars."

Howard shook his head. "Don't count on me, son. I've already got plans."

Dan raised his eyebrows at Grady. "Well, can I count on you, then?"

"I'll get back to you."

Dan sent a significant look at his wife, who smiled and said, "I have a couple friends coming who I'd like to introduce you to."

Single, female friends, no doubt. Grady turned back to the window that looked out over the deserted golf course, hiding his grimace.

His family loved him. They tried to be supportive, and he tried to be appreciative, but he was getting real tired of being everybody's favorite charity case.

It was time he got a life.

He wondered if Paige Ellis was as much of a sports fan as she'd claimed.

"He did not! You take that back!"

Paige heard the angst in her son's voice even before she recognized the anger and resentment. She'd run out to find a grocery store open on New Year's Day and grab cans of the black-eyed peas Vaughn had insisted they were supposed to eat for dinner. Vaughn and Matthias were arguing when she returned to the house. Dropping the bag with the cans on the end of the counter just inside the kitchen door, she glared at the pair of them, Matthias in particular.

"What's going on?"

Vaughn's face set in mutinous lines, while Matthias's eyes clouded. "I was just pointing out a few facts of life to this youngun," the old man grumbled.

"My dad did not kidnap me!" Vaughn declared heatedly.

Paige sent Matthias a quelling glance. "I don't see anything to be gained by discussing this subject." She turned to the counter and began removing the cans from the bag, saying brightly, "I got the peas. They may not be the brand you like, but I was lucky to find any at all. I didn't realize how many people abide by that old custom."

"I'll tell you what's to be gained," Matthias said doggedly. "The truth. Any other woman would've put that man away for what he'd done."

"Matthias, stop it," Paige ordered, whirling around, but it was already too late. Vaughn was already screaming at her.

"It's all your fault, anyway! He wouldn't have had to take me if you hadn't kept us apart!"

Paige fell back against the counter. "What are you saying?"

"He didn't have any choice but to take me! You kept him

away 'cause he wouldn't give you money! That's why he wasn't around for so long! You wouldn't let him be a dad! And now you're doing it again!"

Paige gasped. After the divorce she'd gone out of her way to include Nolan in Vaughn's life. She'd begged him to come around. He'd complained that her demands on his time were unreasonable, saying that Vaughn wasn't old enough to miss him. He'd even threatened to tell Vaughn that he wasn't his father if she didn't give him some space.

Only after she'd proved his paternity and won back the right to child support had he taken any real interest in his son, and only then to punish her. She hadn't cared, so long as Vaughn was happy. Now to hear her son say that she'd kept Nolan from being a dad to him was almost unbelievable to her.

She gulped and stammered, "W-we always have ch-choices."

"I don't!" he yelled. "'Cause if I had a choice, I wouldn't be here!" With that he tore from the room, rocking her sideways as he shoved past her.

"Now look what you've done!" she cried at Matthias, but the old man shook his head sorrowfully.

"Not me, girl. That Nolan's the one who done this, and you aren't helping that boy by not telling him the truth."

Paige closed her eyes and put a hand to her head. "Even if he could hear and believe the truth, Matthias, I couldn't tell him. You just don't understand the harm it does a child when his parents defame each other."

"His father don't have no problem defaming you."

"All the more reason for me to take the high road."

"Just be careful you ain't setting yourself up for a bad fall," Matthias warned. "If you don't make that boy understand that his daddy's a lying, scheming—"

"*Stop,*" Paige interrupted firmly. "Just stop. Don't you

see? No one can make a child 'understand' such a thing."
She shook her head. "I don't even want him to know it, Matthias. I want him to believe that his father loves him as much as I do. I want my son to grow up believing that both of his parents treasure him beyond anything in this world."

"Wanting a thing don't make it so," Matthias insisted. "You're setting yourself up for disappointment, if you ask me."

It was on the tip of her tongue to say that she hadn't asked him, but she swallowed the impulse as he limped out of the room. Matthias only wanted what was best for her, but she had to think of what was best for Vaughn.

Grady leaned against the window ledge behind his brother's desk and tried not to stare at her. He'd been surprised when Dan had called and asked Grady to join him and Paige Ellis in his office. His dealings with Paige Ellis should have been at an end. Even if legal assistance was required, her case was Dan's responsibility, not his. Yet, he'd answered his brother's summons without complaint, interrupting an important telephone conversation in the process.

Her hair was a little longer, he noted, as if she hadn't found time to get to the stylist recently. Shadows rimmed her exotic sea-green eyes. For a moment he thought she'd taken to wearing smudged eyeliner; then he'd realized that she was tired, so tired that even the tiny smile she'd found for him had seemed to require great effort on her part.

"Anyway," she said, glancing at Grady and then at her hands. "I just thought I should run it by you before I made a firm decision."

Dan cast a veiled look at Grady, who knew instantly what he was thinking. The safety issue loomed large in both their minds.

"The contact would be limited to the telephone, I take it?" Dan asked.

She nodded. "Since you made it impossible for Nolan to return to Arkansas without risking prosecution, it has to be."

At least she'd acquiesced to that much, Grady told himself. Dan shot him a helpless look, and Grady cleared his throat, prepared to be the bad guy. "That was my doing, and I thought letting Vaughn call his dad was a lousy idea from the beginning."

"I know you did," she said softly. "My former counselor agrees with you."

"But the new counselor does not?" Dan surmised.

Paige sucked in a deep breath, her chest rising beneath the lapels of her brown velvet jacket and the plain front of the simple plaid sheath dress under it. "That's right. He feels Vaughn will benefit from regular, unhindered contact with his father."

"But the old counselor apparently thought it was harmful," Grady pointed out. Paige took it as a bid for clarification.

"She concluded that talking with his father would keep Vaughn from making peace with his new circumstances."

"Obviously my brother finds merit in her argument," Dan said. "I think I agree with them, though I have to tell you that this is not a legal issue. There is nothing at this point to legally prevent Nolan from maintaining contact with your son."

"We could fix that if you want us to, though," Grady added.

She shook her head. "I'm not here to find a legal impediment. I—I just want to do what's best for my son."

If you were sure what that was, we wouldn't be having this conversation, Grady thought. He truly wanted to help her.

"Can I ask you something?" At her nod, he went on. "Why did you switch counselors?"

The slowness of her reply told him that she was choosing her words with great care. "My son relates best to men."

Dan made a sound somewhere between recognition and conclusion, and Grady knew what he was going to say before he said it. Groaning inwardly, Grady could only listen.

"I'm wondering if a male in this role is the best choice. I mean, we've had experience with this issue ourselves. Our dad's failure to bring a solid female influence into my brother's life created some difficulties for him, as they both would tell you."

Grady briefly closed his eyes. "I don't think Vaughn could have a more solid female influence than his *mother*, Dan."

"Right!" Dan waved a hand, swiveling side to side in his chair with what Grady hoped was extreme embarrassment. "I didn't mean to imply… Actually the situations aren't that similar. Ours was a male household after our mother died. Grady was only six, so it's no wonder he never learned how to relate to women."

Grady groaned aloud this time. "Thanks loads, Dan," he rumbled.

"I—I probably wouldn't have, either," Dan went on lamely, "if not for my wife."

To Grady's surprise, Paige Ellis sat up very straight. "Who says Grady doesn't relate to women?"

Dan chuckled uneasily, as if he thought she was making a bad joke. When he realized that she was serious, both eyebrows shot straight up into his hairline. Paige glanced at Grady and caught him with his mouth hanging open. She flopped back in her chair, huffing with what sounded suspiciously like indignation.

"That's ridiculous," she scoffed. "I spent at least eighteen straight hours with your brother, and I assure you he's perfectly capable of relating as well to women as men." She nodded decisively here and added, "Better, in fact, than a great many men of my acquaintance."

Now Dan's mouth was hanging open. He managed to get it closed, babbling, "Ah. Um, I see. That's…good."

Grady grinned. He couldn't help it. In fact, a chuckle escaped as he came to his feet. But, it was time to bring this discussion to an end before his brother got the wrong idea.

"All right. I think we're through here."

"Yes, I really shouldn't take up any more of your time," Paige agreed briskly, rising from her chair, "especially since I came in without an appointment."

"Think nothing of it," Dan replied graciously, leaning over the desk to offer her his hand.

She shook hands, then allowed Grady to steer her toward the door. He did not dare to so much as glance in his brother's direction as he moved with her across the room and through the next, which was mercifully empty, Janet being away from her desk.

"It was good of you and your brother to see me on such short notice," she said as he walked her straight past the receptionist in the outer office and through the door at the glass front of the suite to the bank of elevators beyond.

"You happened to catch us both free," he lied, pushing the elevator button. The door slid open at once, and the moment for them to part ways had arrived, but he found himself oddly reluctant to do so. Impulsively, he stepped into the elevator with her, an action which required explanation. Belatedly he provided one, saying, "I'm ready for a cup of coffee. Can I buy you one?"

She paused a moment, then smiled and said, "Why not?"

"Good."

He punched a button, and the elevator gave a little lurch before dropping slowly toward the ground. He let silence eat up the seconds while he tried to think of what to say without letting on how pleased he was by her defending him.

She just stood there grasping the strap of her handbag while it dangled in front of her, watching the floor numbers light up one by one. Thankfully the building was only five stories tall. That was enough time for him to panic at a topic for discussion, which he used the moment they stepped off the elevator.

"I, um, know you don't want to hear it, but I have to point out that by not pressing charges against your ex-husband, you've left yourself open to legal action on his behalf." She stopped dead in her tracks, going pale, and he instantly regretted his words. Grasping her by the arm, he started her forward again. "I didn't say he *would* file an action, only that he *could*."

"What sort of action?"

He steered her toward the coffee trolley in the building lobby. "Petition for visitation." She caught her breath. "I didn't say he'd get it."

They reached the trolley, and she stood quietly while he purchased two small coffees. He could see her mind working over the problem of her ex as she added milk and sugar to her cardboard cup and turned with him toward a padded bench set back among a veritable jungle of potted plants.

"I thought you took it black," he commented sitting down.

"Oh. I'm, uh, experimenting."

He watched her sip, barely controlling her grimace, and he could've kicked himself. "You don't even drink coffee, do you?"

She wrinkled her nose. "I'm cultivating a taste. For black, I think."

Appalled at his own stupidity, he removed the cup from her hand and set it aside before swigging down a hefty slug from his own. "Obviously my addiction to this stuff just made me assume that you drank it, too."

"There are worse things," she pointed out, "than being polite enough to offer something you like to someone else."

"*You* were being polite when you accepted," he murmured. "Guess we're just polite folks, you and me."

She smiled and swayed sideways, giving his shoulder a little bump with hers. As if…as if they were friends. Or something. He gulped, then choked down more coffee to cover it.

"About Nolan," she said abruptly. "How could he get visitation if he can't even enter the state?"

Grady forced his mind back to the issue. "He can't unless he can convince a judge he won't interfere with your custody. You could still close that door by pressing charges."

She shook her head. "I know you're right, but I just can't risk alienating my son any further."

"Well," Grady said, "we still have time. We've made it clear to Nolan's attorney that if he does anything stupid we can still file charges."

She closed her eyes. "I pray it doesn't come to that."

He shifted, holding the cup of coffee between his knees with both hands. "Not going well, I take it."

Sighing, she shook her head. "It's as if Vaughn's forgotten all about our life together, as if the last three and a half years have completely canceled out the previous eight."

"Sounds like a defensive thing to me."

She sent him a sharp look. "What do you mean?"

He wasn't use to opening up to people, but he'd make an exception for her. "There was a time when I tried to forget how it had been before my mother left. Died. Before she died."

Paige's slender fingers curled around his hand. "Why?"

He saw how badly she needed to know, and he told her as

best he could. "Because it hurt so much to remember. Forgetting was the only way I could…" He used her analogy. "Find any peace."

Her grip tightened. "Thank you for telling me this."

He let go of the cup with that hand and folded his fingers around hers, saying, "You know, my brother's right. The truth is I do have a difficult time relating to women. I—I never know what to say. I can't figure out how women think or what they want o-or expect."

"I don't believe that," she declared, shaking her head. "You don't have a problem with women any more than you've forgotten your mother. You're just a little shy."

Shy? A big burly guy like him? He pushed the thought away, and shook his head.

"No, I'd rather cut out my tongue than make conversation with a woman. Usually."

She laughed, and her grip on his hand relaxed, but she didn't relinquish it entirely. "Nonsense. Now can I ask you a question? Do you think the male psychologist might be a mistake? I got several references, and they say he's the best."

Grady shrugged, flattered that she was actually sitting here asking his advice on what was a strictly personal matter. "Who knows? If you like him, use him."

"I don't like him. He acts like our problems are ridiculous, as if the solutions should be glaringly obvious to anyone with half a brain."

"Well, there you go," Grady declared, offended for her sake. "Dump him and go back to the first therapist, or else find another."

"I don't want someone else," she stated flatly, surprising herself as much as him apparently. "I know Dr. Evangeline. I trust her, even if I don't always agree with her, and she shares my religious convictions."

"Then why change?"

"Vaughn hates her."

"And likes the new guy," Grady surmised.

"I don't think so, actually. I think he hates all of us."

Grady looked at her, but she didn't appear as wounded as she did relieved. Nevertheless, he heard himself saying, "He doesn't hate you. He hates the situation. My dad thought I hated him, but I just missed my mom."

She smiled. "You don't know how glad I am to hear that."

He shrugged and hid his delight behind his coffee cup, muttering, "No charge."

She laughed again, and he privately marveled. What was it about her that made it so easy for him to talk to her? Maybe he wasn't as inept as he had always believed. He suddenly knew why he'd come down here with her. Sucking in a deep breath, he summed up his courage and plunged in before he could think too much about it.

"Listen, my, um, my brother's having this football-watching party at his house…." She was looking at him with those enormous green eyes, as if trying to figure out where he was going with this, and all at once he wasn't so sure himself. "Um, he's got a giant-screen TV," Grady finished lamely.

She looked down at her hands. "That's nice."

Nice. The death knell for romance.

He bit back a groan. What was he thinking? He couldn't ask her out, especially not to a party at his brother's house! Might as well shoot himself now. Yet, he couldn't just let her walk away.

Suddenly he thought of the cards he'd recently stuffed into his wallet. He normally carried only business cards, but Katie had had personal ones printed for him as a Christmas gift, and he'd made a show of tucking a few into his wallet. He'd never expected to have any use for them. Fishing his wallet from his hip pocket, he found the card and offered it to her.

"Maybe you'd like to have this. You know, in case… Well, just in case."

She took the card and stared at it so long that he had to restrain himself from snatching it back.

"I don't recognize this number," she finally said.

"Right. It's, um, my cell phone."

To his vast relief, she smiled. A moment later, she took her leave. Grady dropped his head into his hands and moaned.

She would never call, of course, but at least he'd made an effort. It was more than he had ever done with anyone else.

Chapter Five

Vaughn covered the mic in the telephone receiver with one hand and looked up at his mother. "You're not going to stand there and listen, are you?"

Paige tamped down her irritation at the question. She'd gone against the advice of everyone she knew and allowed Vaughn regular contact with his father, provided he agreed to return to Dr. Evangeline for counseling. He had seemed slightly less belligerent since then, but he obviously didn't want her overhearing his conversations with Nolan.

She turned to leave the kitchen, saying, "Call me when the water starts to boil so I can put the rice in." She reckoned that would give him twelve to fifteen minutes to talk, but she checked her watch as soon as she was out of sight, knowing perfectly well that if she left it to him he wouldn't call her until the pot had boiled dry.

After fourteen minutes she went back into the kitchen to start dinner. Vaughn hung up and swung around, his sienna eyes challenging her in a manner with which she had become all too familiar. She waited for it, going about her business.

"You hate it that I want to go home."

"You are home, Vaughn."

"This'll never be my home! I want my dad, and he wants me!"

She looked him straight in the eye and softly said, "I know exactly how he feels. Believe me, I know too well what it's like to pray for the sound of your voice. Every day and every night for three and a half years, I prayed just to know that you were safe."

Vaughn's face went blank as she spoke. He stood staring at her for a moment as if he didn't quite know how to react. He didn't speak another word to her that whole evening, answering direct questions with nods, shrugs or shakes of the head. As the days passed, Vaughn grew more sullen and withdrawn.

Matthias was certain that Nolan was somehow directing the boy's behavior, and Paige didn't doubt that on some level it was true, but she couldn't find a way to change it. Every instinct she possessed told her that cutting off communication with Nolan would only backfire. She decided to try to speak to Nolan himself about it, calling him one evening after Vaughn had gone to bed.

Not at all contrite, he literally laughed at her. "Why would I want to help Vaughn be happy in Arkansas?"

"Because it's best for him."

"He wants to be here with me. Haven't you figured that out?"

"That's not the issue."

"Oh, you always think you know what's best for everyone, don't you?" he complained. "You still can't accept the fact that the divorce was best for me, and you never will."

"Actually," she said, pinching the bridge of her nose, "under the circumstances the divorce was best for both of us, but that doesn't matter. All I care about now is what's best for Vaughn."

"And that's why you'll eventually send him back to me," Nolan announced smugly.

She knew then that Nolan would not try to help Vaughn through this because he counted on Vaughn's misery convincing her to do the noble thing. He knew her well. He understood that if she truly became convinced that Vaughn could not reconcile himself to living with her, she would send him back to his father rather than see him continue to be miserable.

First, however, she'd have to find the strength to do it, and at present she was far from convinced that Vaughn would be better off with Nolan. What she'd learned about Vaughn's life with his dad told her that he had not been properly supervised. The written reports from Vaughn's teachers in South Carolina described a boy with a lengthy record of absenteeism who came to school often unkempt, unprepared and sometimes hungry.

If that wasn't enough, Vaughn's behavior was. This Vaughn habitually rebelled at the notion of having to do what was expected of him, unlike the sweet and compliant boy he had previously been, and the only leverage Paige had was those telephone calls with his dad. Afterward, he was often glum and even more belligerent than before. It had become a vicious circle that threatened to wind tighter and tighter until it spiraled completely out of control.

They almost reached that point on the Monday that Paige received Vaughn's first report card, which she accessed online, having signed up for e-mail notification. Because she was pleased when he climbed into the truck that afternoon, she leaned over and smacked a great big kiss on his cheek.

He looked at her as if she'd gone crazy. "What was that for?"

"That was for one A, three Bs and three Cs. I saw your

report card online today," she told him, checking traffic and pulling away from the curb.

"Oh, yeah," he mumbled, looking away, "I guess you're supposed to sign a copy of it."

"Did you bring your copy home with you?"

"Uh, guess I forgot." He didn't forget, and they both knew it, but she didn't scold him. He couldn't just accept her approval and let it be, though, grumbling, "I don't know what the big deal is. Three Cs isn't all that great, and the A was in PE."

"I don't care. It's an improvement over your last report card, that's what counts."

He scowled. "That's just 'cause school here is easier."

She cast a doubtful glance his way. "I'm sure it doesn't have anything to do with you actually doing your homework and showing up for class."

He erupted at that. "There you go again! Always hounding me about homework and stuff. Dad never stayed on my back like you!"

She snapped. Before she even realized what she was doing, she'd whipped the truck over to the shoulder of the road and turned on him. "Would you tell me, please, what it is that *will* make you happier here?" She raised a hand before he could even open his mouth. "I didn't say *happy*. You've made it clear you're not going to let yourself actually be *happy* no matter what! And leave your father out of this, will you please? I just want to know what it's going to take to make you a little bit happier with this situation!" She held up her thumb and forefinger, about a quarter of an inch apart, to demonstrate how small a thing she was really asking of him.

He clamped his jaw mulishly and folded his arms, staring straight through the windshield. She opened her mouth to blast him again, and that's when he answered her. "I don't have anything to do here, nothing fun, nothing I used to do!"

"Name one thing," she demanded.

"Hockey."

She blinked, not only because it was unexpected but because it was such a simple, pointed answer. "I take it you don't mean watching hockey, because I know you watch the games on TV."

"Duh." He curled his lip, just in case she hadn't fully realized yet how stupid he found her statement.

Exasperated she demanded, "Well, how am I supposed to know these things if you don't tell me? Do you want to *play* hockey?"

"Of course, I want to *play* hockey," he all but sneered, turning his hands palm up for emphasis. "I'm good at hockey, believe it or not."

"Of course, I believe it. Why wouldn't I?" He glanced at her, some of the wind seemingly taken out of his sails. She was feeling calmer but hadn't decided yet if losing her temper had been a good or bad thing. Gripping the steering wheel, she checked the traffic and pulled out, muttering somewhat sheepishly, "Now all we have to do is find you a hockey team."

She knew just where to begin her search, too, with the only hockey fan she knew.

That card with Grady's personal cell phone number had found its way into her hand repeatedly since he'd given it to her. She'd stared at it often, knowing full well that she had no excuse to call. Grady was her attorney, not her friend, and if he somehow made her feel wise and capable and able to unravel the enigma that her life had become, it was only because he was a particularly able legal counselor.

Yet, the last time she'd seen him, for one tiny moment, she'd thought Grady might be asking her out. He'd only been making conversation, of course, but just for an instant, her heart had raced and her spirits had soared.

It hadn't mattered how ill-advised dating one of her attorneys might be—or dating anyone for that matter. Of all the times in her life to consider taking that step, this was undoubtedly the worst. Still, she couldn't deny that Grady was a very attractive man, and nice, to boot. At least he could point her in the right direction.

She waited until after Vaughn went to bed that night. He didn't like her hovering, as he put it, while he was getting ready to turn in, so she kept her distance after reminding him that it was time to call it a day. What she really wanted to do, of course, was stand and watch him perform the myriad little rituals she had so missed in his absence, but he grumbled that he wasn't a baby. Instead, she sat patiently, one eye on the clock in the living room, until the yellow line of light that showed beneath his door went black, before she retreated to her own room.

Opening a drawer in her bedside table, she took out the card that Grady had given her and read the numbers printed upon it. In truth she knew them by heart, so many times had she looked at them. Another glance at the clock told her that the hour was fairly late, but it wasn't going to get any earlier if she sat there dithering. She picked up the telephone receiver and dialed.

Grady couldn't believe his eyes when he saw the tiny screen of his cell phone light up with her name. He'd given up wondering if she'd call. After the way he'd botched a simple invitation the last time they were together, he figured she'd finally accepted what everyone else took for granted about him: he was hopeless at getting to know women, and there was really no reason for a woman to try to get to know him, especially this one.

A woman like Paige Ellis could have her pick of men. Still, she'd called, and it would be rude not to talk to her.

Deciding to go for a light, breezy tone, he punched the correct button, lifted the tiny phone to his ear and said, somewhat cheekily, "Well, hello, stranger."

"Umm…hi! This is Paige Ellis."

He smiled at the warm, welcome tone of her voice. "I know. Your name came up on the caller ID."

"Oh, of course." She cleared her throat, and for one awful moment he feared he'd blown it already. Then she responded in a teasing tone. "I suspected you were not a morning person on our drive to Tulsa. I hope that means you're a night owl and it's not too late to call."

"So you figured out I'm not a morning person, huh? Guess my growl was worse than I thought. I didn't bite you, did I?"

She laughed. "Not even a nip. Actually you were very gracious. I hope you're not just being gracious now. Should I call back tomorrow?"

"Nah, I never hit the sack before eleven."

"Not even when you're getting up at two in the morning?"

It was his turn to chuckle. "In that case I make it ten. So what's up? You didn't call to check my bedtime, did you?"

She laughed again. "I'm looking for a youth hockey league in the area, and I'm desperate."

"Desperate but lucky," he quipped. "I happen to have a buddy who's a hockey freak. He turned me on to the sport, actually. And it just so happens that he's coach, commissioner and sponsor of the local youth league all rolled into one."

"You call it lucky. I call it blessed, and you, Grady Jones, are a blessing."

For several moments, he literally floundered. Finally, he sputtered, "Uh, n-no one, th-that is, what I mean…" He cleared his throat and pulled his thoughts together. "I take it this is for Vaughn."

"Who else? Seems he played hockey back in South Carolina. I'm hoping that getting him on a team here will make him more satisfied with his situation."

"I see. Well, the season began in September, but it runs practically year-round. This being January, we're less than four months in, so it ought to be possible to still get on the team. Should I call my guy and see what he has to say about it?"

"Of course, I want you to call your guy. I know it's an imposition, but my son wants to play hockey. It won't make him happy, mind you, but if I thought it would improve his attitude by one iota, I'd impose on a total stranger."

After that, she said that she had to go, he imagined that she seemed as reluctant to end the conversation as he was. He promised to talk to his hockey buddy about the possibility of Vaughn getting into the local league and get back to her soon. A moment of silence followed, and somehow he felt the gentle, gathering import of it even before she softly spoke.

"I meant what I said, Grady. You've been an answer to prayer for me more than once, and I thank God for that."

He spoke before he could think. "Makes me wish I believed in prayer."

She didn't laugh this time. Instead she was silent, then said, "Oh, Grady, that breaks my heart."

Breaking her heart was the very last thing he wanted to do, but he didn't know how to tell her so or even if he ought to. He swallowed, his own heart beating entirely too rapidly, and finally managed to say, "Aw, don't pay no mind to me."

"I will pay you mind," she said, though what that might mean he couldn't begin to guess. "Better, I'm going to hold you in my prayers, Grady Jones, and you'll see. I'll prove it to you. Prayer works. Because God's real, and He loves us."

"I wouldn't know about that," he told her softly, surprised by the sound of yearning in his own voice.

"You'll see," she vowed again. "You'll see."

Oddly enough, he hoped she was right, but he had to wonder if that wasn't pushing hope too far.

Grady nodded as Matthias retreated and Paige rose from behind her desk. He looked around the narrow room. It was colder than the rest of the house, which explained why she was wrapped up in a bulky cardigan sweater. Her face had lit up when she'd first seen him, and she was smiling so broadly now that he couldn't mistake his welcome. Then he spotted the fax machine atop a high table in a corner, and he suddenly knew how ridiculous it had been for him to come here.

He'd expected to spend the whole afternoon of Valentine's Day in court, but when the other party had failed to show, the case had been summarily dismissed. No shortage of work awaited him at the office, but when he'd found on his desk the papers that Jason Lowery had sent him concerning the youth hockey team, he'd made the impulsive decision to personally deliver them to Paige.

It had never occurred to him that he could fax them to her. Instead he'd driven all the way out to Nobb to hand-deliver them, which had absolutely nothing, surely, to do with the fact that it was Valentine's Day. Did it?

He felt like a schoolboy who'd just discovered girls didn't necessarily have cooties, horrified and elated at the same time. It couldn't have been more embarrassing if he'd shown up with chocolates and roses.

She removed the headset and came around the desk

toward him. "I didn't expect to see you today. What are you doing out our way?"

He had no choice but to brazen it out. Thrusting the papers at her, he said, "I thought you should have these right away."

She scanned the papers, her tilted eyes rounding. "Oh! I knew there'd be gear to buy, but this list is endless!"

"Most of it's small stuff," Grady pointed out, "but before you worry about that, we first have to convince Jason to give Vaughn a tryout. Right now he's just willing to meet and talk."

"Okay," she said, sounding determined. "That's a beginning." She laid the papers on the corner of her desk and bent to remove a stack of files from the only chair in the room except for the larger one behind her desk. "Can I take your coat?"

"No, thanks. I can't stay long."

"Well, have a seat anyway. Matthias usually has a pot of coffee on, if you're interested. I warn you, though, it probably won't be what you're used to."

He shook his head, stepping forward and gingerly lowering himself into the rather spindly wooden chair. "No, thanks. I just want to explain Jason's situation to you."

She leaned against the front of her desk, crossing her slender, corduroy-clad legs at the ankles. "Jason is your friend, Jason—" she craned her neck to consult the papers on her desk "—Lowery, I think it is."

"Right. Jason's a couple years younger than me."

"That would make him how old?" she asked, smiling.

He blinked, taken off guard. Then he realized that she could only have one reason for asking—and it didn't have a thing to do with Jason Lowery. "Uh, thirty-seven, I think. I'll, um, be forty in August, so he's thirty-seven or eight."

She nodded, her smile not faltering in the least. "I think you mentioned that he's married."

"Yeah, uh, with a couple kids, boys. The oldest one's about Vaughn's age."

"That's good."

"Yeah. The thing is, there's just the one team in that age bracket around here, and it's sort of an elite group. They don't have the level of interest or parental involvement they need to field more than one team, so naturally they take the best, most dedicated players, and it's mostly tournament play, which involves travel, making it a fairly expensive endeavor."

She deflated a little. "I see."

"But, hey, one thing at a time, right? Meet and speak, that's the first step. If Jason thinks Vaughn's really got the drive, he'll try him out. After that, we'll see."

She nodded, murmuring, "At least Vaughn can't say I didn't try for him. When is this meeting?"

"Up to you. Jason's at the rink three evenings a week, Tuesday, Wednesday and Thursday. And usually Saturday, if the team's not traveling. But, uh, not tonight, since it's Valentine's Day."

"I'm sure his wife appreciates that," Paige said. "I'd normally have choir practice tonight, but it's been suspended so couples can go out."

Grady toyed with the idea of a dinner invitation and discarded it. Valentine's Day was not the time for a first date. When was the time for a first date? he wondered. Pushing that thought away, he asked instead, "Sing, do you?"

She wrinkled her nose. "That's a matter of opinion. I can carry a tune, at least, and Dr. Evangeline felt I needed something in my life that isn't focused on my son."

Grady wondered if she might have room for another kind of personal involvement besides choir. The idea alone scared the fool out of him; yet he heard himself saying, "I could go with you guys, if you like, to the meeting with Jason, I mean."

She smiled. "A personal introduction by a friend couldn't hurt. If you're sure you can spare the time."

"Wouldn't have offered otherwise. Tomorrow night too soon?"

"Not soon enough for my son, if I had to guess. So, yes, tomorrow would be great."

"Okay. Jason says practice starts at seven so we ought to get there about eight. I can be here by, say, seven-fifteen."

She shook her head. "This time, we'll come to you. I insist. It just doesn't make sense for you to come out of your way. How about we meet you in your office parking lot about seven-thirty?"

He said heartily, "Excellent! I've got a deposition tomorrow, and that covers me in case it runs over."

"Okay. It's a date then."

He wished it were. "I'd better let us both get back to work."

"I'll walk you out," she said, straightening away from the desk. "It's about time for me to pick up Vaughn, anyway."

She signaled that he should go first, and they moved through the narrow hallway to the living room. Even before they fully entered that room, the front door opened and Vaughn stepped inside. Grady felt the brush of her shoulder as Paige rushed past him to reach her son.

"What are you doing here? How did you get home?"

Vaughn shrugged. "Justin Gordy's mom brought me. I forgot to tell you we got out early today."

"You should've called me!"

"It's not like I have a cell phone," he retorted, which sounded to Grady like the continuation of a previous argument.

"There are phones at the school," she pointed out.

"The lines were, like, a mile long," he complained. "Guess I wasn't the only one who forgot to mention it was an early-release day." Paige lifted a hand to press her fingertips to her temples. "It's not like you don't know the Gordys," Vaughn argued smartly, and she nodded.

"You're right. You're right. Samantha Gordy's in my Sunday school class. It just shook me. I-I was about to go get you when you came in."

Vaughn had stopped listening to her, having realized Grady was there. "Why's *he* here?" he demanded suspiciously.

Paige smiled at Grady. "Mr. Jones has arranged an interview for you with a local hockey coach."

For a moment, uncluttered joy transformed the boy's expression, so much so that Grady found himself suddenly worried. What if it didn't work out? If Vaughn didn't make the team, not only would he suffer, his mom would, as well.

"Oh, man!" Vaughn exclaimed, putting a hand to his head. "I don't have any of my gear! I can't even practice!"

"Hang on," Grady said, "this is just an interview. I can't guarantee a tryout."

"I get it," Vaughn assured him, somewhat disdainfully. "It's not my first interview."

Grady relaxed a little. Obviously the kid had some real experience with hockey—and a huge attitude problem that Grady tried hard to ignore.

Vaughn looked to his mom again. "I gotta get my hands on some gear. I don't stand a chance without it. I'm too rusty."

Paige glanced at Grady, then smoothed a hand over her son's head. "I understand. We'll just have to cross these bridges as we come to them, though. Something will work out, I promise."

"Not unless I get some practice," he insisted.

"The coach will loan you gear and give you time to practice if you think you need it," Grady informed him.

Vaughn closed his eyes. "Oh, man, I gotta ace that tryout."

Taking his hands, Paige sat down on the edge of the couch. "I think we should pray about this, right now. It'll help put your mind at ease."

For a moment, Vaughn seemed reluctant, but then he bowed his head. Paige began to speak quietly while Grady stood there like a log.

Here, he thought bleakly, was the reason why it would never work between them. Paige wasn't just a believer; she was a practitioner. She didn't just talk about it, she *lived* her faith. A woman like that would never give a doubter like him a serious chance, and even if she did, he was bound to disappoint her.

Grady swallowed a lump in his throat. He could no longer pretend that he'd beat a path to her door on Valentine's Day just because he'd had an unexpected couple of hours on his hands. Now he had to face the truth. Though he had romantic thoughts about Paige Ellis, they could never be more than simple friends.

Friendship was something, though, he consoled himself. It was certainly more than a mere attorney-and-client relationship, and much more than he'd had with any other woman since his divorce.

He'd taken a real step forward. Finally.

Just because it felt like a step in the wrong direction, didn't mean that it was.

Did it?

Paige ended her prayer and looked up, smiling beatifically. Vaughn took a deep breath and let go of her hands.

"Can I call Dad and tell him the news?"

Her smile grew strained. "Finish your homework first."

Vaughn made a face, but he trudged off toward the kitchen, shrugging out of his backpack and muttering, "Dumb report."

"Haven't you forgotten something, Vaughn?" Paige asked, halting the boy in his tracks. He turned, and she jerked her head at Grady, who instantly wished she hadn't.

Vaughn frowned, but he faced Grady and addressed him. "Thanks for getting me the interview."

"No problem. I'm glad your mom asked for my help."

Vaughn started to turn away again, but Grady cleared his throat. Reluctantly Vaughn faced his mother and said, "Thanks."

Paige accepted that with calm grace. "You're welcome."

Vaughn made his escape.

There's another reason not to get romantically involved with Paige Ellis, Grady told himself, watching the kid hurry from the room. He didn't know how much of Vaughn's insolence toward his mother he could put up with. One day he'd collar the kid, and Paige would be mad at him. That, Grady feared, was something he could not endure. Bottom line, it was best that he not do something where he might have to.

Shaken, Grady took his leave. It would have been better, he believed, if he hadn't come, and if he had any sense he'd find a reason not to accompany them on Thursday. But he knew he wouldn't.

Apparently, he didn't have a lick of sense. Not when it came to Paige Ellis, anyway.

Chapter Six

Vaughn literally could not sit still. Repeatedly ignoring his mother's admonitions to keep his seat belt buckled, he bounced around in the backseat of Grady's car, babbling about his favorite hockey players and the brand of new skates he wanted. Paige prayed that he would make the team and that she could afford the gear required to play.

Vaughn asked Grady about the coach and the facilities; Grady told him about Jason but didn't know anything about the rink. Riding in the front with him, Paige occasionally flashed him a wry smile, grateful for his patience.

When they reached the rink, Vaughn was out of the car before the engine died, but then he literally sauntered toward the entrance, flipping a nonchalant wave at a sweaty player walking toward a top-end luxury SUV with his parents. Grady made it around the car about the same time that Paige got to her feet, and it belatedly occurred to her that she might have waited for him to open the door for her. He closed it instead, and they stood side by side watching the strutting sway of Vaughn's shoulders, then traded looks before breaking out in grins.

"I'd say he's got the attitude that Jason's always talking about," Grady said beneath his breath.

"Who knew cocky could be an improvement?" Paige whispered.

Grady chuckled softly. "I'm sorry it's been so rough for you."

"It hasn't been a picnic," she admitted, "but it's better than not knowing whether he's dead or alive."

"It takes a strong woman to go through something like that and come out on the other side without bitterness," he told her.

"Oh no, I'm bitter," she said flatly. "God knows I resent what Nolan did to us. I have to work every day at not acting on that bitterness. How about you? You must have some resentment over your divorce."

He shrugged. "I guess. I don't think about it much anymore. I realize now that we were never really suited. I couldn't talk to her."

"How did you wind up married then?"

He spread his hands helplessly. "Like my brother said, ours was an all-male household after my mom died, so I didn't grow up around women. I liked girls, but I always felt dumb around them, so I just kept my distance. When Robin showed an interest in me, I let myself be swept along. Eventually she started talking about us getting married like it was a given, and I figured it was the thing to do. I wasn't *un*happy about it."

"You might not have been unhappy," Paige said, "but it sounds like you didn't love her."

Grady didn't deny it. He stroked a hand through his thick, wavy hair. It was sandy brown, much warmer than his brother's premature silver, she mused, the perfect foil for those electric-blue eyes.

"I tried," he said, "I wanted to be married, and I wanted

to make her happy, but I never said the right thing. No matter what the problem was, I never could say the right thing to her. It's always been that way."

"I don't get that," Paige protested, drawing her brows together. "You're not like that with me."

One corner of his mouth curled into a lopsided smile. "Maybe I finally grew up. Robin always said I needed to."

"Looks like," she teased, sweeping her gaze over him. She didn't realize that she was staring until he spoke.

"We better get inside before Vaughn body checks some unsuspecting pedestrian."

She smiled, nodded, and walked with him into the building, where they found a surprising number of people milling about in the foyer. She spotted Vaughn talking animatedly with a pair of boys about his age, pads and helmets tucked under their arms, skates slung over their shoulders by the laces. One of them dropped his equipment to shuck his jersey, and Paige was surprised to find that he was much slimmer beneath the bulky pads than she'd assumed. Next to him, Vaughn looked substantially more solid.

A woman called from across the room, and the boys hurried off in her direction. Vaughn turned, looked around and jogged over to Paige and Grady.

"Guys say Coach is tough but cool. He likes aggressive play and emphasizes defense."

"Sounds about right," Grady confirmed.

"They say they're weak on offense."

Grady looked at Vaughn. "What position did you play before?"

"Forward."

"That should work."

"I take it forward is an offensive position?" Paige asked.

"That's right," Grady said, but Vaughn rolled his eyes.

"Don't you know anything, Mom?"

"Not about hockey," she admitted blithely, noting Grady's glower. She pushed through swinging doors into the arena, Vaughn and then Grady following.

Grady was instantly hailed and went off to speak to his friend. Suddenly Vaughn clutched Paige's forearm with both hands. She recognized the combination of hope, eagerness and fear in his expression and knew that he wanted this badly.

She patted his fingers where they gripped her arm and whispered, "You can do this. I know you can. And don't forget, I'll be praying for you."

He visibly relaxed, nodding decisively and pressing back his shoulders. When Grady called to them, waving them over, Vaughn moved out in front and greeted Jason Lowery with a firm handshake and obvious eagerness. After introducing everyone, Grady came to stand next to Paige, letting Vaughn speak for himself.

Lowery was a good-looking man, tall, dark and unabashedly male. All that saved him from being devastatingly handsome was a white scar bisecting one eyebrow and a nose that had obviously been broken a number of times. He struck Paige as intelligent and affable but rather intense.

They chatted for several minutes before Lowery clapped a hand onto Vaughn's shoulder and escorted the boy to a seat in the bleachers some distance away. Paige got the unmistakable message that her input was no longer required.

Grady stepped in front of her, distracting her attention from Vaughn. "We've done everything we can," he told her, and she nodded, folding her arms against her fluttering middle. "Now it's up to him. Don't worry. He can handle it."

"I'm sure you're right," she said, meeting his gaze.

He smiled, his whole face softening. She saw something in his eyes that momentarily confused her.

"What?" she asked.

Grady quickly looked away. Then he winked at her. "A man always likes to hear he's right."

She laughed, and suddenly she knew what she'd seen. Her pulse sped up. Oh, yes, she knew that look. It had been a long time since she'd seen the interest to kiss her in a man's eyes, but she recognized that look when she saw it.

Thrilled, she smiled in a way that she hadn't since she was a mere girl. Then she glanced past Grady to her son and sighed inwardly. This was the wrong time for that look. Unfortunately, the right time might be a long while coming. If ever. Vaughn seemed none too friendly toward Grady, and Grady wasn't exactly delighted with Vaughn's attitude.

Grady took her by the arm and turned her away from the pair talking intently. "Let's walk. This could take a while."

Nodding, she let him lead her back the way they'd come. They reached the area near the doors where a bulletin board was mounted on one wall, and they wandered over to check the notices posted there. Paige saw a lengthy list of used gear for sale.

"This helps," she said, studying the list. "I priced some of the gear new on the Internet, and I don't mind telling you it took my breath away."

Grady was perusing another long sheet of paper. "Looks like you might also have to rent rink time so he can practice."

"Rats." She moved over to take a look for herself, then caught her breath. "That's not all! I have to pay for lessons! He can't be on the ice alone."

"It's only for a short while," Grady said, his hands landing atop her shoulders as he stepped up behind her.

Paige knew that she would pay whatever she had to, if it would help Vaughn make the adjustment to being with her again. "Can't be more expensive than private investigators and attorneys," she added. "Not that they aren't worth every penny."

Grady chuckled and lightly massaged her shoulders, drawling, "Honey, there are times *I* can't afford me."

She didn't really hear anything after the endearment, which washed over her in a hot rush. She turned, wondering if he'd meant that the way it had sounded, but before she could even make eye contact with him, Vaughn's anxious voice distracted her.

"Mom. Mom! Coach needs to see you."

Focusing on her son, Paige hurried to follow him around the bleachers to an area in the back, where the coach was digging gear out of several large cloth bags. He told Vaughn to find a helmet, jersey and pads that would work for him before turning to Paige. The jersey, pads and helmet were on loan. She could rent skates, but Vaughn would need at least one stick, gloves, shorts large enough to fit over the pads and, of course, skates.

Jason wanted to try Vaughn out in exactly one week, provided they could find at least four hours of practice time in the interim. Fortunately, the rink rental was included in the instructor's fees. After recommending two different instructors, the coach warned her that if the boy lived up to his expectations, she would need to have him in Little Rock the following weekend for competition.

"We take the ice at 8:00 a.m. Saturday," he told her, "which means he'll need to be there Friday and stay overnight."

Gulping, Paige said, "I understand."

She and Grady helped Vaughn haul his borrowed gear to the car. The boy chattered in delight every step of the way but fell silent as they were driving back toward the law office where they'd left their vehicle. When they came to a stop at a traffic light, Paige twisted around in her seat to see what had distracted him. Her breath caught, and tears filled her eyes. Vaughn sat with his head back against the seat, eyes closed, his hands clasped and lips moving silently in prayer.

Paige quickly faced forward, not wishing to intrude on her son's conversation with God. Her gaze collided with Grady's along the way. Glancing at his rearview mirror, he let her know that he realized what was going on in the backseat. She wiped away her tears with her fingertips, smiling tremulously. Grady produced a paper napkin, and she laughed softly when she saw the logo of a coffee shop on it. He smiled and then his hand gripped hers for a second before the light changed.

Bowing her head, Paige followed her son's example. Anything that could send him to God was something to be thankful for.

The instructor blew his whistle, and Vaughn slid to an abrupt halt, his skates spewing tiny slivers of ice. Paige had been watching him skate laps for some time, and before that he'd been facing off against another boy and the instructor, a man named Juli, short for Julian, Jefferson.

If the coach minded the feminine-sounding sobriquet, he didn't show it, and considering his height—which must have been six-five, at least—he could have made his displeasure vividly known. In contrast, the other instructor wasn't much taller than Vaughn himself but built like the proverbial brick wall.

Juli skated over to Paige, seated in the home team box, and leaned against the partition wall. "Kid's sharp. If this is rusty, I can't wait to see him a month from now."

"So you think he'll make the team?"

"He will unless he smart-mouths Jason. Lowery doesn't take any lip. He likes attitude, but he wants to see it, not hear it, and he expects his skaters to play smart, which means legal. I don't know what Vaughn's last coach's philosophy was, but some coaches think bad manners are the price you pay for aggressive players. That doesn't cut it with Jason Lowery, though."

Paige sighed. "I heard Vaughn sassing you earlier, and I'll speak to him."

Juli nodded. "It's frustrating to go up against somebody twice your size, but losing your temper doesn't make you a better player, and Vaughn has to learn that." He smiled and added, "I think he's got the message."

"I'll make sure he does," Paige said, hoping that Vaughn would take this lesson to heart. He'd been relatively happy lately—except after talking to his dad.

Jefferson skated off to set up the four boys present in a man-on-man scrimmage, with himself as goaltender. Paige turned her head just as Grady stepped over the bench to settle down next to her. She smiled in surprise.

"What are you doing here?"

He shrugged inside his overcoat. "Case was continued. I didn't see any point in going back to the office at this hour of the day. Besides, I'm curious. How's it going?"

"Vaughn has to learn to control his temper."

"Ah. Well, sports are good for that, believe it or not. With the right coach."

"Jason appears to be the right coach."

"He is." Grady patted her hand where it rested on her knee. "Besides, Vaughn wants this bad enough to deliver what's expected of him."

"It's just that hockey is so violent," Paige worried aloud.

"Any sport can be," Grady said, "if hotheads prevail. You're a sports fan, you know what I mean."

She nodded. "He would pick the one sport I know the least about."

Grady laughed. "I'm betting that the more you learn about hockey, the more you'll find to appreciate. Hockey is similar to soccer in some ways, as physical as football, fast or faster than basketball. Requires as much hand-to-eye coordination as tennis, as much judgment as golf. Roll all that into one and put it on ice, and that's hockey."

Nodding, she let go of her worries. "It's made such a difference in his attitude. Why, he's almost pleasant."

She wouldn't think about what might happen if he didn't make the team. Why borrow trouble? It was enough that Vaughn no longer brooded at the dinner table; he chattered. He continued to seem troubled and pensive after talking with his father, but he'd actually forgone the daily telephone conversation on a couple occasions lately, either because he was eager to get to the rink or had too much homework.

Matthias seemed thrilled with the changes in Vaughn. She'd even heard the two of them laughing together, and Vaughn had thanked her effusively for the skates she'd bought him. He should have. They'd cost a fortune.

After a half hour or so, the instructor called a halt. No sooner did Vaughn reach her than he blurted, "I'm starved!"

Recent experience had taught Paige to be prepared, and she handed over a protein bar at once. He downed it in two bites, even before he got his skates off. After guzzling at least a quart of sports drink, he asked for something else to eat, catching her off guard.

"Uh, we'll stop for something on the way home, I guess."

"I have a better idea," Grady announced. "I'm ready for dinner myself. Let me buy you two a couple of steaks."

Before she could even reply, Vaughn exclaimed, "Great!"

"But you're all sweaty," she pointed out.

"Aw, come on, Mom, I'm hungry!"

Grady lifted his eyebrows at Paige, who gave in. "Oh, all

right." She opened her shoulder bag to get at her cell phone. "I'll just call Matthias while you get out of your pads."

They piled into the car a few minutes later, Vaughn proclaiming that he was going to eat a whole cow. They discussed where they should go and decided on a popular chain restaurant.

It turned out to be a good selection. Grady ordered the most expensive steak in the house and pronounced it acceptable. Vaughn got his favorite, battered, fried onions, and Paige was able to have a good salad. She and Grady sat across from Vaughn in the roomy booth, while Vaughn gave Grady a running commentary on today's practice, admitting, "I blew my cool."

"Just so you know," Grady said casually, "Jason won't put up with that kind of thing."

Vaughn nodded. "That's what Juli said."

"Juli?"

"Julian Jefferson," Paige explained, "the instructor."

"One of those guys out there today?"

"The tall one."

Grady looked at Vaughn. "He lets you call him Juli?"

"No way!" Vaughn answered. "I call him Coach to his face."

"But Juli is what he goes by," Paige said.

Grady shook his head. "Now there's a guy confident in his manhood."

"Actually," Vaughn weighed in, "he said the players on the other teams used to call him Juli to get his goat, so he just decided to go with it, and now it's not an insult anymore."

Grady nodded. "Smart. I'm liking this Juli."

Vaughn considered and agreed. "Yeah. Me, too. At first I thought, well, he's not my real coach so, like, what difference does it make, you know? But, he's the coach right now, and he can still teach me stuff."

"That's a good way to look at it," Paige said, pleased. "I'm impressed that you realize that he deserves a certain respect, Vaughn, and also that you see he has something to teach you, even if it's just that you should control your temper when you play."

"Losing your temper gives the competition an edge," Grady commented. "Once they see you can be pushed into losing your cool, they'll use it against you."

"I know," Vaughn said, an edge to his voice. "My old coach, he used to say the same thing, but sometimes it's hard, especially when someone razzes you. One guy, his dad was in jail, and all the guys on the other team knew about it, and they kept saying stuff." Vaughn glanced accusingly at Paige, and she knew that he was thinking about his own father's short jail stay.

"I hope you see how inappropriate and unfair that sort of tactic is," she told him gently, but he just shrugged.

"When I win at something," Grady rumbled, "I like to know it's because I have superior skills and play a better game."

"I don't think having superior skills is a problem for Vaughn," Paige commented, trying to lighten the mood.

"What would you know about it?" Vaughn asked. "Just 'cause I'm your kid doesn't automatically mean I'm a good player."

"Hey, she may be prejudiced," Grady snapped, "but she's enough of a sports fan to recognize a real athlete when she sees one."

Vaughn looked skeptical. "Yeah?"

"Yeah," Grady grumbled, sounding irritated.

"H-Haven't you noticed that I watch basketball on TV

every chance I get?" Paige asked hastily, disturbed by the air of confrontation.

Vaughn put on a sulky, defensive face. "I thought Matthias was the one turning on the games."

Paige waved a hand and reached for a piece of bread, purposefully keeping her tone light. "As far as Matthias is concerned, golf is the only sport that ought to be televised."

"You probably even watch golf," Grady surmised, cutting into his steak.

"What's wrong with golf?" she asked, feigning indignation.

"Not a thing," Grady replied calmly. "I've watched tons of golf with my dad, and it's every bit as exciting as watching paint dry." Vaughn laughed, and the moment of tension faded. "Playing golf, now that's something else," Grady went on.

Paige relaxed. They bantered about the merits of various sports until the meal was finished and Paige admitted, "Okay, okay, so I don't know anything about hockey."

Both Grady and Vaughn said, "I'll teach you."

They scowled at each other, and Paige jumped in with, "It'll probably take both of you!"

"I'm sure you'll catch on quick," Grady encouraged.

Vaughn shrugged as if he couldn't have cared less whether she ever developed an understanding of hockey or not. Would he ever get tired of punishing her for turning his world upside down? She wondered if he'd done the same thing to his father once he'd realized he wouldn't be going home to her again after that camping trip.

She put the thought away. The past didn't matter. What counted was right now, this moment, and the future that she was building with her son.

That future likely did not include Grady Jones in any substantive way. The renewed tension at the table told her that.

Unaccountably saddened, she reached for her handbag, saying, "It's getting late. We'd better go."

Vaughn sucked up the last quarter inch of soda in the bottom of his glass and slid toward the edge of the booth while Grady signaled the waitress for the check.

"Can I split the bill with you?" Paige asked Grady, dipping into her bag for her wallet.

"Nope."

"At least let me get the tip."

"Uh-uh. I invited you out, remember?"

"But—"

"Vaughn," Grady interrupted, tossing the boy his car keys, "explain the meaning of the word *no* to your mom, will you?"

Vaughn looked at the keys, then he took his mother by the hand and tugged her toward the exit, saying, "Come on, Mom. Let's wait in the car."

She let him lead her out of the restaurant. He unlocked the car and climbed into the back, cracking, "We ought to take this thing for a spin while Money Bags is settling the bill."

"Don't call him that," she ordered, catching the door before Vaughn could pull it closed, "and if you're ever stupid enough to go joyriding, try not to pick an attorney's car."

"What difference does it make so long as you don't get caught?" he retorted.

"It makes a lot of difference, Vaughn," she said more sharply than she'd intended. "Joyriding is a crime."

"Like I'd ever do it!" he protested. "I was just kidding."

Paige grimaced, knowing she'd overreacted. "I know you wouldn't, but mothers are supposed to give advice."

"Well, if you're gonna give me advice, I'm gonna give you some. When a guy invites you out, don't try to buy your own dinner, especially when he's got lots more money than you."

She crouched to bring herself eye level with him. "Grady didn't invite *me* out. He invited *us* out."

"Yeah, right, and he's *just* your lawyer."

"I—I guess we're friends," she stammered. "Does that bother you?"

He shrugged, saying coldly, "What do I care? At least, there'll be somebody here for you when I go back to Dad."

Paige felt every bit of her hope vanish. "Oh, Vaughn."

"I'm sorry, Mom!" he blurted. "But Dad needs me. Your life's together. You've got friends and a business, church and stuff like that. He's got nobody but me!"

"If your dad can't get his life together, Vaughn, you can't do it for him," she pointed out.

"You don't understand!" Vaughn exclaimed. "He depends on me to keep him on track!"

"You're not the parent!" she argued desperately. "You're the child, Vaughn. He's not your responsibility."

"But he's my *dad!*"

"And I'm your mother! And I love you!"

He stared at her, helpless. "I know, but so does he. It's not fair. I should get to choose who I want to live with, and when I'm twelve, I can."

"Is that what you think, that you can just wait me out until you're twelve, then convince a judge to send you back to South Carolina?"

He didn't answer that because Grady appeared just then. Splitting a look between them, he asked, "What's going on?"

"Nothing," she replied tersely, rising and closing the door.

Grady opened up the front for her, and she slipped onto the seat and buckled her safety belt. He walked around to drop down behind the steering wheel before reaching back for his keys, which Vaughn slapped into his palm without comment.

"What'd I miss?" he asked, eyeing Vaughn.

Paige sent him a despairing glance and shook her head. Vaughn said nothing. After a moment, Grady started the car.

When they reached the parking lot of the ice rink, Vaughn bailed out of the car and strode toward his mother's SUV without a single word to anyone. Paige stayed where she was to speak to Grady.

"He thinks that when he's twelve he can tell a judge he wants to go back to Nolan and that will be the end of it."

Grady made a face. "It wouldn't be quite that easy."

"But could it happen?"

"Maybe. Not likely, but...I warned you that you were leaving yourself open by not filing charges."

"What difference does it make?" she asked bitterly. "If, after everything, he wants to go back to Nolan then—"

"Let's cross that bridge when we get to it," Grady interrupted. "He won't be twelve until July, and I can't imagine that he'll want to go back by then."

She shook her head, fighting tears. "You didn't hear him earlier. He thinks he has to go back. He says his dad needs him. It's like he's the parent and Nolan's the child."

"Don't worry," Grady urged, squeezing her hand. "If it comes to a court fight, we've got plenty of ammunition."

She gulped, knowing that her fight with Nolan must never come to a courtroom. "I thought things were getting better, but he's just biding his time here."

"Maybe he thinks that now," Grady said, "but you're a great mom. He'll change his mind. You'll see."

Paige gave him as much of a smile as she could manage. "Thank you for dinner."

He tapped the tip of her nose with his forefinger. "My pleasure."

"You're a good friend, Grady, and a good attorney, even if I don't always take your advice. It's just that I have to think of my son first and foremost."

"Yeah, I got that," he rumbled, and for a moment she thought he'd say more. When he didn't, she did.

"I'm sorry if Vaughn got on your nerves tonight."

He made a face. "It's not that. I just don't have much experience with kids. I didn't mean to come across as surly."

"You didn't," she told him, "but I don't think it matters. He seems to be hoping you'll take me off his hands, frankly."

She'd meant it as a joke, but Grady didn't seem to see it that way. In fact, he looked stunned by the idea, which disappointed her more than it should have. She figured she'd better cut her losses and run.

"Well, good night."

"See you."

She got out of the car, wondering if she really would be seeing him again. Not anytime soon, if she had to guess, and who could blame him? Vaughn could be difficult if not downright hostile.

Maybe, all things considered, it would be better if she didn't see Grady again. Apparently she'd misread him. For so long she'd been too consumed with finding her son to even think of forming a romantic relationship, and now was obviously not the time to begin.

She couldn't deny that she was disappointed, but then she'd never been tempted to lean on someone else the way she was tempted to lean on Grady Jones. Something about him made her feel safe and validated, which was nonsense because they seemed to disagree as often as not. He didn't even share her faith!

From now on, she decided, she would keep her relationship with Grady strictly business.

On the other hand, someone had to show Grady how much God loved him, and if not her, then who?

Confused, she knew that she'd just given herself something else to pray about.

Chapter Seven

"So how come you don't have any family?" Paige heard Vaughn ask as she walked into the kitchen.

Matthias shrugged over his oatmeal bowl. "Me and my wife didn't have no kids, so when she died I was alone."

Paige poured a bowl of corn flakes for herself and stirred yogurt into it. She hated milk, always had. Vaughn, fortunately, loved it, which was why he picked up his bowl just then and slurped down what was left. Afterward, he started to wipe his mouth on his sleeve, glanced at her and opted for a paper napkin instead.

Paige leaned against the counter and hid a smile behind her spoon. These small, everyday things thrilled her. They were what she had missed most during his long absence.

"Didn't you have any brothers or sisters?" Vaughn asked Matthias, returning to his theme.

Matthias reached for his coffee cup. "Had some sisters once, but we lost touch a long time ago."

This was news to Paige. Pushing away from the counter she said, "I didn't know that."

Matthias stared into his cup. "Like I said, we lost touch a long time ago."

"Were they older or younger than you?" Paige asked.

"Older. I don't know if either one of 'em is even still alive." He put down the cup and pushed up to his feet, using the table for leverage.

"Even so," she said thoughtfully, "you could have nieces or nephews."

He shook his head. "So far as I know, neither of 'em ever married. Ain't it time to leave for school?"

"In a minute," Paige said, scraping up another bite of cereal and yogurt. "Get your stuff together, son."

"Okay."

She poked the bite into her mouth, and while she chewed Matthias followed Vaughn out of the room.

Paige pondered what she'd just learned, wondering why Matthias had seemed uncomfortable talking about it. Likely he found the subject sad, but it could be something else, something he didn't want to say in front of Vaughn. She determined to speak to him about it in private, away from Vaughn's sharp ears.

A few moments later, Vaughn yelled that he was ready. Paige rinsed her bowl and left it in the sink before hurrying out to grab her coat and take her son to school.

Her cell phone rang before she got back to the house. Apparently some mix-up had occurred at the office of one of the doctors who used her transcription service, resulting in two of her employees receiving incomplete recordings. She had to drive into Bentonville to resolve the matter, which put her way behind in her own work and left no time for conversation.

She worked through lunch, making do with crackers and cheese, one eye on the clock as she raced to make up for lost time. Vaughn came in from school starving as usual, and she took an hour to spend with him before hurrying back to her desk until dinnertime. She forgot all about talking to Matthias.

It was exactly twenty-two minutes past two the next afternoon when he limped into the office, Grady Jones at his heels. The look on Grady's face told Paige that something was very wrong. She came to her feet, ripping off the headphones without first turning off the recording.

"I came myself," Grady announced unceremoniously, "but if you want Dan, I'll take you to him."

"What's happened?"

He extracted a sheaf of papers from his inside coat pocket and tossed them on to her desk.

"I was wrong," he apologized. "Nolan didn't file for visitation. He's filed for full custody."

Grady sat next to Paige on the sofa in her living room, holding her hand. Worry rumpled her forehead.

"I don't understand," she said. "After what he did, how could he possibly hope to win legal custody?"

Grady tamped down his anger and reached for the professional detachment that he'd abandoned back at his office the moment he'd realized what Nolan had done. The anger was multifaceted.

He was angry with Nolan, of course, but also with Vaughn, who might well have shared potentially devastating details of Paige's life with his father. On another level, he was angry with himself for not having pushed harder for filing charges. He was also angry to a degree with Paige, who had left herself unprotected in her zeal to please an ungrateful little brat who might never be reconciled to his situation.

Grady was even angry at God, if He existed, for allowing this to happen.

"Nolan's claiming that you are an unfit mother."

"That's ridiculous!" Matthias erupted, addressing them from the center of the floor, where he stood with his weight braced against the head of his cane. "He can't prove that. Paige is a fine mother. No kid ever had better."

"He's claiming that you belong to a cult," Grady went on.

"A cult!" Paige exclaimed in disbelief. "That's insane!"

Grady consulted the papers on his lap. "The Community of the Redeemed."

"That's my church. It's not a cult!"

"He says you give them considerable sums of money."

"I don't *have* considerable sums of money, but I give above my tithe, if that's what he means."

"He contends that you don't make a move without the approval of the group," Grady went on. She had to fully understand the charges that Nolan was making.

"I consult my pastor and others from time to time," she said, "but they don't dictate what I do!"

Grady shuffled the papers, cogently presenting the argument as outlined in the emergency petition. "They quote an expert who contends that the church has no affiliation with any recognized body and describes its tenets as secretive."

"That's nonsense! We're independent and nondenominational, but many churches are. There's nothing *secretive* about it."

Grady scanned the attached report. "Says that two investigators from the Foundation for Research on Cults tried to clarify the group's beliefs and were pressed for personal encounters by the leader—let's see, that would be Richard Haynes. They interpreted this as secretive and manipulative."

"Talk about blowing things out of proportion!" Paige declared, rolling her eyes. "I know what happened. These two 'investigators' called the pastor to ask him questions of a spiritual nature, and he did what he always does. He offered to meet, pray and discuss it with them. He likes to counsel people in person. He says it gives him better insight. There's nothing wrong with that, and it's not secretive or manipulative. It certainly doesn't make the church a cult."

"A cult!" Matthias crowed. "Ha! That's rich. Their so-called expert don't even know what a real cult is! Maybe they think all churches are cults. I could tell 'em about cults, the ignorant, no-account weasels."

Something in the way Matthias spoke alerted Grady. He fixed his gaze on the grizzled old man ranting in the middle of the room, his mind racing.

"What do you know about cults, Matthias?" he interrupted.

Matthias shut down in midrant, a hunted look coming over him. "What's that?"

"You heard me. I want to know what you know about cults. More importantly, I want to know *how* you know. Because you do, don't you?"

Paige scooted closer to the edge of the sofa. "Don't be absurd. What would Matthias know about cults?"

"They named him as your handler," Grady revealed, clutching the papers in one hand, his gaze trained on Matthias. "I thought it was pure convenience, him being here in the house with you and possibly attending the same church. But it's more than that, isn't it, Matthias?"

The old man closed his eyes. "Father in Heaven, forgive me," he said. Stumbling backward he came up against the recliner and fell down into it, dropping his cane and bringing both hands to his face. Paige flew off the couch and to his side.

"Matthias! Are you all right?"

"Paige, honey," he said, gripping her hands with his, "I did this! I been a fool near all my life, and I paid the price, but I never expected it to fall on you, never in a million years."

"Perhaps you'd better answer my questions," Grady instructed firmly, ignoring Paige's glare.

Matthias slowly nodded, and Grady listened with growing concern as the old man told the story of a young couple, prosperous farmers, married several years and desperate to conceive a child.

"No one could tell us why there was no babies," he said sadly. "Back in the fifties, they didn't know much 'bout such things. Then a preacher came to town, a traveling evangelist with a band of followers. They called themselves the Seed of Israel."

Charismatic and persuasive, the preacher had convinced Matthias and his wife that their barrenness was due to the sin of greed, and he'd declared that once they'd "surrendered all to God," they would be exceedingly blessed. Before it was over, the Porters had sold off everything they owned and given all their money to the fellow and his followers. Eventually the band of believers had dwindled to a hardy few who'd become increasingly insular, estranged from extended family and friends and controlled by the man they called Brother Israel.

"I actually told my sisters I didn't want nothin' to do with 'em," a shamefaced Matthias confessed to Paige. "I thought, at the time, that Satan was using 'em to pull me away from the true religion."

"Oh, Matthias," she said, "how awful that must have been for all of you."

"I looked for 'em later," he told her miserably, "after Brother Israel died and ever'thing fell apart, but they'd moved away, and I couldn't find out where."

Brother Israel, it seemed, had dropped dead from a stroke during one of his raging, hours-long sermons. The remaining believers had disbanded, leaving the Porters with nothing.

"Truth is," Matthias confessed, "my wife and me never recovered. We moved up this way and farmed on shares or leased land 'cause no one was gonna loan real money to a fool like me."

"You're not a fool," Paige said, on her knees beside his chair. "We all make mistakes."

He patted the hand she placed on his forearm, saying, "It don't matter no more, girl. We made a decent life for ourselves here, put all that behind us. It was years before I even heard the word cult, but that's what the Seed of Israel was. Seemed like they was springing up all over in the seventies. Believe me, wasn't nothing new."

Grady cleared his throat. A headache threatened by the time Matthias had finished his tale. "Obviously Nolan has somehow dug up this story and twisted it to suit his purposes."

"But how could he have found this out?" Paige asked.

"He, or his attorney, has probably done just what we did and hired a private investigator." Grady shook his head, putting up a hand to massage one temple. "I've got to tell you, Paige, it wouldn't take much for a good trial lawyer to spin this into a real nightmare, especially if Vaughn testifies for them."

"But he wouldn't do that!"

"Nolan got this idea somewhere," Grady pointed out. "If not from Vaughn, then from who? I'm not saying Vaughn deliberately told his father things that he could use against you, but I imagine they can make whatever he's said sound pretty indicting. Our defense is going to have to be equally compelling, and the first thing you have to do is distance yourself from the church."

"Don't be ridiculous! We'll just have Pastor Haynes explain what the church believes."

"That might work with a judge, Paige, but with a jury?" Grady shook his head, sick at heart. "I sure wouldn't bet on it. In fact, if I was on the other end of this, I would *insist* on a jury trial."

She put her hands to her head, sinking back on her heels. "I can't believe this."

"I'm so sorry," Matthias said mournfully.

"It's not your fault," Paige insisted. "Nolan did this."

"But I gave him the ammunition, girl. Even if he don't already know 'bout my past, he's bound to find out, and you don't know how sorry I am about that."

"We don't know what he knows," Grady said, "and that's part of the problem, but you're no more to blame than the rest of us, Matthias. I should have insisted that we put Nolan Ellis away when we had the chance. We'll have to file charges on him now. It's our only leverage."

"You know I can't do that," Paige said simply.

Grady couldn't believe he was hearing this. "You *have* to! This isn't just about upsetting Vaughn anymore. There's too much at risk."

She lifted her chin. "I'd risk anything for my son, if you don't know that by now."

"Oh, I know it!" he snapped. "And obviously so does Nolan!"

Matthias lifted a hand, forestalling further argument. "We can't fight them if we're fighting each other."

Sighing, Grady pressed a hand to the back of his head, which had begun to throb. "On that we can agree," he said.

Matthias nodded, his jaw working. "It must be me that put this idea in their heads, so I guess the best thing I can do now is to take myself as far away from here as I can get."

Even as Grady reluctantly agreed, Paige shot up to her knees. "Don't be silly! Where would you go?"

"That doesn't matter right now," Grady said. "We'll find a place for him."

"He has a place," she insisted, "and I won't hear of him leaving home because of Nolan's nonsense."

Grady closed his eyes and counted to ten, trying to retain his grip in the face of growing dismay. "Paige," he reasoned, "just for once, would you please listen?"

"Fine. I'm listening." She subsided, folding her arms and sinking back down on to her heels, a mulish expression on her face. He'd seen that very look on Vaughn's face. Apparently mother and son were more alike than he'd realized.

Grady marshaled his thoughts. "Okay. Now, in order to mount an effective defense against these potentially devastating charges, we have to do certain things. Number one." He held up an index finger. "As I've already said, we have to distance ourselves from anything that can be made to resemble a cult. Two." He held up a second finger, rushing on before she could react to his first assertion. "Vaughn has to be made to understand how serious this situation is." She started shaking her head, but he plowed on. "We have to know what he's said to fuel this claim!"

"No." She got up, leveraging her weight against the arm of Matthias's chair, and faced Grady squarely. He groaned, recognizing that calm, stubborn expression. "Under no circumstances will I put my son in the middle of this."

"Paige, you've got to listen to reason. When this thing comes to trial—"

"It won't come to trial!" she exclaimed, suddenly moved to tears. "I'll send him back to his father before I put him through that. And I won't disavow everything important to me just because someone else is willing to twist the truth!" She whirled away from him. "Matthias, you're not going anywhere. Do you hear me? This is your home. I need you here, especially if worst comes to worst and Vaughn—" She broke off, trembling from head to toe.

Both Grady and Matthias rose to their feet. Matthias was closer, and he'd wrapped his ropy arms around Paige before Grady could even begin to get to her. He shook his head, confident that she must change her mind, certain that she wouldn't. Her back to him, she laid her head on Matthias's bony shoulder, and the old man sent Grady a worried, tearful look.

Grady bowed his head. He understood why she didn't want her son caught up in something this ugly. He understood that her church was important to her because of her faith. He understood that Matthias was precious to her, second only to Vaughn.

What *she* didn't seem to understand was that she was going to lose her child, and perhaps much more, if she didn't let him help her.

"Paige, please think about this. You've got to fight back. If you don't and this gets out… Think what something like this can to do your business."

She laughed, a mirthless, watery sound that broke Grady's heart. Lifting her head, she turned.

"Do you honestly think I care about that?"

"So that's it?" He threw up his hands. "You let Nolan haul you into court and lose everything?"

"No! It won't come to that. I never said I wouldn't fight, but I won't put my son in the middle of it, let Matthias leave *or* give up my church."

"Then what's the point? How else can we fight this?"

Paige swallowed. "This town is full of people who will testify on my behalf. They know the church is not a cult. And there's Dr. Evangeline. I've been seeing her for nearly two years. She's a clinical psychologist. Who better to tell the court that I'm not in a cult?"

"These townspeople, are they members of the church, too?" Grady asked.

"Some. But there are others who aren't."

"And didn't you tell me that Dr. Evangeline has some connection to the church?"

"She's a Christian and a member of a Christian practice. Many churches recommend her organization."

Grady shook his head. "You're taking a big chance going at it this way."

"And Paige, honey," Matthias put in, "just 'cause you won't bring Vaughn into this don't mean his daddy won't."

She bit her lip, but after a moment she shook her head. "I have to do this my way."

"Then you better think of this," Grady ground out. "Doing it your way is going to be expensive. Doing it *any* way is going to be expensive. You can't afford to lose your livelihood, and if it gets out that you're connected to some cult, that could happen."

She shrugged, folding her arms tight. "So we'll just have to keep it quiet."

"Interview, prepare, depose and call a whole town full of people to the witness stand," he drawled sarcastically, "on the q.t.? Right. Baby, you're going to need more than a lawyer to pull that off. You're going to need a magician!"

She lifted a hand to the small gold crucifix hanging from a delicate chain at the base of her throat. "But I have better than that, and He will take care of everything."

Grady lifted a hand to the back of his neck, dropping his head in defeat. What had made him think that he could talk to her? He couldn't even make her understand what a risk she was taking. He should've let Dan handle this. In fact, he never should have gotten involved with Paige Ellis at all.

For her sake, he wished he could believe in a loving, omnipotent God who protected the faithful from heartache, pain and loss, but he'd never been more doubtful or afraid.

Paige shook her head. She'd been doing so for the past hour and more, but she couldn't seem to stop. Unfortunately, she didn't know what the answers were, only what they were not.

"Even if Dan agreed," she said to Grady, sitting across the kitchen table from him, "I couldn't let you work for nothing."

He wrapped a big hand around the mug of coffee that Matthias had poured for him and heaved a deep sigh. The poor man had been holding on to the very edge of his temper all this time. Such steely resolve was to be admired, but Paige couldn't let that sway her.

"And why not?" he asked, his tone verging on a growl. "All attorneys work pro bono cases. It's expected."

"I'm not indigent, Grady," she pointed out. "I managed before. I'll manage again."

"That was *before* hockey," he said glumly.

So it was. The traitorous thought that it might be a blessing if Vaughn did not make the team flitted through her mind, but she dismissed it instantly.

"Of course," Grady said, not quite meeting her gaze over the rim of his mug, "Vaughn might not make the team. For any number of reasons."

She half smiled, understanding clearly that he was offering to speak to the coach, and shook her head again. "I couldn't take that from him."

Grady set the mug down and folded his arms against the scarred tabletop. "Won't make any difference if Nolan gets him back, now will it?"

Paige rubbed her eyes. "No," she conceded, "but I won't

punish my son for a situation created by his father. I want him to be happy, whatever that takes."

"Well, you won't have to worry about legal fees for a while anyway. We've, ah, got this new billing service, and they're, like, way behind. It could be, I don't know, months before they get current."

Grady was a terrible liar, but she wouldn't tell him so. He was trying so hard to help. And a delay in billing *would* be perfect.

"There, you see?" she said, trying desperately to inject a note of levity. "By the time billing catches up to me, I may have won the lottery."

"Now that'd be something," Matthias chimed in from the living room, "winning the lottery without ever buying a ticket."

She wanted to laugh, but it really wasn't a laughing matter. Not only could she lose legal custody of her son, but her good name was at stake. Worse, Matthias would be hurt if his past came out. In addition, her church and all its members could be labeled cultists, its mission to spread the good news of salvation severely handicapped.

While the expense of defending herself was worrisome, it fell far behind those considerations. Nevertheless, she couldn't ignore the facts. Even with the extra time that Grady was essentially promising her, certain expenses connected with something like this would not wait: special fees, court costs, investigators and experts... The list was endless.

And it could all be for nothing, Paige thought morosely.

Perhaps she should send Vaughn back to his father before this went any further, for everyone's sake. Yet, she couldn't quite give up the fight yet.

Neither, unfortunately, could she fight this in the manner that Grady wished.

"You never know how or when God will work something out," she said, as much to herself as the man sitting across the table from her.

"And what if it goes against you?" he asked.

"All I have to know is that God will take care of us, one way or another."

Grady frowned. "Doesn't seem to me like God's doing a very good job at the moment."

"It wasn't God Who filed that custody suit," she said. "That was all Nolan, exercising his free will."

He nodded, whispering, "I wish I could have your faith."

"You can," she told him. "It's yours for the asking."

He looked up in surprise, then he shook his head. "Oh, no, not for me. I've been a doubter too long."

"Yes, for you, and maybe that's the point of this, Grady. Maybe God's teaching us all to rely more completely on Him. So far as I'm concerned, if that's all that comes from this mess, then it will be worth it."

Grady ran a blunt fingertip around the rim of his cup, pensive and solemn, and she knew that he was thinking over what she'd said. After a moment he looked up and asked, "How can you say that? I know how much you love your son, how hard you fought to get him back."

"Yes," she said, "but Grady, don't you see that my prayers have already been answered? For all the time that Vaughn was missing, I prayed to find him, to know that he was well, to have him home again. Yes, I found him. I know that he is well, as well as can be expected, anyway. I've had him home. I believe he's better off here with me, but God sees what I can't see, and whether Vaughn stays with me or returns to his father, my prayers have been answered. For that I praise God."

"It's not fair," he said. "You're a good mother, a good person. You don't deserve this."

"Thank you." She gripped his hands with hers, her heart turning over. "But it's not about fairness. We can't expect a painless life, Grady, not in this world. With pain comes solace, though."

She couldn't help wondering if that wasn't part of why Grady was here, to provide her solace. No one had ever made her feel safer, stronger, more certain than this man, and she had no doubt that God had brought him into her life for a reason.

He ran his thumbs across her knuckles. "I just don't want to see you get hurt again because of something Nolan's done."

"Nolan may have chosen this path, but I choose to walk it with God. That means I have to do what's best for everyone involved, not just myself. Doing it any other way would hurt me more than anyone else."

Grady sighed. "Okay," he grumbled. "We do it your way."

She closed her eyes, thanking God for the man who sat across the table from her. She prayed for wisdom and that, whatever happened, God would be glorified in this situation. She prayed as well that Matthias would find the peace he needed, and that Vaughn, Grady, even Nolan, would come closer to God.

For herself she requested strength, because whatever happened now she knew she was going to need it.

Chapter Eight

On the evening of the hockey tryout, Vaughn was subdued but surly. Grady understood that the kid was nervous, but he didn't see why he had to growl at his mother, who had done everything in her power—to her own detriment—to make her son happy. The second or third time it happened, Grady wanted to reach through the rearview mirror and shake the kid until his teeth rattled. He might have tried it if Paige hadn't been so serenely pleasant. Her, he wanted to hug.

That was getting to be a problem, frankly, an impulse he was having more and more trouble curbing. He really had no business working on her case, but he couldn't bring himself to step aside and leave it to Dan, who seemed all too willing to do whatever she wished with a minimum of argument.

Grady didn't *want* to argue with her, but he couldn't seem to help himself. He often found himself railing at her, and that just wasn't like him. She must not have minded too much because she'd allowed him to come along to the tryout, although he'd practically insisted. That wasn't his usual style, either.

Looking back, Grady realized that he'd seldom insisted, let alone argued, with Robin. He'd just gone along with whatever she'd wanted, including getting married. He regretted that his marriage had failed, of course, but he finally understood why. Obviously Paige had been correct in her assessment that he hadn't really loved Robin.

They hadn't loved each other. He'd been a means to an end for Robin, and she had been an easy, passive answer for him. He hadn't had to strain himself to win her, hadn't had to think of the right words to say, hadn't had to guess her needs or wishes or emotions. By keeping his opinions and thoughts to himself and going along with whatever she'd wanted, he'd thought he was making her happy, but he hadn't troubled himself to find out if that was true.

It was different with Paige. More than anything else in the world, he wanted her to be happy—even if he had to fight with her to make it happen. He wasn't arrogant enough to assume that he alone knew what was best for Paige, but he did know a thing or two about the law and what remedies it offered. It hurt him that she was so reluctant to accept those remedies when that was basically all he had to offer her. Yet, he admired her determination to do what she felt was right.

She was so quick to put everyone else first, though, that he felt someone ought to look out for her. Consequently, he'd defend her as vigorously as she would allow against Nolan's absurd accusations, while doing everything he could to alleviate the other burdens that she bore. That was exactly why he'd decided to secretly give her a helping hand with her finances.

If Vaughn made the hockey team, which seemed likely, then he was going to need gear. Grady had seen to it that Paige was going to get a very good deal on that gear, such a good deal that neither she nor Vaughn could possibly pass it up. He'd also offset the other expenses as much as he'd dared. Knowing how stubborn she could be about these things, though, he'd talked his way into accompanying her and Vaughn to the tryout.

As he pulled into the rink parking lot, he could hear Vaughn breathing in as if he was steeling himself. His eagerness apparently trumped his apprehension, however, as he was out of the car almost before Grady got the transmission in park. He popped the trunk to allow Vaughn to dig out his mostly borrowed gear and took a moment to encourage Paige with a smile.

"Here we go," she murmured, at least as anxious as Vaughn. "It may not make any difference in the long run, but I pray he makes it."

Glancing around to be sure that Vaughn was out of earshot—she insisted that the kid be kept in the dark about the custody suit—Grady succumbed to the need to reassure her.

"I've been thinking about it, and I really believe we can win in court. You're the best parent, and I'm pretty good in a courtroom, if I do say so myself."

Paige lifted a hand, cupping his jaw as tenderly as if he were a fragile, priceless sculpture. "Grady," she said, a touch of exasperation in her tone, "I keep trying to tell you that this can't go to trial. I won't put anyone I care about through that, not Vaughn, not Matthias, not my church, not even myself. And not you. I know you'd do the best for us that you possibly could, but I also know in my heart of hearts that in the long run a trial would do more harm than good." She shook her head. "Don't you see? Either Nolan backs down before it gets to that point, or I've already lost because my son will never forgive me if I do those things that will win an argument in court."

Grady fought every urge that rushed through him. He wanted to hold her, to protect her, to demand that she let him pulverize her ex in court, to tell her how much he cared for her, but he didn't dare. Oh, he didn't doubt that on some level she cared about him, too. She cared about everyone who came into her orbit with a selfless goodwill that amazed and even shamed him. It wasn't the same thing, though. He very much feared that he had fallen in love with her and that she could never feel the same way about him.

Vaughn tapped on the passenger window just then, juggling an armload of hockey gear. "A little help?" he complained.

Paige got out of the car to help Vaughn, and Grady followed them into the building. A half hour later, he sat next to Paige in the stands, gripping her hand as Vaughn made a mad dash toward the goal with the puck, his stick expertly shepherding that little black disc toward the net.

The boy had come out of the box on attack, catching everyone else on the ice off guard, including Jason, who'd lost his whistle in a gasp of surprise when Vaughn had punched through the face-off, darted out to snatch the puck from his own partner and whisked it in to make his first shot on goal. The assistant coach who was functioning as goalie caught just enough of the puck to send it careening off the goalpost. Otherwise, Vaughn would have scored while his erstwhile teammate for the two-on-two scrimmage was left standing midzone with his mouth open.

The pair of thirteen-year-olds deputized to give Vaughn a workout couldn't do anything but try to catch up as Vaughn fielded his own rebound, banked it off the wall and intercepted it again with a lofting swing that sailed it over the goalie's shoulder. Jason bobbled the whistle, finally getting it back between his teeth in time to call play to a halt just as the puck dropped into the corner of the net.

Grady was on his feet next to Paige yelling loud enough to drown out the whistle while Vaughn beamed a smile up into the stands that rivaled the lights overhead. A laughing Paige applauded, while Jason put his hands on his hips and shook his head, clearly impressed. A moment later he put the four skaters to another face-off, with strict instructions for Vaughn to pass the puck to his teammate this time.

Vaughn dutifully followed instructions. Then in the next two minutes he managed three shots on goal, all of which the assistant coach was lucky to stop. For the remainder of the exercise, Vaughn thwarted every attempt of the opposition to so much as get near the goal, let alone shoot on it, proving that his defensive play was as good as his offense. By the end of the exercise, the two older boys were clearly in awe of Vaughn, his own teammate seemed half-afraid of him, and both coaches were over the moon.

It came as no surprise, then, when Jason asked the boy to stay for practice with the whole team and quickly provided Paige with a schedule for the remainder of the season. Quite a crowd had gathered by the time the regular practice was ready to commence, and it quickly became clear to the other parents that the team had a new star. Off the ice, Vaughn seemed a little smug, but on it he was all business, and Grady had no doubt that Jason Lowery would soon take care of that immature arrogance.

One especially awkward moment came when one of the team fathers sidled up to Grady and asked, "Where did your son play before?"

Paige looked past Grady to the man and answered simply, "South Carolina," letting Grady explain that he was only a family friend.

"And a hockey nut," Paige added, flashing a smile up at him.

A hockey-mad friend of the family, he thought. Yeah, that was him, all right. No doubt that explained why he'd secretly paid for a boatload of top-of-the-line gear, the very latest of everything a player could want, the sum of which Jason offered to Paige at a fraction of its actual cost immediately following practice.

"It's used but it's the best available," Jason said.

Vaughn tore into it, thrilled to find price tags still attached. Jason flashed a guilty, apologetic look at Grady, who felt his face heat as the whole ruse threatened to come undone.

"Wh-what do you know," Jason stammered. "Some of it does still have the tags attached." He cleared his throat, obviously trying to think up a plausible reason why "used" gear would still have the store price on it. "Did I, uh, say 'used'? I should've said secondhand."

"Some folks buy out the sporting goods store before they even know whether or not their kid'll make the team," Grady supplied helpfully. "Right, Jason?"

"Uh, right."

Paige widened her already large, green eyes. "Why didn't they just return it?"

"Yeah," Grady muttered. "Why didn't they just return it?"

"Uh. It was on sale?" Jason ventured uncertainly.

Paige laughed. "Of course!"

Seeing her delight, Grady relaxed, and when he relaxed, Jason relaxed, so much so that he was entirely believable when he informed her that he was waiving the usual enrollment fee due to the fact that the season was almost half over. She accepted that with only a mild exclamation of surprise and didn't even question the ridiculously low room rate that Jason quoted her for that weekend's tournament stay in Little Rock.

Vaughn was too busy exclaiming over the new gear to give any thought to how it had just happened to come together in one place. Smart enough to take advantage of that, Grady grabbed up an armload of pads and gloves, heading to the car with them. Leaving Paige behind to complete the purchase, Vaughn followed Grady with his new team uniform, chattering happily.

It was too chilly to stand outside in the dark waiting for Paige, so after loading the new stuff into the trunk Grady and Vaughn got into the car. Several minutes later, Grady began to wonder what was taking so long. Vaughn, who was tired because of all that physical activity, had curled up on the backseat and was half-asleep, so Grady decided to look for her without him.

"I'll lock the car doors and hurry right back. Okay?"

"Whatever."

"Don't open up for anyone else."

Vaughn lifted his head off the seat "I'm eleven, not a baby." He dropped his head again and closed his eyes.

For a moment Grady was torn between going to look for Paige and giving the little smart aleck a piece of his mind. Then suddenly he realized that he was being more idiotic than Vaughn, who was, despite his skill on the ice, merely a child. Children were allowed to be cheeky and foolish; adults should know better.

Vaughn was just a boy in a tough spot, torn between two parents who couldn't live together. For the first time Grady wondered what he would have done in Vaughn's position. He could not be thankful for his mother's death, but he was suddenly glad that he hadn't had to choose between his parents.

From that perspective, the whole situation looked very different from Vaughn's end. Of course, no decent father would steal a child and run away, leaving his mom to suffer, though Vaughn obviously didn't see it that way.

All he knew was that he loved his dad, who had been there during the years when his mom had not. It didn't matter to Vaughn whose fault that was. He loved his dad. Period.

Grady marveled that Paige, who had been most hurt by Nolan's actions, had been able to see from the first that Vaughn's feelings and his ideal of his father mattered. The normal response to the kind of loss and pain that Paige had suffered at the hands of her ex-husband was anger and the tendency to make a monster of the perceived enemy, exaggerating every fault and failing.

Instead, Paige saw the common humanity that she and Nolan shared as parents. Paige Ellis, Grady realized, wasn't completely "normal." Indeed, the woman was almost superhuman, and he could see only one reason for it.

A *feeling* swept over Grady, as if someone or something unseen had tapped him on the shoulder and whispered, "That's right. It's Me." It was a voice he'd never heard and yet somehow recognized. He turned away from the sight of the boy curled up languidly on the backseat of his car and closed his eyes.

Okay, he thought, shaken. *I take it back. She's right. God is real. So why haven't You fixed this for her?*

If he'd actually expected some sort of response, he was disappointed, but *he* suddenly found himself wondering if maybe that was what he was here for, to fix things for her. Hadn't she said, more than once, that he was the answer to a prayer for her? If God could use him for her benefit without him even knowing it, how much more might he be capable of if he willingly surrendered to be used?

Here's the deal, he thought, *I'll do anything You want for her. Anything.*

When he realized what he'd just done, he had to shake his head. He couldn't remember the last time he'd said a prayer.

Reaching blindly for the door handle, he got out of the car and trudged back toward the building. He pulled open the heavy glass door and immediately saw Paige standing against the wall just inside the front entry, her arms loosely folded. Intuition told him that it wasn't some facile misunderstanding that put her there. Frowning, he waited until some guy and a pair of giggling little girls walked past him and disappeared into the arena before he went over to Paige and asked the obvious.

"What are you doing?"

She dropped her arms and rocked away from the wall. "Waiting for you."

"Forget where the car was parked?" he asked drily.

Shaking her head slowly from side to side, she leaned forward and said, "No."

Obviously his cover was blown. "Did Jason—"

"He didn't say a word," she interrupted. "He didn't have to. What's that old joke? I was born in the morning but not *this* morning?" Pursing his lips, Grady hung his head and prepared his arguments. She knocked them all to flinders by softly asking, "I wonder, is it ethical to kiss one's attorney?"

His gaze zipped to hers, finding it warmly glowing, and his heart just melted. "Absolutely not," he reassured her, "but if you don't kiss me, I'm going to kiss you."

"Well, in that case," she said, lifting her arms around his neck and leaning into him.

His heart stopped as she pulled his head down until they stood nose to nose. The top of her head barely reached his shoulder, and he was painfully aware of how dainty and fragile she was, but when she touched her lips to his, none of that mattered. How his hands came to span her waist and lift her or even when he closed his eyes, he didn't know, but when she broke the kiss her feet were dangling off the floor.

He carefully set her down again, hugging her close, even though it hurt to breathe just then, as if his heart had suddenly overfilled his chest. She hugged him back, and he reveled in that embrace until she muttered in his ear, "If you ever do anything like that again, I'll have to fire you."

"Now wait just a minute." He fastened his hands at her trim waist and held her back, the argument falling out of his mouth. "When it comes to the law stuff, you call the shots," he told her. "I don't always agree with you, but you're the boss. I can live with that. But you *don't* get to tell me what to do in my personal life."

She lifted her eyebrows and brought her hands to her hips. "Not even when it impacts *my* personal life?"

He folded his arms. "You turn that around, then you tell me the answer."

"Hmm." She looked down at her toes, then up at him. "Okay, so you get to spend your money however you want, and I get to decide whether or not I'll let it benefit me and my son."

"Fine." They stared at each other for several seconds. He thought his heartbeat was going to strangle him. "So will you? Let it benefit the two of you."

"Yeah," she said, grinning, "and thank you."

He shook his head. "No, I wanted to. It's important to me."

She slipped her arm through his as she stepped to his side, "I'll make sure Vaughn knows who he has to thank for this."

"I—I'd rather you didn't. I'd rather you didn't even know, to tell you the truth."

She tilted her head, gazing up at him. "Why, Grady Jones, that's the dearest thing I've ever heard you say."

He smiled, ridiculously pleased, and walked her through the door out into the cool night. "I know you probably gave Jason a check for the gear, but you really don't have to pay for it."

"Why go to the bother of writing a check when you would just tear it up?" she asked wryly.

He laughed, hurrying her across the parking lot to the car. "Could it be that you know me too well?"

She came to a halt before the passenger side door of his car and turned to face him as he reached for the handle. "What I know is that God keeps using you to bless me and mine."

He froze, that prickle of *something* blowing through him again. "If God's using me to somehow benefit you, that's fine by me," he said.

She blinked at him. "Do you mean that the way I hope you do?"

"You said you'd prove it to me. So, okay, I'm convinced."

She beamed, and he tapped her affectionately on the end of her nose. After putting her inside the car, he walked around the front end to the driver's side. Lifting his eyes heavenward, he whispered, "Anything. Anything at all."

As he slid behind the wheel, Paige urged Vaughn to sit up and buckle his safety belt for the ride home. It hit Grady then that winning over Vaughn would be the greatest service he could do Paige.

Vaughn might even change his mind about going back to his father if he and Grady were more than tolerant acquaintances. Meanwhile, of course, he'd keep working to knock down Nolan's case against Paige. Now all he had to do was figure out how to make a friend of a resentful eleven-year-old whom he didn't even particularly like.

For the first time since he'd realized that his mom would never come home again, Grady considered going to God for guidance.

Grady showed up in Little Rock that next Saturday for the tournament there. Paige knew he must've risen before dawn in order to make it in time for the game. She was pleased but couldn't help worrying about Vaughn's reaction. He seemed happy enough to see another friendly face and played well, but the team came in second, losing by one goal. Vaughn apparently thought it was because of him.

"I blew it. Our whole line played like second graders because of me."

Paige instinctively sought to reassure him. "It wasn't your fault. You obviously knew what you were doing."

"The team will adjust," Grady stated flatly. "If Jason didn't think you were worth shaking things up, he wouldn't have put you on the roster."

Vaughn seemed to accept that, giving his head a businesslike nod, and Paige breathed a silent sigh of relief. Later, while Vaughn was meeting with the rest of the team, she worried aloud to Grady that Jason might be putting a little too much pressure on Vaughn.

"He can handle it," Grady said. "In fact, if you really want to know, I was pretty impressed. There was one point when Vaughn set up a perfect shot and his wingman missed the pass entirely. I thought Vaughn might lose his temper then. He was looking awful frustrated, but he kept his cool, and the next time the kid was where he was supposed to be. If he hadn't missed the shot, they'd have tied the score."

Grady predicted that the team would win the next game, and they did, coming in second in the tournament standings.

The next tournament was some three weeks away, which suited Paige since she'd landed a much-needed new contract. When Jason scheduled scrimmage games in the interim, though, she found herself stretched thin by practices and scrimmages and longer hours of work. Still, she was reluctant to take Grady up on his offer to ferry Vaughn to and from practices.

"Look," he said, "I come to the practices anyway because

I love the game. Why not let me drive Vaughn and save you some time a couple times a week?"

"But you'd be putting a hundred miles or more on your car every time you do it," she argued.

"So? Do you know how many times I've driven almost seven hours each way just to attend pro hockey games in Dallas?"

"In other words, this is a cheap way to get your hockey fix," she surmised, laughing. He just shrugged and smiled. She knew it was more than that, of course, and that both pleased and worried her, but she gave in anyway.

The first time Grady took Vaughn to practice, she made dinner for him, nothing fancy, just meatloaf with macaroni and cheese right out of a box. The second time she was still at the computer when they got back to the house, with hours of work still left to do, but Matthias had stirred up a skillet of beans and franks that couldn't have been blacker if he'd set fire to them. She wasn't entirely sure that he hadn't. On the third occasion, Grady called from the rink to say he was picking up something on his way back, and nothing she could say would dissuade him.

She hung up the phone and turned back to the computer, as grateful as she was disturbed. She was taking shameful advantage of a good man. Not only had he gotten Vaughn an interview that ultimately led to him getting on the team, he'd made it financially possible for him to play. Now he was making it possible for Vaughn to go on playing by allowing her to earn the extra money that made the tournament travel possible.

Grady wasn't doing it for Vaughn; she very much feared that he was doing it for another reason entirely. She just didn't know what to do about that, and the truth was that she wouldn't have changed it if she could have. It had been a long time since a man had cared about her, and no one had ever cared as selflessly as Grady Jones seemed to.

She was surprised by what Grady and Vaughn brought home. Grady had swung by a place in Bentonville that offered full, home-style dinners for carryout to the harried professionals who worked in the area. Vaughn grumbled about it not being typical fast food, then announced that he had chosen the roast pork option himself, complete with potatoes au gratin, mixed vegetables, yeast rolls and carrot cake.

"This is wonderful!" Paige exclaimed once they were all sitting around the table in her old-fashioned kitchen.

She heard Grady's stomach rumble, but he didn't pick up his fork, knowing the routine by now. Instead, he reached for her hand. Paige gripped his fingers and reached for those of Matthias, who linked up with Vaughn, who gingerly took Grady's other hand. They all bowed their heads. Matthias did the honors.

"Lord, we thank You for the food You've provided, and we ask You to bless it to the nourishment of our bodies, that we might be better servants of You and Your kingdom. Amen."

"Amen," Grady rumbled, and Paige squeezed his fingers before she slipped her hand from his. He didn't even seem to realize how often he did that sort of thing. The man who hadn't believed in prayer was becoming surprisingly comfortable with it. She couldn't have been happier about that.

They talked hockey while the food disappeared, mostly about the team's prospects for winning the next tournament, which were looking pretty good according to Grady. Then Paige walked him out while Matthias and Vaughn cleaned up after their meal.

"You know it's not right for you to carry in our dinner

after putting yourself out to get Vaughn back and forth to practice," she said. "Feeding you is the least I should do."

"You're working long hours," he protested, stopping on the bottom step leading down from her porch and twisting to face her. Since she stood on the porch itself, their heads were about even. "I can't let you cook for me, and I like eating too much to let Matthias play chef."

She chuckled at that. "He cooks a few things well, but only a few, and we've gotten pretty tired of those, I'll admit."

There was no porch light, but the moon hung big and full overhead. Its delicate light bathed his face in silver, his blue eyes gleaming like jewels. It was a strong face, square and heavy-featured but unabashedly, unmistakably male. She loved the way his thick, earthy brown hair waved away from its side part and fell boyishly over his broad forehead.

"Carrying in for you beats eating alone any day," he said.

Her hand came up, seemingly of its own volition, and skimmed his cheek. "I feel like I'm taking advantage."

He scoffed at that. "You're humoring me, and we both know it."

She dropped her hand and bowed her head, realizing that she had to say this even if she didn't want to. "Grady, I'm afraid I can't give you what you want from me, not with everything so unsettled with my son."

"It won't always be unsettled," he said carefully.

"Won't it? I just don't know. That's what divorce does to lives, it turns them upside down. When there's a child involved I'm not sure they ever get right side up again."

She was trying to tell him not to get his hopes up, but somehow she couldn't come right out and say it. Even if Nolan finally went away and left them alone, she wasn't sure that Vaughn would ever be comfortable with her dating. Sometimes Vaughn still spoke of Grady in a scornful tone, even though he had to see that they couldn't have managed to this point without him.

She'd prayed about the situation a good deal and still wasn't sure what God's intentions were. Was Grady for her? Or was she for Grady? Or was it more than that? She was almost afraid to hope, afraid she'd wind up hurting a good man.

"We'll see," Grady said lightly. "Meanwhile, I get my hockey fix and meals I don't have to eat alone. Works for me."

"If that's true," she whispered, "then I'm glad, but Grady, please, don't let me hurt you."

"Don't worry about that."

"I have to worry about it."

He shook his head, smiling. "And here I thought you had enough to worry about."

She laughed. "True."

"Look, if I can't manage this or I get tired of it, I'll let you know. Okay? It's not like I've got anything better to do. Or don't you realize that you're dealing with a social misfit?"

"Puh-leze. Don't try to sell that snake oil around here, mister."

He laughed and stepped down onto the ground. "Tell Vaughn I'll see him Thursday." Flipping her a wave, he moved off toward his car. "Good night."

"Good night."

She stepped back into the shadows, watching until his taillights disappeared into the darkness before she went inside. Matthias and Vaughn were watching television. She had work to do, but she sat down with them until Vaughn went to bed, knowing that it was only because of Grady that she dared do so.

Chapter Nine

Over the course of the next month, Grady took so many meals at Paige's house that he felt like one of the family, and while he didn't seem any closer to really getting to know Vaughn, at least the kid wasn't rude. All in all, he considered that he was making progress, especially as Paige seemed to count on him more and more. They attended every scrimmage and hockey game together, but Grady continued to transport Vaughn to and from practices on his own, bringing in dinner as often as not.

Over the past few weeks Grady had interviewed Paige's pastor, Richard Haynes, as well as several of the members of his church, and they were honest, perfectly harmless, everyday folk whose faith, so far as Grady could tell, was genuine. Pastor Haynes was a slight, soft-spoken, middle-aged man with thinning hair and pale, friendly gray eyes. From the outset he had expressed the determination to protect his church and help Paige in any way possible, so Grady wasn't particularly surprised to walk into Paige's house one Thursday evening in the middle of March to find the man waiting for him.

After surrendering a family pack of fried chicken to

Matthias and Vaughn, who carried the containers into the kitchen, Grady shook hands with the pastor and got right down to business. "Have you been in touch with FFROC?"

The Foundation For Research On Cults was the entity Nolan's attorney had sicced on the church. Once a fully credible organization, it had largely devolved into what trial attorneys often referred to as a "hired gun." In other words, its experts tended to tailor their reports to the needs of those who paid them, but Grady hoped that they were still serious enough about their research to want to actually do some when the opportunity presented itself. Haynes had promised to contact those investigators and answer their questions over the phone as they had originally requested.

The pastor nodded. "I've spoken to them all right, but they no longer want to interview me over the phone. Now they want to come to the church."

"And bring cameras," Paige added significantly.

Pleased, Grady shrugged. "Let 'em. We've got nothing to hide."

Haynes smiled and relaxed. "My thoughts exactly. We're set up for the end of April."

Paige glanced toward the kitchen door, reminding them to keep their voices down so Vaughn wouldn't overhear. "Does this mean we can knock down their claims about the church at least?" she asked Grady.

"I hope so. They'll try to twist everything to their advantage, though, so we have to get them on record."

"How do we do that?" Pastor Haynes wanted to know.

"Number of ways, but the most obvious is to tape the interviews yourself."

Haynes seemed vaguely troubled by that, but he didn't protest. "I don't suppose there's any privacy or confidentiality issue in something like this."

"None," Grady confirmed, "but I have to tell you here and now, that I'm going to want the tapes."

Haynes nodded thoughtfully and suggested that they pray about the matter, starting that very moment. Grady allowed Paige to pull him into a tight circle with her and the pastor, who quietly voiced an eloquent prayer for guidance. He petitioned God on Paige's behalf, as well, asking for God's leadership in her life. He even asked that God soften Nolan's heart and make him aware of the harm he was doing with his custody petition and baseless accusations.

They looked up to find Vaughn standing in the doorway to the kitchen. So much for secrecy. Haynes quickly took his leave, and Grady found himself lifting a protective arm about Paige's waist.

She put on a brittle smile, which faded the instant Vaughn asked, "Can I call Dad now?"

Paige audibly gulped, pointedly stepped away from Grady and answered, "After dinner."

Vaughn turned away without another word, and Grady traded glances with Paige. She was clearly worried. "Do you think he knows what's going on?"

"He's not stupid, Paige. If his father hasn't told him already, he's bound to know something's up."

She sighed. "It's important to me that I not be the one to put him in the middle."

"You haven't."

"Thank you for not saying anything to him."

"I promised I wouldn't."

"I know, and I appreciate it."

He smiled. If she didn't know by now that he'd do anything for her, he wasn't nearly as obvious as he figured he was. "Let's get some dinner while it's still warm, hmm?"

She let him steer her into the kitchen, saying. "You can't keep bringing in dinner for us like this, Grady."

"As long as you insist on working these long days, I can," he stated flatly, "and haven't we already had this discussion?"

She sighed at that and let him seat her. Matthias showed no qualms about eating food carried in by Grady, and neither did Vaughn, although he was quiet during the meal. Then again, at the rate that he was shoveling it in, conversation was clearly impossible. He asked to be excused before dessert, saying that he'd save his cherry cobbler for later.

"Can I call Dad now?" he asked. "In your office? Since everybody's still eating in here."

Paige labored over a smile. "That's fine."

He was gone in the blink of an eye. Looking as if he'd bitten into something sour, Matthias pushed back from the table, muttered that he wanted to catch some TV and limped out of the room. Only then did Paige drop her head into her hands. Grady shoved his plate away and reached a hand around to massage the nape of her neck.

"Every time I think he's starting to make the adjustment, he reaches out to his father and we're suddenly going in reverse," she complained softly. Looking up, she said firmly, "Hockey does seem to have a positive effect on his behavior, though."

"Does it?"

"It's either that or you," she noted drily.

Grady chuckled, secretly delighted to think that he could contribute anything positive. "Me?" he teased. "A positive effect? There are legions of mothers who undoubtedly would argue that with you."

She snorted and picked up her fork again. "Obviously you haven't carried in dinner for them."

"Nah, I'm particular about who I carry in dinner for. Even as a boy I wouldn't pick up dinner for just anyone."

He winked, and she sputtered in laughter. He wondered

if there was any limit to how much of a fool he'd make of himself just to hear that sound.

He was still thinking about that some twenty or so minutes later when Vaughn finally wandered into the living room to stand staring at Paige and Grady, who sat side by side while Matthias flipped through the television stations. With Vaughn on the phone in the office, Paige couldn't go back to work, so Grady had dropped down onto the sofa beside her to wait. Vaughn looked sad, dispirited, sullen, even confused.

"Would you like your dessert now?" Paige asked, but the boy shook his head. "Everything okay?"

He shrugged, sent Grady a dark look and said, "I'm going to bed."

"So early?"

"Tired," he mumbled, dragging himself off to the bedroom.

Her expression troubled, Paige glanced at Grady before slipping off the sofa to follow Vaughn into his room. She came back a few minutes later.

"What'd he say?" Matthias asked baldly.

She shot Grady an unreadable look before muttering, "Same old same old. He wants to go back to South Carolina. He doesn't have any friends here."

"He has friends," Grady refuted. "I see him with the other guys on the hockey team. Some of them are jealous because of the way he plays, but most of them seem to like him. They joke around together off the ice."

"I know," she said. "I've seen it, too, but whenever I suggest inviting his teammates over, he makes some excuse."

Matthias cleared his throat. "I think I can help you there. He told me the other day that they're all rich kids. He says they got pools and media rooms and stuff like that. Said the guys would 'freak' if they could see where he comes from."

"He's ashamed of this place," Paige concluded, dropping down on to the couch dispiritedly.

"He could just as well mean South Carolina," Grady pointed out, patting her shoulder. "The point is that most of his teammates are from Bentonville, and their families are affluent."

"Guess that's why he don't want them to see him riding around in your old truck," Matthias said to Paige.

"No wonder he always wants you to take him to hockey," Paige admitted sadly. "I thought he was being thoughtful of my work schedule, but he wants the other kids to see him get out of your Mercedes instead of my old rattletrap."

Grady winced. Here he'd thought the kid was warming up to him. That's what he got for not realizing that Vaughn would feel out of place on an elite Bentonville team. Those kids must seem rich to him, and obviously Vaughn had a problem with that, so instead of hockey making him happier here, it was just making him more discontent.

Grady couldn't help feeling responsible since he'd steered Vaughn to the team. How could he fix things for Vaughn? He made a good living. He could afford a house in Bentonville, a new car for Paige, just about anything she or Vaughn could want. Vaughn could live as well as anyone on his team, and Paige would never have to spend another hour transcribing medical notes if she didn't want to.

How ridiculous a notion was this? They weren't even dating, for pity's sake. He hauled her kid back and forth to hockey practice and invited himself to the dinner table, but they were basically still client and attorney. He had about as much chance of convincing Paige to marry him as sprouting a second head, especially if she lost her son because he couldn't find a way to stop it.

Surely, he told himself, God wouldn't let that happen. But what did he know about it? All he really knew about God, he'd learned from Paige, and that was just enough to confuse him. How was he supposed to know what God had in mind?

Maybe it was time he figured that out. He'd been thinking about it for a while now, and it seemed like confirmation that it was time to take the next step. Thankfully, he knew just who could tell him what that next step should be.

Paige accepted the coming Sunday's sheet music from the church secretary, confessing apologetically, "These days I'd lose my head if it wasn't attached to the end of my neck."

Thin and thirtyish with short, mousy, tightly curled hair, Betty was meticulous to a fault. The pastor claimed that she would alphabetize the months of the year if the order hadn't been firmly established for centuries. It was downright embarrassing for Paige to admit to someone with Betty's organizational penchant that she couldn't keep track of her own choir music.

"Surely my folder will turn up before long," she offered lamely, adding, "If not, of course, I'll pay for it."

"Oh, don't worry about it," Betty said. "We'll just make copies of everything."

"In that case, I hope your user's license is current," commented a familiar voice.

Paige whirled around, absurdly pleased but also surprised to find Grady Jones standing in the doorway of the pastor's office on a Tuesday afternoon. "Grady!"

Pastor Haynes squeezed past Grady. "I'm sure we renewed the license when we were supposed to. Right, Betty?"

Betty tapped the twelve-month calendar mounted on the wall behind her desk. "April," she said. "We renew our license every year in April."

Pastor Haynes folded his hands with satisfaction. "There you are. All in order."

Grady tilted his head as if trying to decide whether or not to smile. He didn't. Instead, he made a statement. "Copyright issues have been getting a lot of play in the courts lately."

"I never thought about copyright," Paige admitted, looking again at the music in her hands. "But that can't be why you're here. What is it? Have we heard from FFROC again?" That acronym always made her want to roll her eyes, but as ridiculous as it sounded, the Foundation For Research On Cults was too awkward a title for easy conversational use.

Grady just stared at her, while Pastor Haynes dithered uncomfortably for a moment before starting as if struck by a sudden idea. "You'll be glad to know," he announced grandly, "that Betty will be taping our visit with the researchers."

"I make the sermon videos," she informed Grady. "It's a simple matter."

"Date and time stamp on the tape?" Grady queried.

She seemed offended that he'd even ask. "Well, of course."

"What happens if they want to look around the place?"

"I'll take the camera and follow."

"No offense, Betty, but wouldn't it be better to hire a professional?" Paige ventured uncertainly. "I would pay for it, of course." She cringed at the thought, but surely this was her responsibility. To her mingled relief and concern, Grady shook his head.

"I think it's better for the pastor's office to take care of it. At this point we're just keeping the process honest. If theirs isn't the only tape, they can't cherry-pick comments to support damaging conclusions. We, on the other hand, just want the truth to come out, and that's always an unassailable position. If it comes to court, however, we'll hire our own expert to refute everything their expert says."

"Not that it will come to court," Paige hastened to add.

Grady made no reply to that, just clamped his jaw before thanking the pastor. The two shook hands, and Grady headed for the exit. Paige glanced around and hurried after him, puzzled by his behavior. Something was up, but she hadn't the foggiest notion what.

She called out to him the instant she hit the sidewalk. He stopped but didn't turn around. Instead he stood waiting for her to catch up with him, one hand jingling the change in his pocket.

Clouds swirled overhead, hinting at rain one instant, jolting them with sunshine the next. They provided a perfect illustration of this situation, illuminating one moment, obscuring the next.

"You never answered me back there."

He glanced down. "Guess I forgot the question."

That was an obvious ploy, and it alarmed her. This was her church. He was her lawyer, not to mention her friend. Why would he come here like this and not tell her about it?

"What's going on?" she asked pointedly. "You didn't drive over on a Tuesday afternoon to ask if the church is licensed to use copyrighted music or hear that Betty is filming the FFROC investigation. If it has to do with my case, I think I have a right to know."

He shifted his feet. "It doesn't." With that he strode away again.

Despite the fact that her vehicle waited in the opposite direction, she went after him, a little angry now. "Grady, I want to know what's going on!"

He rounded on her. "Did it never occur to you, Paige, that it might be *personal?*"

She blinked at him. Personal? This was her church, after all, not his. She stepped back, catching her breath. What if this was about the two of them?

She'd known that Grady wanted more than a professional relationship with her for some time. And she wanted one with him. One day. But not now, especially not after the things Vaughn had said the other evening in his bedroom.

She hadn't told Grady what her son had said because she hadn't wanted to hurt his feelings. Grady had been so generous to them, especially with Vaughn, but even Vaughn knew why. He'd asked what Grady was still doing there, and she'd said something meaningless about just having finished dinner, and Vaughn had snapped at her.

"Don't lie to me. You keep pretending there's nothing going on, but I know better. He ain't coming around because he likes hockey!"

"But he does like hockey," she'd argued.

"Not as much as he likes you," Vaughn had sneered. Then he'd blurted, "Don't think I care, 'cause I don't! At least he's got money, and that's what you care about most."

She'd tried to tell him that wasn't true, but he'd thrown in her face how much she worked. It would have done no good to tell him that it was for him.

"From now on I'll take you to hockey practice myself," she'd promised, and he'd confounded her by exclaiming that he wanted Grady to do it. She hadn't known what to make of that until Matthias had explained later. Now she didn't know what to do about anything. She looked at Grady and realized what a wretched mess she'd made of everything.

"I—I'm sorry. I didn't mean to pry. I was just surprised to…see you," she finished lamely, watching him leave, driving off in his Mercedes.

Maybe it was better this way. She just didn't know anymore. All she knew was that nothing she did seemed to make anyone happy, not Matthias who thought she was too soft on Vaughn, not Vaughn who was doing everything in his power to distance himself from her, and not Grady who seemed to want—and definitely deserved—more than she was able to give.

She was simply too exhausted mentally, emotionally and physically to figure out what to do about any of it. Worse, she wasn't sure it even mattered.

Just yesterday Vaughn had announced that he would be riding the school bus from then on, something he had vehemently protested before. She'd realized that, far from winning him over, she was losing him. That time at the beginning and end of every day had been sacrosanct to her. No matter how pressing her work, how badly she needed the money or how busy their schedule, she'd always driven him to and from school. It hurt to think that Vaughn hadn't understood what those few minutes meant to her. Or that he had, which was why he'd put a stop to them.

The whole thing was deeply demoralizing, but he was due home in less than an hour, and she meant to be at the door waiting for him. She trudged back to her own vehicle.

Matthias was in his room with the door closed when she let herself into the house a few minutes later. Assuming that he was taking a nap, which he often did, she tiptoed into the kitchen to fix herself a cup of herbal tea. Even though the house felt overly warm to her, she hoped that the tea would prove restorative.

Intending to get in a few more minutes of work before Vaughn came home, she carried her steeping tea toward the back of the house. A knock at her front door halted her in midstride; she knew instantly who it was. Only three people in the world could walk up onto her porch without Howler trying to shatter all the windows in the house, and neither Vaughn nor Matthias would bother knocking. Hesitating only a moment, she turned back and set the teacup on the coffee table before opening up.

Grady shuffled his feet and asked grimly, "Can I come in?"

The irony of the situation didn't escape her. First she'd pressed him for answers, and now that he apparently wanted to talk, she was reluctant to get into it.

"You don't owe me any explanations, Grady," she said, folding her arms. "I—I just stopped by the church b-because…" He looked up, smiling slightly, and she saw instantly that something had changed, something important.

"You lost your choir music," he finished for her, crowding so close that she automatically backed up. He stepped into the room, closing the door behind him. "I was there because I needed to talk to someone," he told her. "I still do."

She licked her lips, blew out her breath and stopped; stopped worrying, stopped being embarrassed, stopped backing away. This was Grady, who had become dear to her, who had so often been the answer to her prayers, whose generosity had, for fleeting moments, made her pigheaded son happy. She sat down on the sofa and waited for him to carefully fold up his big body.

"I had some questions," he began, "I wanted to talk to someone about them. Pastor Haynes seemed the right person."

She knew then what it was about. Gladness filled her. "Was Richard able to help you?"

"Yes and no. Some of it makes sense." Grady gripped his knees with his big, square hands and went on. "For instance, a conversation is more productive if there's a personal relationship involved. Otherwise it's like talking to air."

"Do you know what this is?" she asked softly. "This is proof that God answers prayers."

"Is it?"

"It is if you're thinking about your personal relationship with God."

He sat back and crossed his legs. "The thing is, I haven't really had a personal relationship with God. God and me, we've sort of kept our distance, if you know what I mean."

"I do," she replied. "Now God's calling you to Him, I think."

He rubbed his eyebrow. "It *has* been on my mind a lot lately, so I made an appointment with the pastor."

She smiled. "I'm absolutely sure he told you where that personal relationship with God starts."

Grady pinched the pleat of his slacks. "It's surprisingly difficult to think about, you know."

"In what way?"

When he looked up, sadness stood starkly in his gaze. "The cross."

She nodded, understanding fully. "The cross isn't easy to think about, until you realize why He did it, why He let us spill His blood. No, it was more than that. He *poured it out* for us."

"But that's the part that doesn't make any sense."

"Just stop and think about what you'd do for those you love."

Grady looked at her squarely then, and the understanding that she saw in his eyes stopped her heart. As alone as he sometimes seemed, as often as he argued with her about what she felt was right for her son, this was a man who understood love. She thought of his mother, his brother, his father, everyone he might love; she tried very hard not to put herself among them, but she couldn't deny that she wanted to.

"I see what you mean," Grady murmured. "I guess it just always sounded like a bad plan to me. Why would you plan to sacrifice your own son?"

"For the good of all the rest of Your children," she answered. "Besides, would Christ, Who is part and parcel with

God, have had it any other way? After all, since He has the mind of God, He knew what the plan was all along."

"Oh, my," Grady said, sitting forward. He mulled it over for some time. Then he pushed a hand over his face. "Wow."

She couldn't have said it better. When his hand dropped again, it sought out her own, she gripped his fingers tightly.

"Would you pray with me?" he whispered.

"Gladly."

She closed her eyes and bowed her head. Tears leaked out from beneath her lowered lids, but she didn't even try to sniff them back. This moment deserved tears, tears of joy, and she was suddenly so very glad that she'd lost her music! She'd have missed this otherwise.

After several minutes she realized that he was not going to pray aloud. A calming serenity stole over her, but only after he increased the pressure on her fingers did she clear her throat and whisper a closing.

"Thank You for loving us enough to pay the price for our sins, and thank You for all Grady has meant in my life and Vaughn's. Bless him as he's blessed us, accept him as he's accepted You. In the name of Your Son. Amen."

She didn't really know who hugged who first, but it hardly mattered. Reveling in the strength of his arms, she laid her head on his shoulder and held on tight. It was as if her problems just lifted away at that point, faded into insignificance. For the first time since she'd found out about the custody suit, she felt safe. There in his arms, she rested from her travails. Worry, even thought, was momentarily suspended as she just let herself be glad.

The next thing she knew, Vaughn was standing there, the knob of the open door in one hand, his backpack in the other. He stared at them, his face like chiseled stone. Yet, she saw the terrible conflict behind his expression, felt the tug-of-war rending his heart. Weariness slid over her once more, a weight so heavy she could barely lift her head.

"Hello, Vaughn," she said dully, pulling back from Grady and letting her hands fall into her lap. She searched desperately for the right words and came up with only, "How was your day?"

Without a word, he bolted into his room, slamming the door. Paige sighed and lifted a hand to her head.

"I didn't mean to upset him," Grady said awkwardly.

She shook her head. "Everything upsets him."

"I thought he was coming to like me at least a little."

"Grady, my son doesn't even like *me*."

"That can't be. How could he not love you?"

"He won't let himself," she said, really feeling the truth of that for the first time. "He's afraid he'll have to stop loving his father if he does. That's what he's been taught, that it must be only one of us. I can't seem to make him see that it can be both." Grady slid his hand to the center of her back. The weight and the heat of it were a comfort and a pain at the same time. "You'd better go," she said gently.

His hand moved up to her hair, kneading the back of her head. "I don't want to," he told her. "I never want to leave you these days."

She closed her eyes, thinking how easy it would be to lean on him, to let him solve all her problems for her, but she couldn't do that. Vaughn was not merely a problem to be solved; he was her son, and she couldn't allow her own affections to be divided right now.

"I'm so very glad you came," she said, "but it's better that you go now. I have to talk to him, and it'll be easier that way."

Grady looked at first as if he might argue, but then he nodded and got up. She walked him to the door, and they just stood there for a moment, facing one another, until she reached up and cupped his jaw with her hand. She smiled, and then she hugged him again.

"I'm so glad for you."

He clasped her to him. "You said you'd prove it to me, and you did." With that he left her.

She closed the door and put her back to it, thanking God and gathering strength for the confrontation to come.

Chapter Ten

Every step felt as if lead weights had been fixed to her feet, but Paige moved across the floor to Vaughn's room and went inside. Flat on his back on the bed, he stared up at the ceiling.

She looked around, taking in tan walls, a hockey poster, dark blue linens. The radio-controlled car she'd bought him for Christmas occupied one shelf; a few books stood on another. His backpack had been dumped on the desk in the corner. Clothes scattered the floor. A mound of hockey gear stood just inside his open closet door.

Everything was familiar. Yet this felt like a stranger's room, as if it belonged in someone else's house.

Vaughn pushed up onto his elbows and glared at her.

"That wasn't what you think," she said calmly.

He shrugged and plopped down on his back again. "I don't care."

"I think you do care, Vaughn. I think you care a lot."

He swung his feet off the bed and sat up. "I just don't know how you could like him better than Dad is all."

For a moment, Paige was too shocked to speak. She couldn't believe that Vaughn might imagine she still harbored feelings for his father, but apparently he did. She put a hand to her head, trying to think through this.

"Vaughn," she finally began, "I didn't want to be divorced, that's true, but after what your father did—"

"He didn't *do* anything!"

Again, she was speechless. "You can't still believe that. He took you away from me! It was your birthday. Don't you remember? He was supposed to take you camping, but instead he ran away with you."

Vaughn got up to go to his desk, where he began pulling books from his backpack with short, jerky movements. "I have to do my homework so I can call Dad."

She'd worked so hard not to criticize Nolan, bitten her tongue countless times, refused to descend to his level of indoctrination, but Vaughn was too smart not to know the truth.

"You'll never understand what it was like," she blurted. "I was terrified. I didn't know where you were or if I'd ever see you again. I looked for you for three-and-a-half years!"

"You made him do it!" Vaughn insisted hotly.

She tried not to be hurt. She tried so hard not to be hurt, but he was utterly determined to cast her in the villain's role. Suddenly she was too tired to fight him anymore, too drained to take the principled stand, the high road. Why even try?

Her voice trembled when she said, "No one ever makes your father do anything, Vaughn. He does exactly what he pleases. You know that."

Vaughn flipped open a book and pulled out the desk chair, completely ignoring her. She didn't bother reminding him that he was supposed to do his homework at the kitchen table; he knew, but he'd only do it if she forced him, and all she would get for her trouble would be his compliance. Never acceptance. Never that.

Defeated, she started to back out of the room, but he whirled around, demanding, "Do you still love him?"

The question took her off guard. "Who? Grady?"

"No! Dad! Do you still love my dad? He thinks you do. He says that's why you didn't send him to prison, why you won't."

Stunned, she opened her mouth, but no sound came out. Suddenly she understood that Nolan, in his self-centered arrogance, probably actually believed that she was still in love with him. No doubt he thought that was why she hadn't prosecuted him for kidnapping their son! The idiotic man couldn't even imagine that she might have done it for Vaughn, that she could put her son ahead of any need to punish him.

She slapped her hands to her cheeks. It was so appalling it was almost funny.

"I kept your father out of prison for *you,* Vaughn, not him. I didn't want the divorce, because I believe that marriage is supposed to be forever, but no, I do *not* still love your father. If he thinks I do, then he is sadly, badly mistaken."

"Do you love Grady then?" Vaughn demanded, his voice breaking.

She closed her eyes. He couldn't know how hard she'd tried *not* to think about loving Grady, and she still wasn't ready to think about it. "I don't know," she whispered.

"Liar!" he screamed. "Liar! I hate you! I hate living here. I wanna go home! I want to go home! I'm glad Dad filed the custody suit! I'm glad!"

The words hit her like hammer blows. He knew about the custody suit, had known about it probably from the beginning. That hurt worse than anything else.

She whirled away, bumping up against Matthias as she stumbled into the living room. He brushed her off, rigid with purpose, and stomped toward Vaughn's room. She made a futile attempt to waylay him before simply collapsing against the end of the sofa.

Vaughn had known. While she'd been doing her best to protect him, he may well have been plotting with his father to ruin those closest to her. It was almost more than she could bear.

"Your mother's nearly killed herself trying to make you happy!" Matthias shouted.

"I didn't want to come here!" Vaughn shouted back.

"When're you going to get it through your head that your dad ran off from you and your mom both? Then he took you just to hurt her when she called him on it!"

"That's not true!"

"He even tried to claim you weren't his."

"Matthias, don't!" she pleaded, but Vaughn shouted over her.

"He did not! *She's* the one who said it! She even signed a paper! He showed it to me. He showed me!"

Paige closed her eyes, shaking her head.

"She didn't know what she was doing when she signed them papers," Matthias exclaimed, "but *he* did! He drew 'em up just so he could get out of paying child support, and then he ran off with you to get back at her for trying to make him pay."

"It was all about money for her!" Vaughn yelled. "He never could've given her enough!"

"Don't be an imbecile!" Matthias roared. "Look around you! Does this look like the home of a grasping, greedy woman to you?"

"Let Grady give her *his* money!" Vaughn sneered. "He's got lots!"

"He oughta! She paid him plenty of hers when she was looking for you!" Matthias declared.

"Shut up!" Vaughn sobbed. "I want my dad! I want my dad!"

Paige pushed up to her feet then and flung herself at Matthias.

"Stop! Stop," she begged. "You're hurting him. Can't you see that you're hurting him?"

She tried to put a hand over Matthias's mouth and felt the hot, liquid path of his tears. It broke her heart, the old man and the boy both crying. Matthias tried to wrench away and stumbled. She clasped an arm around his shoulders and steered him toward his room, turning back to Vaughn when Matthias put out a hand to steady himself against the wall.

He stood just inside his room, tears running down his face. She took a step toward him, shaking her head in apology. He stepped back and closed the door. She knew then that it was useless, that she had lost.

The weeks and months and years of hoping against hope, the struggle, the counseling, the patience, all the noble intentions, they meant nothing to a boy who just wanted his father. She went to her knees, and this time all she asked for was the strength to do what she must.

Paige finally pulled herself together enough to throw together a late dinner for them, not that anyone actually ate. Matthias was too miserably contrite, and Vaughn too sullen. Paige, operating by rote, concentrated on simply surviving from one breath to the next.

Sometime during the course of that long night, though, she finally made peace with what had to be. She'd turned Vaughn's life upside down when it should have been the other way around, and now the only way to fix it was to let him go.

It was taking a chance, she knew, a huge chance, and ultimately it would mean uprooting her whole world because if Vaughn went back to South Carolina to live, then so, too, must she. At least that was what she hoped to do, not that she *wanted* to move. She'd lived her whole life right here in this little town in Arkansas, most of it in this very house, but what other choice did she have?

Vaughn hated it here. Right now he even hated her. So she was going to let him go. But how could she lose him again? Somehow she had to build a bridge between them, and when that was done, maybe she could make a place for herself in his life. To do that, though, to have any real influence with him, she had to let him go.

On the other hand, to know that he was well and cared for, she had to be where he was. It was that simple. If she suggested such a thing now, though, Vaughn would doubtlessly tell her that he didn't want her there, and she couldn't bear that. Not now.

So she would keep that part of the master plan to herself and pray for the best.

Heavy of heart, she went to tell him of her decision early that next morning, only to find his room unoccupied. The bed didn't appear to have been slept in. Horrified, she mentally kicked herself for not realizing that he might run. Wearing nothing more than her ratty old chenille bathrobe over flannel pajamas and fuzzy slippers, she grabbed her purse and tore out of the house to look for him, praying that he hadn't gotten far.

He had gotten no farther, in fact, than the front porch.

She almost collapsed with relief to see him sitting there on the top step, Howler wedged in next to him, the dog's big black head taking up the whole of Vaughn's lap. That he'd intended to run couldn't have been more obvious. He was wearing his backpack; another bag stood at his feet.

Paige shivered and closed her eyes, thanking God that he'd had sense enough to stay put. Swallowing, she set aside her purse and searched her mind for the right words, coming up with only, "It's all right, Vaughn."

He bowed his head and scrubbed at his face with his jacket sleeve. She leaned against the porch rail, her back to him, and folded her arms, huddling inside her robe.

"It's not just that I miss Dad," he said quietly. "It was *easier* before."

"I understand," she whispered. Before she'd found him again, he'd distilled his life to a certain pinpoint of reality. He hadn't had to think about any of the broader truths until she'd forced them on him. It was what kids did, what they were, what it meant to be a child, and she'd never wanted anything else for him.

"It was really simple there," he went on wistfully. "Here, everything's so complicated."

For a moment the tragedy of it all overwhelmed her, but then she pulled herself together, cleared her throat, and said what she'd been planning to say. "Do you think your father would give me visitation rights, Vaughn?"

He twisted around. Howler scrambled up and wandered away while Vaughn stared up at her, his face tear-streaked. "I can go back? Are you saying I can go back?"

The hope that trembled on the air momentarily robbed her of speech, but she swallowed and managed to say, "He has to sign papers, though, Vaughn. I won't lose you completely again. I can't bear that. I can't."

He rose stiffly. "You mean it?" She saw the hope in his eyes, and it nearly killed her. Finally, she managed a nod. He jerked into action, bolting for the house.

"I have to call Dad before he leaves for work!"

Feeling weak, she turned to lean against the porch post, terrified and already grieving in her heart. She stayed there, staring at the horizon of the dawn sky until she found the strength to stand on her own again.

Now all she had to do was find the strength to let him go—and give up dreams she hadn't even had the courage to dream yet.

Matthias would be shocked, probably even angry at first, but eventually he'd see that this was the best way. If he wanted to go with her to South Carolina, fine, if not, he could stay on here in the house if he wanted. He could bring in someone else if he didn't want to live alone, and they'd remain in close touch.

Grady, on the other hand, worried her. Grady, who didn't understand that he was just shy, just a big, sweet teddy bear of a man who never quite got over missing his mother, had already been abandoned once. She hated, *hated,* to be the next woman to abandon him, but what else could she do? She must take care of her son, and she couldn't ask Grady to uproot his whole life and follow her, not when he had so many reasons to stay here and Vaughn barely tolerated him. Not when she couldn't promise him it would ever be different.

"Oh, Father God," she prayed, "make him see that I have to put my son first. Make him understand that I'm not the woman You meant for him."

She doubled over, gasping for breath, and wondered how it was possible to feel so keenly the loss of something that had never even been hers.

"You can't," Grady insisted, bending over her. "Sweetheart, listen to me. I can back him down. I know I can. I'm not saying that you should take it to court. You can't do that. I get it now. Really. But you don't have to give up custody of your son."

"Yes, I do," she said sadly, lifting a hand to his face.

It melted him, just turned him into mush, when she touched his face like that, as if it was precious to her, treasured. Grady went down on his haunches and covered her hand with his, pressing it to his cheek. He didn't care that his brother stood behind his desk, watching and listening.

"Will you see to it, Dan?" she asked softly.

Dan cleared his throat. "We'll craft you an airtight agreement."

She nodded, and Grady wanted to throw things, scream, rave. For all the good that would do.

"You can't trust Nolan, Paige," he pointed out helplessly.

"I know." She smiled to show that she appreciated his concern. "But I don't have any other choice, Grady. Besides, my faith's not in Nolan."

Grady closed his eyes. How could she do it? He knew how much she loved Vaughn, what lengths she would go to for that boy. And that was his answer. She could do it precisely because she loved her son.

"You really think this is best, don't you?"

"I wish I didn't," she whispered.

"Jason's going to be crushed," he said, half hoping to make her smile.

She merely nodded and dropped her gaze. "I hoped it would be enough, you know, the hockey. Enough to keep him satisfied here. With me."

"Boys can be so self-involved, Paige. They don't mean to be, but they can't help it. Take it from me. I was so angry when my mother died, and I punished my dad for it, like it was somehow his fault, like he wasn't as destroyed as I was."

"You may have punished him, but you really thought it was your fault, didn't you?" she said, smoothing his hair with the same tenderness he'd seen her smooth Vaughn's.

Grady gulped and nodded. "I thought that if she hadn't taken me to school that morning, she wouldn't have been hit by that truck."

Paige nodded knowingly. "But your father finally convinced you, didn't he? No matter what you said or did, no matter how angry you got, he just kept loving you until you understood."

That's what she was trying to do for Vaughn, Grady knew, love him to the truth.

"Yes," he whispered, "that's just what my dad did."

"Then surely you understand that Vaughn needs his father."

"Nolan isn't fit to be that boy's father," Grady bit out.

"Nevertheless, he *is* Vaughn's father," she said calmly, "and Vaughn has to believe that Nolan's worthy of his love. He can't bear to believe anything else. I hope, by doing this, he'll see that I'm worthy of his love, too."

"He will," Grady promised, trying hard to believe it.

"From your lips to God's ears," she said sadly.

His smile was bittersweet because not too long ago, he'd have scoffed at that and now he spent a significant portion of every day chewing God's ear, but he didn't kid himself that he had any special "in" with the Almighty. In fact, much of the time he felt like a toddler demanding his own way.

Even when he started out making his case like the very capable barrister that he believed he was, he'd find himself quickly reduced to sheer begging. Fortunately, he sensed that God was willing to be patient with him. He prayed for a portion of that patience for himself now.

He certainly hadn't exhibited patience when he'd pushed his way into this meeting. He'd been hurt, at first, that she'd come to Dan instead of him. Now he frankly didn't want any part of this. It went against everything in him, everything he felt for her, to send the boy back to his father.

It was apparently going to happen, however, and that meant she was going to need all the support she could get. *That* he could give her. He wanted to, he *needed* to. With Vaughn out of the picture somewhat, maybe she'd even start

to think of him as more than her lawyer. Yet, he'd keep
Vaughn here if he could because that was what she wanted.

"I should go," she said, sliding forward.

He pushed up onto his feet and helped her out of the chair,
allowing his gaze to sweep over her.

She'd chosen a rather formal outfit for this visit, an asym-
metrical suit with a slim skirt and fitted, collarless jacket of
a pale violet trimmed in wide, yellow-gold bands. Her backless shoes were the same shade as the trim and the most
trendy things he'd ever seen her wear, with long, pointed
toes topped with tiny, feminine bows. She'd brushed her
golden hair back behind her ears, and little gold buttons
decorated her dainty earlobes.

She took his breath away, but then she did that in denim
and flannel. Seizing her hand, he announced that he'd walk
her out. After a few more words with Dan, she allowed him
to escort her from the office.

"Let me drive you home," he urged when they reached
the elevator. She shook her head, but he pressed. "I'm worried about you. You're upset. Let me do this. We'll come
back for your truck later, or I'll find some other way to get
it home to you."

"Grady, I'm sorry. I can't."

"For my peace of mind, if nothing else?"

She looked down at her hands and then up again, apology in her eyes. "I have an appointment, Grady."

"Oh? Prospective client?"

She shook her head. "I'm going to be traveling back and
forth to South Carolina, frequently, and it's going to be expensive."

"Don't worry about the cost," he said, seeking to put her
concerns to rest. "I'll help you. I have some frequent flyer
miles built up and—"

"No." She shook her head emphatically. "I can't take your

money or anything else anymore." She looked up, her big, soft, green eyes beseeching him, and added, "Because I can't give you what you need, Grady."

He felt a flare of alarm. "Yes, you can," he insisted, "not right now, maybe, but one day."

"No," she said again.

Panic setting in, he pulled her against him, folding her close. "You're the only one who can give me what I need, Paige. The only one."

"I'm not. I wish I were, but…" She closed her fists in the fabric of his coat as if she would hold him close, but then she pushed away. "I have to concentrate on my son. And I won't take advantage of you anymore, Grady. It's not right."

"Hush," he said, sliding his hands down her arms. "This isn't the time for this discussion. You have other things to concentrate on right now."

She made a sound somewhere between exasperation and laughter. "I think that was my argument."

"Okay, then, we're in agreement. Right?" He smiled down at her encouragingly. "Right?"

He could see that she wanted to continue arguing but didn't have the heart for it. He took hope in that.

"I have to go," she said, slipping free.

Grady swallowed a protest. "I'll, um, I'll call you. Okay? Or you can call me if you want to talk."

She just looked at him, then she suddenly went up on her tiptoes to kiss his cheek. "Thank you."

She was always saying that, and he really couldn't let her anymore. "I'm the one who should be thanking you. I wish you'd remember that from now on."

Worry and regret put a crease between her eyebrows. She sighed and shook her head, but then she turned away to punch the elevator button.

They stood side by side in silence until the elevator arrived. She stepped into it. He let her go with a smile, tucking his hands into his pockets, and then when the doors slid closed, he turned on his heel, striding straight back to his brother's office.

Dan looked up from his computer and leaned back in his chair, waiting for it.

"Ironclad," Grady dictated, pecking the edge of the desk with an emphatic forefinger. "You hear me? I want Nolan Ellis tied up so many ways he can't cough without her knowing it."

"You want to specify the cough medicine he can take?" Dan asked drily.

"This isn't a joke. I wish to God it were, but it isn't!"

He wished, too, that words set down on paper could truly control behavior, but he'd been practicing law too long to believe that.

Dan dropped his ink pen to link his hands together over his belt buckle. "You know what I think, Grady?"

Reaching deep down for patience, Grady pinched the bridge of his nose, growling, "What?"

"I think you're in love with that woman."

Grady snorted and parked his hands at his waist. "For all the good that does either one of us."

Dan cocked his head sympathetically. "Does it help," Dan asked, "to know that I'm praying for both of you?"

"Yes," Grady answered, his irritation dissolving. "Yes, it helps a great deal."

Dan smiled, slowly. "How did she do it?" he asked.

"What?"

"Convince you that you couldn't go on ignoring God."

Grady clapped a hand to the back of his neck. "I don't know. By example, I guess."

"You mean she doesn't preach like I do."

"I didn't say that."

"You never say anything. That was part of the problem. I never knew what you thought, what you believed."

"You haven't preached at me in a long time, though."

"Not because I haven't wanted to," Dan confessed.

Grady looked down at his feet. "I thought you'd given up on me."

"Hardly. I just realized it wasn't doing any good."

"It did more good than you know. I just…" He looked up. "I had to come to it on my own, I guess."

"We all have to come to it on our own," Dan said.

Grady had never felt closer to his brother than he did in that moment, and he knew that it was because they were brothers in more ways than one now.

Oh, Lord, he thought, *hear my brother's prayers. I'm an idiot, but he's a good man, and he's known You a lot longer than I have. Please hear him, because she's been through so much, and she's so good. I don't know how she can bear to lose her son because I don't know what I'd do if I lost her.*

As if she'd ever been his!

Yet he had to believe that she would be; he couldn't imagine how he'd go on if he didn't believe it. Abruptly he understood that it was the same for her where Vaughn was concerned. She had to believe that Nolan wouldn't disappear with him again. She couldn't do what she had to if she didn't.

He was suddenly more frightened than he'd ever been before in his life.

Compared to his tryout just a few weeks earlier, Vaughn's leave-taking from the team was anticlimactic. Grady had asked to accompany them to the game, and Paige felt that it was only fair since he'd been such a big part of the hockey thing from the beginning. Surprisingly, Vaughn had agreed without much prodding from her.

He played his final game with fierce energy and, after a final victory, calmly delivered the news that he was leaving. Paige had told him that the unpleasant chore was his personal responsibility, and he performed it ably, shaking the coach's hand and thanking him. Vaughn balked, however, at saying goodbye to his teammates, and Paige didn't see any reason to force him to do it.

Jason seemed shocked and confused but resigned by Vaughn's brief announcement that he was moving back to South Carolina. Both Paige and Grady thanked him for his trouble and followed Vaughn out of the building. He practically dived into the backseat of the car the instant that Grady unlocked the doors, obviously hoping to avoid the other boys now exiting the building.

Paige knew just how he felt. Goodbyes were awful, and every day felt like goodbye to her now.

Just how little time was left became obvious on the following Tuesday as Paige looked down at the signed custody agreement that Grady had delivered in person. Just as she'd expected, Nolan had conceded to all their demands.

"Do you really think you can trust him to abide by this?" Grady asked again.

She almost told him then what she was planning, but somehow she couldn't. Not yet. Not until she knew for sure that it was going to happen. She still had so much to work out, and until she did, not even Vaughn would know that she intended to move to South Carolina to be near him. Why hurt Grady until she had to?

She shook her head. "No, but maybe he will for a little while."

All she needed was enough time for Vaughn to start to miss her. By then she hoped to have sold her business and made provisions for Matthias.

"What if he runs again?" Grady demanded.

"There's no reason for Nolan to run again," she said. "He's won. Why would he take Vaughn and disappear now?" Except to hurt her, but surely depriving her of her son a second time would be enough even for Nolan.

She carefully placed the papers on her desk. "Well, I guess it's time to make the flight reservations."

"Let me do it," Grady offered, rising from his chair. "How is Saturday? I can go Friday, if you want, but—"

"Grady, I can't let you go with us," she stated as kindly as she could.

"But you can't go alone," he argued.

Matthias had said the same thing, but while she could definitely use the support of a good friend in this, she couldn't see letting Grady accompany her. Vaughn's attitude toward him guaranteed that his presence would make a difficult journey even more so.

"It's best," she said simply, dismissing Grady's concerns.

He literally gnashed his teeth. "Why won't you let me help you through this?"

"You have. You are, but..." She gave him the truth. "I won't spend those last hours in my son's company with him sulking because I brought you along. He would, too. It's not fair, I know, but that's just how it is."

Grady sighed and muttered, "At least let me drive you to the airport."

"Better not plan on it," she said. "You could do one favor for me, though."

"Anything."

She looked down at the agreement on her desk. "I'd like you to explain this to Vaughn. I don't want his father to be able to lie to him about our agreement, and frankly I'm not sure he'll believe me."

"I'll take care of it," Grady said solemnly. "Bring him by the office. It'll feel more official that way."

They settled on Thursday, two days hence. After thanking Grady and walking him to the front door, she went back to her office and began calling airlines. She almost cried when she found a special fare leaving out of Northwest Regional, the local airport, the following week. She bought tickets for Wednesday.

That left her exactly eight days with her son, and she silently vowed to make their remaining time as fun and carefree as possible. It was too little too late, perhaps, and God knew she needed to work every minute, but she would have plenty of empty hours to catch up after her son went back to his father.

She could only pray that all her hours wouldn't be empty ones after that.

Surely, surely, Nolan wouldn't disappear with their son again, although he might if he knew what she was planning, which was a very good reason to keep it to herself until it was too late for anyone to do anything about it.

Vaughn plopped down in front of Grady's desk with an aloof air, which he immediately ruined with a sarcastic remark to his mother. "Your boyfriend's office is pretty cool."

Seeing Paige wince, Grady mentally grabbed hold of his temper and flattened his hands on the gleaming surface of his desk. "I am one of your mother's attorneys," he told the kid sternly, "but, believe me, any man would be blessed to be your mother's *boyfriend*. Now, I suggest you button that smart lip and listen to what I have to tell you."

Sullenly, Vaughn folded his arms, but other than narrowing his eyes, he offered no other reaction. Paige averted her gaze, flags of color flying in her cheeks. Grady cleared his throat and once more addressed the boy.

"You need to understand the agreement that your parents have signed."

Vaughn shrugged, but his insouciance was belied by a certain wariness in his eyes.

"First of all," Grady began, "your parents have agreed to shared custody, with physical custody to reside in South Carolina. This means that you'll live with your father, but he cannot change your address without informing your mom and working it out with her."

"I just can't lose track of you again," Paige explained shakily. "That's all this means."

Vaughn looked at her but didn't say a word.

"Your mother has the right to see you every other weekend," Grady went on, "beginning the second weekend in April."

"That's, like, just over two weeks," Vaughn said, sounding troubled.

"That's right," Paige said, swallowing. "Is that a problem?"

Vaughn inclined his head, eyelids lowering, and Grady thought he saw a bit of guilt in the boy's expression. Finally, though, he shrugged and muttered, "Dad says my old team will let me come back, and the games are always on Saturdays."

"That's fine," Paige told him softly, her voice thick with unshed tears. "You know I love to watch you play."

Vaughn blinked. "You mean *you're* gonna come *there?*"

"I thought you'd prefer that."

Vaughn smiled. "Yeah! That's great!"

Grady traded looks with Paige. Clearly, Vaughn wasn't displeased by the idea of spending time with his mother. He just hadn't expected her to actually put his needs and desires first, despite all evidence to the contrary. Grady went on.

"Your mother is also entitled to spend holidays with you."

"That's negotiable, though," she put in hastily. "I'm willing to alternate with your dad." Offering him a lame smile, she added, "We'll work something out."

Vaughn frowned, his gaze seeming to turn inward, but he said nothing.

Grady licked his lips and said, "You'll spend summers with your mother."

"We'll work that out, too," Paige added quickly. "I don't want you to miss out on any important camping or fishing trips."

Vaughn bowed his head, leaning forward slightly to grip the arms of his chair. Grady couldn't tell what the boy was thinking, especially as he seemed to have taken a sudden vow of silence. After a moment Grady continued his explanation of the agreement. When he got to the part about the child support, Vaughn suddenly looked at his mother.

"You mean, Dad doesn't have to pay you a bunch of money?"

She spread her hands. "Vaughn, I never cared about that, except when you were small and we couldn't pay our bills."

He frowned, muttering, "It's just, he doesn't make much."

"Child support is always predicated upon income," Grady informed him. "The court sets the payments based on the income of the parent who has to pay, and if the income level changes, the child support amount can be adjusted. All your father had to do was approach it legally, unless, of course, he could afford to pay and just didn't want to."

Paige gave her head a little shake, looking worried, and Vaughn opened his mouth, but then he seemed to think better of whatever he was going to say and subsided. Grady lifted an eyebrow and moved on.

"Your mother is under no legal compulsion to pay child support to your father," he began. "Nevertheless, she has arranged to make monthly payments into a special account in your name, one hundred dollars of which will be made available to you every month for your personal use."

Vaughn's jaw dropped. "A hundred bucks a month!"

"We can make it twenty-five dollars a week, like a real allowance, if you want," Paige suggested carefully.

Vaughn's excitement was palpable. "Honest?"

"I think he likes that idea," Paige said to Grady, smiling.

Grady bit his tongue, any number of snide remarks threatening to slide off it. Why hadn't they just offered the kid money to stay?

"And," Paige was going on, "when you're ready for college, the rest of the money will be there." Vaughn's eyes went wide. "Of course," she added, "you'll have to keep your grades up."

"I will!" he promised. "Honest!"

Paige nodded, smiling, though her eyes were suspiciously bright. "That and a hockey scholarship could very well pay for your entire education," she observed brightly.

Vaughn looked at Grady. "Can you get hockey scholarships?"

"I would imagine so."

He sat back as if dumbfounded, mumbling to himself, "Dad had to pay for his college himself."

"Actually," Grady snapped, knowing he shouldn't, "your father defaulted on his college loans."

Vaughn blinked, but a mulish expression overcame him as he turned to his mother to grudgingly demand, "What's that mean?"

Paige flashed Grady a censorious glare, but she answered her son. "It means he borrowed money that he didn't pay back."

Mouth tightening, Vaughn cast his gaze downward. "Maybe he couldn't afford to pay it back."

"Maybe so," Paige whispered.

Vaughn scratched the arm of the chair with one fingertip, silent once more.

Grady mentioned that the contract between his parents could be amended only by mutual agreement, then asked if Vaughn had any questions. He shook his head. Grady flipped the folder closed and sat back.

"I guess that's it, then. Unless you have something you'd like to say?"

Vaughn sat in stony silence, scratching, scratching, scratching. Grady glanced at Paige, who lifted a shoulder. Leaning forward, Grady softened his words.

"You know, Vaughn, it's not too late."

Vaughn looked up at that. "What do you mean?"

Grady spread his hands. "You don't *have* to go back to South Carolina." Vaughn abruptly dropped his gaze. "Or," Grady went on, "you could wait until the end of the school semester. That's only a couple more months."

After a moment during which Paige sat forward hopefully, Vaughn shook his head. "I oughta go now." He looked up then. "I mean, I want to go now." He turned to his mom. "O-on Wednesday, like we planned."

Paige nodded, slumping. "Okay. Sure. On Wednesday."

They sat in painful silence for a few more seconds. Then Paige got to her feet, shifting the strap of her handbag onto her shoulder.

She'd worn jeans and a navy blouse beneath a neatly tailored camel corduroy jacket. Grady drank in the sight of her.

"We'd better go," she said with forced brightness. "We'll miss the movie."

Grady followed them out into the hallway, wishing he was going with them. She smiled at him.

"Thank you, Grady."

He nodded, and she started off down the hall at a brisk pace. Vaughn glanced in his direction before turning to follow her. Grady would never know what impulse made him step forward and call out to the boy, but he did.

"Vaughn?"

The boy stopped, turned around and walked back to him. "Yeah?"

Grady glanced at Paige, who had halted and half turned. He patted the boy's shoulder awkwardly. "I, uh, just wanted to say so long."

Vaughn dropped his gaze uneasily. "Yeah. Okay. See ya." He started to turn away.

"And," Grady added abruptly, "i-if you should need anything…" The thought drifted away while he wondered what he was doing.

Self-consciously, he slid a hand into his coat pocket, his fingertips encountering a single card. He had no idea how it had come to be there, but after slipping it free he saw that it was a card with his private number on it. He watched as his hand reached out and tucked the card into Vaughn's shirt pocket.

"Call me," he said, dropping his voice. "Any time."

The boy stared up at Grady for a moment, then he shrugged and turned away, trudging toward his mother. Paige lifted an arm as Vaughn drew near and draped it around his shoulders.

Grady leaned against the doorjamb and watched them walk away, his heart heavy. He imagined what it would be like for her, returning her only child to the man who had stolen him away from her. Abruptly, he made a decision.

She'd forbidden him to go with them, but she hadn't said anything about going on his own. Striding back into his office, he went to the telephone. It wasn't necessary to dog her all the way to Greenville, but he could meet her in Atlanta, make sure she got home okay, offer a shoulder for her to cry on.

It was a lot less than he wanted to do, but at least it was something, and for now it was enough.

Chapter Eleven

They laughed a lot those last few days, and it grieved Paige that they hadn't been able to do so from the beginning. Perhaps if she had been wiser or Vaughn had not been so angry and resentful, they might have managed it. Instead, it was only as he was leaving her that Paige and her son had found a sense of fun between them. That knowledge haunted her in quiet moments.

If he had known from the beginning that she would let him go, would it have made a difference in his attitude? Or would it have simply hastened his departure? It ceased to matter when she loaded his bags, several more than the two with which he'd arrived, into the back of her truck on that first Wednesday morning in April.

Because she had tried to make the most of every moment with him, she was sending him back to South Carolina with dirty clothes and mismatched luggage, including her cheap, flowered overnighter and a decrepit old thing of Matthias's that was held together with duct tape. They'd made a game out of packing, and she'd managed to keep her eyes dry, at least when she was around Vaughn. Now that the dreaded moment had arrived, however, she had to fight just to keep moving forward when she truly felt like crumpling into a sodden mass of grief.

Thankfully, the journey itself had been stripped of its most tiring part, the long drive to and from Tulsa. The special fare she'd found took them from the local regional airport, through Dallas and on to Greenville via Atlanta. Having to change flights twice lengthened the trip, but that just gave her more time with her son.

Paige tried to believe that Nolan would not simply take Vaughn and disappear with him again as soon as her return airplane lifted off the tarmac in Greenville. God knew she'd done everything in her power to minimize the risk, and she took a good deal of comfort in knowing that Vaughn hadn't run when he'd had the chance. Still, the fear would not entirely leave her, and reminding herself that she was building Vaughn's confidence in her by giving him up was small comfort.

The greater fear, however, was that Nolan would continue to poison the boy against her. She prayed that Vaughn would be less susceptible to his father's propaganda after having spent this time with her, but if not, she was powerless to do anything about it. That, like so much else, could only be left in God's capable hands, but despite the strength of her faith, surrendering her son was undoubtedly the most difficult thing she'd ever done.

They made it through the short flight to Dallas, even maintained the fragile air of adventure during their race through the sprawling DFW airport to catch the next plane, but her spirits flagged during the leg to Atlanta and bottomed out completely even before they boarded the final flight. Paige fought tears throughout that last hour. Hiding behind a magazine, she prayed for composure. When the aircraft touched down in South Carolina, she bullied the tears into submission, or as near as she could manage, and moved out into the aisle ahead of Vaughn so he wouldn't see her struggle for control.

Her arrangement with Nolan, made through their attorneys, called for her to walk Vaughn to the baggage claim area, where his father would be waiting. Then she'd simply go back through security and catch the next plane home without ever meeting Nolan face-to-face. She thought it a shame that they could not, even now, put aside their differences and just agree on what was best for their son, but Nolan apparently wasn't ready for that. He'd have to come to it eventually, though, because she was not going away. Just the opposite, in fact, if all went as planned.

Vaughn walked beside her in silence down the broad concourse, flashing her wary, worried glances. She told herself that he knew she was hurting and cared about her feelings, and she so wanted to be brave for him, but despite her best intentions, she lost it on the escalator, just managing to turn away before the tears began streaming. Then, try as she might, she couldn't beat them back again. All she could do was swipe at her face ineffectually and force a smile.

She spotted Nolan across the baggage carousel at the same time that Vaughn did. He seemed shorter than she remembered, slighter somehow, though he'd obviously put on some extra pounds.

His stare burned triumphantly across the distance. It was hard to remember that they had once been in love, once planned a future together. Then Vaughn turned to face her, and it became much easier to think of Nolan with kindness, pity even.

Whatever else he had done, whatever he had destroyed, he had given her this son, and even if this should be the last moment she ever beheld Vaughn's face, she would be eternally grateful.

Despite the determined campaign of sarcastic animosity that he'd waged, Vaughn was a caring boy beneath that hard shell. His attitude and actions had been dictated by fierce loyalty, and she couldn't fault him for that. He was only doing what seemed right and best to his eleven-year-old mind. If that conflicted with her determination to forge a healthy relationship with him, well, he was not to blame.

It was all in God's hands now, anyway.

Vaughn said uncertainly, "So I guess I'll see you soon."

She smoothed his hair one more time. "Absolutely."

He smiled as if looking forward to her visit. Had the fun in which they'd indulged these last few days made a difference then? She tried to take comfort in the idea, to believe that somehow she would again be part of his daily life.

"Do you know when?" he asked.

"Not yet, but I'll call you as soon as I make the flight reservations."

"Okay."

He hitched a shoulder, casting a nervous glance behind him. Then suddenly he threw his arms around her.

She managed not to sob as she held him close, whispering brokenly, "I love you, Vaughn, and I want you to be happy. Nothing will ever change that."

He mumbled something that might have been, "You, too." The next instant he tore away, calling out, "Dad!"

She watched as he ran to his father and was greeted with a hug and a pat. She thought he might have waved to her, but she didn't wait to see. Reeling away, she found the nearest ladies' room, stumbled blindly into a stall and clapped both hands over her mouth, letting the agony begin.

Soon, she promised herself, just as soon as Vaughn was ready, they would be together again, even if she had to move to Greenville to make it happen.

No sacrifice was too great if only her son could learn to let her love him.

* * *

Grady jingled the change in his pocket, pacing from trash can to pillar and back again.

Paige's plane had landed in Atlanta five or six minutes ago, but thanks to current airport security rules he was the only one waiting at the gate to greet it, a feat accomplished simply by not leaving the concourse after his own flight had gotten in some two hours earlier.

He knew it was foolish to fly all this way at the last minute, paying top dollar for the privilege, just to hold her hand, but he couldn't help feeling that she needed him. Besides, he'd have gone mad at home, waiting to hear from her, knowing she was alone and in pain.

A uniformed airline employee unlocked a door across the way and folded it back to secure it against a wall. Grady yanked his hands from his pockets, dried his palms on his shirt and sucked in a deep breath, well aware that she might not be happy to see him, especially since it was not the attorney who stood here today. It was the man who cared for her more than was probably wise at this time, a man desperate to help. He'd wanted no mistake about that, which was why he'd worn jeans, brown boots and a simple navy-blue T-shirt beneath a khaki-colored windbreaker with upturned collar.

People straggled up the narrow, sloping hallway and out into the gate area, most of them lugging carry-on baggage. Paige was one of the first to appear. Looking haggard and disheveled, eyes red and swollen, she carried nothing more than her handbag with the strap slung over one shoulder.

Grady thought she was at once the most pathetic and the most beautiful thing he'd ever seen. One look at him stopped her dead in her tracks, but sorrow seemed to dull any surprise.

Uncertain what to do next, Grady simply stood there.

Then her chin quivered, and he opened his arms. She hit his chest sobbing, and he could do nothing but hold her.

"It's okay, sweetheart. I'm here now."

"But y-you *shouldn't* be h-here," Paige finally managed.

"Neither should you," he replied, "but if you have to be here, then so do I."

"I'm g-glad you came."

He let out a silent breath of relief and gathered her against his side. "Let's find something to eat before we head home."

"I'm not hungry," she mumbled, but she wrapped her arm around his waist and let him lead her toward one of the better restaurants on the concourse.

By the time they were seated, she was more composed, but she ordered a side of fries and nibbled at them after they arrived only because he insisted. He didn't have much appetite himself, but he waded through his club sandwich mechanically, figuring that at least one of them ought to keep up their strength.

After a while, he asked how it had gone, getting a desultory shrug and a few whispered words out of her before she picked up a fry. She dipped it in the tiny cup of ketchup on her plate and lifted it listlessly to her mouth, only to abruptly drop it again and turn a stricken gaze on him.

"We forgot to say grace!"

It seemed a completely understandable lapse to Grady, all things considered, but she was clearly horrified by the omission. He quickly laid aside his sandwich, wiped his fingers on the paper napkin draped across one thigh and reached across the table. She placed her hands in his and bowed her head.

After a moment he realized that she was waiting for *him* to speak. Grady licked his lips and tried to think what to say.

"Lord, this is a tough time...but thank You for the food.

And…keep Vaughn safe. And, um…she's done her best for him. That's got to be worth something, so somehow just… help. Amen."

He figured that had to be about the most miserable prayer anyone had ever voiced, but then she squeezed his fingers and whispered, "Amen."

Afterward, she started to cry once more.

"Honey, don't," he begged. "Try to eat."

She picked up the French fry again, but when she swallowed, it was with tears streaming from her eyes. Grady vowed then that he would give her and Vaughn whatever they needed to be happy.

If it took fine houses and cars, he would get them fine houses and cars. He would be friend, protector, guide and provider. Anything. Everything.

Just to see her smile.

She couldn't stop crying. It was weak, and it was silly, and she hated the attention that it garnered, the pitying, sidelong glances, the uncomfortable silences and appalled stares, but she couldn't help herself.

After years of being strong, sure, determined to find and be reunited with her son, Paige discovered that at the core she was mush, after all, as helpless as a newborn babe. If not for Grady, she couldn't imagine how she would have managed to get herself from gate to gate, onto the right plane and into the right seat, so she let him take care of everything, too sick at heart to care just then about right or fair.

He had their seating assignments switched, upgrading them both to First Class so they could sit together and have some semblance of privacy. It must have cost him a fortune, but she made no protest. Deeply grateful, she sat in the curve of his arm, her head on his shoulder, and concentrated on breathing steadily while tears dripped off her chin.

It was shockingly easy to ignore the whispered exchanges between him and the flight attendant. On occasion she managed to open her eyes and look at him. She could tell then that he was worried, but she couldn't seem to reassure him. It was as if all the grief and fear and failures that she'd stored up over the years had suddenly erupted and now flowed like lava, searing her heart and soul. She couldn't pray but kept recalling over and over again snatches of the eighth chapter of Romans.

"…but the Spirit Himself intercedes for us with groanings too deep for words…according to the will of God."

She tried to make herself focus on the following verses, the promise that all would be worked for the benefit of those who loved the Lord, but at the moment her own groaning went too deep for comfort. Without Grady to anchor her, she feared that she might simply float away on a tide of despair, so although it was unfair, she clung to him.

He'd thought of everything, it seemed. Having arranged to have himself dropped off at the airport earlier, he'd left his vehicle at her house so he could drive her SUV home. Bleary and blessedly numb by the time they reached Arkansas, she handed over her car keys, then let him buckle her into the passenger seat like an overgrown child. She closed her eyes, making not even a token protest, as he paid the parking fee and guided the truck out of the lot and onto the road toward her house.

Once there, she somehow managed to get herself out of the vehicle and onto the porch, though climbing Everest couldn't have been much more arduous than those few steps.

Howler greeted her with a whine, but she pushed him away, visions of Vaughn assailing her.

She pushed away Matthias, too, not physically but emotionally. In truth, it had begun days before, almost as soon as she'd made her decision to let Vaughn go back to South Carolina and then follow him. Provided, of course, that he did not again disappear like vapor.

If that happened her son would forever be lost to her; she felt it to the marrow of her bones. Sick with fear, grieving the loss of her son and soon the loss of her home and business and even more that she dared not now contemplate, she felt a gathering anger.

For so long she had held such emotions at bay. For so long she had turned the other cheek. Now she felt a viciousness building. It threatened to overwhelm all she knew and believed until it lashed against the innocents in her life. How much longer she could hold it in, she didn't know, so when Grady suggested that they sit down on the couch, she shook her head vehemently.

"I'm not fit company right now."

She caught the glide of a worried glance between him and Matthias and folded her arms over the howl building in her chest.

"Maybe I should stay a little while, anyway," Grady said, "in case you need something."

"What I need," she retorted, feeling brittle enough to shatter, "is for you both to stop worrying about me."

"Paige, honey," Matthias began mournfully, "I can't help feeling that this is all my fault. If I hadn't—"

"Please!" she interrupted sharply, putting a hand to her head. "I can't talk about this. Not now. I just need to be by myself for a while."

"Paige," Grady said softly, cupping his big, hot hand

around the nape of her neck, "I don't think you should be alone now."

"But without my son I *am* alone," she cried bleakly. "If he disappears, I always will be alone."

"Girl, you know better than that," Matthias rasped.

"Neither of you have ever had a child! You don't know what it's like to give up your only son!"

"God does," Grady reminded her. "You told me so yourself."

"Yes, and what if He requires the same thing of me? What then?"

"Then you do what everyone else who's ever lost someone does," Matthias said brokenly. "You accept, and you go on."

"You hold on to your faith," Grady added softly. "You trust God to do what's best for everyone."

She stared at him for a long moment, lost in desolation, but then she gulped and nodded. "You're right. I'm sorry. My grasp on reason just now is tenuous at best. As I said, I'm not fit company. I—I think I just need to sleep."

Grady still looked worried, but he finally nodded. She didn't wait for more, simply turned and walked out, hurrying down the hall to her room, that lonely place where she had for so long nursed her hope. She would find only fear—and recrimination—there now, for it had suddenly become crystal clear to her that, even if everything worked out as she prayed it would, she was going to lose someone dear.

Worse, what she was planning was nothing short of a betrayal of those two good men, each of whom cared about her in his own way. Yet, she could find no other way.

Her son had to come first. If Vaughn would not, could not, live here, then she had to be a part of his life some other way. That didn't make what she had to do any easier. It was, in fact, almost as difficult as letting Vaughn go—and that was only if everything went according to plan!

Everything could still fall apart. The sale of her business might not go through. Vaughn might not want her any closer than she was now. Nolan could defy all reason and vanish into the ether with their child.

Meanwhile, all she could do was pray and try for a few hours of oblivion.

Grady sighed and hung up the phone, having reached the limit of his patience. He was mighty tired of speaking to Matthias when what he really wanted was to talk to Paige.

For days she had held herself apart, apparently even from Matthias, who reported to Grady that she had not even joined him at the table for meals, moving wraithlike from her room to the office, on occasion even locking herself away and refusing to answer the door. Even more troubling, she hadn't attended church the Sunday following Vaughn's departure.

On that Sunday, Grady himself had gone with his father and his brother's family to services, and for the first time he hadn't felt like a complete and utter stranger, but neither had he felt as if he quite belonged. He found no fault with the large, enthusiastic congregation or the sumptuous building with its state-of-the-art technologies, but he couldn't help wondering what worship would be like in the little church in Nobb with Pastor Haynes speaking kindly from the pulpit and Paige sitting at his side.

Perhaps it was as well that he not suffer that distraction just now. When she was around, he couldn't seem to concentrate on anything or anyone but Paige.

On the other hand, she was never far from his mind, never completely out of his thoughts. Or his prayers.

Funny how a thing like that so quickly got to be a habit. Funny, too, how he'd learned to make room for it in his life.

If someone had asked him just a few months earlier, Grady would have said that, even had he believed it efficacious, he didn't have time to devote to prayer. Now he found himself in what seemed to be an ongoing conversation with his Maker.

Most of it had to do with Paige and what was best for her. Finally he understood not only why she had done what she had for her son but how she had managed to always think of what was best for Vaughn.

He understood, too, that someone had to shake her out of her depression, and Matthias wasn't getting anywhere. It was Tuesday. Time to rattle her cage.

It only took a few minutes to cancel his next appointment and rearrange the rest of his afternoon. Then he got into the car and headed out on a drive that had become as familiar to him as the way home.

Along the way construction rerouted traffic through the countryside south of Bentonville. Grady chafed at the delay, but then he noticed the uncommon beauty of the area. He noted something else, as well.

He was driving by the great stone walls and artistically crafted wrought iron gates of what promised to be a truly fine new housing development. Mentally committing the telephone number to memory, he decided to give the builder a call later.

Putting that out of mind for the moment, he hurried on to Paige's place, parked in his usual spot and climbed the steps to the porch, stooping to give Howler a scratch as he moved to the door. It opened just as he got to it, and Matthias stood there glowering at him.

"Well, it's about time," he grumbled. "I was starting to think I was going to have to beat down that door myself."

That felt like permission to Grady. Glad for it, he queried baldly, "Where is she?"

"In her bedroom, where she's been just about every minute since you was last here." He lifted a gnarled hand and pointed to the hallway. "Second door. I'm gonna heat up something for her to eat. See she does."

As Matthias limped off toward the kitchen, Grady moved into the hallway, trying to decide just what tack to take with her. He felt out of his depth on the one hand and that he was doing the right thing on the other. Stationing himself in front of her door, he lifted his hand, but then he paused to arm himself with prayer before letting his fist fall.

"Open this door, Paige, or I'll open it myself," Grady warned, his tone leaving no doubt that he would do just that. "I'll take the casing off and pull out the framing if I have to."

Exasperated, Paige got up off the bed and stomped to the door. Why couldn't everyone just leave her alone? Wasn't it enough that they were right and she was wrong? Even the psychologist had warned her that she was taking the risk of never seeing her son again, but she'd truly believed that, as difficult as it was, letting him go had been the best thing, the *only* thing, she could do.

After five days without a single word from Vaughn, five days of a ringing telephone that had gone unanswered, she knew that she had gambled and lost. The last twenty-four hours were a blur of tears. Now suddenly her misery had once again become the one emotion with which she had least acquaintance, anger. The thing about anger was that it tended to go off in the wrong direction, usually just striking at the closest target.

Grady was the closest target this time. How dare he come pounding on her door like this? Fully prepared to inform him that he wasn't going to bully her, she wrenched the door open.

A moment passed before she fully grasped the fact that he had swept her off her feet and was literally carrying her down the hallway in his arms. Her emotions surged, threatening to swamp her; she grasped at the anger defensively.

"What do you think you're doing?"

Grady neither slowed nor blinked, his profile a study in granite. "I could ask you the same thing."

What *was* she doing?

The answer was at once starkly apparent. She was wallowing in self-recrimination, but she clamped her jaw and refused to say so. If anyone deserved to indulge in a little self-pity, surely it was her.

Grady turned the corner into the living room with her, dipping to make certain that her head made it around without cracking against the plaster and again so that her feet followed safely after. Curiously touched despite her lingering petulance, she let her arm slide across his shoulders, feeling the strength in them. He carried her into the kitchen, where Matthias placed a bowl on the table and hastily pulled out a chair.

Soon she was sitting down, her chair pushed up to the table as if she were a toddler. Matthias plunked a spoon into a bowl of what appeared to be chicken noodle soup.

"Eat," Grady ordered, dropping down into the chair at her side, "or we'll feed you."

"Don't you even…" she began, only to find herself with a mouthful of noodles. She glared at Grady over the spoon, then swallowed of pure necessity. "…think about."

The second time soup dribbled down her chin. A paper napkin appeared. Snatching it, she wiped her face.

"There, that's better," Matthias said complacently, limping around the table to help himself into a chair.

She opened her mouth to tell them both what she thought of them—only to swallow again a moment later. When Grady went after the next, dripping spoonful, she reached for the utensil, muttering, "Okay, okay, I'll do it."

He relinquished the spoon after only a minor tussle. She began to eat, finding, to her surprise, that she was actually quite famished.

"Okay," Grady said as soon as she had slurped up the last mouthful, "talk."

She thought of several scathingly witty remarks, but then her chin began to wobble, and the enormity of her loss came rushing back.

"They've gone," she whispered, and then she wailed, "They've disappeared again!"

Instantly Grady enveloped her, his long, thick arms pulling her close to his side, so close that she found her head on his shoulder. "Sweetheart, I'm so sorry."

"When?" Matthias demanded. "When did they leave?"

"I don't know. Probably right away. I—I didn't call until Friday. I thought I'd give them a day or so. They didn't answer the phone, so I called again on Saturday. And *again* on Sunday, early, late." She shook her head. "Nothing."

"Oh, no," Matthias muttered.

"I told myself they'd taken the weekend, gone camping or fishing or something. Then yesterday I called again, in the morning and in the afternoon, late into the night. No answer, not even an answering machine." She looked at Grady through her tears. "You were right. Nolan took my son and ran!"

"You don't know that," Grady said reasonably.

"Then why don't they answer the phone?"

"Could be any number of reasons. Maybe it's out of order."

"I checked. It's not. This is exactly what he did before, left all the utilities on and just disappeared!"

"Have you called the school?"

"Yesterday. Vaughn hasn't been enrolled."

Grady took out his cell phone and laid it in front of her. "Call again."

The number was on her bedside table, so Matthias hurried out to retrieve it.

"What happens if he's still not there?" she said anxiously.

"I call the cops," he told her calmly. "Then we drop everything and go after them." He tapped her on the end of the nose. "And we don't stop until we find them."

She took a deep breath, feeling considerably more hopeful, until Matthias returned with the telephone number of the school that Vaughn had last attended in South Carolina. Suddenly gripped by fear, she couldn't make herself dial.

Grady picked up the phone and punched in the number. Within moments he was speaking in his best lawyer's voice, explaining that he was an attorney in Arkansas whose client's son should be enrolled in the school.

"The custody agreement between my client and her ex-husband stipulates that their son attend your school, and we're just checking for compliance," he went on. He spelled Vaughn's full name and gave his birth date, then looked to Paige. "Social security number?"

She closed her eyes, brought the recently memorized number to mind and repeated it. Grady transferred the information to whomever was on the other end of the phone and smiled.

"Excellent," he said pointedly, looking at Paige. "Tell you what I'm going to do, I'm going to send you a copy of the court order validating the agreement, so you'll know how and when to contact us. In fact, I'm sure that Vaughn's mother would be delighted to hear from you in the future for any reason whatsoever. She's very concerned about her son's welfare, and that includes his performance and attendance in school. Thank you so much for your time."

He ended the call and dropped the phone into his pocket, addressing her. "Nolan enrolled Vaughn in school this morning."

She nearly collapsed with relief. Somehow she found herself sitting with her head on his shoulder again.

"Thank God! Thank God."

"I expect the school will be calling you over every unexplained absence and missing piece of homework," Grady informed her kindly, patting her back.

"Wonderful!" she sighed, purely delighted.

"Eh. Never thought I'd be grateful for lawyers," Matthias said, limping out of the room.

"Everyone is, sooner or later," Grady remarked drily, and Paige laughed.

She gasped in fresh air, feeling as if she'd just gotten her first breath after days of oxygen deprivation. It wasn't long before she was feeling pretty stupid.

"Oh, my. Oh, my." She dropped her head into her hands, elbows braced against the tabletop. "I can't believe how easily I accepted defeat." She lifted her head and looked at Grady. "Or how easily you took care of it."

"Everybody stumbles and falls sometimes, Paige."

"Don't I know it. Lately it seems that every time I do, you're there to pick me up again."

He smiled and cupped her chin with one large, capable hand, his blue eyes shining. "Paige," he said softly, "don't you know yet that I'd do anything for you?"

A feeling of warmth and security flooded her, and it was then that she knew without any doubt that she was going to break both their hearts.

Chapter Twelve

Paige's sigh gusted through the telephone and into Grady's ear, eliciting a frown from him.

"Oh, Grady, I'm sorry," she said, "but I just can't spare the time to go out for dinner. Everything's crazy here. I'm still trying to establish contact with my son and catch up on my work."

Grady pressed the telephone receiver to his ear with his left hand and drew another curlicue on the doodle that he was making with his right. Her excuse was legitimate, but he couldn't escape the notion that she was putting distance between them, and he couldn't figure out why.

Only a couple days ago he'd thought that their relationship had reached a new stage. The worst had seemed behind them when they'd established that Vaughn was where he should be, but she still had not been able to speak with the boy. Now, she no longer seemed to fear that her ex would steal her son away again; instead she feared that Nolan wouldn't have to, that Vaughn had rejected her completely.

Grady blamed himself in a way. He should have mandated in the custody agreement when and how often Vaughn was to call his mother. It would have been unusual and might not have succeeded, but he couldn't help feeling that he should have tried—or wondering if Paige blamed him for not doing so.

"They're still not answering the phone then?" Grady asked, working to keep his tone even.

"Nolan is, but he says Vaughn doesn't want to talk to me."

Grady winced at the angst in her voice, the confusion. "Surely you don't believe that."

"I don't know what to believe."

Her abject distress pierced his heart. "You left a message for Vaughn at the school, as I suggested?"

"Yes, and they say he got it, but he still hasn't called."

"We could ask the police to pay them a courtesy visit, remind Vaughn that you're waiting to hear from him and Nolan that you do have rights."

"I can just imagine how Nolan would spin that," Paige said bitterly.

Grady laid aside his pen and pinched the bridge of his nose. Short of actually making a trip to South Carolina, throwing a headlock on Nolan Ellis and grabbing Vaughn by the ear to haul him in front of a telephone, Grady didn't know what to do.

"If only I could go down there this weekend as planned," she lamented, proving that their minds were working in similar fashion. "It's my own fault, I know. I should've made the reservation before I even let him go. Now it'll be another week before I can make the trip."

"Paige, I can get you there this weekend," he pointed out. "There are first-class seats left. Let me take care of it."

"No. I can't take money and gifts from you anymore, Grady."

"You could when it was for Vaughn."

"That's different. Besides, if I can't get in touch with him beforehand, I have no guarantee I'll be able to see him when I arrive. Nolan could simply claim they didn't know to expect me."

Grady put a hand to his temple. "Let me think about this, see what I can come up with."

She didn't sound very hopeful when she hung up. Grady turned the page on his legal pad and began to jot down possible actions, weighing pros against cons. No easy answers presented themselves, only disadvantages. He had to find a way to do this without giving Nolan ammunition to use against Paige. By evening he was no closer to finding a solution to this situation.

Worn out from straining his brain, Grady dragged himself home, picking up a burger and scarfing it down on the way. He turned on the television in his bedroom, intending to listen to the early news broadcast. Instead he found himself sitting on the side of his bed, head bowed in prayer.

I don't know what to do, he admitted. *She needs to hear from her son and know that he loves her, that he wants her in his life. Please make him realize how blessed he is to have her for a mom, and don't let Nolan keep on hurting her.*

He went on and on, pleading with God, and finally rose to move into the bathroom, still wearing his clothes. Maybe a hot shower would loosen some of the tension knotting his muscles. He reached to turn the shower on, but the muted buzz of his cell phone stopped him.

The phone was usually the first thing to go on his bedside table once he got home. Otherwise, it wound up hanging in his closet inside a coat pocket instead of accompanying him to work the next day. The fact that he hadn't automatically placed it in its customary place atop his bedside table was indicative of his state of mind. Yet, had he done so, he'd likely have missed this call. Bemused, he removed the small device from his pocket and flipped it open, reading the words on the screen.

Who on earth was C. D. Bishop? Must be a wrong number. Shrugging, he almost closed the phone and put it away, but something prodded him to answer. Even as he watched his thumb press the right button, he shook his head, but then he put the phone to his ear and rumbled a greeting.

"Grady Jones."

The voice that answered him sounded tentative and edgy. "Hi. It's me."

He nearly dropped the phone. Instead, he tightened his grip on it, rolled his eyes heavenward and exclaimed, "Thank you!" confident that he wasn't talking to the ceiling.

"Huh?"

Grady laughed and said, "Good to hear from you, Vaughn."

He'd never meant anything more.

Paige gripped Grady's fingers with one hand and the slip of paper bearing Vaughn's e-mail address with the other. Closing her eyes, she silently thanked God before saying what they both now knew. "It was Nolan all along."

"He takes the phone with him when he leaves the house so Vaughn can't call you," Grady confirmed drily, "but he underestimated his son." He squeezed her hand. "And his son's feelings for you."

She beamed at the thought. "I can't believe Vaughn set up his own e-mail account so we can keep in touch!"

"Everybody knows you can get e-mail free on the Internet," Grady quipped. "Vaughn said so."

Paige laughed. "I have to find a way to thank his hockey coach for letting Vaughn use his cell phone." Sobering, she voiced the one, niggling, little worry that remained. "But why didn't he just call me? Why call you?"

Grady sat back against her couch, maintaining contact with her through their hands. Paige couldn't make herself pull away. She told herself that it was because he'd driven here to bring her this message from her son, but the truth was that she craved his touch.

"Apparently Vaughn found my card in his shirt pocket when he was changing clothes at the ice rink after practice," Grady said. "Nolan was late picking him up, so Vaughn took advantage of that to borrow his coach's phone and make the call. He said he had this number written down at home."

That made sense. "He wouldn't know this number by heart," Paige concluded. "It's not like he's ever called here." Or ever would if his father had anything to do with it. She remembered the day that Grady had tucked that card into Vaughn's shirt pocket and shook her head, marveling anew. "I meant to wash that shirt before he left, but I didn't get around to it."

"Nolan hasn't, either, obviously."

"Thank God."

"Seems to me God's fingerprints are all over this."

She tightened her grip on Grady's fingers. "And yours."

A slow smile spread across Grady's face. Her heart skipped a beat. How did he do it? Every time her world looked its bleakest, here came Grady to the rescue. How was she supposed to resist a man like that?

Because she had to. Because it wasn't fair to him to do otherwise. Chances were that she would be leaving here, after all. And him. She knew that she should tell him, but she didn't know how. Not now. Not after this.

But soon. She would have to tell him soon.

Gulping, she fixed her thoughts on something else, something more pleasant. "This'll teach Nolan to be such a skunk."

"At least now Vaughn knows which one of his parents is fair and compassionate," Grady said, "and which one *isn't*.

This proves that you were right to let Vaughn have contact with his dad while he was here with you, by the way."

She shook her head. "Don't give me too much credit, Grady. Most of the time I'm operating blind, bouncing from one wall to another, never certain of my path."

"You may not always know where you're going, Paige," he refuted gently, "but we both know you're guided by godly beliefs and ethics. That's why eventually you always get where you need to be."

She looked away, thinking that where she needed to be now was in South Carolina, near her son. And far from everyone else she cared about. Troubled, she pulled her hand from his, covering the action by adjusting the hem of her sweatshirt. It was not one of her nicer garments, but she hadn't been expecting company.

"Where I need to be right now is at my desk," she said apologetically. "Sorry to throw you out, but I really have to get back to work."

"It's almost nine," Grady said, sitting forward again and checking his watch. "You work too much."

"I have no choice. I have to get it done."

"You should look into hiring some extra help."

"Oh, no, not now."

"Why not? You obviously have enough work."

Paige bit her lip, knowing that she'd just been presented with an ideal opportunity, even if she was loath to take it. "I'm thinking about selling my business," she said carefully.

Grady straightened in surprise. "Really?" She nodded, and to her surprise, he smiled. "That's wonderful."

"It is?"

"Absolutely. I imagine it's worth quite a lot, and selling would free you to spend time with your son. You could spend the whole summer together."

"Exactly."

But not here. Vaughn looked forward to camping trips with his dad in the summer. If she was going to spend any time with him, she'd have to be there in South Carolina, ideally by the time school let out.

Grady got up, saying, "Well, I won't keep you. I know you'll want to have the business in great shape before you go looking for a buyer."

"Actually," she said, cringing inwardly, "I already have someone who's interested."

"Excellent!" Grady exclaimed. Reaching down, he drew her to her feet. "When you're ready, we'll put together a contract that gives both parties a fair shake."

Guiltily, she managed a nod and let him lead her toward the door, steeling herself to tell all. Before she could, he put his head back and sighed happily.

"I'm so relieved. All afternoon I agonized over what to do about Vaughn, but there just didn't seem to be a good solution. Then I sat down and really prayed about it, and the next thing I knew some guy I've never heard of before was calling. Can you believe I almost didn't answer?" He shook his head. "Hearing Vaughn's voice, well, it was hearing answered prayer."

With that, Grady dropped a casual parting kiss on her forehead and pulled open the door. Paige swallowed the confession she'd been about to make. She just didn't have the heart to tell him at the moment. He stepped out onto the porch.

"Oh," he said, "Almost forgot. According to Vaughn, all the guys think his new hockey gear is 'juicy.'" He winked, smiling, and moved to the steps, repeating to himself, "Juicy." Chuckling, he took the steps and headed for his car.

Paige wandered out onto the porch, both reluctant and relieved to see him go. Limned by moonlight, he lifted a hand and called out in farewell.

"I'll phone you tomorrow, babe. Since it's Friday maybe we can go out to dinner. Bye." He opened the car door and dropped down behind the wheel.

Babe.

She watched him start up the engine and drive away, whispering sadly, "No, Grady. We aren't going out to dinner. We aren't ever going out on a date. I just can't do that to you."

It was bad enough as it was.

She turned back into the house, looking down at the paper in her hand. One problem was solved, but others remained. She thought of Matthias sleeping in the other room. She hadn't seen the point in telling him what she was planning before because only now was it really looking like a possibility.

On the other hand, what was the point in upsetting everyone until she knew for sure that the move was going to happen? After the tension and turmoil of the past weeks, didn't they all deserve a little peace before she broke the news? Besides, so much could still go wrong.

She knew that she was looking for excuses to delay, but the last thing she wanted to do was hurt either of the two men who had supported and helped her during the worst times of her life. She'd just have to pray for the right time and words.

And the courage.

"So what do you think?"

Grady glanced at the church secretary standing on the patch of lawn in front of the building. He knew what Paige was asking but teased her by pretending to misunderstand.

"I think Betty's a frustrated paparazzi."

Paige chortled. "She was *very* disappointed that she didn't get to dog those FFROC investigators with a camera, it's true, but I think Richard was glad when they canceled after the suit was dropped. That's not what I meant, though. I meant, what do you think of the church?"

Grady turned to look back at the rambling building. Built partly of brick, partly of cinder block and partly of wood, it had been painted white in an apparent bid to add continuity, the result being a somewhat lumpy-looking structure that could have served any number of purposes. The only thing about it that really resembled a church from the outside was the steeple. Inside, though, the place felt permeated with a welcoming, almost comfortable, very uncommon *holiness*.

While neither grand nor vast, the sanctuary felt more like church than any place Grady had ever been. Pastor Haynes had opened the simple service by welcoming the congregation to "God's house," and that's just what it had felt like to Grady. Maybe sometimes God's house was a palace where only the most formal of reverences was acceptable or a modern hall with all the bells and whistles of a theater, but apparently sometimes God's house could also be as comfortable and casual as, well, home.

"I think," he said to Paige, "that this church is a far drive from the east side of Fayetteville where I'm living."

She looked a little crestfallen. "You didn't like it then?"

"Of course, I liked it." He smiled. "It was a wonderful service, and it's really not all that far from Bentonville."

She cut him a sharp glance from the corner of those big, soft green eyes. "Bentonville? What's that got to do with anything?"

"Haven't I mentioned that I was thinking of moving to Bentonville?"

"No. What's brought that on?"

He looked down. "Well, my dad's not getting any younger. Bentonville's closer to him in Belle Vista but not too far from the office in Fayetteville. Seems like a good place to be."

"But doesn't your brother already live in Bentonville?"

"He does. That doesn't mean I can't, though. Not that I intend to set down roots in the same neighborhood as my brother. Actually, I've been looking at this new development on the south side, rolling hills, little lake, community stables."

"Stables? Sounds expensive."

He shrugged. "Maybe, but I think it might be worth it. One-to two-acre lots, security gates. Of course, I'd have to build a house, but I've always wanted to. Why don't we drive by there on our way to lunch? You can tell me what you think of the site I've got in mind."

He could almost see her shutting down. She'd been doing that a lot lately. Everything would be fine, then she'd start pulling back. She'd done it again that weekend. After Thursday's turnaround, he'd thought for sure that they'd go out on Friday or Saturday night, but she'd continued to plead work. When he'd shown up at church this morning, she'd first seemed thrilled. Later, she'd clearly been uncomfortable. He didn't know what to do except forge on and hope that whatever was bothering her would work itself out.

"Oh, uh, no. Grady," she began, "I can't let you feed me, not after everything else you've done."

"Yeah, you're right," he cut in, squinting up at the sun. "You owe me. So what's for dinner?" He looked down and grinned.

She melted, spluttering laughter. "Get in the car. We'll decide on the way."

"Yes, ma'am."

Unlocking the Mercedes, he dutifully slid in behind the steering wheel. She called out across the lawn to Matthias, who was chatting with another elderly gentleman.

"Matthias, we're going to lunch." With a nod, the old fellow started limping their way. She got into the car. "You don't mind if he comes with us, do you?"

Grady shrugged. "You're buying."

He wasn't stupid. He knew perfectly well that she was using Matthias as a shield of sorts, but he'd take what he could get, happy just to keep his foot in the door. She already wanted to invite him in; surely before long she would. He just had to be patient. Grady was discovering, to his surprise, that he was pretty good at being patient.

Paige linked her hands behind her back and strolled around the shady hillside, looking out over the rolling vista. Neatly bisected with broad, smooth streets, low, split rail fences and narrow, shady riding paths, it looked like the little piece of heaven that it wanted to be. The small lake in the distance reflected sunlight like a sheet of glass, its subtle landscaping managing to look natural and perfectly balanced at the same time. Even the large, low horse barn in the center of the enclosed pasture below the rise upon which they stood appeared to have grown right up out of the ground. The developer had been wise enough to install a couple of sleek, spirited Thoroughbreds in the near paddock to add to the ambience.

She could almost see the large, sumptuous, sprawling homes that would soon begin rising across this place, their rock faces discreetly turned away for privacy's sake. The house that stood atop this hill would be the pinnacle, trading the sometimes icy ascents of winter for neighborhood primacy.

Vaughn would love it here, bless his mercenary little heart. If only... If only.

Paige leaned her shoulder against the rough, twisted trunk

of a hickory that the builder had chosen to leave be and tried to decide what to say to Grady.

"So what do you think?" he asked, using almost the same words she'd used with him after the worship service that morning. "Does it feel like home to you?"

She shook her head, then softened that negative response with a positive one. "It's beautiful, though, Grady."

"Too rich for my blood," Matthias announced, turning back to the car. "How come a pretty day like this always makes me sleepy? Musta eaten too much lunch. Sure was good, though, wasn't it? If anyone wants me, I'll be in the backseat."

Paige chuckled as Grady stepped up beside her. "Real subtle, isn't he?"

Grady braced an arm against the tree trunk above her, smiling wryly. "He knows these are the only minutes you'll spend alone with me."

She hung her head. "Grady. Please try to understand. I'm not free to follow my heart in this. I have to put my son first."

"I get that."

She turned her back to the tree, looking up at him. "No, you don't. You can't."

"That again," he said. "Okay, I don't have any kids. Yet. But I will, one day." He tapped her on the end of the nose, grinning, "I'm counting on you to show me the ropes, you know."

Her heartbeat stuttered. "Grady."

"You're such a great mom. You really ought to have a couple more kids some day."

She looked down. "I always thought I'd have three or four by now, but that obviously wasn't a part of God's plan for my life."

"It's not too late," he said lightly, but she heard the very great import behind the comment and shook her head.

"Oh, but it is. I already have a son, Grady. His wants and needs outweigh everything else."

Grady sighed. "I knew he wasn't crazy about me, but lately I thought he was starting to like me, at least a little."

"Oh, sure. You're great buddies. At a distance of several hundred miles."

"No, really, when we talked on the phone the other night he was real friendly, a little defensive where his dad's concerned, but friendly."

"It's that defensiveness that's the problem," she pointed out gently. "He doesn't want anyone to replace his dad in any way, not even me."

Grady nodded and said, "Yeah, I know, but that'll change. You were right to let him go, Paige. I see that now."

"I hope so. He was such a perfect little stinker while he was here, but I miss him so much. Then when he didn't answer the phone, I thought…but my son *does* want me in his life."

"Of course he does. You're his mom. Someday he's going to realize just how blessed he is by that, and I think sooner rather than later. That's what I'm praying for, anyway."

She smiled because he'd said it as if he'd never doubted that a loving God heard and answered prayers. Reaching up, she framed his beloved face with her hands. "You don't know what it means to me to hear you say that."

"I know what it means to me to hear you laugh," he said smoothly.

She caught her breath. "Oh, Grady, don't."

"I can't help it." He turned his face, pressing a kiss into the palm of her hand. "I know you have other things on your mind right now, and I can wait. But don't ask me not to care."

Perhaps it was wrong of her, but she couldn't find it in her heart to turn away his gentle kiss after that. Neither could she deny that for those few moments she felt whole and strong again. How could she tell him then that if everything worked out as she hoped, she would soon walk out of his life completely?

How could she not?

"Grady," she began, but just then Matthias opened the back door of the car and stuck his head out.

"You kids about done? The sun's coming right through this window and broiling me where I sit."

Grady chuckled. "Okay. Keep your shirt on. Or not."

"We'd better go before he sets up housekeeping in your backseat," she quipped, secretly relieved.

"Actually," Grady commented, as they strolled back toward the sedan, "I expect Matthias to stay right where he is for the rest of his life."

"Oh, I intend to see to it," she said. It was the least she could do, after all. If only she could do as well by Grady.

It was a weary but happy Paige who climbed out of her truck near midnight the following Sunday evening. She hauled her brand-new overnight bag from the backseat, looked at the Mercedes parked in her yard and shook her head. Obviously, having refused to allow Grady to drive her to and from the airport in Tulsa had not discouraged him from waiting for her here at her house.

She almost wished she could be put out with him. It would be easier for both of them if she didn't care so much for the man and vice versa. Yet, how could she regret a relationship that had so often proved to hold the answers to her prayers?

These days much of her prayer life centered on Grady himself. She owed him so much, and the very last thing she wanted to do was hurt him. If only she could figure out how to avoid it.

Doggy nails clicked on the porch as she climbed the steps, but before she could locate the dog so as not to fall over it, her front door opened, spilling light into the darkness and revealing none other than the big man himself. He stepped outside to greet her with a hug.

"You okay?"

"I'm great."

"Went good, then?"

She set down the overnight case and placed her handbag atop it before looking up into his shadowed face. She knew that the light fell full on her own.

"We had a wonderful time. The apartment building where Vaughn lives isn't much, but there's a forest behind it, and we hiked all over the place yesterday. Then today, after church, we had a picnic. I've never seen him so relaxed and happy."

"What about Nolan? He give you any trouble?"

"He didn't seem happy when he opened the door and saw me standing there, but what could he do?"

"Not a thing unless he wants to lose custody permanently."

"I just don't understand why the two of us can't talk like adults, why we can't discuss our son and make decisions according to what is best for him."

"I don't, either," Grady said, "but that's on Nolan, not you, and Vaughn must realize it now."

"Maybe. We didn't discuss it."

"Of course not." He slid his hands around to the nape of her neck and lightly massaged the weary muscles there.

"Mmm. That feels good."

"You must be worn-out."

"Oh, yes, but it's worth it." She could hear the television

softly playing inside. "Where's Matthias? He go off to bed and leave you on your own?"

"In a manner of speaking." Grady tossed his head. "He fell asleep in the recliner a couple hours ago."

"Ah. He does that sometimes."

Howler pushed his way between them then, seeking a pat from someone. Grady was the first to oblige, going down on his haunches to give the animal a good rub. Paige bent at the waist, bringing her nose within a hairbreadth of the dog's.

"Someone asked about you, Howler. I think he misses you."

"I'll bet he misses more than this old hound," Grady said, rising to his full height once again. "Vaughn's going to be asking to come home to Arkansas before you know it."

Straightening, she shook her head. "I don't think so. You have to understand, Grady. Vaughn loves both of his parents. I wasn't so sure before. I am now, but I can't ask Vaughn to choose between us. I won't."

"I never expected you to."

"What's going to change is that Nolan's going to have to learn to deal with me," she went on, "because Vaughn won't give him any other choice."

"And we know how determined Vaughn can be," Grady put in.

She laughed. "Exactly." He lifted his arms above his head, locking his hands and twisting to work out the kinks in his back. "You should go home and get some sleep," she told him.

"Yeah, I should," he agreed, dropping his arms and flopping his head from side to side. "I just wanted to be here, you know, in case things didn't go the way we hoped they would. I'm glad to know it went well."

"Thanks."

"You need to get some rest, too, so good night, babe."

He stepped up and would have dropped a kiss in the center of her forehead, but for some absurdly stupid reason that she could never fathom, she tipped her head back and brought her mouth into contact with his. It was like summertime in April. Warmth enveloped her, and then she realized that he'd wrapped his arms around her.

How easy it was to just forget all the reasons she shouldn't be letting it happen, how easy to justify. A simple expression of affection should be permissible between adults, shouldn't it? But nothing was simple about this. Fraught with complexity, the many layers of emotion, needs and desires were doomed never to be fulfilled. They were both breathing roughly when she finally made herself break away.

"I'm so sor—"

He clapped a finger over her lips, whispering, "Don't." An instant later he took his hand away. "For once let me be the one to pull back."

Chapter Thirteen

Grady stopped by unannounced on Wednesday evening with an armload of rolled-up house plans, which he dumped on her kitchen table, declaring that he needed help. After everything he'd done for her, Paige couldn't very well turn him down, but his dropping by was getting to be a dangerous habit that she felt she had to curtail.

"You might have called first. What if I hadn't been home?"

He gave her a knowing look. "And where else would you be since you've dropped out of choir? Pastor Haynes mentioned it on Sunday. What's up with that, anyway?"

She found that she couldn't quite meet his gaze as she muttered, "I no longer need a distraction from my son's nasty attitude, that's all."

"Speaking of needs, I need input from a female perspective," Grady said, waving a hand at the mound of rolled-up sheets of oversize paper. He grinned and announced, "I bought the lot and talked to an architect. He sent these over for me to look at."

Paige tried to be happy for him, but all she could think about was that she wouldn't be here to see the house that he was going to build on that beautiful piece of land. She managed a smile and a muted, "That's wonderful."

"I'm so anxious to get started," he said, rubbing his hands together, "but there's this weird questionnaire he wants filled out." Pulling a folded set of stapled forms from his hip pocket, he tossed that onto the table with the rest. "I knew I was in trouble when I got to a question about laundry rooms. Do I want laundry facilities near the master bedroom, the other bedrooms, the kitchen, the garage, what?"

He looked so perplexed that Paige chuckled, taking pity on him. "I guess it depends on whether you're using a split bedroom plan or—"

He held up a hand. "Let's just start at the top of the list and go through it that way."

She knew it wasn't wise to get caught up in his building plans, but how did she turn down a plea for help from the one person who constantly came to her aid? Taking the questionnaire in hand, she began to read. Soon she was planning a dream home, the likes of which she'd never before allowed herself to imagine. She had to remind herself that it would never be *her* dream home, nor had Grady said outright that he hoped it would be. She prayed he would not.

Only the day before she'd made a counter offer to a company interested in buying her business. As soon as she knew that the sale was going to go through, she told herself, she'd find a way to tell Grady that she was moving to South Carolina. Somehow.

"Take a look at this one," Grady said, unrolling the papers and holding them open with one hand. He scanned the floor plan. "Here." He planted his big, blunt forefinger and reached into his shirt pocket for a pencil. "What if we moved these walls like this?" He began sketching the changes onto the paper. "And offset the sinks like this."

Paige spread the sheet she was holding and framed an area of that floor plan with her hands. "And put this whole section here, right?"

"Right."

She tilted her head, trying to picture the evolving schematic. They'd been going over plans and formulating others for over a week now. "It's everything you've said you want, the master suite opening onto the pool, the master bath easily accessible from there."

"And, Miss Sunshine, we have plenty of windows," he teased.

She didn't know why she'd criticized so vociferously the dearth of windows in one particular plan. It wasn't as if she would ever live in the house that Grady was going to build, after all. Still, she felt the need to defend her opinion.

"You can't have a master suite of this size with just one little window, I don't care how oddly it's shaped."

"You don't put much store in architectural interest, do you?" Grady observed, grinning.

"Livability trumps architectural interest every time in my view," she grumped.

Grady chuckled. "Yeah, me, too. Besides, I like a bright, cheery room. I have another appointment with the architect Monday, by the way. He says once we approve the final plans, construction can start immediately, so we'll probably break ground by the end of June."

"You," she corrected softly. "Once *you* approve the final plans. All I'm doing is offering a female perspective, remember?"

His grin withered, and he began rolling up the papers. "All right, once *I* approve the final plans." He speared her with a direct look. "Happy?"

Paige didn't dignify that with an answer. Instead she quickly rose to go to the refrigerator and refill her glass with iced tea. He muttered something that could have been, "Didn't think so." She ignored that, too.

The truth was that she had never been more unhappy, and it wasn't just because her son no longer lived in her house. Oh, that was part of it, to be sure, but Grady and his expectations were a larger part.

She'd tried to discourage him, turning down his invitations repeatedly, making sure she was never alone with him, constantly reminding him that her son was the focus of her life and that he needed both of his parents in his. Then Grady would drop by with a new plan or a bag of hamburgers and she'd find herself offering an opinion or laughing at something he said, and before she knew what was happening an hour had passed. Afterward she'd berate herself and vow to tell Grady that her plans for the future did not, could not, include him.

Yet, she hadn't even told Vaughn that she intended to move to South Carolina to be near him. She meant to feel him out about the possibility this weekend. Nolan wouldn't like it if she moved down there, of course, but he had no say about it. No more, unfortunately, than Grady did.

If everything worked out as it should, she'd be living in South Carolina before the builder broke ground on Grady's new house, which was a very good reason to keep her distance from Grady now. Why she couldn't seem to do that was a mystery to her. It made no sense. She'd never been a coward, and it was the right thing to do, after all.

Wasn't it?

She closed the refrigerator, turned and found him watching her. He got up out of his chair and moved to stand beside her, one arm braced against the kitchen counter.

"Want to grab a bite to eat?"

She shook her head, glad that she didn't have to lie to him. "I've already eaten."

"How about just coming along to keep me company then?"

She had to look away and steel herself in order to turn him down as firmly as she knew was necessary. "Sorry, no. I have to be up in the wee hours to catch a plane, remember?"

Even two weeks out, most of that weekend's flights had been booked solid, at least as far as Atlanta, so she'd had little choice but to take an early-morning reservation.

Grady leaned a hip against the counter beside her and said matter-of-factly, "Yeah, about that. I'm driving you into Tulsa."

She pushed aside a spurt of yearning and girded herself for a fight. "No."

"Yes."

"I'm not letting you get up at 2:00 a.m. just to drive me to the airport," she insisted.

"I'm not letting you hit the road at 3:00 a.m. all by your lonesome."

"You tell her, counselor," Matthias put in from the living room. Paige rolled her eyes and folded her arms stubbornly.

"I am an adult. I can get myself to and from Tulsa."

"*I* am an adult," Grady retorted calmly, "an adult *male*, and I wouldn't let any *woman* I care about drive alone at that time of the morning. Call it sexist if you want, but I'll be here at three, and you can either ride with me or I'll follow you in my car. Your choice."

She threw up her hands. "Why ask me? You're obviously making all the decisions."

He dropped his chin, staring at her from beneath the crag of his brow. "You don't even want to know what would be different around here if I was making all the decisions." She gulped and looked away while he went on earnestly. "But that's beside the point. Do you honestly think I could rest knowing that you were on the road by yourself at that hour? Anything could go wrong with that old truck of yours, and your options for assistance in the open countryside are limited. Besides, I'd rather spend ninety minutes driving you to the airport than almost anything else I can think of, including sleep."

Paige sighed, knowing when she'd lost an argument, and grumbled, "You're a lousy adversary."

"I am an excellent adversary."

"Exactly."

He chuckled, and crooked a finger beneath her chin, turning her face to receive a kiss dropped casually on to the tip of her nose. "I'll see you at three then."

She didn't answer him, but they both knew she'd be climbing into his car in that black hour of the morning.

As he gathered up his house plans and took his leave, she wondered why it was that she couldn't seem to do what was best in this situation. Her business was all but sold, after all, and the longer she put off telling Grady that she was moving, the worse it was going to be. Still, no matter when she did it, she was going to rip out his great big heart, and she didn't know how either one of them was going to survive that.

Thankfully, he had not declared himself, and she hoped to heaven that he never would. She didn't know how she could bear it if he did, which was all the more reason to tell him her plans before they reached that point.

But surely she should tell Vaughn first. If his reaction was negative, she'd have to put her plans on hold, after all, in which case there was no reason to upset anyone. Which was just another excuse for keeping quiet.

"Oh, Lord in heaven, what am I doing?" she whispered, but for once she found no answers.

All she knew was that she couldn't make herself do what she knew she should. She'd never expected to be so torn between two loves. Yet, what choice was there, really, for a mother with a son who needed both of his parents?

The last time they'd made this trip, Grady would rather have taken a beating than be going to South Carolina. Now he wished he could get on that plane with Paige. He knew better than to suggest it, though. For one thing, Dan was flying down to Georgia tomorrow in order to take a deposition on Monday from a witness to an auto accident, and it was their policy that, if possible, both of them not be out of town at the same time. More importantly, Paige would only have said no.

He wasn't sure, even now, what the problem was. In the beginning he'd assumed that she feared Vaughn would object to her being with any man other than his father. Now he suspected that it was more than that, mostly because the kid definitely seemed to be warming up to him.

The two hadn't actually spoken again, but they had exchanged several e-mails. That Vaughn was clever had never been in doubt, but he'd turned out to be something of a wit, too, which Grady found quite entertaining. Like most eleven-year-olds, Vaughn definitely had a selfish bent. He'd hinted broadly that he wanted something which Grady had taken it upon himself to supply. Now Grady feared that Paige would think he'd overstepped, which was why he waited until they reached Tulsa to bring it up.

"I have something for Vaughn. Will you give it to him?"

She glanced over at him just as he put on his blinker for the airport exit. "What is it?"

"Reach behind your seat."

She frowned as she leaned to one side and groped blindly behind her. They'd come to a halt at a red light on the service road to the highway by the time she got a hand on the box and managed to drag it into her lap.

"A *cell phone?*"

"It's not your usual sort," he told her quickly. "It will only dial 9-1-1 and four preprogrammed numbers. I put in your number, mine, his dad's and his hockey coach."

Her next question was predictable. "What did this cost?"

"Irrelevant."

Her mouth tightened. "What's the monthly charge then?"

He considered stonewalling her, but the look on her face clearly indicated that he'd pushed it as far as it was going to go, so he told her. She seemed pleasantly surprised. Opening the box, she took out the small, sturdy, neon bright phone.

"It has a tether," he pointed out, "and a counter to let him know how many minutes he's got left for the month. That can be tracked online, too."

After a moment, she sighed and conceded, "It's perfect."

Grady relaxed. The light changed, and he drove through the intersection. The airport lay straight ahead.

"I thought so. It may not be what he had in mind when he wrote me that if he had his own cell phone he wouldn't have to wait for his dad to 'loosen up' before he could talk to you whenever he wanted, but it's a pretty fail-safe plan."

She dropped the phone back into its packing slot and closed the box, saying, "He asked me for a cell some time ago, but I didn't know about this option, so I told him no."

"Guess that explains why he tapped me," Grady said. "He probably figured I could afford it, too, and he was right about that."

"Nevertheless, I will pay you for this and take over the monthly plan."

Grady signaled for a right turn. "If you pay for the phone, then it won't be a gift from me, now will it?"

"Grady, you've already given him too much."

"I'll concede on the monthly plan," he said, making the

turn, "but he asked *me* for the phone, and I want to give it to him. So let's compromise, okay?"

"And if I don't accept your compromise?"

He moved over a lane, following the sign for departures, and said, "Then I'll mail him the phone. And hope Nolan doesn't get to it first."

She threw up her hands, demanding, "How do you always do this? No matter how hard I try to be fair and smart and reasonable, you always manage to get your way!"

His temper suddenly flared. "*My* way?" he snapped. "Oh, baby, I'm so far from getting *my* way that it's not even funny!"

He swerved the car into the first vacant spot in front of the terminal and threw the transmission into park. Hanging one elbow on the steering wheel, he twisted sideways in his seat to face her. The look of misery on her face stopped him cold. Whatever anger or frustration he'd felt evaporated like a puff of breath on a frosty morning. Instantly contrite, he wrapped a hand around the nape of her neck and pulled her head to his.

"I'm sorry. I didn't mean to shout."

"No, I'm sorry," she said miserably. "So very, very sorry. You have every reason to be upset with me, more than you even know. Oh, Grady, I'm going to br—"

Suddenly panicked, he kissed her just to shut her up, and a very effective means it was, too, until he tasted her tears. Puzzled, he drew back, holding her face in his hands.

"Paige?" To his shock, she began to sob. He wrapped his arms around her. "Honey, a few sharp words are not worth this."

"It's not that. You d-don't understand."

"Tell me."

A car ahead of them pulled away from the curb, and a passing courtesy bus blew its horn. The place was surprisingly busy for so early in the morning. She glanced at the clock on the dash, scrubbing at her face.

"I can't. I have to g-go." She sucked in a deep breath. "But when I get back, we have to talk."

"Fine," he said, brushing at her tears. "Just don't cry anymore. I can't stand it. Rips me up inside."

She closed her eyes, and when she opened them again, the sorrow that he saw there cut like a knife. He'd have done anything, said anything to banish that look. What he did, what he said, had been coming for a long time. He'd have chosen a different time and place if he could have, and he might have worded it more eloquently, but that wouldn't have changed the truth of it.

"You must know that I love you." Her impossibly wide eyes grew larger still, and her bottom lip trembled, but she slowly nodded. It was an oddly solemn moment, one of the most significant of his life, and every bit of the doubt that had dogged him for weeks fell away. "You love me, too, don't you?"

She didn't deny it. She tried to. He watched her try to pull back, to rein in the wealth of emotion in her eyes. And he watched her fail. He wrapped his arms around her again, and this time she reciprocated, clasping him tightly.

"Try to remember that when I get back, will you?" she whispered brokenly.

As if he could forget!

Suddenly she pulled away and had her car door open before he could react. Grinning like an idiot, he hopped out and unlocked the trunk, hurrying around to lift out her single bag and carry it to the curb. She took it from him and immediately backed away. He stood watching her, one hand lifted in farewell, until she turned and strode swiftly toward the terminal.

She loved him.

He pumped a fist and tilted back his head. "Yesss!" It was the most heartfelt prayer of thanks he'd every uttered.

Despite her eagerness to see her son again, Paige couldn't seem to lift the funk that had settled over her in Tulsa. All through the flight to Atlanta she felt on the verge of despair, and when she tried to pray she found herself alternating between morose confession and angrily demanding that God fix this mess that she had created.

How had it happened? She'd known from the moment she'd decided to let Vaughn return to his father that she'd have to move to South Carolina herself. It was the only way she could be as much a part of his life as he needed her to be, the only way she could be sure that he was well cared for and safe. Yet she'd let herself grow closer and closer to Grady and vice versa.

Now, not only would she have to tell Grady the truth as soon as she got back to Tulsa, she was going to spend this whole trip dreading it. No doubt it served her right, but it wasn't fair to Vaughn, let alone Grady, who had no inkling of what was coming. Tormented by guilt, she paced the length of the terminal in Atlanta during her layover, but nothing could remove the sound of his words from his ears.

You must know that I love you.

Of course she'd known! How could she not? He'd shown her every way imaginable. Hearing him say it had produced a thrill unlike any other—and shame, deep, horrific shame.

She didn't think she'd ever get past it, nor should she for it was nothing less than she deserved. Grady, on the other hand, deserved only joy and respect and consideration, none of which she had given him.

By the time she reached Greenville, rented a car and found the ice rink where Vaughn was playing hockey, the game was in the middle of the second period. He spotted her when he came off the ice during a line change and waved so she'd know it was him.

Even at a distance she couldn't miss the welcome in that simple gesture, and neither did Nolan. He was sitting right behind the team bench and turned his head to glare at her when Vaughn waved. She ignored him.

Nolan had done plenty to hurt her, but she hadn't been a perfect wife to him, either. Much of the time she'd been absolutely clueless. Still, she'd have worked at their marriage for the rest of her life if he hadn't walked away. Thinking about it now, though, she knew that at the best of times her feelings for Nolan paled in comparison to what she felt for Grady. But that didn't change anything.

Nolan had cost her three-and-a-half years with her son, and if she worked hard at it, she could even blame him for the hurt she was about to cause Grady. Unfortunately, that wouldn't let her off the hook. She was as guilty of crimes of the heart as Nolan, but all she could do now was fulfill her responsibilities to her son as well as she was able.

Paige sucked in a few deep breaths and concentrated on the hockey game. It wasn't long before Vaughn was back in action. Even before that Paige realized that the general level of play in this league was higher than what she'd seen in Arkansas, but Vaughn stood out here, too. He seemed to be showing off for her benefit, a supposition confirmed as soon as he left the ice at the end of the game.

"Did you see me make the winning goal?"

"I did, honey. Good job!"

Nolan appeared at her elbow and took Vaughn's helmet, into which Vaughn had dropped his mouthpiece. "Good game there, sport. Guess those new skates were worth the money, after all, huh? But then your mother's always known how to get her money's worth."

Vaughn immediately shuttered his expression and began

slipping plastic covers on to the blades of his skates. "I gotta shower and change so we can go, Mom, but I'll be real quick."

"I'll wait right here."

Vaughn looked at his father long and hard before stiffly walking away. Paige stared straight ahead, waiting. Vaughn was barely out of sight before Nolan made his first verbal jab.

"I can't believe you thought you'd win him over with expensive skates and other junk."

"I just wanted him to play hockey, Nolan, because I hoped it would make him happy."

"But it didn't, did it? Because *this* is where he wants to be. With me."

"I know that."

"The two of us do things you never could," Nolan went on smugly, "things that boys like."

"I know that, too."

"Then why are you here? Why punish yourself like this? You could be doing something fun back in Arkansas. You've got friends there, *boy*friends, even." She looked at him then, surprised to see anger in his brown eyes. "Vaughn told me. Did you think he wouldn't?"

She shook her head and said only, "I'm here because I love my son and he needs me."

"For what? He's been just fine without you. We both have. Now that he's getting older we can do even more together, the really good stuff."

"He's not your playmate, Nolan."

That's what Vaughn was to him, she realized suddenly, not a son to be guided and taught and provided for into manhood but a permanent buddy, and Vaughn was so anxious for the love and approval of his father that he found ways to pick up the slack and forgive the failures he probably couldn't even identify but nevertheless felt. She knew because she had once done the same thing: overlooked the slights, ignored the selfishness, pretended that Nolan cared when his every action had demonstrated otherwise. She'd given in, gone along, whatever it had taken to hold on to the illusion that her husband would ultimately love her back.

This insight showed her, as nothing else could have, how much her son needed her. She truly had no choice but to move, no matter what it cost her personally. Already she grieved what she would leave behind in Arkansas, but her responsibility was to her son, and she would not, could not, shirk it.

"Vaughn wants and needs a mother," she told Nolan, "just as he wants and needs a father, and I intend to see to it that he has both from now on. We can be partners in this one area, Nolan, for his sake, or you can fight me. But you have to know that the more you fight me on this, the more you'll suffer in comparison."

"I don't have to 'fight' you," he sneered. "Vaughn's already chosen me. I'm the one he lives with. You're just a temporary distraction, a change of pace, and when you're not around he can't even be bothered with you. How long do you think he's going to get excited about the silly little weekends you cook up? He's almost a teenager. How much longer do you think he's going to want to spend his weekends with his mama?"

"Not long," she admitted.

That seemed to satisfy him immensely. "Better enjoy it while you can. That's all I've got to say."

He turned and strolled away as if he didn't have a care in the world, one hand in his jeans pocket, the other lightly swinging Vaughn's helmet. Paige shook her head. His world was about to change, had already changed, and he didn't even know it.

When Vaughn emerged still wet from his quick shower some moments later, his arms loaded with hockey gear, he glanced around apprehensively. "Dad take off?"

"Uh-huh." She reached for a set of pads, blithely changing the subject. "We have some time to kill. Any ideas?"

His smile stretched from ear to ear. "The guys told me about a cool arcade that's opened up in the old ice-cream shop. Wanna go?"

"Sure. You can wreck some race cars while I make a few phone calls." They turned together toward the exit, hauling his gear.

"Who you calling?" Vaughn asked offhandedly.

Paige strengthened her smile. "Thought I'd check out a few Realtors around town. Know any good ones?"

Vaughn's steps slowed to a halt. He looked up at her, his face twisted. "Realtors? You mean, like, for houses?"

Paige nodded. Her heart beat slow and hard against the wall of her chest. "I thought it might be nice to have my own place here. What do you think?"

"Really? But how can you afford two places?"

"Well, there's someone back in Fayetteville who wants to buy my business. For quite a lot of money, as it turns out."

"That's great!" She wasn't certain if his enthusiasm was for the money or the idea of her having a house of her own here. Then he dropped his gear and threw his arms around her, declaring, "It'd be almost like you lived here!"

Pleased, she hugged him close. "Would you like that, son?"

He bent to retrieve his stuff. "Are you kidding? That'd be perfect!"

She hadn't intended to tell him all, only to sound him out on the subject of her moving here, but now she saw no point in holding back.

"Can you keep a secret, son? Just for a little while? I

think I should move here." His jaw dropped, and then he literally leapt into the air, crowing like a rooster, so obviously pleased that she had to laugh. "You wouldn't have to live with me, of course, if you don't want to, but it would be a more normal life for both of us, I think."

He hugged her so hard, that she thought he'd crack a rib. She realized with a jolt that he was taller than her now. Had he really grown so much in a few short weeks? Trampling her foot in his excitement, he skipped backward. She laughed again, blinking rapidly. He was so happy! How could she be both thrilled and on the verge of tears herself?

"What about Matthias?" he asked, suddenly going still.

"I don't know. I haven't discussed it with him yet. He may come with me, but more likely he'll stay in Arkansas."

"If Matthias comes that means Howler will, too, and it'll be like having my own dog!"

"You could have your own dog anyway, if you want," she told him. "We'll just look for a house with a fenced yard."

He whooped, then he threw an arm across her shoulders, physically propelling her toward the door. "Dad and me almost got us a place for a dog once," he babbled, "but he decided on the boat instead. I was mad for a while, but you can't fish from a dog. Oh, man! I can't believe it!"

They hurried to the car, him laughing and talking. This was how it should be—except for the ache in her chest. But she would face that later. Then Vaughn unwittingly robbed the moment of much of its joy.

"What happened?" he suddenly asked. "Did you and Grady break up or something?"

Paige froze in the act of unlocking the trunk of the car. "I don't know what you mean. We were never a couple, Vaughn. I told you that."

He seemed confused. "Looked that way to me."

"Well, it wasn't. Not really. Besides, I thought you resented Grady. Except for his car and money, of course."

"Grady's okay," he muttered.

"Yes, he is," Paige agreed softly, "but Grady has his life in Arkansas, and mine's here with you now."

He hugged her again. It was bittersweet balm.

"I'm sorry, Mom, for before," he told her in a small, cracking voice. "I guess I forgot some stuff, but it wasn't ever that I don't love you."

"I know, son."

"It's just that I love Dad, too."

"Of course, you do. I wouldn't want it any other way."

He looked up then, sadness in his eyes. "I know he's a mess. He's not like you. I guess it's all that Christian stuff. It's not so dumb as he says it is. Nothing's ever quite what Dad says it is. But he's still my dad, you know?"

Paige managed a nod and a wobbly smile before hugging him close one more time while she silently thanked God.

Her little boy had finally, at long last, come home. She couldn't ask for more than that.

No matter how much she might want to.

Chapter Fourteen

Grady had never considered himself an impulsive sort of fellow. His ex-wife had often complained about it, calling him unimaginative and inhibited. Now he knew that she'd been correct. But that was before.

This Grady, the *new* Grady, the reborn Grady, the in-love Grady, was startlingly imaginative. He made up entire scenarios in his head, visions of himself and Paige and, oddly enough, Vaughn, living together in that big house on the hill that was already taking shape in his mind. He even imagined other occupants of that dream house: Matthias; his father, Howard. And babies. Little blond babies with big, sea-green eyes.

He had become a daydreamer. His father remarked on it Saturday, the very next morning, after he'd driven Paige to Tulsa. Howard had just made a perfect long drive on the seventeenth hole. Grady missed it entirely, realizing that something noteworthy had taken place only when the group of golfers waiting behind them broke into applause.

Glancing around sheepishly, Grady caught the congratulatory statements of the foursome awaiting their turn at the tee. He dropped the club upon which he'd been leaning into the wheeled bag at his elbow, saying, "Good one, Dad."

"Yessir, the old man's still got it!" Howard crowed, doing a little jig and playfully poking his son in the midsection with the head of his club. "And you, son, have got it bad."

Grady lifted his eyebrows. "I don't know what you're talking about."

Howard winked at the golfer teeing up beside him and threw a companionable arm around his son's shoulders as they started off down the hillock. "I am talking," he said in a conspiratorial tone, "about Paige."

Grady grimaced. "Who told you about her?"

"Who do you think? Dan says she's quite remarkable and about as far from Robin as she can get." He slid his club into the bag that Grady pulled behind him. They were so alike in build and size that they played with the same clubs.

Grady should've realized his family would be talking about this.

Howard shoved his hands into the pockets of his jacket, matching his steps to his son's, and remarked, "Dan says she reminds him of your mother." He smiled. "What a gal she was, that Bea, wonderful wife and mother. I miss her."

Grady smiled. "Me, too."

"Used to be, when you were daydreaming like that," Howard said, waving a finger at the top of the hill, "I knew you were thinking of her, remembering her. Did my heart good." He sighed, adding, "Been a long time since I caught you daydreaming about your mother, and you know what? This is better."

"Yes, it is." Grady chuckled, remembering how embarrassed he'd been as a teenager because thoughts of his mother could still reduce him to tears on occasion. He was rather proud of that now. Thoughts of Paige brought all sorts of other emotions to the surface, and he couldn't be ashamed about those, either.

"After you're settled," Howard was saying, "I may have to think about getting married again myself."

Grady barked laughter, completely shocked that his father was talking about marriage. He was even more shocked at his own reaction. With sudden clarity he realized that not too long ago he'd have been angry and hurt if his father had dared to mention remarriage. It had been thirty-three years since his mother's death, and only now was he somehow able to let her go. And he'd thought Vaughn was pigheaded! All the kid had ever done was try to hang on somehow to those he loved.

"What?" Howard asked, glancing over at him, "you don't think this old rooster could talk some old hen into building a nest with him?" He didn't wait for a reply but admitted baldly, "I'm tired of being alone. I'll never love again like I loved your mother, but once like that is enough in any lifetime."

That, too, Grady understood. Such love was rare and to be treasured. It should be grasped with both hands and held close. This time it was Grady who slung an arm across his father's shoulders in a grateful, affectionate hug. Then he simply left the bag standing in the pathway on its little wheeled cart and strode off across the green toward the parking lot.

"Where are you going?" his father demanded.

"Jewelry store," Grady called over his shoulder.

"This means I'm the winner, you know!" Howard crowed.

"We're both winners, Dad," Grady replied.

Actually, they were blessed. So blessed.

Paige waited until just before she left town to give Vaughn the cell phone. Thrilled, he saw instantly that it did much more than she'd realized.

"Games. Cool."

"Really?"

"Sure. See? It even downloads ring tones. Can I get one?"

"Uh, okay."

"I guess Grady told you to buy it, huh?"

"Actually, Grady is entirely responsible for this," Paige told him. "Grady bought the phone. I'm paying the monthly charge. Four hundred and fifty minutes a month, Vaughn, and not a minute more. All right?"

He dropped the tether over his head. "That's like fifteen minutes a day."

"Your math is still good, I see." He chuckled and scuffed a toe in the dirt, his hockey gear piled on the apartment landing behind him. "Do me a favor will you?" she asked. "Call Grady and thank him, but not until tomorrow. Okay?" She didn't want Vaughn breaking the news to Grady before she could.

"Sure. Okay."

She smiled and ruffled his hair. "Be responsible with this, and we'll see about getting you a regular cell phone later. Deal?"

"Deal." He looped his arms around her neck, and she kissed his cheek. "See you soon." Dropping his arms, he backed away and slapped a hand over the phone hanging against his chest, saying, "Thanks, Mom. For everything."

She smiled. "You're welcome. For everything. Gotta go." She moved toward the car. "You better be calling me," she tossed over one shoulder.

"I will."

She drove off toward Greenville and left him standing there in front of the apartment building, smiling happily. Everything was going to be fine now, she told herself, setting her sights on the airport. Everything was going to be just fine. Once she got through tonight, all would be just as it should be. She swallowed down dread and prayed for strength.

Grady prowled the arrival area at the airport like a cabby looking for a fare. A little red velvet box burned a hole in his jean jacket pocket. He pictured the ring inside and suddenly worried that it was too big and gaudy. Then he saw Paige emerge from the terminal onto the sidewalk and all at once that two-carat center diamond didn't seem nearly big enough, let alone the pair of smaller ones set deeply into the smooth platinum band. They could always take it back, he reminded himself, maneuvering his way to the curb a little way past her. The sales manager had said so. He killed the engine and got out, lifting a hand in greeting.

"Hey, beautiful, need a ride?" Looking serious, she hurried toward him, her little bag rolling behind her. He popped the trunk and tossed the overnight case inside, asking, "You hungry?"

"Yes, uh, no. Grady, we need to talk."

"My thought exactly." He winked at her, refusing the impulse to drop a kiss on those sweet lips. She'd realize how badly he was trembling! He hurried around and opened the door for her. "Get in. I know a quiet little place where we can go and talk privately."

"Oh, I'm not really dressed to go out." She looked down at the neat, slender khaki slacks that she wore with a simple moss-green sweater set and backless flats.

"It's casual," he assured her, standing there in blue jeans and a polo shirt, "and you look great."

She got into the car, murmuring, "Thanks."

He jogged around and slid behind the wheel. "Vaughn like the phone?"

"Oh, boy, did he ever. He'll call you tomorrow."

"Excellent. Everything go okay then?"

"Very much so."

"Terrific. How was the hockey game?" He felt her relax.

"I'm no expert, as you know, but from what I saw, Jason Lowery would love to get his hands on that whole team. Either one, actually."

They talked hockey all the way downtown. He dropped the car with the valet at the lot across the street from the restaurant and took Paige by the hand, somewhat surprised when she pulled back.

"Grady, I'm not so certain this is a good idea."

"No, it is," he assured her. "Trust me on this. I checked the place out."

She gulped, pulled the sides of her little cardigan together and nodded, stepping off the curb. He slipped his hand around the bend of her elbow and escorted her.

The foyer of the restaurant was small and dark. Music played softly in the background, accented perfectly by the gentle clink of flatware against china. The fortyish man behind the reservation stand wore pleated slacks and a dress shirt with an open collar. Grady breathed a silent sigh of relief as he showed them to their table, which was in a quiet corner, just as Grady had requested. He had never been big on potted ferns, but the enormous one that separated the table from the rest of the room got an approving smile from him. Menus were placed in front of them. They both decided on the stuffed pasta shells, beef medallions and house salads.

"This is a nice place," Paige commented, looking through the greenery at the room beyond.

Grady nodded, aware of a waterfall pattering softly somewhere out of sight. He hoped this little restaurant would be a special place, a very special place. They discussed its merits until the food came, the consensus being that it was comfortable but not pretentious, relaxing but not boring, old-school but not old-fashioned. The place was busy in a quiet, familiar fashion.

The quality of the food gave them something else to talk about. By tacit agreement, they said grace silently, bowing their heads in unison, each with his or her own personal entreaty. They didn't hold hands. Paige kept hers in her lap, and in a way Grady was glad. Nerves made his hands quiver, and he didn't want to give himself away until the right moment.

The moment came as they waited for dessert, which they had been warned could take some time but would be worth the wait as the chocolate soufflé with fresh berries and sweetened cream was the house specialty and best served straight from the oven.

"Maybe I'll have room for it by the time it arrives," Paige mused. "I don't know what possessed me to agree to dessert. It just sounds so good."

"I'm glad you like this place," Grady told her, reaching for the hand that she'd briefly rested beside her tea glass. He slipped the other into his pocket. "I spent hours yesterday researching the Internet until I found just the right place for this."

She blinked at him, going very still.

His heart was pounding like a big brass drum as he placed the small velvet-covered box in the center of the table and softly asked, "Will you marry me, sweetheart? Say yes. I promise I'll—"

She pulled her hand from his and pressed it to her mouth. Even then he didn't realize that the whole world had come crashing down, not until she closed her eyes, fisted both hands against the edge of the table and whispered, "Grady, I can't marry you. I'm moving to South Carolina at the end of the month."

* * *

She never looked at the ring, never even opened the box. She couldn't. It hurt too much just to have it sitting there, a reproach in red velvet, a dream never to be realized, a promise never to be spoken. This was a sacrifice that she made unwillingly and perhaps not even graciously when all was said and done, but for the life of her, she could do nothing else.

The rushed, apologetic explanations and whispered recriminations did nothing to take the ache from her heart or the glazed, wooden disappointment from his face. Even that proved preferable to the silent, shattering pain that seemed to envelop each of them individually. Regret too deep to be imagined kept tears trembling on the rims of her eyes, but she couldn't shed them. She didn't feel she had the right to cry, not after a single glance at his ravaged face. Oh, why hadn't she told him sooner? How had she let this happen?

They left before the dessert came. It was more than an hour later as they drove through the deepening night before he cleared his throat and asked if she was sure.

"It's the only solution I can find, Grady. Vaughn needs me so much, and he's so thrilled, so happy. I have to do it."

He swallowed and asked what arrangements she'd made. She told him. "I accepted an offer to buy my business before I left. What happens to the house will depend upon Matthias. If he elects to go with me, I'll probably find an agent to lease it. If not, it will remain his home. He doesn't know, by the way."

Grady's mouth twisted wryly at that. "At least I'm not the only one you've kept in the dark."

"I wasn't sure it would happen at first, and then I just didn't know how to tell you. I did try to warn you, though."

"Yes, you did," he admitted.

"I should have told you I was thinking of it."

"Why didn't you?"

"I guess I just kept hoping…" She didn't say what she'd hoped for; he didn't ask.

She thought of a dozen compromises and as many reasons why they wouldn't work. How could she even suggest that he leave his family and business, his career, the dream house he'd just contracted to build? How could she ask him to give up all that in order to be second in her life? She couldn't ask it of him, and he didn't offer.

The silence ate at her like acid, so that by the time they pulled up to her yard she felt raw and prickly, as if she were held together with barbed wire. He grimly got out and walked her to the porch, carrying her bag stiffly in one hand. There in the darkness the tears finally slipped free.

"I guess some things just aren't meant to be," he whispered.

She gulped, keening inside, and said raggedly, "I'm sorry, Grady. So very sorry. You've been good to us, and you can't begin to believe how I'll miss you, but I have to do this for my son."

"My brother says you remind him of our mother," Grady said in a voice that had an otherworldly quality to it, almost an eeriness. "I thought she was the best mother in the world. I guess she was. And that must mean Dan's right."

She felt him step back then. A shudder passed between them, a blackness as despairing as hopelessness and loss could be. It lifted gooseflesh on her arms and neck. Suddenly he seemed to be far away, a great gulf yawning between them.

"Goodbye, Paige."

She almost cried out, knowing that she would not see him again. Still, she couldn't give him the farewell he deserved. The words simply were not in her. She found herself sitting on the step before she even realized that her legs had given out.

Everything was all wrong suddenly. Matthias hadn't come to the door as he usually did. Home wasn't waiting just up these steps anymore. This time she had pushed Grady away and he had not reached out to pull her in again.

When a cold nose pressed tentatively against the back of her neck, she was pathetically grateful. Reaching around, she locked her hands in Howler's collar and buried her face in the dog's thick black neck. With a snuffle and a scrabble the fat old thing flopped down on her lap, crushing her beneath warm, smelly weight. The dog sat patiently while she sobbed, much as Vaughn must have done on that night when she had begun to let him go.

She tried to let go of Grady in the same way, second by second, tear by tear, prayer by prayer. But this time there was nothing to cling to, no great gamble, no half-formed plan, no feverish hope.

This time there was only loss.

Grady sat in the dark, his head in his hands. He'd plopped down onto the cassock that stood in front of the easy chair in his neat-to-the-point-of-stark living room after coming home from work. The day had been interminable, even for a Monday, and he was exhausted. Just moving by rote, which was all he was capable of just now, required enormous effort.

The only saving grace was that Dan had been held over in Georgia another day, so at least he hadn't had to face a family inquisition. Yet. It would come, though. Even if he tried to pretend that his heart hadn't been ripped out, Dan would know. He'd known after Robin had left.

Grady had come home alone for the weekend. Nothing unusual in that. Robin had rarely accompanied him on those visits. It had been surprisingly easy to pretend that she was home doing whatever it was that she did while he was gone. Howard hadn't suspected a thing, but within the first ten minutes Dan had demanded to know what was wrong.

Grady didn't think he could manage a pretense this time. He wasn't even sure he could manage to live. He ought to get up and eat, but he couldn't seem to make himself do it. Instead he sat, trying not to think or feel or even breathe. He didn't even know what he was doing in here. He hardly ever came into this room, preferring instead to watch TV from his bed when he was home.

Home. This house had never been a home. It was just a place to sleep and change his clothes. The house itself was nothing special, certainly not pretentious—three bedrooms, one of which he'd outfitted but never really used as a home office, and two baths—but it was large enough for a small family. Yet, he'd never thought of making a family here.

He'd never thought of making a family at all, really, not even when he was married to Robin. Somehow the subject of children had never come up with them. But Paige, now Paige was all about being a mother, and he had started to think, to believe, that the two of them together would somehow become three or four or five or....

That was a dream which would never be realized. Like the house on the hill that they'd planned, it would simply never take shape. That was a house for a family, and he knew now that he would never have a family of his own. If he couldn't have it with Paige, it just wasn't meant to be. She was the only woman who didn't make him feel alien and awkward and stupid.

That didn't explain why he hadn't seen this coming. The moment she'd said that she was moving to South Carolina, he'd seen all the signs in retrospect. He couldn't understand how he could have gotten it all so wrong. Again. He hadn't understood his life at six years of age or after his divorce, and he didn't understand it now.

What hurt most was that she hadn't asked him to go with her, hadn't even hinted at such a thing. She had to know that he would. Once before he'd moved for a woman, walked away from his family business, established himself in a strange town. Did Paige think he wouldn't do it again? Obviously she hadn't known what sort of fool she was dealing with. Or was there more to it?

The very idea that she might be getting back together with Nolan made Grady queasy, but it had to be considered. He knew to what lengths she would go to please Vaughn, but was that all it was? She hadn't prosecuted Nolan when ninety-nine out of a hundred women would have. She hadn't wanted to cause him pain, hadn't wanted to see him punished, had gone against expert advice to keep the lines of communication open, had sent her son back to him rather than meet him in open court. Yet, not once had Grady considered that Paige might still care for her ex-husband.

Fool didn't quite cover what he was.

The cell phone in the front pocket of his coat vibrated. Not wanting to be disturbed, he'd set it on vibrate before he'd picked up Paige at the airport yesterday evening, and he'd left it on vibrate because he still didn't want to be disturbed. He didn't want to talk to anyone, see anyone, be with anyone, not now, not when he hurt this badly.

All the way home from Paige's house last night he'd kept looking down, expecting to see a great, bloody, gaping hole in his chest. At first he'd been too stunned to feel much of anything, but it hadn't taken long for the anguish to come, and now it wouldn't go away.

The phone vibrated again. It lay heavily against his ribs, and the vibration sent a sharp tingle deep into his chest. Grady straightened, stretching out his arm to move his jacket away from his body, and then he remembered once before when he'd meant to ignore this phone. If he hadn't answered it then, would Paige be moving to South Carolina?

"Oh, God," he whispered, "what do I do now?"

He didn't expect an answer, but he didn't expect something to crawl up his back, either. In an instant he was on his feet, certain that he was not alone. Whirling around, he expected to see... What?

It was pitch dark, shadows upon shadows. He reached for the lamp on the side table and nearly tipped it over before he got it on. Even before light flooded the room, he knew what he would see. No one. Nothing, at least nothing out of the ordinary. Still, he stood uncertainly for a moment. Was he losing his mind? Or was someone trying to tell him something?

Turning in a slow circle, he took stock. The couch sat against the wall as always. The drapes were drawn. The glass inset in the coffee table gleamed. The house was stuffy, as usual, and sterile, as usual, and empty. As usual.

You are never alone, he thought suddenly. *Perhaps you won't be with Paige, but you will never be alone.*

Sucking in his breath, he pushed his hands over his face, surprised to feel the dampness of tears on his cheeks. That was when he realized that the phone had not vibrated again. Whoever had called had thought better of it.

It could have been Dan, their dad, any of a dozen people, but he knew, even as he tugged the phone from his pocket who had called. Paige had told him to expect it, after all, before she'd destroyed his world. He flipped the phone open and pushed two buttons in succession in order to bring the number on to the tiny screen, and then he pushed another to dial it. The screen told him that he was calling Vaughn and then that Vaughn had answered. Grady put the phone to his ear and cleared his throat.

"Hello?"

"Hey, it does work. I was starting to think you'd bought me a bum phone, big guy."

Big guy. Grady smiled in spite of everything. "I just didn't get to it before."

"That's okay. Mom didn't answer, either, so I thought maybe it wasn't working or I wasn't doing it right or something."

Grady bit his tongue to keep from asking about Paige. "Hard to do anything wrong with that phone from what I understand."

"Yeah, I know, but I thought maybe something got messed up when I downloaded a new ring tone."

"Ah."

"Or, uh, when Dad threw it."

Grady's free hand went to his waist, and a whole lot of anger that he was doing his best to suppress came roaring to life. "Your father *threw* the phone?"

"He's kinda upset," Vaughn mumbled. "He's always upset about something these days."

Grady frowned, unable to imagine what Nolan Ellis would have to be upset about. "What do you mean?"

"I already know he lied to me," Vaughn wailed, "so what difference does it make if I see Mom?" Grady pressed his temples as Vaughn rushed on. "He's the one making everything tough. She's the one doing everything to make it better. I don't know why he's so mad just 'cause I wanna be with them both. What's he care if she buys me a phone? Which she didn't. Thanks, by the way."

"You're welcome," Grady rumbled absently. So Paige *wasn't* going back to Nolan. Sighing with relief, Grady rubbed a hand over his chin, feeling the rasp of the beard that he sometimes had to shave twice a day.

"Did she really keep him from coming to Arkansas?" Vaughn asked in a thin, choked voice.

Grady tried to think. Had Paige kept Nolan out of Arkansas? "Actually," he said, "I did that. She didn't fight me on it, like she did everything else, but I took it upon myself to secure an order barring your father from coming to Arkansas. I was worried, Vaughn. When she wouldn't put him in jail I tried to see to it that he couldn't come here and take you away again."

"But there's no reason she can't move here if she wants to, is there?" Vaughn asked.

Grady gulped. "No. None."

"So he can't keep her from seeing me?"

"He sure can't. Not legally."

"Okay. I didn't think so, but he says stuff when he's mad. You know?"

Gripping the phone a little tighter, Grady asked, "Did he say he'd keep your mom from seeing you, Vaughn?"

"Yeah, but he can't, can he? I told him, I want her to come. If she moves here, it'll be like it used to be when... when I was a real kid and she took care of everything. When she took care of me."

A real kid. Grady swallowed. "I remember when my mom used to take care of me," he said. "I didn't know what a wonderful thing that was until I didn't have it anymore. But after she died, my dad took care of me. He took good care of me, Vaughn. It didn't make up for my mom being gone, but he was a good father. He still is. Doesn't your dad take care of you, Vaughn?"

Vaughn snorted. "No. More like I take care of him. He's in there drinking now, and when he passes out I'm not putting him to bed, and I'm not making him coffee in the morning when he's hungover, either."

Grady shook his head. No wonder Paige was moving

to South Carolina. What else could she do? "I'm sorry, Vaughn," he said. "Does he drink often?"

"Yeah, but he don't get drunk all that much, not at home, anyway. He doesn't really stay home much. He likes to be out doing stuff, you know. He's got the boat and the bike and the bow and arrow and his bowling team and golf and his online games, and he *really* likes to go to the drag races."

"Do you get to go along?"

"Sometimes."

"But mostly you stay home alone, don't you?"

"Yeah," Vaughn admitted in a small voice.

"Well, I tell you what you do, Vaughn," Grady said. "You call me anytime you want, and if I'm not in a courtroom or with a client, we'll talk. Okay?"

"Okay. But Mom says I just get 450 minutes a month. That's like fifteen minutes a day, and she can talk that much without even saying anything."

Grady chuckled. "Well, there's still e-mail. That's almost as good." He closed his eyes, adding softly, "Besides, she'll be down there with you before long, won't she?"

"Yeah. Hey, you don't play games online, do you? Dad's got this headset, and you can, like, talk to your buddies while you're playing. I play all the time when Dad's not home. It don't cost anything once you've got the setup. But you probably don't play."

Grady smiled at himself. *Now* the kid wanted to be buddies. "I do as soon as I get my hands on a system and you tell me what games."

"Cool!"

Vaughn excitedly rattled off everything Grady could ever want to know about operating systems and headsets and half a dozen different games. He gave Grady a list of screen tags he used, his favorite being SCaB, for South Carolina Boy. Grady promised to call as soon as he got set up. The whole thing was going to be a fiasco, of course. Vaughn was going to trounce him. Grady knew beans about video gaming, but what else did he have to do? Paige might be out of his life, but it looked as if he'd made a friend in Vaughn, at least. That was something, and maybe…

No, he wouldn't think about using Vaughn to stay close to Paige. If she wasn't going back to Nolan, then she just didn't want him, Grady, going to South Carolina with her.

After Vaughn got off the phone, Grady took a deep breath, and it still hurt, but it did seem that he was going to live.

And you're never alone, he reminded himself again, looking around. *Even when you're by yourself, you're never alone. You're always with God.*

That was more than he'd had before, and more than enough to get him through this. Who knew? Someday God might bring another woman into his life, and if not, well, one Paige in a lifetime was all any man could ask for.

Chapter Fifteen

"Grady?"

The voice woke him from a deep, exhausted sleep. Only when he cleared his throat in order to reply did Grady realize that he held the phone pressed to his ear. Obviously he'd plucked it off the bedside table in robotic response to its buzz.

Blinking into the darkness, Grady demanded, "Who is this?"

"It's me."

"Vaughn?" Grady sat straight up in the bed, one thing clear in the jumble of his sleep-fogged brain. "Something's wrong."

"Matthias was right, Grady. My dad did steal me from my mom, and he's trying to do it again."

Grady pivoted to drop his legs off the side of the bed, his mind kicking into high gear. "Your dad's going to run. He wants to hide you from your mom again because she's moving to Greenville to be near you." Somehow, he realized, he'd expected this, maybe even counted on it.

"Yes," Vaughn said. "He started packing boxes after I went to sleep, but I woke up, and I saw him. He says we've got to. He says she's gonna try to get money out of him, that I'll go to live with her and then the courts will try to make him pay again. He says…" Grady could hear the confusion in the pause. "He says he's not gonna let her win."

That was some *game* Nolan Ellis was playing, Grady thought darkly. To Vaughn he said, "You can't let him leave with you."

"I know. I went out the window. Could you come get me?"

Grady paused in the act of rubbing a hand over his face. "Are you telling me that you've run away from your father?"

"I had to! He was gonna make me go with him. I had to. Can't you just come get me?"

"Vaughn, I'm a whole day away from you, *provided* I can even get a flight. You've got to call 9-1-1."

"But they'll send me to that home again, and they'll arrest him."

"I can't promise that Nolan won't pay a price this time, but you know your mom won't do anything without talking to you first. And what if he finds you, Vaughn? What then? Do you never want to see your mom again until you're grown?"

"No."

"Listen to me. My brother Dan is in Augusta, Georgia. I'll get him to you as quick as I can. He's an attorney, too. He can take care of this, but it's going to take some time, so just tell me where you are, and I'll have the authorities come get you."

A pause followed, during which Grady held his breath. Then Vaughn said, "There's a park with a pavilion and basketball courts. It's on Scot's Trace Trail."

"You stay at that park until someone comes for you, Vaughn. Promise me."

"Yeah, okay."

"I mean it. It'll kill your mom if she loses you again. Please, buddy, let me handle this. Will you?"

"That's why I called you."

Grady heaved a sigh. "Thank you, Vaughn. Don't worry, and keep that phone with you. I'll be in touch soon."

"I don't want my dad to be like this," Vaughn wailed in a tiny voice. Grady could tell that he was crying.

"I know. Maybe we can help him be different, Vaughn. We'll ask God to help us with that, okay?"

"Okay." Vaughn sniffed. "Maybe you better call my mom," he said. "I think I've used up my fifteen minutes."

Grady had to swallow his chuckle. "No problem."

The next several minutes were fraught with heart-pounding anxiety. Because his file with all the pertinent Greenville telephone numbers was at the office, he had to race to the computer and get on the Internet to find what he needed. While he was doing that, he called Dan. It was four in the morning on the east coast, but Dan rose without complaint to dress and pack and head to the airport. Grady was already punching the number of the Greenville County Sheriff's office into his home phone when he got off the cell with Dan.

The sheriff's deputy to whom Grady spoke agreed to give the heads-up to the Greenville police, freeing Grady to play two-phone tag with three different airlines until he got Dan booked on a flight to Charlotte and another in to Greenville. That looked like a roundabout way to do things to Grady, but it was apparently the fastest route. He called Vaughn to tell him that Dan should be with him shortly after seven-thirty.

Vaughn did not answer.

In a panic, Grady picked up the phone to finally call Paige. He hit his knees instead, begging God to spare her the agony of losing her son again.

He made every argument he could think of, pointing out what a really good person she was: kind, thoughtful, generous. She'd given Matthias a home and stood by him even when his past had presented problems for her. She'd built a business from scratch, without compromising her ethics even once. She hadn't punished Nolan, hadn't sought any retribution, and she'd done everything, everything, for the sake of her son.

Paige was blameless, even in her dealings with him. He'd known she was holding back, holding him off, and he'd ignored that, worked his way around her, pushed and pushed a little more, until she'd had no choice but to hurt him. He would never regret what had happened between the two of them because, if nothing else, she'd shown him the reality of God, the way to a personal relationship with his own Maker. Now he was making his best case to that Great Judge on her behalf.

This life was not fair. Grady knew it well. Otherwise, would his own mother have died in a senseless accident when he was only six years old? Would Nolan have stolen Vaughn from his mother in the first place? Would Matthias have lost everything to a charlatan and a fraud? Life was not fair, but God would always be God, with the power to answer prayer and reward right.

"And she's tried so hard to do what's right, Lord," he said, *"for everyone, in every situation. You know her heart. You know how hard she's tried and how much she's already suffered. I beg You to spare her this. I don't ask You to punish Nolan, just don't let him keep Vaughn away from his mother. Please."*

He didn't know how long he implored the Almighty, but when his cell rang again, he knew that it was the answer to his prayer, one way or another. He was entirely correct. It was the Greenville County Sheriff's office. Vaughn had been picked up by a police cruiser at the park in Curly and was on his way to Greenville at that very moment. Nolan Ellis, however, was nowhere to be found.

Grady couldn't have cared less about Nolan. He only cared that Vaughn was safe and sound, and he took time to thank God for that before he decided how best to tell Paige that her son was once more coming home to her. His first instinct was to pull on clothes and drive to Nobb, but on second thought, he realized that was not the wisest course. For one thing, it would delay the news even longer, and she would want to know as soon as possible. For another, if he saw her he would have to hold her, but he wasn't sure she would welcome that, and he just didn't know if he could bear another rebuff. He picked up the phone.

Paige was sleeping soundly when the call came. It felt like the first time in weeks, which perhaps accounted for the fact that she felt unusually refreshed when she opened her eyes to a surprisingly pitch-dark room. She groped for the phone, got her hand on the receiver of the hopelessly outdated corded telephone on the bedside table and lifted it to her ear. Her voice didn't work quite as expected, sounding raspy and soft.

"Hello?"

Grady's solid baritone greeted her. "Paige? Honey, wake up. I've got something important to tell you. Vaughn called me a few minutes ago."

She sat up. "What's going on?"

He told her in calm, succinct words. For some reason—she didn't know why—she could barely believe it. Nolan was insane to try something like this. What did he have to gain? The only reason for it was to hurt her, but he had succeeded only in punishing himself. Nolan had forced Vaughn to choose, and their son had chosen *her*.

At first she felt that she ought to go to Vaughn straight-away, but Grady counseled her to speak to Vaughn before she did anything, and for once she took his advice to heart. The situation was under control. Vaughn was safe. Dan was already on his way and entirely capable of handling the le-galities. God willing, Vaughn could be in Arkansas before bedtime rolled around again. One thing puzzled her.

"Why did he call you with this?"

"You'll have to ask him," Grady answered. "Maybe he figured I could afford to come get him easier than you could. Or maybe he didn't want to worry you. All I know is he's afraid to go over his fifteen-minute-a-day telephone allot-ment."

Paige shook her head. He was either the most responsible boy she'd ever known or the most mercenary. Maybe both. "That child is a piece of work," she mused aloud.

Grady chuckled. "Yes, he is, and you'd lay down your life for him."

"In a heartbeat," she confirmed.

A moment of silence passed, and then Grady softly asked, "What's going to happen now, Paige?"

She knew what he was asking. Would she and Vaughn stay in Arkansas or move to South Carolina together as they'd planned?

"I don't know, Grady. I just don't know."

Things got a little complicated. It turned out that Vaughn had called his father and warned him that he might be ar-rested again. Paige couldn't fault him for that. She under-stood that he didn't want his dad to go to jail. It was enough for her that he had thwarted Nolan's plans to abscond with him. It did, however, delay Vaughn's return.

The sheriff wanted to be sure that Vaughn had no real knowledge of his father's whereabouts, but they couldn't question him until Dan arrived and took stock of the situation. After that all the proper hoops had to be jumped through before Dan could leave the jurisdiction with Vaughn. Child Welfare had to be called in and brought up to date, and this time they had to go before a judge in chambers. They allowed Dan to take Vaughn with him to a local hotel for the night.

It was Wednesday evening before they stepped off the plane at Northwest Regional. Paige was waiting with open arms. She was a little disappointed that Grady was not there, but all things considered, it was probably for the best. She still didn't know what the future held for her and her son.

Vaughn had been through a rough few days and had essentially lost his father. He would need time to calm down and adjust. Then they could discuss the situation and come to some well-reasoned decisions. She was fully prepared to move to Greenville with Vaughn if that was what it was going to take to reconcile him to this new situation, which was why she intended to go ahead with the sale of her business.

She thanked Dan profusely. He was in a hurry to get home, having been gone several days longer than expected, but he was philosophical about the whole thing.

"I figure this was why God had me down in Georgia to begin with. I certainly didn't accomplish what I went there for."

Paige commiserated with him. "I'm so sorry. I guess this means you'll have to go again."

Smiling, he shook his head. "Nope. God had everything under control. The defendant decided to settle. They contacted Grady this morning, and he rushed them into arbitration. They were still at it as of five minutes ago, but I expect we'll have an agreement shortly."

Paige sighed with relief for more than one reason. Was it

vain and selfish of her to hope that Grady hadn't yet given up on them? She looked at her son, who appeared tired and sad, and reminded herself that she had much for which to be thankful. Slipping her arms around his shoulders, she shepherded her poor boy to the truck and home.

He rode quietly all the way, answering her careful questions with terse, sad replies. She was gratified that he greeted Howler with a good scratching and Matthias with a quick hug. But then he picked at the supper she had put back for him and glumly asked what was going to happen now. When she told him that it depended on him, he nodded solemnly, said that he was tired and rose from the table to take himself off to bed. Before leaving the room he kissed her cheek and told her that he loved her. She hugged him tight, whispering that she knew he was hurting and how sorry she was about that.

"It's not your fault," he told her, fiercely scrubbing away his tears. "Nothing's been your fault." He looked at Matthias and said, "You were right. I'm sorry for before."

"No, son," Matthias said, looking at Paige. "Your mama is the one who's been right. About everything, and I gave her just about as hard a time as you did."

She shook her head, keeping an arm around her son. "I wish it all wasn't so painful for you, Vaughn."

"How come he has to be this way?" Vaughn cried in a tiny voice, and she knew he was talking about his father.

"I don't know, honey. I wish I did. Then maybe we'd all still be together the way a real family should be."

"We can be a family anyway, can't we?" he asked hopefully, "Just us on our own?"

"Yes, we can. We already are," she assured him. "God will work out everything else."

She would not be greedy enough to ask that He work it out as she wanted Him to. Even if she and Vaughn decided to stay right where they were, it might be too late. A man like Grady could be expected to come in second only so often.

It was the middle of the afternoon when the phone in Grady's office rang. It was Paige's number, but Matthias's voice that greeted Grady. Once again, however, Grady knew immediately that there was trouble, if not catastrophe. The quiver told him as much as the words.

"Grady? You b-better get o-over here. Nolan's showed up."

He was out the door before the connection was broken, leaving a client on hold on the other line and the receptionist gaping. Everything he knew and felt told Grady that Nolan turning up at Paige's house could not be good. Even before he hit the parking lot at a run, he was talking aloud to God.

"Keep them safe, Lord. Keep them safe. I'll do anything. I'll give up anything. Just keep them safe."

Somehow he managed not to get stopped for speeding as he tore through one community after another. He was driving so fast that he dared not even take the time to call and check on them. Instead he just kept handing it off to God, trusting Him to protect them until he could get there. As he sped through the single, timeworn block of downtown Nobb, he noticed that folks were standing out on the side of the road, staring off in the general direction of Paige's house.

He caught the flash of colored lights through the trees as he swung the car onto the drive. Panic seized Grady by the throat. The panic intensified when the cop cars came into view. An ambulance was parked beside a two-tone blue pickup with a creased tailgate. Grady bailed out, stupidly ignored the officer who approached him and was saved a confrontation when Vaughn shot out of the house and threw himself at him. Howler was ripping the sky apart and turning tight circles around everyone in the yard, but the mutt shut up and plopped down on his haunches as Grady caught a sobbing Vaughn against him.

"He hurt her bad! I tried to stop him, but he hurt her!"

Grady nearly dropped. "Where is she?"

He turned instinctively toward the ambulance, only then aware that someone or something was being loaded into it. At the same time, Vaughn pulled him toward the house. Grady left Vaughn behind in two strides, took the steps up onto the porch in one leap and was standing in her living room before the officer guarding the door could even move to block him.

One wild glance around the room showed him Paige sitting calmly on the sofa. A female medical emergency technician was perched next to her, taking her pulse. Grady dropped to his knees beside Paige. She offered him a lopsided smile and a look of such compassion and apology that he sighed. Then she leaned forward and pressed her forehead to his.

"Thank God!" he exclaimed, sliding his arms around her.

She caught her breath, and that's when he realized that she was wearing a sling on her left arm. Before he could even think about it, he was on his feet again, rage unlike anything he'd ever felt tearing through him.

"Where is he?"

A solid hand fell heavily on his shoulder and spun him around. It was the policeman.

"If you're talking about Nolan Ellis," the officer said, "that's him they just loaded into the ambulance."

Grady blinked at that. Nolan was in the ambulance?

"What happened?" he demanded of the room at large. Vaughn, who had entered the house behind him, answered.

"Matthias hit him with his cane."

Grady turned until he found Matthias standing uncertainly against the wall. He looked sick, every bit as shaken as he'd sounded on the phone. "You hit him?"

"Knocked him cold," the policeman confirmed.

"He had to," Vaughn insisted. "I missed him with the lamp."

"Missed *who* with the lamp?"

"Nolan," Paige said softly, reaching out a hand to her son. Vaughn stepped to her side and took her hand in his. "Nolan had some crazy idea that he was going to force Vaughn to go with him," Paige explained softly. "When I intervened, he attacked me. Vaughn threw the lamp in his bedroom to try to stop him from twisting my arm."

"It needs an X-ray," the EMT said, getting to her feet. "The wrist could be broken."

"It doesn't hurt now," Paige put in quickly. "It'll keep until we're done here."

Grady looked at the policeman, slipping easily, almost gratefully, into lawyer mode. It made it easier to tame the riot of his emotions. "What do you need to wrap this up? I'll be representing Mr. Porter, if it comes to that. You should know that Ellis has broken several laws just by entering the state."

The policeman held up his hand. "All right, cool your jets. I've had the story from these three, and we're transporting Ellis under custody. He'll be arrested as soon as he regains consciousness. I'll need statements, but it can wait a day or two. You get her taken care of first." He looked pointedly at Paige. "I wanted to call a second ambulance, but she insisted she'd wait for you."

It was Vaughn who said, "That's 'cause Grady always takes care of us."

"I always want to," Grady said automatically, looking down at Paige, who smiled without meeting his gaze. The bottom fell out of Grady's stomach. He swallowed and forced himself to prioritize. "Let's get you to an emergency room."

Paige nodded and rose shakily to her feet.

"I wanna come, too," Vaughn insisted.

Matthias cleared his throat then and stepped forward. Grady took one look at him and said, "We'll all go." Still looking shaken and pale, the old guy simply nodded. Grady glanced at Vaughn and gave his head a little jerk. "Lend a hand?"

Vaughn went straight to Matthias. Looking up at the old man with something akin to hero worship, he took Matthias's hand and lifted it to his shoulder, saying, "Lean on me. I'll be your cane for a while."

Grady watched Matthias beat back tears, nod and pat the boy's shoulder. "Let's go then."

It took several minutes to get them all in the car and several hours to get Paige seen, treated and released again. Grady made sure that she was looked over from head to toe, but the X-ray showed only a hairline fracture in one of the bones in her left wrist.

Vaughn hovered over his mom as if he was her caretaker instead of the other way around. Grady sensed that it was a role with which he had great familiarity, and that alone would have told him about the boy's relationship with his father if Vaughn himself had not already done so. By tacit agreement, the three adults allowed Vaughn to hover and fuss and generally act like he was in charge, fearing that an emotional storm was yet to come.

Grady secured a report on Nolan and passed the information to Vaughn, who accepted it in silence. Although concussed, Nolan was expected to make a full recovery. Vaughn seemed relieved but subdued after hearing this.

It was dark by the time they left the hospital. Grady called ahead and ordered pizza and salad to be picked up for dinner. Vaughn rode in the backseat with his mother, leaving Matthias to ride up front with Grady. The storm broke while they waited in the drive-through lane for the food.

Paige just held her son against her right side and let him cry, whispering comfort and encouragement, telling him over and over again that nothing was his fault. Every once in a while her tear-drenched eyes would meet Grady's in the rearview mirror. He put everything else aside and did his best to telegraph his strength and love straight to her.

Once they got back to the house, he settled Paige on the couch and sent Matthias for a blanket while Vaughn carried the food into the kitchen. Grady joined Vaughn, and together they got down plates and poured drinks for everyone.

Finally Vaughn looked up at him, eyes swollen and red, to softly ask, "What's going to happen to my dad now?"

Grady didn't sugarcoat it, but he took no pleasure in saying, "He's going to spend some time in jail, Vaughn, probably a few months. Hopefully it'll be enough to convince him that he never wants to do something this stupid again."

Vaughn bowed his head. Grady looped an arm around his shoulders, thinking what a curious mix of man and child Vaughn was. Grady supposed that came of being torn between two parents, one of whom could not seem to live up to his responsibilities. The other, fortunately, was wise, indeed.

"That doesn't mean you can't see your dad," Grady told the boy, "or that God can't change him."

Vaughn nodded, and asked, "What's gonna happen with us?"

"What do you want to happen?" Paige asked from the doorway.

Grady frowned at her, but he knew how much good it would do to scold her for getting up. Instead, he just pulled a chair out from the table and parked her in it. Then he leaned against the counter and folded his arms. He had just as big a stake in Vaughn's answer as anyone, after all.

Paige called Vaughn to her and smoothed his hair from his forehead with her one good hand. "We don't have to make any decisions now, but what do you want to happen, Vaughn? Do you want to stay here so you can see your dad from time to time, assuming this is where he'll be." She looked to Grady for confirmation of that, and he nodded. "Or do you want to go home to South Carolina? If you want to go home, I'll see to it that you get back here as often as possible to visit your dad."

Vaughn screwed up his face. "I dunno. I like Curly. My friends are all there, and the hockey team's better." Paige nodded and smiled wanly, flashing an apologetic look at Grady, who could only swallow and wait for it. "But we already got our own house here," Vaughn went on, "and what about Matthias and Grady?"

Paige squeezed his hand with hers. "What about them?"

"Well, you said that we could be a real family, just the two of us, but aren't they, like, sort of our family, too."

Paige nodded, tears filling her eyes. "Chosen family," she whispered.

Grady cleared his throat and stuck his big foot in the door. "We could be more than *sort of* family," he said, holding her gaze, "if I could convince your mother to marry me."

Vaughn jerked around. "Ha! I knew it!" Grinning slyly, he asked, "Are you still gonna get that new game system?"

Grady laughed, feeling his worries float away. "We'll see."

"Vaughn," Paige said, forcing his attention back to her, "I thought you were upset with the idea of me and Grady together."

Vaughn shrugged and glumly said, "I guess I thought that if you loved Dad he'd change."

"Honey, I did love your dad."

"I know, and he ruined it," Vaughn stated flatly. "He ruins everything. I don't think he can help it." He looked at Grady and said, "He doesn't know how to take care of anybody like you do, not even himself."

"You know how," Grady said. He looked to Paige, adding, "Must get it from your mom."

Vaughn smiled. "Yeah. She's the best."

"You know what I think?" Grady asked, latching a hand on to the boy's shoulder. "I think you'd be a really good big brother."

Paige gasped at the same time Vaughn declared, "That'd be cool!"

Suddenly Paige began to sob. "I love you both so much!" she wailed.

Grady looked at Vaughn, and they shared what he was sure would not be their last moment of masculine understanding.

"Well, do something," Vaughn instructed.

Grady did the only thing he could think to do, the thing he wanted most to do. He went to Paige and picked her up, cradling her in his arms like a weeping child.

"Bring the pizza," he told Vaughn, carrying her into the living room.

Matthias walked into the room carrying a blanket at the same time Grady walked in carrying Paige. "What's wrong with her now?" he wanted to know.

"She loves us," Grady said, dropping down onto the couch with her in his lap. Paige chortled and spluttered.

Matthias grunted and plopped down into his chair, dropping the blanket beside it. Vaughn appeared and thrust a plate of pizza and salad at Matthias, announcing, "Mom and Grady are getting married."

"'Bout time."

"And I'm gonna be a big brother."

"Well, of course you are, a good one, too."

Paige wiped her eyes on Grady's shoulder and petulantly demanded, "Where's my ring?"

Grady chuckled, the hole in his chest finally closing, and kissed her temple. "On my bedside table." He glanced down at her swollen left hand and added, "You'll get it just as soon as you can wear it."

She sniffed and said, "Are we still building the house?"

"What house?" Vaughn asked, bringing them a plate piled high with pizza enough for two.

"Oh, Vaughn, it's the most amazing thing, stables and a pool and a media room."

"Sweet! Where?"

"Here or there," Grady said, taking the plate that Vaughn offered them. He kissed Paige's nose. "If Vaughn wants South Carolina, we'll give him South Carolina."

Paige looked at Grady, wonder in her eyes. Foolish woman. "You'd really do that?"

"Sweetheart, I moved once for a woman I didn't care about half as much as I love you. Do you really think I wouldn't move for you and Vaughn?"

"I just couldn't ask it of you," she whispered. "Your family and career are here."

"My family want me to be happy, and they need lawyers in South Carolina, too."

Paige wrapped her arms around his neck and squeezed before turning to Vaughn, who'd taken a seat on the end of the sofa opposite them. "What do you say now, son? Here or there?"

Vaughn shrugged as if it was immaterial to him and bit off a huge chunk of pizza. He looked at Grady and with a full mouth asked, "Suppose Jason will let me back on the team?"

"Don't talk with your mouth full," Grady said mildly, smiling, "and yeah, I think we can get you back on the team."

Vaughn cut his eyes at his mom and swallowed. "Can I get that new cell phone?"

She stared at him and sternly warned, "Don't push it, buster."

Vaughn grinned. "I don't know why we'd go back to South Carolina when everything that matters most is here."

"There you go," Matthias put in. "Kid's got brains. Always said he had brains. Takes after his mother."

Paige laughed, and said to him, "I'm counting on you to walk me down the aisle, you know."

"I'll walk you down the aisle, but I ain't giving you away," Matthias told her. He winked at Grady and added, "I'm keeping the lot of you, and that's that."

They all laughed. And then Paige realized that they hadn't said grace over the pizza. Grady did the honors, finding so much to be thankful for that the words just fell out of him. When he was done, he opened his eyes to find Vaughn gazing at him.

"I guess, in a way, I got my mom and dad in the same place, after all, just not like I thought it would be."

"That's a good way to look at it," Grady said, smiling.

Vaughn nodded and said, "This way is better, I think."

Grady reached out and laid a hand on the nape of the boy's neck. "I hope that one day your dad will say the same thing, Vaughn."

"We'll pray about it," Vaughn said matter-of-factly, going back to his pizza.

Grady looked down at the woman who had made them both understand just how powerful a simple thing like prayer could be.

"We certainly will," he said.

It was the right thing to do, after all, and maybe one day even Nolan would find his way home, home to love and healing and understanding, home to God, where love reigns and we all belong.

* * * * *

Dear Reader,

The very bedrock of Christianity is forgiveness. Through the work of Christ, God forgives our transgressions, and we are admonished to forgive those who harm us, as well. Yet, if we're honest, we could all recognize something that we find nearly impossible to forgive.

In writing Paige's story, I had to imagine what would be truly difficult for her to forgive, which meant imagining what would be truly difficult for *me* to forgive. Didn't take much thought, actually. It's pretty much been a given since the day after Christmas of 1972, when my first son was born. Harm me, I think I can find a way to forgive; harm my child…that's another struggle entirely.

Yet God loved us enough to actually sacrifice His own Son. That greatest of sacrifices should inspire and empower us to do that which may be most difficult, simply because it is right and best. May we all find that strength and know the rewards of truly forgiving.

God bless,

Arlene James

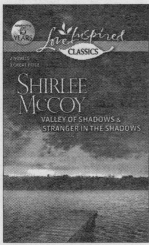

REQUEST YOUR FREE BOOKS!

2 FREE INSPIRATIONAL NOVELS
PLUS 2
FREE
MYSTERY GIFTS

YES! Please send me 2 FREE Love Inspired® novels and my 2 FREE mystery gifts (gifts are worth about $10). After receiving them, if I don't wish to receive any more books, I can return the shipping statement marked "cancel." If I don't cancel, I will receive 6 brand-new novels every month and be billed just $4.49 per book in the U.S. or $4.99 per book in Canada. That's a saving of at least 22% off the cover price. It's quite a bargain! Shipping and handling is just 50¢ per book in the U.S. and 75¢ per book in Canada.* I understand that accepting the 2 free books and gifts places me under no obligation to buy anything. I can always return a shipment and cancel at any time. Even if I never buy another book, the two free books and gifts are mine to keep forever.

105/305 IDN FEGR

Name	(PLEASE PRINT)
Address	Apt. #
City	State/Prov.	Zip/Postal Code

Signature (if under 18, a parent or guardian must sign)

Mail to the Reader Service:
IN U.S.A.: P.O. Box 1867, Buffalo, NY 14240-1867
IN CANADA: P.O. Box 609, Fort Erie, Ontario L2A 5X3

Not valid for current subscribers to Love Inspired books.

**Are you a subscriber to Love Inspired books
and want to receive the larger-print edition?
Call 1-800-873-8635 or visit www.ReaderService.com.**

* Terms and prices subject to change without notice. Prices do not include applicable taxes. Sales tax applicable in N.Y. Canadian residents will be charged applicable taxes. Offer not valid in Quebec. This offer is limited to one order per household. All orders subject to credit approval. Credit or debit balances in a customer's account(s) may be offset by any other outstanding balance owed by or to the customer. Please allow 4 to 6 weeks for delivery. Offer available while quantities last.

Your Privacy—The Reader Service is committed to protecting your privacy. Our Privacy Policy is available online at www.ReaderService.com or upon request from the Reader Service.

We make a portion of our mailing list available to reputable third parties that offer products we believe may interest you. If you prefer that we not exchange your name with third parties, or if you wish to clarify or modify your communication preferences, please visit us at www.ReaderService.com/consumerchoice or write to us at Reader Service Preference Service, P.O. Box 9062, Buffalo, NY 14269. Include your complete name and address.

LIREG11B

Louisa Morgan loves being around children.
So when she has the opportunity to tutor bedridden Ellie,
she's determined to bring joy back into the motherless
girl's world. Can she also help Ellie's father open his
heart again? Read on for a sneak peek of

THE COWBOY FATHER

by Linda Ford,
available February 2012 from Love Inspired Historical.

Why had Louisa thought she could do this job? A bubble of self-pity whispered she was totally useless, but Louisa ignored it. She wasn't useless. She could help Ellie if the child allowed it.

Emmet walked her out, waiting until they were out of earshot to speak. "I sense you and Ellie are not getting along."

"Ellie has lost her freedom. On top of that, everything is new. Familiar things are gone. Her only defense is to exert what little independence she has left. I believe she will soon tire of it and find there are more enjoyable ways to pass the time."

He looked doubtful. Louisa feared he would tell her not to return. But after several seconds' consideration, he sighed heavily. "You're right about one thing. She's lost everything. She can hardly be blamed for feeling out of sorts."

"She hasn't lost everything, though." Her words were quiet, coming from a place full of certainty that Emmet was more than enough for this child. "She has you."

"She'll always have me. As long as I live." He clenched his fists. "And I fully intend to raise her in such a way that even if something happened to me, she would never feel like I was gone. I'd be in her thoughts and in her actions every day."

Peace filled Louisa. "Exactly what my father did."

Their gazes connected, forged a single thought about fathers and daughters…how each needed the other. How sweet the relationship was.

Louisa tipped her head away first. "I'll see you tomorrow."

Emmet nodded. "Until tomorrow then."

She climbed behind the wheel of their automobile and turned toward home. She admired Emmet's devotion to his child. It reminded her of the love her own father had lavished on Louisa and her sisters. Louisa smiled as fond memories of her father filled her thoughts. Ellie was a fortunate child to know such love.

Louisa understands what both father and daughter are going through. Will her compassion help them heal—and form a new family? Find out in
THE COWBOY FATHER
by Linda Ford, available February 14, 2012.

Love Inspired Books celebrates 15 years of inspirational romance in 2012! February puts the spotlight on Love Inspired Historical, with each book celebrating family and the special place it has in our hearts. Be sure to pick up all four Love Inspired Historical stories, available February 14, wherever books are sold.

SHLIHEXP0212